He had wrapped a blanket around his waist and was busy laying out his clothes on top of a bale of hay. He looked around with a grin and started toward her.

"What are you doing?" she said, shivering helplessly with something other than just the cold.

"I'm taking off your very wet jersey," he said softly, pulling it over her head. "And your soaking shirt, too," and peeled that off her skin, leaving her sensitive breasts exposed to the cold air, but she didn't feel it; in fact, her skin felt on fire. "And all the rest of it," he continued almost inaudibly, doing exactly that.

She stood as if in a trance, unresisting as her clothes fell one piece after another.

"Oh," she said, and then he was there, pulling her into his arms, his breath coming in quick gasps, his lips kissing her hungrily. Then he pulled away and took a blanket, spread it out on the hay, and lowered her onto it...

Also by Julia Jay Kendall

PORTRAITS

Published by
WARNER BOOKS

Julia Jay Kendall

A Warner Communications Company

WARNER BOOKS EDITION

Cover illustration by Max Ginsburg

Warner Books, Inc.
666 Fifth Avenue
New York, N.Y. 10103

A Warner Communications Company

Printed in the United States of America

First Printing: November, 1988

10 9 8 7 6 5 4 3 2 1

To Kathy Kunis, without whose friendship, support, and dedication to long lunches I would have been lost. My love and thanks.

And to Bess and Jock Mullard and their daughters, Katie and Susanna, for whom this story was written.

Acknowledgments

I owe thanks to so many people during the course of writing this book, but I'd especially like to thank Edward Dawson of the Turl Wine Vaults in Oxford for his time and his information on the port industry. Mr. Raffety and his staff, of Raffety Clocks in London, were also very helpful, as was Mr. Alan Smith, an extraordinary gardener. I am very grateful to my friends in the Dordogne, particularly the Chaminades, for their generosity in allowing me to pry into the past as well as take pleasure in the present. Also, my thanks to Stephanie Waldron and Christine Dawkins for early editorial help, and to Fredda Isaacson for later guidance. And thanks to Bessie, for giving me Oxford.

CHAPTER One

The water was completely still save for the prow of the boat cutting cleanly through and leaving a rippling wake behind it. The sun had pushed over the horizon some hours before, but a slight chill still lingered in the air and Kate sat on the deck in an oversize blue cotton shirt, the hem pulled over her knees. She stared out at the water, oblivious to the startling Caribbean blue, her mind back in New York, once again playing out that last deadly scene with David . . .

A sudden, unexpected lash of wind blew a heavy arc of spray up and over the rail into Kate's face, snapping her wetly out of her reverie and she gasped and fumbled for her basket, dragging out a towel. Hairbrush, sunglasses, and an assortment of odds and ends came tumbling out in its wake and rolled along the deck.

"Oh, *hell*!" She jumped up and scurried after her things. "Why do I get the feeling that it's going to be one of those days?"

"What d'you mean?" asked Stephanie, looking up and for the first time noticing Kate's dilemma. "Oh, I see." She graciously put down her book and helped to pick up the wayward items. "Actually, I'm feeling quite pleased with the day so far. After all, we did manage to pick up a boat on the spur of the moment, and for a song, and after the hotel told us we'd have to book well in advance. I think this was a stroke of genius.''

''Things always seem to go that way when I'm around you, Steph. I'm convinced that your mother dragged you off in your infancy to kiss the Blarney Stone. You speak a right load of drivel, and everything drops right in your lap—Hey!'' She looked up in the nick of time and neatly caught the hotel keys thrown rudely at her. ''Of course, being an Amazon might have something to do with it, not to mention your powers of persuasion. Those poor Jamaicans couldn't drag us onto their boat fast enough! If you'd held out another few seconds I think we would have had the day for nothing.''

''I wouldn't have gone that far. They looked as if they could use some money, but I wasn't about to give them what the others were asking. This boat isn't exactly the height of luxury.''

''That, my dear Steph, is a typical understatement.'' Kate looked around her. It was a fishing boat; a tower holding a wheel and spaces for extra rods dominated the prow, and beneath it was a cabin containing, from what she could see, the controls, a table and sofa arrangement and, next to that, a galley. Below that, she supposed, lay the sleeping quarters. The rest was simply a wide area of deck with two chairs bolted to the planking. It was painted a steel gray, but the paint was weather-beaten and blistered and the plastic coverings on the seats were mildewed and cracked. A faint smell of fish exuded from the floorboards and she wrinkled her nose.

Stephanie laughed. ''Consider it local color. You know: quaint, charming, unique.''

''Unique, yes. And don't leave out the local aroma—it reminds me of cod-liver oil. The boat's probably held together by fish glue.''

''Most likely. But our money will feed both those men's families for a week. That's probably why they were so eager to have us.'' Stephanie yawned lazily, picked up her book, and settled back into one of the mildewed chairs.

"Oh, please, that's far too maudlin a scenario for you. I'd expect something more along the lines of ruthless drug runners luring innocent young women onto a boat and then selling them to white slavers."

"Kate, that's not bad—I could do something with that!" Stephanie closed her book again and assumed a faraway look. "Let's see. A romantic lead, a chase on the high seas—"

Kate smiled. "I hate to admit it, but I've really missed you."

"Really?" said Stephanie dryly. "If you've missed me so much, you might be a little more forthcoming. You practically demanded I come, gave me next to no notice, and haven't given me a clue as to what it's all about. You haven't exactly been full of cheer, you know. I don't want to pry, but there's obviously something going on, and it would help to know what it is."

Kate paused, feeling a little rush of guilt. It was true, she'd been miserable company and Stephanie was, after all, her closest friend. She owed her at least an explanation, despite how little she wanted to dredge it up.

"I guess it has been a little obvious. I'm sorry, Steph."

"Don't be silly, you have every right to be as miserable as you choose. But I must admit, I've been waiting for you to mention it. You used to talk to me, remember?"

"I know. I suppose I haven't wanted to say anything because—well, because it seemed pointless unloading my problems on you." A little smile crept onto her face. "I know how much you hate scenes unless you're writing them yourself."

"Nonsense. I just hate pointless scenes. Is it David?"

"Oh, Steph, the whole thing's the most awful mess. I—" Tears stung at her eyes and, angrily, she brushed them away. "You see? All I'd do is cry all over your shoulder. Quite pointless."

Stephanie looked at Kate calmly. "I don't think it is at all. I'll tell you what—why don't we forget about it and have a wonderful, carefree day and then you can tell me all about you and David over dinner and a bottle of wine. Okay?''

Stephanie's casual manner cheered Kate enormously. The last thing she could have borne just then was sympathy. She had been feeling sorry enough for herself in the last two weeks and that certainly hadn't helped matters. ''Okay. I guess maybe it will help to talk about it. But as you say, we'll save it for later. There's no reason to ruin a perfectly good day. Although,'' she added, looking worriedly up at the sky, ''the wind does seem to have suddenly picked up out of nowhere. I hope this isn't going to develop into a squall.''

''God help me if it does! Don't think I've forgotten that awful Channel crossing coming back from school when you managed to spend the entire time, all those long, unforgettable hours—''

''Enough said, you horror. You have no idea what a curse a weak stomach is.''

''Willpower, Kate, willpower. It's all in the mind.''

''I wish!'' Kate said with feeling. ''Cars, boats, airplanes, anything that goes back and forth or up and down too fast. I live in constant fear of embarrassing myself. Anyway, enough about that, I could go for something hot to drink. I'm a little cold.''

''Me, too. I wonder if they run to that sort of thing on this tub.''

''Maybe they'll surprise us.'' Kate looked up at the two men in the tower. They were talking quietly in a patois that was unintelligible to her. ''Hello, up there,'' she called. ''Hey, Eustice!''

One of the men turned and peered down at her, his teeth showing very white against his attractive black face as he smiled down at her. ''Miss?'' He spoke English with a beautiful, lilting accent.

''I don't suppose you have any hot coffee around somewhere? My friend and I could use some warming up.''

''But yes, Miss. Fresh hot coffee!'' He raised a Thermos and waved it at them. ''You'll be warm in no time!'' His rich laughter was carried away on the wind, and Stephanie threw a wicked smile at Kate, murmuring, "Want to bet it's laced with something sinister?"

Kate rolled her eyes, but when minutes later two steaming mugs of coffee were produced, Eustice pulled a bottle of white Appleton rum from the pocket of his tattered shorts and asked with a wide grin, "Maybe the ladies would like a bit of our island poison in the coffee?"

Kate whooped with laughter. "Pour away, Eustice, and one to you, Steph—"

"Just what the devil do you think you're doing with my rum, Eustice, and who the *hell* are these two uninvited persons?"

Kate turned around sharply at the sound of the clipped British voice and took in a tall man, shaggily blond, somewhere in his early thirties with a good week's growth of beard, a thin, high-bridged nose and extremely blue eyes which, at that moment, were red and bleary looking. He was leaning against the door of the cabin with his arms folded, wearing a faded pair of jeans and a sweatshirt that had seen better days, as had his old sneakers. His expression was less than pleasant.

"The ladies were cold, Mister Dristoll, sir."

"That is quite beside the point, my good friend. I want an explanation, and it had damned well better be a good one."

Kate glared at him in indignation. "Wait just one minute—"

"No, my dear girl, you wait—"

"I will not! I think we deserve an explanation from you! What are you doing on our boat?" Kate folded her arms across her chest and stood squarely facing him.

"Look madam, this happens to be my boat and I don't recall asking you aboard." He eyed her coldly.

"Your men did. We hired the boat for the day and you were most certainly not part of the agreement."

He turned his gaze on Eustice. "Well?"

"It is so. Bouge and I did not know you would be returning, and as we knew you were hard up for cash, we thought we would make you a little on the side. The ladies are not interested in fishing, just in boating around. Very simple, yes? How were we to know you had slept on the boat last night? We thought you had other plans.'' Eustice grinned innocently. It was quite clear that he wasn't the least bit shaken by the interrogation.

''Blast it, Eustice! This is my boat and I sleep on it when I like! Furthermore, neither my financial nor my personal affairs are any of your business. Now you've loaded me with these damned girls and I have a killing hangover. What do you intend to do about it?''

''Some rum in your coffee might help.''

''Oh, this is just delightful.'' He turned and examined Kate and Stephanie with a long, impassive stare and finally shook his head. ''It's too late to go back, I suppose, since we're out this far, so I'll have to put up with you for the duration of your little idyll. Simon Dristoll at your service.'' He bowed mockingly.

''I am Kate Soames and this is Stephanie Matthison. And you, Mr. Dristoll, are the necessary evil in our 'little idyll' I suppose?''

He raised an eyebrow. ''I expect there are a good many people who would agree with you. So, you are vacationing not only on my boat but also in Port Antonio?''

''Yes. At least until a minute ago. Now I could just as well be back in New York having a run-in with a cab driver.''

''Quite the tongue you have on you, Miss Soames. I must confess I have never been compared to a taxi driver, and certainly not to one who hails from New York. I shall have to mull the likeness over. In the meantime, you'll have to excuse me. I have a hangover to nurse. Eustice, I want to see you below—now.'' His tone brooked no argument and Eustice followed him into the cabin with a small backward shrug and an apologetic smile.

''My goodness,'' said Stephanie in a low voice.

Kate looked over at her and reluctantly smiled. '' 'What bloody man is that?' ''

''Oh, stop with the Shakespeare. And maybe not so

bloody. Behind those red-rimmed eyes and abrasive manner lurks an interesting piece of diversion.''

''No, you can't mean it, Steph! He's the most irascible man I've come across in a long time. You can have him.''

''Thanks, I might, if that Australian I've been cultivating doesn't work out. This Simon character is deliciously good looking and has a mighty pair of shoulders, but I must say, my Aussie looks exceptionally well endowed.'' She saucily tossed her thick mane of straw-colored hair back over her shoulder and lifted her mug. ''This isn't half bad, you know. Cheers!''

''Your mind is in the sewer as usual and I'm not at all sure that's an appropriate toast.''

''Oh, stop being so cranky, Kate, and let's have the promised happy day. It's bound to improve when the god gets over his headache.''

''I suppose. But his manners could certainly use a little polishing.''

''Forget it. Give him half an hour in your company and he'll be tame as a lamb and head over heels with you. They always are, you know. All you have to do is smile instead of going off like a rocket.'' She gate Kate a little squeeze on the shoulder. Kate shrugged and leaned over the railing, concentrating on the wake of the boat.

Stephanie joined her at the railing. ''Kate, whatever is going on? I've never known you to be without your sense of humor, even when everything else around you was falling apart. You've changed, my girl, and it's not just that sleek new haircut. I can't believe that problems with David have brought all this about.''

''I don't know what you mean, Steph. I'm the same as ever, just a little unhappy at the moment.''

''No, that's exactly what I mean. You always used to laugh about everything. Like just now, for instance. Poor Mr. Dristoll came in for quite a beating, when in the past you would have found the whole thing a hoot. It's as if all the fun's gone out of you.''

Kate gave Stephanie a troubled look. ''Do you think so?

Maybe it's too much exposure to the diplomatic circuit. I've probably been on my best behavior for too long."

"That could be. You know, you've never been quite yourself when you've been around your father. I didn't say anything at the time, but are you sure it was such a good idea moving back to America?"

"Oh, Steph, he needed me! You know how lonely he's been since my mother died, and I think he was dreading moving home to that big empty house. He wanted to have me nearby. What was I supposed to do, tell him to get lost?"

"Maybe it wouldn't have been such a bad idea," she said carefully. "Your two years away don't seem to have done you worlds of good. Anyway, we all miss you in England."

Kate smiled. "Thanks for that, anyway. I miss all of you too, more than I can say. I could go for one of Elizabeth's amazing Sunday dinners, and lounging around in the garden afterwards with the Sunday *Times*, arguing over the crossword puzzle, and then having to rush to get back to London before the traffic hit. Remember?"

"Of course I remember. Weekends at your godmother's house kept me going for the rest of the week. But do I sense a touch of homesickness here?"

"Maybe a little. I think I could use a good dose of Elizabeth's sensible advice right around now."

"I think you could too, but for the moment you're just going to have to settle for me."

"Thanks, Steph. I know I haven't been much fun, but don't worry about me, I'll be fine."

"If you say so. But do me a favor; lighten up, okay? We'll talk about the other stuff tonight, but why don't you give our hung-over friend below a break? He didn't ask for us, after all."

"Oh, the poor lamb," said Kate with a grin.

"That's more like the Kate I know." Stephanie went back to her book.

* * *

"All right now, Eustice, suppose you give me the real story. I have full confidence it's going to be a good one." Simon paced the cabin, one hand rubbing his eyes.

"To tell you the truth, I didn't know what else to do. About an hour after you'd gone to bed, I finished encoding the radio transmissions and went up above. There were very few people about at that hour, but there was a man whom I didn't recognize—he was discreet, but I'm almost positive he was watching the boat."

"What did he look like?"

"About six foot, white skin, dark hair and eyes, I'd say late twenties, early thirties. He was casually dressed and stayed well out of the way but there was something about him that didn't seem right. Then the women came up and asked if the boat was for hire. He looked quite startled, and then he turned away. The women seemed a good alibi for us under the circumstances, so I said the boat was available. I figured that if he was at all suspicious, they would put him off. As soon as they were on board he disappeared. There wasn't time to wake you, and once the job was done, there didn't seem any point. You've had little enough sleep for the last few days."

"There's been no time for sleep. It's almost over and we hardly have what we need. God in heaven, that bloody man Erharder is a wily old bugger and I'd be damned surprised if he shows his face—if he's even here. Not a sign of anything so far and I'm no closer to knowing where the hell to look." Simon leaned against the wall and considered for a moment. "Well, you did some quick thinking, Eustice. If it was someone on to us from the Group, I hope to hell you put him off. Otherwise we've got big trouble. Up until now I'd have sworn I was in the clear, and it's a strong possibility that the man you saw was there by coincidence. Still, if you see him again, mark him."

"I'll keep an eye out, you can count on it."

"I will. You know, Eustice," Simon said slowly, "we could actually use this situation to our advantage—you say the ladies hired the boat for the full day? Well . . . We have to keep someone at the radio until that transmission comes through, but between the three of us that shouldn't be such a problem. Maybe it's not so bad. I might just be able to turn this into a convenient cover. God knows I can use one if we are being watched. Unless, of course, our two friends up above are part of the whole thing."

"I can't imagine they could be. You should have seen the way they negotiated the price—I practically had to pull them on board."

Simon smiled. "How much did we make off it?"

"Ten dollars." Eustice grinned.

"Amazing. Well, it'll buy the three of us dinner tonight. So where did Rose White and Rose Red appear from?"

"Literally out of the blue. But I really don't think they're trouble."

"Nothing would surprise me at this point. I sincerely doubt there's anything to it, but I'll try to find out what I can about them—that would be a fine kettle of fish and not the first time I've been taken in. Keep a very sharp eye on them. In the meantime, I'm going to try to sleep awhile longer. Wake me if there's any problem, and for God's sake don't let them down here. And send Bouge in to monitor the radio." He pulled off his sneakers, lay down on the bunk, and was asleep almost immediately.

At about noon, Bouge reemerged from the cabin and went back up to the tower. He and Eustice conferred quietly, Bouge gesturing in a northeasterly direction. The wind had picked up considerably and the sky had begun to darken. The little boat swayed heavily among the whitecaps that had appeared almost out of nowhere.

Kate's face had paled beneath the golden tan and her hands gripped the railing. Stephanie watched her with concern but did her best to make light of the matter. "I once swore I would desert ship if you ever did this to me again, you know. Come on, buck up, there's a friend. Willpower, remember?"

"Believe me, I'm trying—oh, God, Stephanie, perhaps you'd better leave me to my own devices."

"Not to worry, I'm not such a rat as all that!"

"Oh, no?" Kate muttered. "All you'd need is a fast line to shore and you'd be crawling down it in a flash." The white pallor shaded abruptly to green and all conversation halted as she heaved over the side of the boat. Within moments the sky had opened and the rain began to pour down, pounding violently on the deck.

"Bouge!" Simon bellowed from the cabin door and Bouge ran down to meet him.

"Sorry, sir, I'm afraid a small crafts warning has been issued and we're in for a rough time. Eustice is turning the boat for shore." His face reflected his concern.

"Okay, rather than heading for the harbor let's aim for one of those small coves—there should be one within about half a mile from here, if I remember correctly. Check the map and then get down below and cover up any of the equipment that doesn't look quite right for a small fishing boat with an impoverished owner. Throw some clothes around, that sort of thing. It can't be helped, I'll have to bring the girls into the cabin. What a bloody stroke of luck." His mouth tightened as Bouge hurried off.

"Right, ladies, let's get you inside," he called. "Only idiots stand out in a tempest."

"It's Kate, Mr. Dristoll," cried Stephanie through the now howling wind. "I'm afraid she's suffering from a bad bout of seasickness and refuses to budge."

"So I see. You go inside, Miss Matthison, and I'll take care of it." Stephanie did as she was told with a worried backward glance.

Simon pulled on a heavy oilcloth jacket and went out to Kate. He could see that she was clinging for dear life to the railing and was very unwilling to be moved. In fact at that moment it would have been an impossible task.

"It's all right," he said gently when she had straightened up. "I'm going to take you in now, out of the rain. I know you're feeling bloody awful, and there's a basin in there you can use to your heart's content. I wouldn't move you for the world but it really isn't safe out here."

She groaned miserably, and he pulled a handkerchief from his jacket and gave it to her. "Come on then, there's a good girl. I've got some medicine in the cabin that will help you."

It was only the mention of something that might end her misery that convinced Kate to leave the refuge of the railing. With Simon's arm around her, half supporting her, half carrying her, she managed to stagger down into his sleeping quarters; and although Simon's jacket was definitely the worse for wear at the end of the journey, she was too sick to even notice. She was carefully deposited on a bunk, a blanket wrapped around her wet shirt and bathing suit and a basin instantly placed in her lap. For the next half hour she was blessedly ignored until the worst was over. When she looked up, Simon's face swam into her view.

"Here, a cold cloth will help," he told her, "and when you feel that you can, swallow these tablets. They'll make you sleepy, but I reckon that will seem like a blessing to you." Her teeth were chattering, and without a word he removed the blanket and stripped the wet shirt from her, gave her a brisk rub with a towel, and replaced the blanket.

"Thanks," she managed to say, beyond embarrassment, beyond much of anything.

"Not at all. It happens to the best of us under far less stormy circumstances. You'll be glad to hear we're anchored now, so you should start to feel better. Have some water with those."

A cup was put into her hand and she gratefully swallowed, then relinquished the cup and leaned back against the pillows feeling extraordinarily weak and tired. "Maybe you are something of a lamb after all," she whispered.

"I beg your pardon?" said Simon, somewhat bewildered at this peculiar statement. "I thought I was more like a New York cabbie in your opinion."

"Did I say that? How very rude of me..." Her eyes closed and then half opened again for just a moment. She smiled sleepily, foolishly at him, and murmured, "Apollo, the lamb." Then she dozed off.

He looked at her in bemusement. "Apollo the *lamb*? So, 'and this man is now become a god.' " he said softly and shook his head with a broad smile. "Some spy you'd make, sweetheart." He sat down to keep watch over the radio, highly amused at the turn of events.

CHAPTER *Two*

A few hours later Kate opened her eyes and found herself feeling very much better. She looked around the cabin with interest, taking in what she hadn't been able to focus on before. It was a mess, clothes strewn everywhere and piled over the backs of chairs and on the other bunk, which of course was unmade. She smiled to herself, thinking of Simon. It was exactly what she might have expected. She ran a wet cloth over her face and cleaned her mouth with her finger and some of Simon's toothpaste. Examining herself in the little mirror above the sink, she groaned; some color had come back to her face, but she definitely looked the worse for wear. She pulled the elastic band out of her dark hair and shook it loose. It fell neatly enough above her shoulders but could have used a good brush. Since there wasn't a comb or brush in sight, which hardly surprised her, she combed it with her fingers, and with complete disgust at the result, tied it back again. Her hazel eyes had managed to regain their clarity, where she'd expected them to be at least shot through with red, and they seemed unconcerned enough. Stephanie had often enough pointed out how easy her eyes were to read, and Kate felt pleased that now they reflected nothing at all. Stephanie had seen enough already.

Kate climbed up the steep steps into the upper cabin, but no one was there, so she wandered out onto the deck. The boat was securely tied in a little cove and the sun was shining once again, already having dried her shirt, which had been thoughtfully hung out on the railing. There was no one in sight and she slowly took in her surroundings, squinting against the bright light.

The cove itself was formed into a small semicircle cut out of the edge of a lush tropical jungle that gave onto a ribbon of pure, brilliant white sand. The palest of blue sea licked gently at it, but where the ledge on which the cove rested gradually sank off, the water shaded deeper and deeper into a sapphire blue of the most exquisite clarity. There was a perfect peace, worthy of Paradise and untouched by human sound, broken only by the distant twittering of birds and the lapping of the water upon the shore. Here indeed lay the idyll.

As far as the eye could see, a fine thread of sand defined the boundary between vegetation and sea. Coral reefs wove in and out of the coastline, easily spotted by eye and very beautiful, but terribly dangerous if one were to be accidentally swept upon one. Kate had heard somewhere that a cut made by a piece of coral would fester and was very difficult to heal. She wondered if it were true . . .

"Hello, Kate!" Stephanie's voice penetrated the stillness.

"Stephanie! Wherever have you been? Where is everyone?"

"Oh, Bouge and Eustice disappeared down the coast to the east, and Simon's just behind me. We've been to see the most amazing waterfall." She pulled herself up the ladder onto the boat.

"Have you now?" said Kate with a wicked leer. "And what else have you been to see, dear Steph?"

"I can see the sleep did you good. You're back in form, my dear. I might as well tell you now to save you further speculation, your Simon hasn't got eyes for me."

"*My* Simon?"

"So it appears. I can't think of another living soul that could be sick all over a man she'd never met before and have him dancing constant attendance on her.'' Stephanie raised her eyebrows teasingly.

''What on earth do you mean?'' asked Kate curiously.

''I hardly saw Simon. After he'd brought the boat into the cove, he spent the next two hours down below with you, Sleeping Beauty, watching over you tenderly. It was only a half hour ago that he remembered my existence and took me off to see the falls.''

''You're joking! I must say, he was incredibly kind to me. Not a single word about throwing me overboard.''

''He must have thought there was enough of you overboard as it was.''

''Oh, you wretch! You miserable, low-crawling creature—''

''It's not I who's the wretch, Kate Soames. Who laid first—''

''What in heaven's name are you two shouting about?'' Simon appeared over the side. ''You sound like a couple of fishwives haggling over the day's catch!'' Kate and Stephanie looked at each other and burst into helpless laughter.

''God help us,'' said Simon.

By the time they returned to the harbor, it was bustling with activity; fishing boats clustered together bringing in the day's catch, nets were being spread out to dry, and bright groups of color littered the docks. Women with straw baskets of every size and shape were bargaining loudly with the fishermen. A great deal of shouting and jostling went on, but all in the spirit of the game that was played every day, all year long.

Simon inclined his head in silent question at Eustice who was carefully combing the crowd, but Eustice could only shrug a shoulder. There was no sign of the man who had been so interested in their boat that morning.

''Right, well it's been very interesting indeed meeting you two, and I wish you the best of luck with the remainder of your stay. Perhaps I'll see you around.'' Although his words were polite it was obvious that his attention was elsewhere and he was anxious to be on his way.

"Thanks again for everything, truly, Simon." Kate grinned broadly.

"Really, Simon," echoed Stephanie, laughing, "you made our day." But he had already turned and elbowed his way into the crowd, disappearing quickly.

The hotel was situated on a much wider cove than the one in which they'd been sheltering earlier in the day. It had its own bay stretching onto a broad beach and the living quarters were a series of white cottages situated on the hills above and stepping in levels down to the wide, grassy lawn. Each cottage, its shutters painted a different color from the others, had two to four bedrooms and a sitting room that opened onto a wide balcony overlooking the bay. The cottages were brightly decorated with prints by local artists and the furniture was predominately white; rush matting covered the floor. It gave the rooms a light, airy feeling and in the evening the sound of calypso singers playing below drifted up through the windows on a soft breeze, mingling with the scent of exotic flowers.

There were two restaurants to choose from, one in the main courtyard of the general reception area and another high above the cottages, a good ten-minute walk, perched on a cliff that offered views of mountain and sea. It was here that Kate and Stephanie had decided to have their promised dinner, and it was everything they could have asked for. They were both ravenous and dug into their food with relish. They started with a delicate conch soup, succulent chunks of the meaty shellfish floating in a rich cream broth, and followed that with a spicy lamb curry made with coconut milk and surrounded by fried plantains and rice colored deep yellow with saffron. A bottle of ridiculously priced but nevertheless delicious Chardonnay accompanied the meal. By the time they had finished a dessert of mango mousse, they were happily filled to bursting and moved out onto the terrace to take the island's rich Blue Mountain coffee, named for the backbone of lushly vegetated hills that formed the center of the island.

"Oh, heaven," sighed Kate contentedly. "That was the perfect way to finish a truly bizarre day."

"It's not finished yet, my dear." Stephanie fished out a cigarette from her pack and lit it from the glassed candle on the table. "Truce is over—start talking."

"Great—just when I was starting to relax. I suppose you want to hear all the gruesome details?"

"Every last one. And start at the beginning. You're the worst letter writer I know, and when you do write, I can never make any sense out of it."

"What a pal. All right, I suppose I do owe you an explanation for my filthy behavior and I might as well get it over with." She took a deep breath and stared down into her cup. "From the beginning. Well, as you know—at least, I think I told you—David's a lawyer, a very successful one with a high-powered New York firm. He was Harvard Law Review, all that; I'm sure you get the picture. He's also an aspiring politician and recently decided to run for Congress. I met him about a year ago at one of my father's parties, the usual mixture of foreign service and government types. He was charming, intelligent, and good looking, the fatal combination."

"I've never known you to be overwhelmed by the combination before."

"No? Well, I guess there's something different about David. And miracle of miracles, my father actually likes him."

"Really..." Stephanie inhaled deeply on her cigarette and watched the hazy blue smoke curling lazily up into the air and vanishing into the midnight sky.

"Really. Anyway, we started going out, and there was the usual romantic stuff, but this time it was serious. So, after an appropriate period of time, we decided to get married. Naturally Daddy was as thrilled as could be. David eventually wants to aim for the State Department without going through the usual tedium, and I'm sure Daddy will be more than willing to help him in. What could be better?" She frowned, fidgeting with her coffee cup, turning it round and round in the saucer.

"Sounds like heaven," said Steph dryly.

"It was at first, it really was, but then the trouble began. I wanted to wait a year. That didn't go down at all well, but I really can't see the point in rushing something that's supposed to last a lifetime. David started to push the issue. He says it's important for a politician to be married, it's better for his image, and he thinks I'm shying away from making a commitment. The murderous thing is that Daddy agrees with him."

"Traitor! But then your father's never backed you in anything, has he?"

"I know, but I'd never done anything by his rules either, at least not until now. Still, I don't think he had any right to take David's side, not in such a personal issue. Anyway, I tried to counter by saying that he hadn't married again and it hadn't hurt his diplomatic career a bit. Naturally, that was exactly the wrong thing to say. You know what Daddy's like. He just bristled and remarked that he'd never find another woman like my mother, whereas I'd found David, and there was no point in putting off something that could be beneficial to both of us now. I don't know, maybe I am afraid of making a commitment."

"Don't be ridiculous," said Stephanie succinctly.

"In any case, the issue had been heating up, and David and I had an unholy confrontation just before I left. He said that if I couldn't make up my mind then maybe we had better forget the whole thing, and you know me, instead of bursting into tears and backing down, which would have been the sensible thing to do, I was up in arms. I felt as if he were trying to tie me up in a neat little package labeled 'politician's wife, image maker.' I told him that maybe it was a good idea to call the whole thing off since he couldn't seem to respect my point of view, and then I dropped a little bomb on him that I'd been putting off telling him about."

"Oh, good, one of your little bombs. Do tell."

"Well . . . My firm's offered me a fantastic opportunity

for the summer. They want to send me back to the London office to learn more about the port industry, which they're thinking about promoting over here in a big way, and as a nice plum thrown in they want me to go to France to buy some wines for them. They think I'm perfect for the job because of my background, but I've also been slaving away for four years and I've damned well earned it."

"Gosh, that's fantastic, Kate, that's really exciting news! Have you accepted?"

"That's the hell of it. I haven't because of David. He exploded when I told him, said it was out of the question. That did it. I as much as told him to get lost and threw his ring at him. Then he suddenly went very quiet, you know the kind of icy calm that makes your blood run cold? Well, he said that since I was so keen on taking my time to make important decisions, perhaps I would do him the courtesy of reconsidering while I was away. We were supposed to go on this trip together..."

"Oh, so that's where my invitation stemmed from. Second choice, am I?"

"Better than last, and you might be gracious about it." Kate smiled a little grimly. "Anyway, then he quietly told me that he loved me very much and didn't want to lose me over a childish temper tantrum, kissed me, and showed me out. That was that."

"So? We've all felt the effects of your temper in the past, Kate, and you're always overcome by remorse. This sounds typical."

"I know, I do know, and I feel like a fool—and terrible about the whole thing, naturally. I was horrible to him, and he's so warm and sweet, when he's not being . . . Oh, I don't know—"

"Authoritarian?" supplied Stephanie helpfully.

"Yes! Yes, that's exactly it! Why should I have to sacrifice all the other things I want just because I love him? I shouldn't have to change myself inside out to suit him, but I don't want to hurt him either. He needs someone always to be there supporting him, and I just don't know how many political parties and social circuits I can stand. You know how much I loathe that sort of thing. I only did it for my father because there was no one else. So you see, it's not just the stupid argument. I have to decide if it's really better to end it now, even though it's the last thing I want to do. And if I want to pick it up again, then I have to go crawling back like a complete worm."

"Yes, I see the problem," said Stephanie sympathetically. "The old story of you can't live with him, you can't live without him. Throw in a little of the old Kate Soames pride mixed up with some second thoughts and you have a typical made-for-television movie by which I make my fortune."

"Stephanie! This is my life we're talking about, not one of your fabricated movies!"

She smiled. "I am aware of that, but you can't fault me for recognizing the material. Seriously, Kate, I think you need to decide on what you're willing to compromise. You can't have it all, you know. Figure out what's going to make you happy in the long run. Fine words coming from me, right?"

"Right, you're a great help. I'd managed to get that far all on my own." Kate gave a little laugh. "Why don't you write the ending for me, friend?"

"No, sorry. This one you're going to have to finish all by yourself. Just don't let your pride get in the way."

"I know, my damnable pride. It's hell, Steph, it really is."

"How about relaxing a little? It's not the end of the world yet. Try going home and talking it out. Maybe he's feeling a little repentant, too."

"I hadn't thought about that."

"Of course not. You're always too busy taking the blame on yourself instead of spreading it around a little. Remember poor Peter in Hampshire? You made that out to be all your fault."

"Oh, Stephanie—trust you to bring up one of the more embarrassing episodes of my life!"

Stephanie laughed. "Come on, let's pay up and go home."

* * *

Late the next afternoon Kate and Stephanie decided that they'd had enough of the usual tourist fare. Stephanie had a late evening engagement planned with her Australian endowment, as Kate now referred to him gleefully, and so they decided on an early dinner somewhere off the beaten track. They asked the desk clerk they'd befriended for advice, and he made a great show of giving away a tightly guarded secret when he divulged the dirt road winding through the back of the town and up into the hills. They were guaranteed not only spectacular views but also a marvelous and unpretentious little restaurant. Thrilled with the suggestion and making appropriate expressions of gratitude, they piled themselves into the ancient and somewhat unreliable Hillman Minx that Kate had rented at Kingston airport (she'd thought it interesting looking) and chugged off fitfully.

They found the road with a little difficulty, much circling, and even more laughter. Port Antonio was certainly full of charm, but the roads were unpaved, uneven, and perilously narrow in places. Kate negotiated the hairpin turns with great trepidation—not only did she not trust the Hillman, but also she quickly discovered that anything from chickens to goats would wander out onto the road without warning and no amount of horn blowing would move them. As a result, Stephanie was forced out onto the road with a great show of arm waving and raucous threats while Kate urged the car forward at a crawl. At one point along the way they were assaulted by a crowd of enthusiastic and curious children, all talking and giggling at once and attempting to climb on the car as it inched forward, which was the most it was inclined to do. But the children dropped off as the car left the last of the villages and Stephanie and Kate were away into the hills, climbing steadily as the little Hillman strained upward. It grew hushed and majestic as they gained in altitude and as they rounded one particularly treacherous corner, the island seemed to fall away beneath them.

Kate parked the car as far as she dared off the road and

they went to stand on the edge of the cliff. The air was crisp and cool, the sun already pale red and descending. And in the distance was the sea, a tiny blanket of sapphire blue cradled in the arms of the emerald jungle. Wisps of clouds drifted around them, shifting in the smoky blue gray air.

They stood for a while, each locked in her separate thoughts, but as the sky began to don its evening pastels, the air grew chill, and hunger beckoned. The restaurant was only another mile up the road, and its lights welcomed them. It looked a pleasant enough place, a low rectangular building with a red tiled roof and whitewashed walls. They were ushered in by a very friendly Jamaican with a generous stomach and a gold tooth crowning his broad smile.

"You ladies have come for supper? Good, good! You shall sit outside and have something to drink while you look at our menu." The enormous Jamaican, who introduced himself as Joe, ushered them out onto the most incredible veranda.

It seemed to support itself in thin air but must have been built into the side of the mountain. The view was spectacular, opening onto rolling hills shrouded in thin cloud, seemingly close yet at the same time infinitely far away. Rush shades had been lowered on the exposed sides to keep the wind from blowing through, and they were seated at a table next to the railing overlooking the mountains. At the only other table occupied three white men sat drinking the local Red Stripe beer. One of them glanced over his shoulder, then slowly turned in his chair and stared at Kate with narrowed eyes. He was old, his hair a pure silver and his face deeply lined, but his eyes, so light they were almost without color, were chillingly clear as they raked her up and down without any attempt at subtlety. A twisted scar ran below his ear and disappeared into the collar of his shirt. She looked quickly away, a shudder running down her spine...

Joe reappeared with a concoction he called Blue Mountain cocktails, a lethal mixture of rum, vodka, and Tia Maria mixed with fresh orange and lime juice. "You will find it delicious, I guarantee," he boomed.

They sipped, and although at first Kate thought it felt like liquid fire going down, it did taste delicious and she said so. Joe couldn't have looked more pleased.

"Now for my menu. I'll explain everything on it in great detail, and then leave you to take your time. Matters like this cannot be rushed." He proudly asserted that no other kitchen on the island was comparable to his when it came to cooking local fare, and he then launched into his commentary on the menu. It took another five minutes before he left them.

"If I may make a suggestion, ladies, I'd leave all the decisions up to Joe." The voice spoke quietly over Kate's left ear, and she spun around in surprise.

"Oh! Simon! What are you doing here!"

"And well met to you, too," said Simon with a little laugh. "May I join you?" He pulled up a chair.

"Of course," said Stephanie quickly. "Don't mind Kate, she's a little slow at times, but we love her."

"You know Joe?" asked Kate, wondering if Simon owned any clothes that were not old and worn. He was wearing jeans and a plain white T-shirt covered by a jacket, and although his clothes were quite clean, he was still unshaven and his hair had apparently been dried by the wind.

"I've known Joe for years. He's quite a character. How on earth did you ferret this place out? It's carefully guarded from tourists."

"We got lucky; a spy at the hotel gave it out. Why? Do you object to our being here, Mr. Dristoll?" she asked when he shot her a peculiar look.

"Not at all, Miss Soames. It's indeed a pleasure to run across you again. The only reason Joe's is kept under wraps is to protect it from being discovered and spoiled by an invasion of tourists. The local people need a place of their own, and this is it. Whoever told you about Joe's must have thought you quite unusual."

"Well, of course!" said Stephanie. "So you recommend that we place ourselves in Joe's hands?"

"Without reservation. Whatever he comes up with is bound to be extraordinary."

Joe bustled out again. "So! Welcome, welcome, my

friend! You know these ladies? It was you who sent them to me?''

''Not exactly, Joe,'' said Simon, throwing Joe a look of caution. ''But we are acquainted.''

''And you will eat with them, no?''

''I'm afraid I haven't been invited,'' he said with a rueful smile.

''Oh, yes, please join us,'' offered Stephanie enthusiastically.

''How very kind, if Kate doesn't mind.''

''No—no, of course not,'' said Kate, hurriedly. She was thoroughly disconcerted; he seemed to have read her mind, and if the funny little smile in his eyes was anything to go by, he knew it. She couldn't understand why she felt this queer reticence; after all, she really did owe him a debt of gratitude, and she promised herself to be more sociable.

As it turned out, dinner was a great success. They had another Blue Mountain cocktail (Simon declining); Joe did indeed live up to his reputation and they had a superb meal, with courses that seemed to never end, crowned with a roast pork Calypso. Simon seated himself facing the other tables, insisting that Kate and Stephanie enjoy the view. They shared a bottle of wine, and Kate found herself disarmed in no time, for Simon was thoroughly pleasant and relaxed company, amusing them with light stories of life aboard a boat and lesser-known facts about Jamaica that had them all laughing.

''Oh, no! Look at the time—it's flown by! Kate, I'm sorry to have to drag you away like this but I'll be late if we don't go now . . .'' Stephanie dug in her purse for her wallet.

''Have you an appointment?'' asked Simon casually.

''Yes, I'm afraid so, in half an hour at the hotel. No time for coffee. Sorry to end dinner so abruptly.''

''Well, that's easy enough. Why don't you take the car you came up in, and I'll bring Kate home later.''

''Oh, what a fabulous idea! How kind of you, Simon, I was feeling so guilty . . .'' She threw some bills on the table and rose. ''I'll settle up with you later, Kate. You're both dears to understand.''

''Just a minute, you two. Don't I have any say in this?''

"Not really," said Simon easily, his eyes smiling at her.

"Oh," said Kate, handing Stephanie the car keys.

"Now that we're alone, you can tell me all about yourself, without worrying about boring Stephanie." Simon leaned back in his chair and folded his arms.

"There's nothing very fascinating to tell."

"Oh, I wouldn't say that. Let's see: For example, you're twenty-five and American, your hybrid accent comes from traveling all over the world with your father who was with the State Department, you were schooled with your friend Stephanie at Châtelard, Switzerland, and then you went on to Trinity College, Oxford—where you took a First in English literature, I believe? After that you and Stephanie lived together in London and were holy terrors until you decided to move home to America when your father retired, and you transferred to the New York office of Rosterman and Marsh, the wine brokers. Does that cover it, or would you like to add anything?" He grinned.

Kate stared. "How did you—oh . . . Stephanie?"

"Exactly, Stephanie. Such a mine of information. Of course, I felt I was entitled, after services rendered."

"Oh, you beast! What else did she tell you?"

"Ah . . . There are some things one never gives away, certainly not a woman's secrets." Simon raised his eyebrow in a particularly infuriating way.

"I see. And now you think I'm inadvertently going to reveal myself in an effort to find out how much you know. Very clever, Mr. Dristoll, but your strategy won't work."

"No? Don't tell me you're not dying of curiosity this very minute."

"Certainly not." Kate did her best to look indifferent.

"Ha!" Simon laughed. "The truth is, you can't decide what your degree of disadvantage is. You must have been very wicked to be looking so worried."

"I can't imagine why you'd suggest such a thing." She looked down at her cup of coffee, smiling.

"Can't you? There's something about you, my dear Kate, that suggests it for you." His smile widened.

"Oh, really? Coming from you that's hardly surprising. I

imagine you're quite capable of reading wicked motives into the Virgin Mary if it suited your purpose."

Simon burst into laughter. "Naturally. But I can't think you're comparing yourself to that dear lady? Wouldn't that be just a bit exaggerated?"

Kate grinned. "You're quite good, you know. But you get nothing more out of me. This may surprise you, as it seems you're accustomed to availing yourself of personal biographies, but I'm not in the habit of revealing my life to total strangers. You happen to fall into that cagetory, my dear Mr. Dristoll. And in any case, what do I know about you other than the fact that you live on a boat that's falling apart at the seams and you make some sort of living fishing the island? That's not an awful lot to go on."

"No, it's not, is it?" said Simon complacently.

"Well then," she said, going for game point, "why should I tell you anything more about myself?"

"No reason other than I asked," said Simon, taking the match, and calling for the check before Kate could reply.

They drove back down the mountain in Simon's car, a battered old Mini in only slightly better condition than the Hillman. Kate's mind drifted lazily in the companionable silence; she felt completely comfortable and, she had to admit, slightly light-headed. Her eyes followed the distant glow of red taillights winding on the road below them, and eventually the lights turned up a road shortly before the fork to Kate's hotel.

"I have an idea," said Simon, breaking into Kate's thoughts. "Did you see where that car turned off? There's a pleasant little place up there that you really shouldn't miss. Would you like to give it a try?"

"Well . . . What is it, exactly?"

"Oh, it's a small sort of club, with music, dancing, that sort of thing. It's a nice atmosphere, good view and never crowded. You'd like it, I think." Simon glanced at her through the dark. "Anyway, if Stephanie's entertaining in your cottage, you wouldn't want to cramp her style." He grinned.

Kate gave a short laugh. "You are persuasive, aren't you? Do you always get your own way?"

"Not by any means. But this time I'm hoping I will. Would you like to try it?" He slowed for the turn.

"Yes, all right. The night's so beautiful, it would be a shame to cut it short."

He was right, she thought immediately, it was a pleasant place. There was an outside terrace that faced out over a floodlit garden that had been painstakingly landscaped. They took a small table bordering the low wall where steps led down onto the grass. As Simon had said, there were not that many people, but Kate noticed with a vaguely uncomfortable surprise that they were seated close to the same three men that had been at Joe's restaurant. It must have been their lights Simon had followed down.

"Do you know those people?" she asked, indicating the table.

"No, why would I?"

"Just because they were at Joe's. I thought they might be local."

"I gather one of them is, of a sort, the one with the silver hair."

Kate turned around and gave him a good stare. She was delighted when he frowned at her and looked away.

Simon choked on his drink. "Kate, you dreadful girl, how can you be so obvious?"

"Well, he stared at me at Joe's, and very rudely, too, so I thought I'd just give him a taste of his own medicine."

"Oh, I see." Simon shook his head with a little laugh. "Sweetheart, you really are quite something."

"Well, who is he, then? I like to know my enemies."

"His name is Willy Schumann, according to Joe. I've never met him, but Joe says he has a house at Alligator Head. As I understand it, he only comes every now and then, and pretty much keeps to himself."

"It's a good thing. I wouldn't like to run into him or his friends, for that matter, on a dark night. I wonder how he got that scar on his neck."

"One of his female victims probably bit him. How about

forgetting our sinister friends and giving me a dance." Simon rose to his feet and took her hand.

The music was soft and slow, a lilting song Kate didn't recognize. Simon drew her into his arms and Kate went easily, as if she'd been doing it all her life. She found she enjoyed the feel of him, the way his firm body moved against her, the long muscle of his back shifting beneath his jacket. Sighing, she rested her head on his chest and let herself be carried away. He smelled clean and good, of fresh air and sea. So nice, so uncomplicated . . . She closed her eyes and thought of nothing at all.

Simon's eyes were watchful.

"Kate?"

"Mmm?"

"The music's finished."

"Oh, so it is!" She looked up to see that they were the only people left on the floor and the musicians were leaving their places. Simon was grinning down at her. She suddenly noticed how the little creases at the side of his mouth deepened when he smiled.

"It was nice, wasn't it, but I think the band's taking a break. We'll do it again later." He led her off, his eyes laughing.

As Kate passed the old man's table, she felt his eyes on her back, and once again a shudder of repulsion passed through her. "Simon?" She looked up at him as he pulled her chair out for her.

"Yes?" His eyes met hers, and an odd jolt ran through her, but a pleasant one, very unlike her reaction to Mr. Willy Schumann.

"I—oh, forget it, it's stupid."

"What is it, Kate? You look troubled." He sat down opposite her.

"It's nothing, really. There's just something about that man that makes me extremely uneasy."

"Yes, I know exactly what you mean."

"I wish I hadn't goaded him earlier. It's just given him an excuse to stare back."

"I shouldn't let him get to you, Kate. He's probably just a lecherous old man who gets his kicks out of ogling pretty women. I'll probably be doing the same at his age." He leaned his chin on his hand, regarding her lazily. "And I can certainly see why he picked you out."

Kate laughed. "Was that meant to be reassuring?"

"Absolutely. Don't you know a compliment when you hear one?"

"I think I might just be getting the hang of it. You've obviously had a lot of practice. But that reminds me—what happened the other night? It seems all your years of training went for nothing."

"What do you mean?" The hand had dropped away and he looked at her blankly.

"You know perfectly well what I mean."

"Do I?"

"Yes. You were in a terrible state, and Eustice was certainly under the impression that you weren't meant to be sleeping on the boat. It sounded as if you hadn't planned on it either."

"Just what are you getting at?"

"I was just wondering whether you were involved with someone and she, well, she stood you up or broke it off. It was the only reason I could think of to put you in such a filthy mood."

"I see. I do think I see," he said slowly, then smiled. "But to put your mind at ease, no. I wasn't stood up and I was in a filthy mood, as you put it, for quite a different reason. And no, I'm not involved with anyone. Is there anything else you'd like to know?"

"No, I was just curious. I—never mind, I shouldn't have asked."

Simon burst into laughter. "Kate, you really are an extraordinary girl. I can't make you out. Have you gone through all your life like this?"

"I don't know what you mean."

"I mean you're a spitfire one minute, an innocent child the next, and then a beautiful, fascinating woman before I've had time to draw breath."

"Oh . . ."

Simon reached over and took her hand. "It's a good thing you're only here on a short holiday. I could become quite fond of you."

"Well, what's so wrong with that?"

He grinned. "I never get involved. Never, never, never."

"Never?" Kate said, laughing.

"Absolutely not. Let's dance."

They talked for another two hours, Kate sipping on white wine and Simon on cognac, and they danced a few more times. Kate was relieved when the trio of men left, for she couldn't help but be aware of Mr. Schumann's continuing and unwanted attention. But once gone, she quickly forgot about him. She found that she was more relaxed than she had been in weeks; Simon was so easy to be with, so undemanding and comfortable. The wine probably helped, and the moonlight and soft air and Simon . . .

"I think it's time to go, sweetheart. High time you should be tucked away in bed."

"Yes, you're quite right. You should probably have tucked me away a good hour ago."

"Really?" said Simon with a grin.

"Honestly, Simon. You are in training to be an old lech, aren't you?" She stood, and Simon's hand slipped quickly under her elbow.

"Steady as you go there, mate."

"Oh, dear, I think I had a bit too much . . ."

"I think you did too, but there's no harm in that. You had fun, didn't you?"

"Oh, Simon, I really did. I can't tell you how long it's been since—" She cut herself off abruptly. "Actually that's not at all true. But not the part about having a good time tonight, because I did, really."

Simon ignored this remarkably silly speech, saying only, "How would you like to go scuba diving tomorrow afternoon, say around two?" He helped her into the car.

"I'd like that. In fact it sounds wonderful! I feel so much better, Simon, thank you."

"I wasn't aware you'd been feeling bad."

"Well, I had been, but I don't want to talk about it."

Simon smiled in amusement. "Absolutely not. I'm just glad you're better from whatever it was. We aim to please." He said nothing more, concentrating on the road, until he drove through the gates of the hotel.

"Here we are. Which one are you?"

"Um, oh, three hundred ten—no, three—it's that one down there. Oh, Simon, I think you'd better ignore everything I've said for the last two hours at least, and I'll hope that I've forgotten it in the morning."

"Nonsense. You've been wonderful company. In fact, I haven't had such an—interesting evening in a very long time."

"Really?" said Kate in delight. "My, you couldn't be having much of a love life after all!"

"Why, you little shrew!" he exclaimed, and she threw her head back and crowed with laughter. But the steps leading down to the cottage were steep and rocky, and Kate, her balance not being all it should, tripped. His arm came immediately around her and she fell against him, still laughing.

"Oh, dear, thank you." She looked up at him and grinned. "I'm sorry, Simon. I'm sure it's not true. In fact, I'm sure that you have millions of women swarming around you all of the time. In fact—"

"Hush, Kate." His other arm came around her and pulled her closer.

Kate found that suddenly she couldn't quite catch her breath. "Simon . . ." she managed, her hands coming up against his chest, and somewhere she registered the hard, broad planes beneath the T-shirt and the steady beating of his heart. She really ought to tell him about David . . .

Lifting her eyes to his face, she found herself locked in his gaze. He was examining her face intently, for what she wasn't at all sure. But somehow her explanation no longer seemed important. Her hands slipped beneath his jacket with a will of their own and then she froze, the moment snapped by the touch of cold steel under his arm.

"Simon—what is that!"

"A gun," he said mildly.

"A gun!" She pulled away from him. "What are you doing carrying a gun around? Isn't that a little bit sinister?"

"It's protection. There's a big difference on this island between resort living and my kind of life-style. You can't be too careful late at night around the harbor."

"Oh . . . I hadn't thought of that."

He smiled down at her. "I hadn't expected you would." Then, with no warning, he scooped her up in his arms and carried her down the rest of the narrow steps, leaning her against the door of the cottage. "There you are, madam, safely delivered."

"Thanks again, Simon, it was lovely."

"No, I thank you, Kate. You have no idea what a favor you've done me. I'll pick you up here tomorrow?"

"Yes, tomorrow. Well . . . Good night."

"Good night, Kate," he said with a little laugh as she disappeared through the door. He went up the steps, then stopped and looked back at the cottage for a long moment. Then he turned abruptly and walked off to his car.

CHAPTER Three

It was late morning and the sun beat hotly down from a shimmering blue sky. But Kate and Stephanie were sheltered in the cool of the balcony where they were having coffee and toast, neither having stirred from bed until half an hour before.

"It sounds like a wonderful evening, Kate. I'm so glad you had a good time." Stephanie turned and helped herself to some more coffee as she spoke. A decidedly mischievous gleam lurked in her eye. "It's very nice of you to ask me along this afternoon, but I've already made plans. D'you mind?"

"Of course not. I'm glad the endowment's going well."

"Very well, thanks. But the thing is, since it's our last night, he's asked me to his place for dinner—I was wondering?"

"Oh, Steph, for heaven's sake! I thought we worked this sort of thing out years ago. Go, have a marvelous time and tell me all about it afterwards. But don't get carried away and forget that we have a plane to catch tomorrow afternoon, will you?"

"It's no wonder I haven't been able to bear another roommate since you left."

"I know exactly what you mean. You know, one of the

things I miss most are the talks we used to have. They always helped to put things into perspective." Kate chewed thoughtfully on a piece of toast.

"So here's your big opportunity. Tell me more about Simon."

"Mmm, sorry, there's nothing more to tell. You saw it all for yourself at Joe's."

"I don't believe it—he didn't offer forth a shred of romance?" Stephanie looked incredulous.

"No, he didn't. It wasn't that sort of thing at all." Kate made a face at her.

"Why ever not? I could have sworn that's what he had on his mind, the way he was looking at you. You didn't tell him about David, did you?"

"Actually, I didn't, but not because I was trying to keep it from him. It just didn't come up." She remembered, with a small stab of discomfort, that one brief moment when it nearly had. Quickly pushing it from her mind, she said, "That reminds me, I have a bone to pick with you."

"Uh oh. What have I done this time?"

"Just a small matter of revealing my life story the other day, does it ring any bells?"

"Oh, that." Stephanie waved her coffee cup at Kate. "Well, look at it this way. I didn't tell him you were halfway engaged—a very salient point, don't you agree?"

"You really are the end."

"I was just trying to be helpful. Anyway, he struck me as rather nice. But it's true, he did ask a lot of questions . . . You know, Kate, it occurs to me, he knows a great deal about us, and we know absolutely nothing about him."

"Aha! A mystery in the making."

"I'm serious. He's very good about worming past history out of you, isn't he? Now why would he want all that useless information?"

"Maybe he's just curious. Come on, Stephanie, the man's a fairly obvious piece of work. He likes to bum around the islands; what kind of a mystery can you make out of that?"

"That's my point, you idiot. How many people do you

know who speak with that sort of well-bred accent drop out of the mainstream of life and opt for tooling around in a smelly fishing boat with two crazy Jamaican types for the rest of their lives—and at his age, too!"

"The only reason you think it's odd is because you live in the middle of London and hang around with bowler and umbrella types. There are a lot of people like him, not just down here, either. Haven't you ever heard of a free spirit? And just what do you mean, 'at his age'? He's only just thirty!"

"That's still too old to be playing the university-student-drops-out-for-a-year game."

"I liked the original plot better—which reminds me, I nearly forgot the best thing of all. Are you ready for this? Simon packs a pistol."

"What?" Stephanie looked delighted.

"He was wearing a gun of some kind strapped under his arm last night."

"In a holster? How absolutely incredible—but why?"

"Protection, he said. Isn't it too good to be true?"

"Utter bliss. He's probably running ganja or cocaine to Miami and making a killing. He'll have the last laugh on you, Kate."

"Over my dead body!"

"Most likely. Well, whatever the story is I must say I like him."

"He's nice enough," said Kate, and changed the subject.

Simon anchored the boat just short of the reef and helped Kate into her scuba gear. "You're not very heavy, are you? Here, I think you'll need a few weights. I do assume you've done this before?"

"Lots. Don't worry, I won't drown on you, Simon." He dropped to one knee and fastened the weight belt around her waist, over her yellow tank suit. He had beautiful hands, she noticed, as he maneuvered the buckles with long, squared fingers; not the hands she would have expected of a fisherman.

"Nothing you did would surprise me, my dear. There you are, that should be about right. Now, the reef runs about half a mile to the west. It's fairly shallow in front, but drops off steeply behind. If for some reason we get separated, get your bearing first by the water level, then swim along the more shallow side until you come to a long flat plain. It runs about a hundred feet to the stern of the boat. But don't."

Kate thought with an inward smile that her guess the night before about his build was proved correct, now that he wore only a swimsuit. His torso was long and well muscled with broad shoulders, and his legs were powerful, covered with the same blond down as his forearms and the triangular patch on his chest that tapered off and ran in a fine line—

"Kate?"

"Oh—what?"

"Don't get lost." Simon grinned, his eyes impossibly blue.

"Aye aye, cap'n. I'll stick to you like glue." Kate smiled up at him.

The water was clear and warm. A myriad of aquatic life lay below, the colors vibrant and varied. Kate reached her hand out to stroke the frond of a wavy red seaweed. Above the water it would have felt slimy, but here in its own environment it had a delicately silky texture. Schools of fish darted by and they passed a rock ledge that contained a colony of sponges. She'd read somewhere that a sponge had to filter a ton of water for food particles before it could absorb enough to gain an ounce of body weight. Some of these sponges were huge. She wondered idly how many tons of water they had filtered in their lifetime.

She followed Simon as religiously as she'd promised, and she had to admit she enjoyed watching him. He was in excellent condition, with not an ounce of fat on him, and the muscles rippled below his skin as he smoothly kicked and twisted. His hair floated around his head, undulating in the water like a cloud of algae.

Kate loved the transformation from land animal to sea creature that came with diving. She loved moving like a fish, loved the shafts of sunlight that filtered down hazily gold, and the way the surface of the water looked from below, a clear glass sheet protecting its precious sea life from the treacherous air above. She loved the way the sandy bottom was suddenly whipped up as some little creature scrambled for cover or the way a school of smaller fish would veer and seem to vanish into thin air at the approach of a possible predator.

Simon arched around and beckoned her over, pointing to a dark hotel below in the rock. Kate maneuvered down to it and peered in curiously. Her heart seemed to stop with a violent jerk and every nerve ending screamed. The most enormous fish head was staring out at her with bulbous eyes, its lower jaw jutting out as if with a bad overbite, and large, rubbery lips. It was hideously ugly. Frantically she swam upward to Simon and grabbed his arm, to find his eyes laughing at her behind his mask. Only then did she realize he had known all along that thing was in there, and had deliberately sent her down, and her panic subsided to be replaced by a rush of heated anger. She twisted away from him and swam off, but soon forgot to be annoyed, lost in the beauty around her.

It seemed no time at all before their air was nearly finished, although almost an hour had gone by, and she followed Simon regretfully to the surface. He pulled himself up the ladder on the boat's side, and quickly took off his gear, returning to help Kate onto the boat with a strong heave.

"Let me get the tank for you."

"Thanks. I feel as if I weigh two hundred pounds."

"I know just what you mean. It's always an unpleasant return from weightlessness to gravity. However, you don't look as if you weigh two hundred pounds, so I wouldn't worry." He stood the tanks upright on the deck and began tightening their valves.

"All right, Simon." Kate had finished removing the rest of her equipment and turned around. "Your moment of reckoning has come. I hope you don't think you're going to get away with scaring me nearly out of my skin with that hideous sea monster, whatever it was—"

"Jewfish. Terrible eating. I imagine that's why they get so big—"

"I don't care what the stupid thing's called! That was a filthy trick!"

Simon's back was turned and he pretended to be engrossed in the regulator he was holding, but his shoulders began to shake helplessly.

"You are lower than low, Simon Dristoll!"

He turned around and looked at her soberly for a moment, but it was too much for him. "Oh, Kate, I am sorry, truly I am, but you were funny!" He burst into laughter.

"I'm so glad I was able to provide you with amusement," she said, advancing on him.

"Come now, Kate—ouch!" Kate attacked his chest with her fists, laughing helplessly.

"Take that and that, you brutal, sadistic—"

"You little she-devil!" He grabbed her wrists and easily pinned her hands by her sides. "So, it's to be a word and a blow, is it?" He looked down at her with a maddening smile. "Tut tut, Kate. It's not nice and it's certainly not smart to go about hitting men who are considerably larger than you are."

"You deserved every well-landed blow you got," she said with great satisfaction, but becoming uncomfortably aware of the warmth of his wet body pressing against hers and the sudden change of expression in his deep blue eyes. "And you deserve far worse," she said more softly.

"Then here's my penance." His fair head came down toward hers and his lips, surprisingly soft and warm, covered her own. Then they were gone, too quickly, and her eyes flew open.

"Am I forgiven, Kate?" He looked down at her with a little smile, still holding her.

"Yes! Yes, absolutely forgiven. Now let me go!"

"And if I do let you go, you promise not to beat me anymore?"

"I promise. But you have to promise not to do that again." Her knees felt unaccountably weak.

"I mustn't do what again?"

"Kiss me."

"No?"

"Absolutely not," she said firmly.

"What a pity. I rather enjoyed it." He released her and chuckled. "You really are the most astonishing woman, Kate. Well, I suppose we should get under way." He casually strode off to pull up anchor. Kate stared after him, wondering what on earth had come over her.

Simon delivered her to her door. "Home again, my little shrew."

"At least today you didn't have to carry me down the steps." She touched his shoulder. "I always seem to be thanking you, Simon."

"I'm coming to rather like it, you know. For heaven's sake, don't stop now." His eyes glinted that secret little smile she was coming to know.

"All right. Thank you, Simon."

"Ah, Kate—I can't tell you what that does to me. Or rather I could, but apparently I mustn't."

"You really are the most impossible man," she said, laughing. "Well, I suppose this is good-bye. We leave tomorrow."

"No, really? What a pity! Just as I was beginning to figure you out."

"Nobody has ever figured me out, including myself, so don't feel you were about to crack the safe."

"Hmm, an interesting metaphor—now, don't you start that again—you know what will happen." He caught her wrist and laughed with delight. "Oh, you are quite adorable, you know."

"I most certainly am not adorable," said Kate with dignity.

"You most certainly are, and I really must be on my way.

It has been a genuine pleasure, Kate Soames." He took the wrist he was holding, and turning it over to expose the sensitive skin just below the palm, he raised it to his lips and kissed it. His breath was warm on her skin, and a little shock ran through her at the touch of his mouth. Her hand gave an involuntary jerk.

"That's not allowed, either?" he asked with mock surprise.

"Oh, Simon, really! It's a moot point now, anyway. Good-bye, and thank you." She turned quickly and went inside, softly closing the door and leaning against it for a moment. She could hear him walking up the steps, his sneakers softly scuffing on the rock. And then he said something to himself and she could only just make out the words as they drifted away, but she knew them by heart.

They came faintly in his pleasant, rich voice. " 'Farewell! Thou art too dear for my possessing, and like enough thou know'st thy estimate.' " And then he was gone.

Kate smiled, her forehead pressed against the cool wood of the door. How could she not love a man who knew his Shakespeare? "Good-bye, Simon," she whispered.

She turned around, still smiling like an idiot. And for the second time that day her heart jerked painfully to a stop.

"David what are you—" She flew into his arms.

After leaving Kate, Simon drove out to Alligator Head where he spent some time discreetly taking a number of photographs. Then he went back to the boat to meet up with Bouge and Eustice. In the cabin he found Eustice with a big smile on his face.

"Give over, Eustice, what have you come up with?" He sat down at the table opposite him.

"You caught the big fish last night, and today I might have a smaller one for you."

"What do you mean?" Simon leaned forward, his eyes keen with concentration.

"The uninvited company from the other day? He reappeared this afternoon. I'm afraid I didn't see him until after you went out, but I followed him to his hotel. He's staying at the Trident."

"That's bloody well it! I had a feeling he was up to no good. Good work, my friend. I must confess, it's a pleasure working with you again. I'm after him. Look, you go on ahead. I'm going to have a quick shower and change; I'll meet you there in about half an hour. I want you to stay with me in case we need to split off. If we're lucky, he'll lead us on." He stood up and stretched and went out into the sunlight, Eustice following him.

"I'll be there. But you'd better be careful. He knows your face now."

"Maybe he does, but beautiful Kate has done her job well as an unwitting cover. And I can't say I haven't enjoyed every minute of it. Damn! I thought when he hadn't come back that we were okay. The last thing I need is to have my face recognized now and connected back. Any word from London?"

"Nothing yet. Bouge is down below and he'll cover it."

"I'll go down and tell him I got the photographs. London will want to know. Half an hour then." Simon went back inside, and Eustice jumped lightly off the side of the boat and disappeared.

In exactly half an hour Simon was at the Trident, the Mini parked off to one side. Not an hour later, Eustice spotted their man getting into his car. He signaled to Simon and pulled out, and Simon followed at a discreet distance, surprised when the quarry turned in through the gates of Kate's hotel. Eustice had driven straight by, then pulled off the road, and Simon turned in, parking out of the way. He waited, watching the man enter the main building, then pulled a jacket over his shoulder holster, covering the straps that ran around his neck and across his back. He followed a few minutes later and walked casually into the bar. The maître d'hotel had seated his man at a small table outside.

Excellent, thought Simon. A dinner for two, is it? He sat near to a window with a good view of the table and ordered a scotch and water. Five minutes later, the man stood up as a woman approached.

"Oh, sweet Christ—I don't believe this!" whispered Simon. It was Kate.

"So they finally made old Jack Wharton a senior partner after all these years. Boy, was he delighted, but I don't think he's figured out that he's due for retirement next year. What a bunch of sharks." David laughed, and shrugged his shoulders. "Shall we order another bottle of wine? It's not a bad wine list for down here, is it?"

"No, it's not, but it's overpriced." They were having dinner in the open courtyard of the hotel. A fountain gushed in the middle, and high arches supported by white columns defined three sides of the square. The fourth side was open to the bay. More tables sat under the arches, which led into the main reception rooms and the bar; long windows faced out onto the courtyard.

Up until now, Kate and David had been walking on eggshells, careful not to say anything that might expose the rawness between them. They might have been casual acquaintances who had met by chance and found refuge in discussing mutual friends. After Kate's first impulsive reaction, she had immediately pulled away and they had retreated to this polite facade as if by silent agreement.

David had not stayed long at the cottage. He said that he had come only to see if she was free for dinner, and it would be better to talk then. Kate agreed; she'd needed time to collect herself.

After a long and uncomfortable silence, David, looking very grim indeed, said, "Katie, we have to talk. I can't take this tension anymore."

Kate quietly put down her knife and fork. The red snapper on her plate had lost its appeal. She felt suddenly sick and she took a deep breath. "But I don't understand why you came all the way down here to talk when you knew I was coming back tomorrow!"

"Do you think it was impulsive of me?"

"No, of course not, David. I think it's wonderful—I mean, that you cared enough to do something like this."

David looked away for a moment, then back again as if he had made some kind of decision. He pushed a dark lock of hair off his forehead, a habit of his when nervous. "The truth of the matter is that I've been here for a week."

Kate was stunned. "But why?"

"Well . . . I'd already planned to take the time off, I had my ticket, so I thought I might as well use it. I sure as hell needed a break after—after everything. I didn't want to ruin your vacation, or infringe on your privacy—we'd agreed that you'd take this time to think things through. I only came over because I just couldn't wait any longer. It's been driving me crazy, knowing you were here making decisions about our future, and not having any idea what they were. It's been hell, Katie." His dark brown eyes were heavy, as heavy as the silence that stretched tensely between them. "Please, say something!"

Her voice was tight. "I had wondered about your tan. Where have you been staying?"

"Not far from here."

"Oh." She looked down at her plate with a frown.

"Katie? What's wrong? Did I make a mistake by coming over?"

"No, David. Not by coming over, by coming at all! I can't help but feel that it's evidence of your wanting to deny everything we talked about, my need for a little freedom, my need to have something of my own life."

"Look, honey, that's ridiculous. You never knew I was here! I waited until the last night. It's the same old problem, you look for trouble where there isn't any—damn it, I feel as if you try to find reasons to push me away!" He lit a cigarette, looking away from her.

"I don't, David. That has nothing to do with it—it's the principle of the thing, don't you see that?"

"No, I don't see that, although I'm trying very hard! Katie, marriage is a commitment between two people, not a pact to live separate lives. I love you, therefore I want to be with you. It just seems that you don't want to be with me."

"Oh, David, I do, really I do, and I've been utterly miserable about this whole thing. What I asked for was time, just time to be absolutely certain. I want to be the kind of wife you need but I can't change my nature. It wouldn't be fair to either of us."

"Don't be silly—I don't want you to change your nature, I love you for it. I know your attitude about being the wife of a politician will change; I think you're just used to the role of being your father's daughter. It will be different when we're married. And I want to be married to you more than anything else in the world. Will you marry me, Katie?" David's eyes flashed in the candlelight.

"David, I just don't know yet." Kate's eyes were swimming with unshed tears, her voice husky. "I can only be honest with you about what I feel. It's terribly important to me to make my own decisions. Don't you see, by your coming down here, I feel as if you've robbed me of that opportunity."

He sighed deeply and looked down. "I don't know what else to say to you. That was certainly not my intention, I swear it. Okay, let me go at this another way. I want to ask you something, and please, be honest with me. Does your attitude have anything at all to do with the man you were with this afternoon?"

"The man—oh, *David*! How could you think such a thing?"

"Believe me, it's the last thing I want to think. I'm sorry, I couldn't help but wonder. I did see you together outside the cottage, you know, and it looked extremely friendly to me."

"David, we hired his boat to go out one day, and he's been kind to Stephanie and me. He took me diving this afternoon, that's all. He's just a British expatriate who fishes the island. He means nothing to me."

"Well, that's a relief. I guess you can't blame me for being a little jealous." He smiled that sweet, crooked grin of his, and it twisted at her heart.

"Not about that. That's one thing that you've never had

to worry about.'' But she felt a twinge of guilt as she spoke, remembering her reaction to Simon's kiss.

''Okay, you've convinced me. I'm sorry, that was stupid of me; it's just that with everything else, I don't know—I guess I was feeling abandoned.'' He reached his hand out to her. ''Look, Katie, I have a proposition to put to you. If you won't say yes, will you at least take your ring back? It would make me feel an awful lot better, and you did say that you haven't completely given up on us. I won't rush you for a wedding date, I promise. You take your time, and you just tell me when you're ready. Can you accept our relationship like that?''

''I don't know, David.''

''Look, this just isn't as complicated as you're making it. We love each other, Katie. I think that's certainly worth trying for.''

''You really think we can make it work?''

''Doesn't my being here right now prove it?''

''Yes . . . I suppose so.''

''Well, then?'' He looked at her earnestly. ''Please, Katie?''

That did it. Kate's resistance crumbled. ''Yes, all right, David. I'll give it another try.'' She cursed the tears that still threatened at her eyes and willed them away. This was no time to cry.

''Then you'll take your ring back?''

''Yes, I'll take my ring back.''

''Oh, Katie.'' He sighed, then very simply said, ''Thank you.'' He reached into his pocket and pulled the ring from his pocket, slipping it back on her finger. The square-cut diamond seemed to come alive in the candlelight, fire flashing in its depths.

''I can't believe you dragged it all the way down here. My David, the eternal optimist.'' She spoke lightly but deep down she still felt vaguely troubled and couldn't understand why.

* * *

The beach was deserted at midnight and Kate was glad for it. David had left an hour before, despite her entreaties to talk. He had wanted to get back to his hotel, saying that he needed to pack. "We'll have all the time in the world to talk when we get home," he'd said, kissing her good night.

She couldn't shake the feeling that there was still something wrong between them, or at least too many things left unresolved. She sighed heavily and looked down at her ring. David had said that they could work things out, but she wondered. The same questions still circled around and around in her mind.

"Well, well, what have we here?"

Kate jumped and uttered a strangled cry. "Simon! You scared me half to death! Do you always creep up unannounced? What are you doing here anyway?"

"I came to have a drink with a friend, and thought I'd come and sit by the water for a while. Shall I go away?" He smiled down at her quizzically.

"No—I'm sorry if I was rude. It's been a day of surprises. Please, pull up a chair."

"Thanks, I'd like that." He sat down next to her, silent for a long moment. "What were you thinking about to make you look so sad, Kate?" he asked softly.

"Oh, nothing, really. I suppose I'm sad to be leaving. It's been such a nice break and going back to New York—well, you know."

"Yes, I do." Simon looked out at the sea. The moon hung softly in the sky, a pale silver sphere mirrored in the dark water.

"Simon?"

"Mmm?"

"Why do you live down here? You were obviously brought up in England—don't you ever get tired of this life?"

He looked at her then, the misty light gently outlining the contours of her face. "Can't you say the same of your life, Kate?"

"Yes . . . Yes, of course, you're right. My life is such a mess right now—I was just thinking what it would be like to run away from it all to a tropical paradise like this, but then I realized it would pall after awhile and the same problems would still be there."

"It's true enough. I suppose you have to find where you're most comfortable and then hope like hell to find happiness."

"Happiness . . ."

"Are you unhappy, Kate?" he asked simply.

"No, not really, just a little back-to-front, if you know what I mean."

"Back-to-front Kate. Yes, I suppose I can see it," he said with a little smile.

"I know you said you never get involved, but have you ever been in love, Simon?" Kate looked at him intently, wondering again at the mystery behind the man. A soft wind ruffled through his hair, picking up the fair strands and shifting them back off his face like a caress.

"I thought I was once."

"What happened?"

He shrugged. "The girl thought I was quite different from the person I was, in fact. She liked the high life, lots of money to spend, constant parties. I was extremely dazzled by her, and we came close enough to getting married, but then the awful truth about me struck her, and she went off with a glamorous earl who could and did give her everything she wanted. I suppose it was a blessing, but it didn't seem like it at the time."

"Oh . . . I see. Is that what brought you down here?"

"Indirectly. Very indirectly. I was up at Cambridge then—"

"You were?" interrupted Kate in surprise.

"I was, and it's very rude of you to look like that."

"Sorry. Of course, Shakespeare's sonnet. Go on."

Simon laughed. "That's a nonsequitur if ever there was one, and I hadn't thought you'd heard." He looked over at her with a curious expression.

Kate blushed, grateful for the darkness. "Only just. But what happened?"

"What happened with what?"

"The girl who ran off with the earl!"

"Oh, yes. The description has a certain ring to it, doesn't it? Too bad I didn't see it that way then. Anyway, in time I got over her, and I finished my degree, but I realized that the life I was leading was basically superficial. There was a lot of rot going on under the facade of jolly old England."

"And so you left it?"

"In a sense, yes, I left it. There seemed to be more important things in life. And what about you, back-to-front Kate? What's bitten you?"

"I don't know—I wish I did. I feel as if I'm constantly getting in the way of myself, that I fight every good thing that comes along because I want to have my own way. There you have it, probably my one glorious moment of truth."

"I don't think it is, quite."

"What do you mean?"

"I don't think your assessment of yourself is quite accurate."

"Well, what do you think then, Simon Dristoll?" She glanced over at him in surprise.

"I think you probably do get in your own way, but I suspect that you generally know what's good for you when you finally get around to it." He smiled.

"Oh." Kate had a sinking feeling she knew exactly what he was alluding to.

"And that has nothing to do with having your own way. In fact, I suspect that very often it's the exact opposite." He bent down and scooped up a handful of the fine sand, sifting it through his fingers.

"Really? And what is your solution to my problem, doctor?"

"Very simple. Learn to trust your feelings and stop judging yourself so harshly. Perhaps I was wrong. Perhaps you really don't know your own worth."

"Oh, Simon, I wish I could believe that was it. That would get me off the hook for a lot of my more glaring faults. I'm afraid if anyone did an appraisal of me, I'd turn out to be dismally lacking."

"My darling girl, believe me, your price is far above rubies."

"At any rate, thank you for saying so, Simon. Although

for someone who never gets involved, you seem like something of an expert on the subject of women.''

''Do I?'' he said with a laugh. ''Oh, dear—I wouldn't want you to think that.''

''What difference could it possibly make to you what I think?''

He met her eyes evenly through the silvery light. Then he finally said, '' 'The fair, the chaste, the unexpressive she.' ''

'' 'An ill-favored thing, sir, but mine own.' *As You Like It*.'' Her heart was beating slightly too fast.

''Not ill favored, Kate. Never ill favored.'' He lifted his hand and brushed the hair off her cheek.

She bit her lip. ''You'd be surprised just how ill favored I can make myself.''

''Did all this come out of dinner tonight?'' His voice was very quiet.

She looked at him in surprise. ''I hadn't realized you were there. I suppose to be honest, it did. 'Dinner with David.' It should be a play; God knows there's enough material in it for three acts and a few tears.''

''Who is David?'' The faintest of lines was drawn between his brow.

''David Russell. He's my fiancé.''

''Your *what*?'' Simon stared at her in astonishment.

''My fiancé. I was quite surprised when he appeared this afternoon. We'd had some problems and he came to straighten them out. In fact, you very nearly botched it. He wanted to know who the man was who was so avidly preying on my wrist. He saw us outside the—why do you look so surprised? I'm not that much of a hag, am I? After all, you managed to kiss me this afternoon without too much distaste.''

''And I'm going to do it again!'' whooped Simon, sweeping her up and swinging her around. And then he put her firmly back on earth and gave her a resounding kiss. ''Congratulations! That's the most marvelous news I've heard in ages! My beautiful Kate, engaged—fancy that!''

''Simon, are you crazy?'' Kate looked at him as if he certainly must be.

''Absolutely mad as a hatter, deliriously out of my mind

with joy for you, my love!'' He pulled her into his arms and swept her around in an improvised waltz, his cheek pressed against hers. ''Can you hear the music, Kate? It plays for you—when do you marry the lucky bastard?''

''Stop it, Simon! My God, you need a shave, and I wish you'd get rid of that gun! I don't know, we haven't set a date—''

'' 'I must dance barefoot on her wedding day—' '' he quoted.

'' 'And, for your love to her, lead apes in hell,' '' she finished, dissolving into laughter.

''Exactly so. Straight from *Taming of the Shrew*, my dear, how appropriate! Cambridge?'' he asked, his eyes dancing wickedly.

''Oxford, you monster, as you know perfectly well,'' she responded with a grin.

''And what a handsome ring! I can't believe I hadn't noticed it before—or were you trying to lead me astray, wicked woman?'' He picked her hand off his shoulder and admired the diamond without missing a turn.

''No, of course not! I'd given it back to David and he returned it to me tonight—wait a minute, this is none of your business!''

''Oh, yes it is, Kate, believe me, it is.'' He sobered and stopped, but still held her in his arms, looking clearly into her eyes. ''Seriously, I wish you every happiness. Don't worry about your muddle—I'm sure it will sort itself out. Just be true to yourself, will you? I've got to go, my love, I really do, but before I leave, may I ask you one favor?''

''What is it?'' She looked at him suspiciously.

''May I kiss the bride-to-be, one last time?'' Without waiting for an answer, he drew her closer to him and kissed her long and deeply. Then he released her and whispered, ''Good-bye, sweet Kate.'' And he walked away without looking back.

CHAPTER
Four

"I don't believe any of this, Kate. You have to be making it up!" Stephanie was shaking with laughter, gasping for breath. "Oh, watch the corner!" The Hillman squeaked valiantly around, narrowly missing a bus going the other way. Kate hardly seemed to notice. "I swear to you, Steph, it's just how it happened. He started dancing around like a madman, congratulating me on my forthcoming marriage, and admiring my ring."

"Oh, ouch, you have to stop—my sides are killing me!" She mopped at her eyes. "It is a beautiful ring, I'll have to give him that—fancy Simon noticing!" and she went off into a fresh peal.

"Wait, I haven't finished. Then he stopped dead, wished me luck, and gave me an amazing kiss that left me completely unglued—and walked off! The last seen of Simon Dristoll. What do you think of that?"

"I think it's interesting the way you describe the kiss. That's one better than you've done for David."

"Don't be ridiculous—this was quite different and thoroughly harmless. Anyway, it has a lot to do with the fact that Simon is so uncomplicated, and David, well . . ."

"You've resolved your argument, but not the problems that caused it, is that what you're trying to say?"

"Yes. I thought I'd feel much better, but I still have the same lead weight in my stomach. I don't know, Simon told me I should trust my feelings, but I don't know what they are anymore."

"Oh, Simon did, did he. I see." She burst into fits again.

Kate had a hard time saying good-bye to Stephanie at the airport. She'd hoped that Stephanie would have the chance to meet David, who was driving himself to Kingston, and they were both bitterly disappointed when he didn't show up before Stephanie's flight to London.

"God, I'm going to miss you. Thanks for everything, Steph." She hugged her, hard.

"Same to you, friend. If things get too tough, just pick up the telephone—or better yet, come and stay. I wish you'd take that summer thing."

"We'll see. I'll have to talk it over again with David. Take care."

"Bye . . ." One last hug and she was gone.

Kate choked back her tears.

Colonel Harrington was smiling, a rare thing for him. He laid the report down on the cluttered desk in front of him and looked across it benevolently. "Good job, Dunn, very good job. I really must congratulate you."

"Thank you, sir." Sebastian fiddled with his pencil.

"Finding and photographing Erharder was a stroke of genius. How on earth did you do it? Hasn't been done since the war. But best of all is discovering the name he's been using all these years."

"Actually, sir, you have Joe to thank. When Erharder showed up in his restaurant, Joe called me. He couldn't believe Erharder was the same old gentleman who'd been vacationing there for years but when he noticed the scar I'd described, something told Joe not to take a chance."

"Are you quite positive Erharder didn't suspect you? You say here that you openly followed him to a club."

"As certain as I can be. If he had recognized me, I think I

would have seen a reaction when I first walked into Joe's. I was ready for it. But there was no sign of recognition, and anyway I got lucky. My cover, the girl Kate Soames, was perfect. There was no reason for him to think anything was wrong.'' Sebastian smiled to himself, remembering Kate—Kate and her slightly tipsy state that night, and Erharder's annoyed expression when she had turned around and peered at him. If anything, that would have assured him of their innocence.

''Then what about the man you suspected of watching the boat? There's nothing in here about that. Why would Erharder put a man on to watch you if he didn't suspect you?''

''You can forget the watcher. Kate Soames was the one he was after. He turned out to be her fiancé, one David Russell, skulking around to keep an eye on her. It seems they'd been having some trouble, and he had obviously followed her down to the island without her knowledge, and was keeping an eye on her activities. I was taken to be another suitor.''

''I see. Well, I want to thank you, Dunn, for coming back in on the job. And not just for confirming Erharder's participation in the Group. With Gustav Schwab's identity also confirmed, we can get onto the third man, Anton Brecht.''

''Schwab and I go back a few years, although he's blissfully ignorant of the fact. Tony would have laughed himself sick. It was certainly my pleasure to get their mugs on film with their crony Erharder.''

''I quite understand, a sweet sort of revenge.'' Colonel Harrington stood up, ending the interview. ''Thank you again, Dunn. I am fully aware how reluctant you were to take this assignment. But now we know for certain that as far as the Group is concerned, you remain anonymous.''

''Ah, well, as for that, I admit to relief that there is not 'some corner of a foreign field that is forever England.' ''

Colonel Harrington smiled. ''If anyone were to be buried in a foreign field, I doubt very much it would be you, Dunn. But I am pleased that you remember the words of Rupert Brooke.''

"How could I not, sir, when you have used them to hand down any number of maxims over the years?"

"Solid words for men in our line of work. As he also said, 'think each in each, immediately wise.' Good men, Cambridge men."

"Indeed," said Sebastian with a little smile. "You certainly have enough of them around here. Is that it, sir? Can I assume I may now return to civilian life?"

"Absolutely, with our gratitude. Now that we can put faces to Erharder, Schwab, and Brecht, we should be able to get somewhere. Things are going to heat up for Herr Erharder."

"I'm delighted, sir." He shook the old man's hand. "Good-bye. If you need me for anything further, you know where to reach me."

"Indeed. It is a lucky thing for us that your work is so flexible. And Dunn?" he added as Sebastian turned to go.

Sebastian paused. "Yes, sir?"

"Very decent tan." The colonel chuckled deeply.

"It was a hell of a way to get one," Sebastian said with a short laugh, and let himself out. He went down the stairs and out into the dusk. The sidewalk was dark with spent rain, and the thin black branches of dormant trees hung barren against the heavy sky. Sebastian paused and looked around, scrutinizing the street. It was a habit he thought he'd lost.

"Oh, hell," he said with an ironic smile and walked off.

"You're going to do *what*!" David roared, pacing the room in a fury.

"David, calm down. I haven't said I'm going to, I said I was considering it. Rosterman and Marsh asked me again today, and they need an immediate answer. I'd have to leave this weekend." Kate took his arm but he shrugged it away.

"Goddamn it, Katie, it's out of the question! I thought you'd given up this foolish idea. You know my congressional campaign is set to get started this summer and I'll need you with me! It's ludicrous to go running off now—how can you even consider such a thing? You'll have to give up the job when we're married, anyway; you might as well do it now." His face was a blaze of anger.

Kate turned away from him and walked over to the open window. Warm sunshine streamed onto her face, but the rest of her was cold as ice. She suddenly knew what she had to do. They had been coming to this for months. Strangely, now that the moment was here, she felt surprisingly calm, almost detached, as if she had made her decision a long time ago, and now had only to speak.

"Well?" asked David impatiently.

She turned around to face him, her eyes clear, the color of the ocean as a storm moves in. "I'm not giving up my job, David, and we're not getting married."

"Don't be childish, Katie. That's a ridiculous way to resolve an argument! What happened to all the talking we did about compromising?" His voice had risen to a shout.

"It's not going to work, David. We've both tried our hardest, but neither of us is happy."

"Oh, come on, Katie, we were doing just fine until now. Don't make such a big deal out of it."

"David, I'm perfectly serious. I think it's time to call it quits. I'm going to take up the offer and go to London—it'll be better if we don't see each other for a while. I hope when I come back, we can be friends."

He paled, then visibly regained control of himself. "You're not serious—you're not really going to break it off? Katie, please, stop for a minute, reconsider. Don't let your temper carry you away; this is too important."

She spoke very quietly. "I've been considering this for a long time, you know that. I'm sorry, David, but this is the way it has to be. I'm not going to change my mind."

"All right, okay, go to London if it's what you think you need and we can talk more when you come back. Come on, Katie, think it over." The lines running between his nose and mouth were pronounced, pinched, and white.

"No. Not this time." She looked down at her hand, and then pulled off the engagement ring. "I shouldn't have taken this back. It was wrong of me, very wrong, but I think you knew this was coming." She carefully handed it to him.

"God, I can't believe you're doing this. You know how much your father wanted this marriage, Katie—"

"Leave my father out of this. This has nothing to do with him, this is between you and me. It's just not right between us, David, and it would never be. We're too different. Please try to understand that it's for the best?"

"Never," he said bitterly. "You do as you have to, Katie, but I'll never understand. You'd better go now." He looked away, straining for control.

For a fraction of a second she hesitated in the face of his hurt, but then words spoken to her months before, spoken with a quiet and steady strength, came echoing back. "Just be true to yourself . . ."

"Good-bye, David. I really am sorry." She kissed his cheek and then let herself out.

Her father lived in Westchester County near Rye; the drive was long enough to give her plenty of time to think of what she wanted to say, but she still had to steel herself as the house came into view from the driveway. It was palatial by most standards, white and square, fronted by columns, with two smaller wings spreading off the sides and a frame of enormous trees. Grand and conservative, the huge house was just like her father.

Peter Soames was a large and solid man, with a thick thatch of white hair and the commanding presence of the elder statesman he was. Although he was officially retired, he still presided over many committees and had published three successful books on international political strategy. He was powerful, autocratic, and irascible. The first thing Kate had done entirely right in her life, as far as her father was concerned, was to become engaged to David Russell, and she knew he was not going to take her news well. But for once, she didn't really care.

She found him behind the house in his garden, pruning his beloved roses. "Hello, Daddy."

He turned around to peer at her through the tortoiseshell glasses that were a permanent fixture on his nose. "Katie, what a surprise! How are you, my dear? How's David?"

"That's what I came to talk to you about." Kate sat down on the warm, freshly mown grass next to the rose bed and waited.

"Hand me those long shears, will you, dear? Thank you." He reached into the back roses and began to cut away the heads that had faded.

After about three minutes of heavy silence he finally spoke. "Trouble?"

"Not exactly trouble, but I don't think you're going to be very pleased with what I have to tell you."

"Humph," he grunted. "I had a feeling something was up with you. Well?"

"I called it off." He never made anything easy.

"I suppose you think you know what you're doing? I had high hopes for you and that young man. Marrying into a life you know, good family, it would have been a fine thing." A large, deep red head fluttered to the ground.

"No, Daddy, I'm sorry, but it wouldn't have been a fine thing. It may be a life I know, but that doesn't mean it's the one I want." Kate leaned over the border and picked up a clump of the dark, rich soil, squeezing it between her fingers.

"Just what do you mean by that? You were happy enough until now, weren't you?" Snip. Another rose fell to the ground, its spent petals sticking to the wet earth.

"Yes, of course I was, but we had no choice in the way we lived. I never saw much of you to begin with, and after Mummy died, I spent more time away at school or in England with Elizabeth than I did with you. Anyway, I wasn't cut out for never-ending receptions and receiving lines, and always being on my best diplomatic behavior. I found myself getting more and more panicked by the thought that the rest of my life would be like that."

"Your mother did her best and she was damned good at it," he said gruffly.

"I know she was, but I'm Kate, your daughter, not Susanna, your wife."

"Don't be impertinent, Katie!"

"I'm sorry, Daddy, but this is important. I know you've always wanted me to be like her, but we're so different. She was calm, sure of herself, so—so aristocratic, if you know what I mean. Nothing ever seemed to trouble her; she was always serene, even when she was dying. I loved her and admired her, but I'm not anything like that, hard as I've tried to be, and I'd make an awful mess of our life together if I married David." Kate looked hard at her father's back. It was true, she thought with surprise: He had tried to turn her into a copy of Susanna. It had certainly taken her a very long time to realize it—she wondered, in fact, when it had come to her. Surely not just now?

"Well, Katie, you're supposed to be old enough to know your own mind, and stubborn enough not to let anybody change it for you. So I don't think there's anything more to be said on the subject. I'd only be wasting my time. What are your plans now?" He finally turned around to glower at her.

It was almost a relief, being able to see his face, and Kate met his glare squarely. "I've decided to take up an offer given me by the firm. I'm going to London for a few months."

"Ha!" said her father dryly. "Back to London is it? Sounds to me as if you're running away."

"Not at all. I've been considering it since Christmas and decided it was an opportunity I couldn't afford to miss. I leave on Saturday."

"I see. Well, you'll do as you please in any case, regardless of what I think." He turned back to his roses. "Where will you stay in case I need to reach you? Your grandmother isn't at all well, you know."

Kate felt like screaming, but gritted her teeth instead. "I do know, Daddy, and I intend to stop by the nursing home on my way back, although I doubt she'll know me. And I'll most probably be staying with Stephanie when I'm in London and with Elizabeth when I'm up at Oxford."

"Oxford? What are you doing there? I thought you'd finished all that nonsense."

"I have, although I didn't consider it nonsense. There's a very knowledgeable wine merchant there who knows a great deal about port, which is one of the things I'm being sent to research. Remember my friend James Lambert?"

"If you want to know about port, why don't you go to Portugal? Seems ridiculous to go to Oxford."

"Yes, Daddy," said Kate patiently. "But you see, it's the British market I want to study; most of the big port firms are British-owned. Then I'll be going to France for about three weeks. I'll leave my itinerary with Elizabeth so you can find me if you need to. All right?"

"You give Elizabeth my love. She's a fine woman and meant the world to your mother."

"She means the world to me, too." Kate got up and brushed herself off. "I have to go, I have a million things to do, and I want to see Granny before it gets dark."

"All right then, Katie. I hope you think this through a little better. You've always been too impulsive for your own good, and you're making a terrible mistake."

"Good-bye, Daddy." Kate kissed his cheek and said very softly, "I love you," then walked back toward the house.

"And I wish you wouldn't wear those blasted blue jeans!" her father bellowed after her.

Kate was still smarting from the conversation with her father when she arrived at the nursing home and sat in her car for a few moments trying to collect herself. It was so damnably unfair that he could never attempt to see her side, that he always had to make things so difficult. Despite the fact that she had stood up to him, it didn't make her feel any better, and she found herself wishing once again that her mother were still alive. She would have listened in her calm, intelligent, understanding way. Her grandmother had once been like that, but despite the fact that she still inhabited her body, she had drifted away and could no longer offer any kind of support. Kate sighed and closed the car door with a thud.

"Mrs. Jessop, your granddaughter is here to see you." The white starched uniform rustled like tissue paper as the nurse bent over the old and fragile figure in the bed. "Mrs. Jessop, it's Kate, come to see you." There was no reply. She straightened up and said, "I'm sorry, dear, but her mind wanders, you know. I'll just leave you together, and maybe you can talk quietly to her. It sometimes helps."

"Thanks, Mrs. Beekins." Kate waited until the nurse had whispered out of the room, and then sat down on the bed, taking her grandmother's hand and kissing her soft, withered cheek.

Caroline Jessop, born British, was Kate's grandmother on her mother's side, but one would have thought Peter Soames was her son, the way he doted on her, almost as if she were a substitute for her dead daughter Susanna. After her husband Guy died the year before and she'd visibly begun to wither, Soames had found her the finest nursing home available and installed her with every creature comfort. But she was no longer able to appreciate such things, having slid farther and farther into what seemed to be a self-willed deterioration.

"Hello, Granny," said Kate cheerfully. Caroline opened her eyes, but Kate couldn't tell if she recognized her. "It's Kate. I've just come to tell you that I'm going away for a while."

"Kate?" she said, looking at her blankly.

"Kate, your granddaughter." She sighed, realizing that her grandmother had no clue. "Susanna's child? You remember Susanna, your daughter?"

Caroline looked at her sadly. "I've never forgotten her, you know. My Susanna was always in my heart. Nobody understands how it was." Her faded blue eyes welled up and she closed them as if to take the tears into herself.

"I know, I miss her too." Kate stroked her white hair. "Granny, listen. David and I aren't going to be married after all, and I'm going to England for a few months. I'll be seeing Elizabeth, and I'll be sure to give her your love. Remember your old friend Elizabeth?''

Caroline's eyes shot open and she looked at Kate with surprising clarity. ''Elizabeth?'' she whispered.

''That's right, Elizabeth Forrest.''

Caroline suddenly pulled herself up in bed with amazing strength and grasped Kate's arm. ''Susanna mustn't ever be told, Elizabeth!'' she said with great force. ''You must promise to keep the adoption a secret! Nobody must know, ever!''

''Granny?'' said Kate, confused and a little alarmed by Caroline's vehemence.

''Promise!'' she insisted.

''Yes, yes, all right, I promise!'' said Kate hurriedly. ''But what—''

''Good. Such a good friend. You will be the baby's godmother, of course.'' Caroline fell back against the pillows. ''It's best if you keep the watch,'' she said. ''Much safer, just in case Guy finds it. Hide it—take the watch and keep it safe, Elizabeth. Nobody must know.''

''Yes, I'll keep it safe, don't worry.''

''It's the only way, for everyone's sake. The child must never, never learn the truth. It would be too dangerous. Much too dangerous . . .'' Her voice faded away and her eyes closed.

Kate found herself more than shaken by what had just passed. She was accustomed to her grandmother's senile ramblings, and yet she'd seemed suddenly more alert than she had in months. But her mother—adopted? It didn't seem possible . . . And what was all that about a watch, and danger? It simply didn't make any sense.

''Granny? Granny, please, talk to me!'' But there was no response. Her grandmother had disappeared into her private world. Kate sat with her awhile longer but she didn't speak again, and finally Kate kissed her and left, unable to shake the peculiar conversation from her mind.

* * *

Kate's taxi pulled up in front of a little mews house just off Kensington Church Street. The early morning light spilled down on it, brightening the geraniums and alyssum planted outside the windows in low white boxes. Stephanie's place, a legacy from her grandfather—Kate had always thought it looked just like a dollhouse, blue with white trim and with a minute flower garden carefully planted on either side of the steps.

Kate paid the driver, ridiculously pleased to be handling the familiar pounds and pence again, and lugging her cases from the taxi, she mounted the steps and rang the doorbell with anticipation. She could hear it pealing inside, and then footsteps running down the stairs.

"Kate!" shrieked Stephanie, opening the door, clad in her old blue wool dressing gown. "You came! You rat, why didn't you tell me? Don't just stand there, come in!"

"I didn't tell you I was coming because I just love watching you get worked into a state. It happens so rarely." She dropped her cases and gave Stephanie an enormous hug. "Is there room?"

"Absolutely—how long are you staying?"

"Until the wind changes," said Kate with a grin.

"God, I'm glad to see you. I'll just make some tea and then you're going to tell me absolutely everything that's happened since the moment I left you at the airport." She started toward the kitchen.

"The big news is that I'm a free woman, Steph."

Stephanie turned around at that and scrutinized Kate's face. "Heartbreak or jet lag?"

"Jet lag, I'm afraid. No heartbreak, no regrets."

"Oh, Kate—why don't you get washed and changed and then you can tell me all about it."

"The wash and change sound heavenly, but the true confessions will have to wait 'til tonight. I've got to get over to the Regent Street office."

"It's Sunday!"

"I know, I can tell by looking at you, but they have someone there waiting for me with a briefing. Dinner?"

"I wouldn't miss it for the world. We'll go out and celebrate."

Kate managed to have her briefing, unpack, and have a three-hour sleep before dinner. Waking up as the light turned golden, and feeling infinitely refreshed and nearly human, she decided that the one last thing she needed was a long, hot bath.

She soaked until the water was turning lukewarm, and she was just contemplating getting out when a terrible banging started at the door.

"Out of the bathroom and let me in!" shouted Stephanie. "It's not as if you haven't been in there for at least an hour!"

Home, Kate thought on a happy sigh.

"It's the strangest feeling—as if I'd never left," said Kate. They were seated at a table in their favorite bistro, a five-minute walk from the house. "Do you know what I mean, as if time has stood still?"

"That's one thing it hasn't done. You're a person quite different from the one who left here over two years ago."

"Hmm, older, wiser, worse for wear, you mean?"

"I don't know yet. You'll have to tell me what happened between you and David. I've been dying of curiosity all day." Stephanie refilled their glasses from the carafe of red wine.

"Oh, I'd forgotten how fabulous their pâté is here," said Kate, scooping some more onto a crusty piece of toast. "It's exceedingly dull telling, I'm afraid." She ran through the story from the time she'd left Stephanie at the Kingston airport.

". . . So you see, by the time I announced I was going to come over this summer and to hell with everything else, David was thoroughly fed up with me, and I was thoroughly fed up with the relationship."

"So what did you do? Did you lose your temper and throw your ring at him again?"

"No. Congratulate me, I was amazingly calm. I ended it right then, gave him his ring back and left, terribly cool and collected, so adult about it all. But once I got outside, I felt like tearing down the street. Isn't that awful?"

"Why is that awful?" asked Stephanie, puzzled.

"Because I felt happy, don't you see? I had just leveled David, the man until minutes before I supposedly was going to love until death us do part, and I felt great!"

"I think that's terrific, Kate. You are one strange bird, you know. Here you are looking a hundred times happier than you did in Jamaica, having found the strength to end a relationship that was obviously half killing you, and you want to be miserable. I don't understand you."

"I don't either—but listen, forget David Russell. I have something really wild to tell you." And leaning forward with sparkling eyes, she launched into the story of Caroline Jessop and the nursing home.

The next weekend Kate took the train to Reading, and Elizabeth Forrest met her at the station and drove them back to her house in Henley. It was Kate's second home, and she loved it. Set on the bank of the river Thames, it had been there for three centuries and in Elizabeth's family for two. Elizabeth was an only child who had never married and although she was Caroline Jessop's contemporary at age eighty-one, she had retained all the health, sparkle, and vivacity that Kate's grandmother had lost. A tall, well-built woman, she wore no-nonsense tweeds and stout shoes and always her string of pearls. Kate absolutely adored her.

"It's lovely to see you, my darling, and most unexpected," said Elizabeth over tea, passing Kate the homemade scones and thick strawberry jam that Kate knew had come from the past autumn's efforts. Then comfortably, she said, "Why don't you tell me all about it?" and settled back with her cup of tea.

So Kate did, talking easily about the two years that had passed. She found Elizabeth the most marvelous person to talk to; she could say anything at all and ramble on for hours and Elizabeth rarely interrupted and ventured an opinion only when asked. When Kate had finished, Elizabeth said merely, "I see. How very interesting."

"I wish I understood myself better, Elizabeth."

"You will, dear, in time. Give things a chance to settle, and for heaven's sake, don't worry about your father. He always was over-managing as far as I was concerned."

"Elizabeth . . ." Kate hesitated, wondering how on earth to put this and decided it was best to go for the straight approach. "I know this is going to sound very odd, but there's something I must ask you."

"Well, certainly, Kate, what is it?"

"Are you my grandmother?"

For the only time Kate could remember, Elizabeth Forrest lost her composure. "Your—grandmother? What an extraordinary idea! Whatever can you be thinking, Kate?"

And once again Kate related the episode with Caroline. Elizabeth said nothing at all during the recounting of the story and she said nothing at all when Kate had finished, but her expression was unusually disturbed. Then after considering for a moment, she said, "And perhaps you would like to explain why that makes me your grandmother?"

Kate blushed, feeling incredibly foolish. "Well, Stephanie and I tried to work it out, and if the story were true, the most obvious explanation would be that since you and Granny were such close friends and you never married, well—" She hesitated for a second and then finished on a rush. "Well, if you had a child out of wedlock, the most sensible thing to do would be to give her to your best friend who was childless. I thought that must be the reason why my mother was sent to school in England and you looked after her on holidays, and then looked after me for all those years after she died."

"My dear Kate, your mother was sent to school at Cheltenham Ladies' College because her mother was British and wanted her educated that way. As I was Susanna's godmother, naturally I looked after her. And as for you, after your mother died, there was no one else who could give you a proper home, certainly not your father. What did he know about twelve-year-old girls? You were also my goddaughter and I was very fond of you, although sometimes I wonder why."

"Oh, dear," said Kate with a little smile. "I can see I've put it together backwards. I'm sorry if I offended you, it was just that it sounded such an intriguing story."

"I can certainly understand that, and your imagination as usual ran away with you. And I am not offended, in fact I suppose I should be flattered that you conjured up an illicit love affair for me. However, it saddens me terribly to hear that dear Caroline is in such a bad way. It's always so tragic when the mind goes. Some more tea, Kate? Then I thought we'd take a walk around the garden. I want to show you my rugosa roses. It's been such a wet spring that everything was late, but summer seems finally to be here . . ."

The gardens surrounded every side of the house and spread out to the back, and the lawn running down to the river was sculpted with bushes of every size, shape, and color, carefully set out to conform to Elizabeth's horticultural vision. There were dozens of trees, including chestnut and hawthorn, apple and pear, seasonally dressed in thick blossom. It was a masterpiece, and Elizabeth tended it with all the loving zeal she might have showered on her children had she had any. Peonies, sweet-rocket, lupine, foxglove, delicate white aquilegia: They all clustered together in their immaculate beds footed by clumps of starry flowers. Oriental poppies stood tall, backlit in the late afternoon sun, their regal red heads swaying slightly on fragile stems in the soft wind. The strawberry bed was covered in snowy blossom, and clematis, ivory white with buttery yellow centers, climbed profusely up the low stone wall that bordered the vegetable garden.

"Now here are the rugosa roses, dear." Elizabeth gestured at them with her stout cane. "I've put them in since you last were here, and they've done very nicely. I think they add a certain color, don't you?" She had planted a row of the heavily foliaged bushes on either side of the path leading down to the river, alternating them white and magenta pink.

"Oh, Elizabeth, they're beautiful! They remind me a bit of camellias." The flowers clustered thickly on the bushes, large and fragrant with delicately wrinkled leaves and yellow hearts.

"Yes, I see the resemblance, but unlike camelias, these will flower all summer long and then in the autumn the leaves will turn gold. It's quite effective."

"I'll have to tell Daddy. He'll be so jealous!"

"That would give me great satisfaction," said Elizabeth. She and Peter Soames had always had a difference of opinion over their roses, among other things. "I'll cut you some tomorrow to take back to London with you. Now tell me about your friend Stephanie. What has she been doing with herself, aside from helping you turn me into your grandmother? That girl always did have an interesting mind hidden behind her practical exterior."

"She's still at the television studio writing scripts, but she's doing much more free-lancing these days, making quite a name for herself. I doubt she'll stay with the studio much longer . . ."

Elizabeth served up her usual sumptuous Sunday noon dinner. First came a joint of richly aromatic lamb, pink with its own juices and surrounded by crisp and browned roast potatoes and baby heads of cabbages from Elizabeth's garden. That was followed by a rhubarb pie, and Elizabeth's special chocolates which she bought, strangely enough, at the butcher's. After they'd cleared the table and left the plates to soak, they moved into the sitting room to have their coffee.

"Elizabeth, that was wonderful. I haven't had a Sunday dinner like that since I last was here! It's a good thing I can't stay for tea, or I'd roll out of here."

"Kate, dear . . ." Elizabeth was looking at her strangely.

"What is it? Is something wrong?" Kate put her cup down in alarm.

"No—no, don't worry. But I've been thinking, you see. My conscience has been bothering me and I think I must talk to you about it."

"Well, of course. Goodness, you listen to me often enough. Confess away."

"It's not that easy. You see, my darling, I realized that I had something that belonged to you, and not to me. I hope you will understand why I kept it from you."

Kate was bewildered. "I can't imagine what you're talking about."

Elizabeth did not answer. She rose from her chair and went over to the portrait of her father above the mantelpiece. She swung it out from the wall and opened the safe that lay behind, and drawing out a small package wrapped in a handkerchief, she gave it to Kate. "This was your mother's."

Kate unfolded the cloth carefully and withdrew a round, tooled-leather case with a small square hinge. Inside of that lay another case, plain silver, and a watch lay nestled within. The dial was gilt, circled by Roman numerals, and there was an engraving of two squirrels in the center. The hands were blue steel, stopped some forty years before at ten to three. It was extraordinarily beautiful.

"This is the watch that Granny was talking about, isn't it?" asked Kate softly. Elizabeth nodded. Kate found that her heart was pounding. She closed the case and turned it over in her hands. On the back of the leather was an ornate monogram stamped in gold. She could not make it out. "Whose was it, Elizabeth?"

"I don't know. But I think it's time I told a story that I've been silent about since 1944. I'm not your grandmother, Kate. But neither is Caroline Jessop."

"No? Then who?" Kate looked even more bewildered.

"I don't know. But I'll tell you what I can." She sat down opposite Kate and clasped her hands in her lap as if to compose herself. Then she began.

"Caroline Cates and I grew up together and were the best

of friends. In the years before war broke out, an American by the name of Guy Jessop, a very wealthy industrialist, came more and more frequently to England. Later we learned that he was a secret emissary from Roosevelt and had something to do with Secret Intelligence Services. He and Caroline fell in love and were married in 1937. Caroline and Guy wanted a child more than anything else in the world, and although the doctors had advised against it, eventually, and with great difficulty, she became pregnant in 1943. She was thirty-eight by then and the pregnancy was not an easy one. Guy sent her away from London to live here with me. She had refused to leave him before, and came then only for the sake of the baby that she so desperately wanted. Then on a night of a particularly bad air raid, Caroline went into labor, but with the bombs there was no way to get her to the hospital. Fortunately Guy happened to be here for the weekend. We made a makeshift bed in the cellar, and there after a very hard time, she gave birth to a daughter. The infant lived only long enough to be baptized Susanna, after Caroline's mother.

"Naturally, Caroline was terribly distraught. To make matters worse, she knew she would never be able to have another child. After the birth, Guy went upstairs to the sitting room and was up there for hours. When he came back down, he announced that he had decided to tell no one about the birth and death of their daughter just yet. He said he wanted to give Caroline some time to recover; he didn't think she could cope with the condolences that would undoubtedly pour in. He buried the child himself. I thought the whole thing was terribly macabre, but what could I say?

"Then two days later, his true reason for the delay became clear. Guy had gone back to London, but he returned suddenly. He and Caroline were closeted away in the bedroom for over an hour, and I could hear Caroline crying. But when Guy came out, all was quiet. He sat me down, here in this room, and told me that an infant girl, recently orphaned, had been brought out of France through the Resistance. She would arrive here the next day and he and Caroline were going to take her in as their daughter. Nobody was ever to know that it wasn't their Susanna.

"The baby came, delivered in a cardboard box by a man on a bicycle. I never saw him again. All she had with her was the nightdress she was wearing, the tattered blanket she was wrapped in, and the watch you are holding. Caroline fell in love with her immediately; and though she would always grieve for the daughter who had died, she took this little girl into her heart as her own. She swore me to secrecy, and gave me the watch. She didn't want Guy to know about it, she said; if he knew he'd be rid of it, because there must be nothing to connect the baby with her past. What that past was I don't know; Caroline and Guy did, but wouldn't say. They seemed to feel there was danger of some kind connected to it, or trouble that could arise. In any case, Caroline, sentimental as always, could not bear to dispose of the one thing that truly belonged to the baby, so I took it and hid it away. Naturally, no one doubted that the child was theirs. Guy announced the supposed birth as any proud father would. We never spoke of it again.

"They took the girl back to America with them when the war was over. She was your mother, Kate."

Kate sat quite still, her mind focused inward as she struggled to come to terms with the story she'd just heard. Finally, she just shook her head. "My God, Elizabeth. Did anybody else ever know the truth?"

"No, not even your mother."

"Then why did you choose to tell me in the end?"

"I suppose because you came to me with it. I hated lying to you, but you took me by surprise. You have to understand that I swore to Guy and Caroline never to speak of it, and I would have kept the secret to my grave if you hadn't stumbled upon it yourself. It's been bothering me since yesterday and would have continued to do so. I couldn't allow you to labor under the false impression that I was your grandmother." Elizabeth gave a dry chuckle. "I can certainly see how you might have come to that conclusion, however. In any case, when you get on to something you're like a dog with a bone, so it seemed more sensible to tell you now rather than letting you worry me to death about it. With Guy and Susanna dead, and Caroline all but gone from us, there's no one who can be hurt by it after all this time. However, I think we should keep it to ourselves."

"Thank you, Elizabeth."

"I did what I thought was right, and I must say, it's a relief to have it off my chest after all these years. I also think you have a right to know the truth of your heritage."

"Yes . . . It's a little difficult adjusting to. I wonder who Susanna's real parents could have been, what they were like! It's ironic, all that pounding on Grandfather used to do at me about the importance of heritage, being true to my blood, and now I find out I don't have a drop of Jessop blood in me and he knew it all along."

"Don't be ridiculous, child. They loved your mother and you as completely as if you had been their own flesh and blood. You brought great happiness into their lives, happiness they would otherwise not have had."

"Yes, I realize that, and I certainly love Granny as if she were my own, nothing can change that. But that's not what I meant. I think . . . I think I'd like to try to find out who my real grandparents were. Aside from the fact that it's an incredible story, if what Grandfather always said about 'blood will out' is true, I'd like to know just what to expect. Do you think there's any way of tracking them down after all this time?"

"I wouldn't know, but you can always try if you have a mind to."

"You don't think it could cause trouble now, do you, if I go digging all this up?"

"I can't think it would at this late date. Whatever it was is bound to be connected to the war. I often wondered whether Susanna wasn't Jewish. That would explain why she might have been in danger and sent out of France during that terrible time."

"Yes . . . That is possible, but then once she was safe in England, why all the secrecy?"

"I really don't know, darling. But do remember that Guy worked for one of the Intelligence departments. Perhaps whatever channels he received Susanna through had to be kept top secret. I doubt we'll ever know. You must remember, Kate, that she was an orphan, so your grandparents will be long dead. I don't want you to be disappointed if you find out nothing. There's not much to go on, and I'm afraid I've told you everything I can."

Kate looked down at the watch cradled in her hand. "I can always start with this."

CHAPTER
Five

"*Oh*, Kate, it really is extraordinary!" Stephanie delicately examined the watch. "The whole thing is extraordinary—what are you going to do?"

"I'm going to keep it to myself, first of all. It's been a secret for so long now, I don't think there's any reason for it to come out. I can just imagine what my father would say. Anyway, when Elizabeth told me, she was trusting my judgment and my silence. You're the only person I plan on telling."

"I won't breathe a word," Stephanie promised solemnly. "But how are you going to trace your grandparents with only this to go on?"

"I have an idea. Thursday I have to go to the rare wine auction at Christie's. Why can't I see one of their other experts while I'm there? Perhaps he can trace the watch for me. After all, it's obviously an uncommon piece. How many like could there be?"

"Brilliant idea! This could turn into quite an adventure, you know. I can see the headlines—innocent girl discovers mystery in background and is led to gothic horror tale."

"Oh, shut up, Steph." Kate threw a pillow at her.

* * *

Christie's was on King Street, St. James's. Its blue flag fluttered regally outside the imposing white facade; inside there was a quiet air of importance. Kate quickly explained to the woman at the front desk what she needed, and the woman agreed to make an appointment with one of the consultants after the afternoon session of the auction.

Kate attended the auction not to buy, but to appraise. She was interested in the going rates for fine vintage ports, of which the British had long been aficionados. Rosterman and Marsh were very interested in promoting the port trade in America where it was in its infancy: rarely did any American order a glass of port after dinner in a restaurant, and even more rarely was a port of any quality available. But things were changing, and many of their clients had inquired into buying up cases of port as an investment; and Kate was determined to be able to advise them when she returned to New York.

She took copious notes, and was thrilled when three bottles of a vintage port, 1931, whose shipper was unknown but was thought to be the great Quinta do Noval, went for over 800 pounds sterling. By the end of the auction, not only had Kate learned a great deal about port, but also she'd picked up a good deal of generally useful information about other members of the wine family.

The auction room slowly emptied out, and Kate busied herself with examining the old, dusty bottles, with their famous labels and prohibitive prices, that lay in glass cases in the front of the room.

"Madam?" It was the woman from the front desk.

"Yes?" Kate turned expectantly.

"If you'll just come this way? You're very lucky. Our top man for *objets de vertu* is in today—he said he'd be happy to look at your watch."

"Oh! That's wonderful. Thank you so much." The woman led her around the corridor, which was crowded with antique furniture due to be auctioned the next day.

"If I may just have your name? I'm so sorry, I didn't manage to get it before."

"Yes, of course. It's Soames, Kate Soames."

"Mr. Dunn is the head of the department, you see, Miss Soames, and a very busy man. But he's considered the expert in his field—he has a worldwide reputation, so you can expect the best. Of course, you can always expect the best at Christie's, but you really are very lucky that he's in today . . ."

Kate was very amused at this stream of idolatry, and expressed the appropriate appreciation at her amazing good fortune. She had a delicious vision of a leonine old man, covered in cobwebs, bent double from his many years of expertise in examining small, fine works of art. She was ushered into an outer office where an elderly woman was sorting out large neat piles of correspondence. "Martha, this is Miss Soames, with the watch she'd like appraised."

"Oh yes, Miss Soames. He's expecting you. Come right in." She knocked on the inner door and opened it. "Mr. Dunn, Miss Soames is here."

Kate walked through into the large, elegant room, bright with sun. A fair-haired man in an immaculately tailored gray suit sat behind a mahogany desk. Kate froze where she stood and her body washed cold with shock.

He looked up from his papers. "How do you . . . Oh, sweet Christ."

"Mr. Dunn?" said Kate, trying to recover herself.

"Thanks, Martha, that will be all." He waited until the door had shut on Martha's astonished face. "Kate," he said simply and rose to his feet.

She stared at him in disbelief. "Yes. Still Kate Soames. But you had a shave and a haircut and suddenly your name became Simon Dunn?"

"It's Sebastian, actually." He smiled apologetically.

"And I'm sure you have some perfectly reasonable explanation for all this?" Kate's eyes flashed dangerously.

"Well, naturally I do. But why don't you sit down first? There's no need to look quite so indignant, Kate."

"Oh, isn't there? In the first place, I don't like being

taken for a fool, Mr. Dunn, and in the second, I came to get a watch looked at. I did not come for an explanation from a two-faced, conniving rotter who passed himself off as a simple fisherman running away from reality and turns up as a so-called expert at Christie's auction house in a blasted suit!'' She paused for breath.

''You don't like it?'' said Sebastian, looking sadly down at his sleeve. ''My tailor will be devastated.''

''Oh, you swine!'' Kate's cheeks were flushed with fury.

''Kate, for the love of God, sit down before you explode into thousands of pieces which, knowing you, would be hell to put back together.'' He walked around to her and pulled out a chair, pushing her resisting form down into it. ''That's better. Now what about this watch of yours?'' He sat on the edge of the desk.

''I don't see why I should trust you with it. For all I know you'll turn into a pumpkin next.''

''Give it over, you awful child.'' He grinned at her, that familiar smile that deepened the creases at the sides of his mouth, and Kate felt herself thawing against her will. It's Simon, she thought with a queer little rush, forgetting her anger.

''I suppose since I'm here . . .'' She opened her handbag, and drawing the watch out, she placed it on the blotter.

''Hmm. A gilt pair-case watch, early eighteenth century, I'd say. Very interesting.'' His long square fingers carefully examined the piece. She'd forgotten what beautiful hands he had. ''You say you want it appraised? Are you planning on selling it?''

''No. Actually, it's not so much the value that I'm interested in. I'd like to know where it came from, its previous owners, if possible.''

''I see. That might not be too difficult, especially if it's been auctioned before. The movement's probably signed, and if I'm correct, by Gosselin.''

''Who's that?''

''He was master of the Paris Corporation in the early seventeen hundreds. This is what is known as a French 'oignon' watch. I'll see what I can do for you, Kate.''

"Oh, thanks. Also, I don't know if this is anything to do with you, but it doesn't run."

"That shouldn't be any problem. I'll have one of the men in the clock department give it a look. They'll be very helpful in tracing its provenance, in any case. It might take some time, you know."

"How long, do you think?" Kate frowned.

"It's hard to say; a month or two, I should think. How long are you here?"

"Three months. But I would like it back as soon as possible."

"I'll do my best. It would be helpful to know how you came by it."

"Oh!" Kate hadn't thought of this. "My, my aunt gave it to me."

"And do you know where she got it?" Sebastian was watching her curiously.

Her mind sped. "Um . . . Well, it was given to her by a gentleman, who bought it in London, but he was killed during the war. That's as far back as I've been able to go." She could feel herself blushing furiously and looked up only to meet Sebastian's very blue eyes full on hers—and that infuriating little smile was playing in them.

"And why are you so interested in tracing its history, Kate?" he asked softly, continuing to hold her eyes.

She looked away. "Oh, just idle curiosity. Look, maybe this is too much trouble—"

"Don't be silly. I was only curious myself. Right, that should do it. Is there anything else you want to ask?"

"No . . ." Kate was thinking how very good looking Simon, or rather, Sebastian, had become. Amazing what a difference the lack of beard could make; she could see now that his chin had a little cleft in it, and his mouth seemed somehow fuller, or was it wider—anyway, more sensual . . .

"Kate?" Sebastian laughed, and she blushed even more deeply.

"What?"

"Would you like to have dinner tonight?"

"No! I mean, no thanks. I—I'm busy."

"Tomorrow, next week? I feel I owe it to you. Surely you have some questions?"

"I can't. I'm sorry."

"Hmm. Is it because of your fiancé? Is he here with you? I assure you it would be perfectly harmless."

"No, it has nothing to do with David. He's—we're not together anymore." She felt like a babbling schoolgirl. What on earth was the matter with her?

"Oh . . . I see. Yes, I should have noticed the ring was gone again. Well, then all the more reason to have dinner with me." He grinned.

"No. I'm not interested in questions or answers, or anything else about you. And you of all people should be able to figure out why."

Sebastian looked at her speculatively. "Let's see; it has to be one of two things. Either you are still furious with me for having temporarily transformed myself into a certain Simon Dristoll, and a splendid chap he was, or you're afraid I'm going to eat you."

"Oh, Simon or Sebastian, it doesn't make an iota of difference which one, you're both impossible! Thank you very much for your time, Mr. Dunn, I must be going." She stood.

"It was my pleasure, as always, Miss Soames. Why don't you let me know where I can reach you when I have something on your watch."

Kate hesitated. "I'm staying with Stephanie Matthison. It's in the book. Good-bye."

He came around the desk and opened the door for her, then shook her hand. His palm was cool and dry, his grip firm. "Good-bye, Miss Soames. You'll be hearing from me soon." His voice was unconcerned, polite, but his eyes were warm, laughing at her.

She had to force herself to walk sedately away. She felt like bolting.

Kate didn't get back to the house until late. She was exhausted, too tired to think, and all she wanted was a hot bath. She kicked off her shoes and called, "Stephanie? Are you home?"

Stephanie's head appeared over the railing. "So, mystery woman, I was wondering when you were going to get back. There's something up here for you, and I think you'd better come have a look."

"Oh, no, I don't need any more surprises. What is it?" She headed wearily up the stairs and into the sitting room.

On the coffee table was an enormous rectangular white box, with a red ribbon wrapped around it. "It came three hours ago. I've been dying for you to get home! I thought maybe it was your past so beautifully wrapped up, having come special delivery."

"Stop it, Steph. I've had a hell of a day. I can't imagine what it could be."

"Well don't gape at it, idiot, open it!"

"All right, all right." She untied the ribbon and pulled the top off. Inside, nestled in soft green tissue paper, lay an armful of yellow long-stem roses. "Oh . . ." Kate's breath came out on a long sigh.

"How absolutely glorious—who d'you suppose they're from? David? There must be a card."

"I hope they're not, but there's no one else who would—yes, here it is." She tore it open. "I don't believe it!" She started to laugh.

"What, Kate? Is it David?"

"No!" She finished reading the note, her shoulders shaking with laughter. "You're *never* going to believe this. They're from someone called Sebastian Dunn. Oh, this had made my day."

"Who's he?" Stephanie wrinkled her brow, trying to think if Kate had ever mentioned the name.

"He, my dear Steph, is the man at Christie's who looked at my watch today." Kate grinned, dangling the bait.

"He must have liked it! Why ever is he sending you roses—look, there's a full two dozen here!"

"Here, read the card." Kate handed it over, her grin growing even wider.

Stephanie scrutinized it. The script was clear, the writing strong and upright.

My dear Kate,

These flowers will have to stand in lieu of dinner as an explanation and apology until your curiosity overcomes your stubbornness. Believe me when I say that I was just as surprised to see you today as you were to see me, but in my case the surprise was a pleasant one. I'm deeply sorry my sudden change of circumstances upset you. But I wondered if I promised to wear jeans and splashed on a little fish oil, you might feel more charitable toward me and reconsider dinner. I really won't eat you, and you can't stay angry forever, can you?

As ever,

S.

"I don't understand. You've obviously met him before—"

"Doesn't fish oil ring any bells?"

"Fish oil?" She rubbed her forehead, looking blank.

"As in cod-liver? Boats?"

She looked down at the note then up at Kate with disbelief as the light dawned. "Surely not . . . Simon? Oh, Kate! But I don't understand!" Stunned, she sat down on the floor and Kate followed suit.

"Neither do I, Steph, but I swear to you, I walked into that office today, and there was Simon Dristoll big as life. Only his name was Sebastian Dunn and he looked as if he was to the manner born. Cleanly shaven—"

"Cleanly shaven?" Stephanie looked even more disbelieving.

"His hair was cut short and brushed back off his face and he was wearing the most beautifully cut suit."

"I can't imagine your Simon in a suit. Oh, Kate, this is too good to be true!"

"Isn't it though? I thought I was going to die of shock. And he took it so calmly. I'm afraid I didn't."

"That comes as no surprise."

"Well, I was angry, and understandably so. He tricked me, Steph, and I told him all those things about myself thinking he was someone quite different. I mean, he kissed me, for heaven's sake, using somebody else's name!"

"I can't see what the name has to do with it. As I remember you described it as heavenly, or amazing, or something."

"Did I?"

"Yes, and I can't see why you didn't accept his dinner invitation. Not only is this irresistibly intriguing, but also it's perfectly clear to me that you're attracted to him."

"I am not!" objected Kate vehemently.

"Of course you are, and there's nothing wrong with that."

"Oh, yes there is. First of all, I'm just getting over David. The last thing I need is another man in my life, especially one I'm attracted to—all right, I admit it, but drop it right there! Anyway, that's beside the point. I shouldn't feel that way, it's ridiculous."

"Why is it ridiculous?"

"It would be crazy to go out to dinner with a man who's a proven liar and womanizer. And I'm not ready to get involved, and anyway I'm leaving in a few months. So I'm not going to play with fire, no matter how attractive it is."

"What makes you think he's a womanizer?"

"Well, he womanized me, didn't he?"

"Oh, of course," said Stephanie. "How silly of me."

James Lambert was the proprietor of a small but very well-known wine cellar in Oxford, built on the level of the old thirteenth-century carriageway that had once run around the entire city. A distinguished-looking man in his middle years, with a fine sense of humor and a passion for his subject, he was considered one of the foremost experts on port, and it was a wise don who consulted him before laying down a single bottle for his college. He was also the person who had given Kate her love for fine wines and their history while she was at Trinity College. She'd spent many an hour in his cellars, drinking in the smell of damp stone and musty bottles and tasting the varied vintages he would produce, until she was able to place an unknown wine practically on its home vine. Gradually he started teaching her about distribution and the intricacies of buying and selling, so that by the time she had her degree in literature in hand, she had forgotten about teaching and was ready to enter the London wine trade.

"I'll tell you, Kate, the Americans are catching on faster than you think. The colleges are finding it difficult to get their hands on port—it's all going to America. If we don't do something soon, in twenty years' time we'll be dry as a bone, and college tradition will be in tatters. Here we are, with all the big port houses as British-named partnerships, and where's all our port going? To America."

"Are you objecting, James?"

"No, now don't get me wrong, it's a fine thing to see our cousins over there finally sitting up and paying attention, and they have the patience to let it age, unlike those French, who'll never understand a good port if it were given them for Mass! Even the Italians are buying into port, but not the French who think they're such experts on wine—Ha! I say." And James was off on one of his favorite subjects, which was that wine had always been a British-controlled industry, from the time of Eleanor of Aquitaine. "Bordeaux was British owned for three hundred years. Who do they think developed the industry, Kate? The French? Nonsense—to this day, we dictate the marketplace worldwide. You've seen that for yourself, by now."

"Yes, I have, James," she said, smiling broadly, knowing they could be on this for hours. "You know, I'd like to get your opinion on some of these prices that went at

Christie's last week. Speak of the British dictating the marketplace!"

"Yes, indeed. And we have Mrs. Thatcher to thank for disbanding those killing currency controls and getting us into the Common Market. That man Wilson was a disaster for wine buyers."

"Here, James, look at this nineteenth-century port that was up for sale." She offered him the catalog.

"Oh, my, yes. I heard about that..."

By six o'clock, Kate was ready to go back to Elizabeth's. She planned on coming up to Oxford as often as she could to talk with James, and staying with Elizabeth was an added incentive. Walking slowly down Broad Street, past the rounded front of the Sheldonian Theatre with its Roman design and carved heads topping the external wall, she crossed the street and went to gaze in the window of Blackwell's, her most favorite bookshop in the world.

Her eyes widened as she discerned that there was a familiar face reflected in the glass, and her heart gave an absurd, almost painful thump. She took a deep breath to compose herself and then turned around. "Why, if it isn't Sebastian Dunn, as I live and breathe, or are we Simon Dristoll today?" she asked sarcastically.

"Why, Kate Soames, as I live and breathe!" said Sebastian with a grin. "What a coincidence."

"I don't believe that for a minute. Have you been following me?"

"Good heavens, no! Whatever gave you that idea? Can't I walk the streets of Oxford without being suspected of trailing you?" His face was a study of innocence. He looked more familiar to her today, wearing khaki trousers and a pullover covered by a suede jacket.

"Well, if you're walking the streets, go walk somewhere else."

"Oh, no. You're not shaking me off that easily. I have

something I want to say to you, and I'm damned well going to say it, whether you want to hear it or not."

"You don't take rejection well, do you?"

"Are you referring to the message you left with my secretary? 'Thank Mr. Dunn for the flowers and tell him that oil isn't the only thing that smells fishy about him'? Really, Kate. Poor Martha was most nonplussed."

"Can't you get it through your head that the only thing I want to have in common with you is a watch?"

"As a matter of fact, that's why I came up today. I have something that might be of interest to you."

"Oh." Kate had the grace to look embarrassed.

"Look, just put down your fists for a moment and come have a glass of wine with me." He didn't wait for her answer, but took her by the arm and pulled her into the White Horse, directly next door. He found them a table and sat her down, ordering two glasses of the house white.

"How did you know where to find me?" she finally asked into the protracted silence, feeling very disconcerted at the way he was looking at her.

"Guess."

"Not Stephanie?"

"Clever girl; you got it in one. She was very helpful. Aren't you the least bit curious about what I have for you?"

"I suppose so," said Kate reluctantly.

Sebastian reached into his pocket and withdrew a yellowed and faded photograph, creased in four squares. "Here. I sent your watch to the clock department to have it looked at, and they found this wedged between the two cases. Do you have any ideas as to whom it might be?"

Kate felt a little thrill of excitement as she examined the photograph. It was a picture of a dark-haired young woman sitting on a wall in a flowered dress. She was laughing. On the back was written "St. Mouton, 1943." Could this possibly be her grandmother? The date would be right, and the town sounded French, which made sense. She looked straight at Sebastian and lied. "I have no idea. Did you discover anything else?"

"Not really. The movement was signed Gosselin, Paris,

as I'd suspected, but that doesn't give us much to go on at this point, other than it appears the piece stayed in France at least until 1943, and then surfaced later in England during the war. I'm having it traced to see if it was ever recorded at any European auction prior to that. As I said, it will take time."

"But this is wonderful, Sebastian!" The wine had mellowed her reserve, and in her excitement she had forgotten her resolution to keep her distance.

"It's put a smile on your face, at least. I was beginning to think I'd never see one again."

"I'm sorry. I have been awful to you, and here you are trying to help. But that doesn't suggest you're by any means forgiven, you know. There's still 'a very ancient and fishlike smell.' " She laughed, waiting for it.

"Ah yes, but 'now does my object gather to a head,' " he said, cocking an eyebrow and grinning wickedly. "*The Tempest*—and again how appropriate. Well, that's something easily remedied. We'll strike a bargain. Since I came all the way up to give you your photograph, the least you can do is have dinner with me tonight. Agreed?"

The last of Kate's resolve melted away. "Oh, all right. But just this once, as thanks."

"Whatever you say," said Sebastian cheerfully.

CHAPTER
Six

Kate drove Elizabeth's little red Metro the twenty miles back to Henley and explained that she was going out to dinner unexpectedly.

"Oh, that's perfectly fine, darling, I was only making soup and omelettes. Did you run into an old friend in Oxford?"

"In a way, yes. I must rush, he's coming by at eight and it's past seven already." She tore upstairs to draw a bath, wondering frantically what to wear and wondering even more frantically why she had agreed to this dinner. She was unaware that Elizabeth was looking after her with growing interest.

The steaming bath gave her time to relax, and she suddenly realized that she hadn't even told Elizabeth about the photograph. "Slow down, Kate," she murmured. "It's one dinner, that's all." Carefully scrutinizing her feelings, she decided the truth of the matter was that Sebastian terrified her. When he was near she felt out of control at a time when she needed all the control she could muster. Falling in love with David had been a slow sort of thing, built up over months of sharing things in common, a quiet, steady relationship. But this was completely different; Sebastian exuded pure animal magnetism, some terrible pheromone that drew her to him, and it would only lead to trouble if she wasn't careful . . .

Twenty minutes later she came to with a start and leaped out of the bath. She rubbed herself down briskly with a big, deliciously rough white towel, fresh from the drying line. She wrapped another towel around her head and dashed across the hall to her bedroom. A full white wool skirt and a soft cotton jersey woven in a subtle mixture of purples, blues and pinks were tossed on the bed, and in twenty minutes her hair was dry, her face lightly touched with makeup, and her clothes in place. She slipped into a pair of blue pumps and ran downstairs, just as a silver Jaguar pulled up in the driveway. Grabbing her coat and bag, she kissed Elizabeth abstractedly and walked sedately out the door as if she hadn't a care in the world.

"You look perfectly beautiful, Kate," said Sebastian, opening her door for her. He'd changed into a tweed jacket and a tie, an interesting taupe silk with a gray and white design.

"Thank you. You're looking rather smart yourself, and so is your car. You do take some getting used to, you know. But what heaven!"

"Are you referring to me or the car?" he asked with a grin, sliding into the other seat.

"The car, you idiot!" She smiled and leaned back against the seat, breathing in the wonderful rich fragrance of leather, suddenly glad she'd come.

"It is nice, isn't it," said Sebastian comfortably, starting the engine. "I thought we'd go to a little place about fifteen minutes' drive from here where I'm staying tonight. I don't think you'll know it—it belongs to a good friend of mine who opened up only a couple of years ago but knows what he's doing. Sort of an upscale Joe's where you let him decide what's for dinner. All right?"

"It sounds fine." Kate looked over at him. His eyes were trained on the road and she watched his profile for a minute, drinking in the sharp, clear line of cheek and jaw, the high arch of his nose. He looked relaxed, very much at ease, and she couldn't imagine why she'd thought him dangerous.

"Sebastian?"

"Yes?" He glanced over at her.

She hesitated. "Never mind."

"Oh, no, Kate; you don't get away what that. What were you going to say?"

"I was just going to say that I'm glad you talked me into dinner. I know how perfectly bloody stubborn I can be."

He smiled. "Yes, you can, but that's part of what makes you Kate. I wouldn't have it any other way."

The restaurant turned out to be a converted Queen Anne house set on its own estate. They were ushered into a large, comfortable bar area, originally the sitting room, and had a glass of dry sherry while their table was being readied. Then they were shown into the dining-room. It had a quiet, elegant atmosphere; brilliant white tablecloths were set with large, crisply starched and equally brilliant white napkins, gleaming silverware and sparkling glasses. Candles glowed on every table that also held a small vase of cut flowers, and a fire burned steadily in the enormous central fireplace, giving off a gentle warmth. They were seated next to a window that looked out over a lovely pastoral setting painted a deep gold as the sun slipped behind the trees and disappeared.

Dinner passed lazily by, Kate having forgotten that she'd ever had a problem with Sebastian Dunn. He regaled her with amusing stories of the antique trade, and she in turn found that he drew her out about her childhood. He was a relaxed presence, a careful listener but with a fine, sharp sense of humor that lurked just below the surface. He somehow managed to blend the casual, insouciant charm of Simon with a sleek sophistication unique to this new Sebastian, a Sebastian so comfortable that she felt she'd known him all her life, despite the fact that he was a virtual stranger.

The restaurant began to empty somewhat and they were just finishing their coffee, when a man of about Sebastian's age with flaming red hair appeared at their table.

"Ah, Geoff, another brilliant meal! I'd like you to meet

Kate Soames, an old friend of mine. Kate, may I present the infamous Geoffrey March.''

He bowed over her hand. ''I'm very honored.''

''No, the honor is all mine, believe me. The food was more than perfect, and the wines were superb.''

''Yes, Sebastian told me you were in the business. I've brought out a little something special I thought you might like to sample.'' He snapped his fingers and a waiter produced three snifters and a bottle of cognac. Kate examined the label

''Oh, Geoffrey, what a treat—a Delamain Reserve! I've never tasted it, but I've heard wonderful things! Wherever did you come across it? It's extremely rare.''

''I'll never tell,'' he said firmly, pouring it out and handing it around. ''I'm sure my methods were thoroughly illegal.''

''The usual story, Geoff,'' said Sebastian with a smile, sipping the cognac. ''This *is* excellent. What do you think, Kate? Does it come up to expectation?''

''Mmm, it's utter heaven! It's really too good to be true—smooth, rich, mellow, everything it should be. Thank you a thousand times, Geoffrey.''

''You are most welcome. It gives me great pleasure to see a connoisseur appreciating my humble offerings. This particular cognac, for the ignorant party across the table, is vintage 1920s and actually unblended. That's how pure its little heart is.''

''Purer than yours, no doubt.'' Sebastian grinned.

''That's the pot calling the kettle black, don't you think?''

''Indeed it is. You couldn't find a blacker heart than the one that resides in my chest, isn't that right, Kate?''

''I wouldn't begin to argue,'' she said with a little smile.

''Isn't she marvelous, Geoffrey?''

''It's just what you need, I think; a woman who won't be swayed by your somewhat dubious charms. Alas, I cannot stay to have another glass with you; duty calls. But help yourselves—with discretion, Sebastian. I trust Kate to keep an eye on my precious bottle.''

''I'm beyond responsibility, and besides, I have absolutely

no control over Sebastian; I think you should take it away. Not only is this glass the perfect touch, but also if I had another I'd fall off my chair! It was lovely meeting you, Geoffrey, and thanks again."

"The pleasure was entirely mine. Where did you meet this gem, Sebastian?"

"We know each other from Jamaica," said Sebastian smoothly, and Kate nearly choked.

"Oh, well if you ever give up on this wastrel here, let me know, Kate. We'd get along splendidly. Sebastian, come upstairs whenever you please. I'll see you at breakfast, I expect." He slipped away as quietly as he'd come.

"Sebastian, how could you bring up Jamaica like that, as if it had been some bland little cocktail party!"

"Well, I certainly wouldn't describe it as bland, Kate, would you?"

"No, but that's not the point, as you well know. I think you have some explaining to do, Mr. Dristoll."

"Certainly. And it's all part of the story I'm going to tell you. Shall we drink up and leave? I could use a good walk after all that food and wine. Let's go down by the river."

The half-moon swam mistily in the sky, and the wide ribbon of the Thames glittered beneath its cast-off light. They walked down the footpath, side by side, their bodies close but not touching. Kate was filled with a delicious contentment and something else besides that she couldn't place but that made her feel as if everything were just slightly unreal. " 'The iron tongue of midnight hath told twelve; Lovers to bed; 'tis almost fairy time,' " she softly quoted.

" 'And then the moon, like to a silver bow new-bent in heaven, shall behold the night of our solemnities.' " replied Sebastian. "Wrong order, but it's the best that I can do at the moment." Sebastian drew her over to the side of a low bridge that spanned the river. "Let's stop here for a moment, Kate. It's time you heard why I was in Jamaica."

"Yes, I suppose it is."

He sighed and leaned against the stone parapet, gazing down into the rippling water as he began.

"There was a certain, shall we say, object, which was about to go up for private sale, an extremely valuable piece. However, the particular gentleman who was selling the piece had once before been suspected of substituting a fake for the original. The story never got out, and nothing was ever proven, but it was enough to be concerned about. It was my sale, you see, and I felt responsible to the potential buyer.

"The seller happened to be vacationing in Jamaica, and he had the piece with him, supposedly for safekeeping, but also where it conveniently couldn't be examined. I'm sure you can see that it would have created a tremendous scandal if this suspicion had become public.

"I went down surreptitiously to check the piece out. Actually, breaking and entering would be a more accurate description. Throwing modesty to the wind, Kate, my name is quite well known in certain circles and if the seller had had any inkling that I was anywhere near the piece, I'm quite sure both would have disappeared. Therefore, I became Simon Dristoll, poor fisherman."

"But then why were we taken onto the boat that day?" interrupted Kate. "Not only was that unnecessary, but also surely it was dangerous for you?"

"Actually, the reason Eustice pulled you aboard was because the boat was being watched. You appeared at exactly the right moment as the perfect alibi."

"Oh." Kate frowned. "I'm not sure I like being an alibi."

"Ironically enough, it turned out the other way around. It wasn't the boat being watched, it was you, Kate."

"Whatever do you mean?"

"Apparently David was keeping an eye on you." Sebastian turned his head and watched her absorb this piece of news.

"Oh!" Kate flushed with anger, violently glad that David was out of her life, and surprised with the vehemence of her feelings. "Well, never mind that, go on."

"There isn't much more. I found what I needed. It was a forgery, very cleverly done, and never would have been spotted if one hadn't been looking for it very carefully. I warned the prospective buyer off, and the word's been spread quietly among dealers to keep an eye out for it. The only thing I don't know is if the gentleman in question still has the original. He could easily have sold it quite secretly to a private collector. That's it. Of course, I have to ask you to keep this to yourself, Kate."

"Yes, naturally. But Sebastian, how did you know the area so well, and the people and things, if you didn't live there?"

"That's why it was such a perfect cover. My family had a house in Port Antonio, pre-political trouble in the seventies. We used to vacation there every year."

"How convenient for you. You even remembered where to find that ghastly fish. I suppose it's been lurking there for years."

Sebastian threw his head back and laughed. "It has been, just waiting for you to come along."

Kate turned abruptly and walked away from him, torn by conflicting emotions. She was silent for a minute, and she could feel him behind her, waiting. Finally she spoke. "I accept the rest of your story, but I don't see why you had to use me, Sebastian."

"How, Kate? How did I use you?" he asked quietly.

"You—you misled me, you used me as an alibi, and you certainly didn't have to kiss me like that!"

Sebastian smiled through the darkness. "No, you're quite right, I certainly didn't."

"Then why? Why did you?" She turned around to face him, not really understanding herself why it upset her so much, but needing an answer.

"Very simply because I wanted to, Kate. Can you understand that? I had no desire to hurt you, and for the life of me, no idea in the world that you would waltz into my office a few months later. You were far and away the nicest thing that happened to me on that bloody trip. Originally I had no way of knowing that you were involved with someone, and by God, the only reason I was so delighted when I found out you were was because it meant my cover hadn't been blown. And then I most certainly wasn't going to give up the opportunity of kissing you good-bye. I swear I wasn't playing with you, Kate, if that's what you're thinking, but I couldn't exactly turn around before I kissed you and reintroduce myself as Sebastian Dunn of Christie's, now could I?''

''No, I suppose not,'' she said slowly.

''Good, I'm glad you understand that. In any case, believe me, at the time it didn't seem important. And are you going to forgive me for having to deceive you?''

''Yes . . .'' She looked at him cautiously, her eyes turning very dark.

''Then come here, Kate.''

''Why?'' she asked foolishly, slightly breathless at his tone.

''Because I'm about to kiss you again, and this time I intend to do a very thorough job.''

She walked straight into his arms.

Some time later, Sebastian took her by the arm and led her over the far side of the bridge to a bench. It sat at the foot of an enormous lime tree whose branches hung out over the river, carving deep shadows in the moonlight. He put his arm around her and pulled her close. ''Now tell me all about David.''

And so she did, and when she'd finished he was quiet for a few moments. Then he looked down at her and smiled.

''It sounds very much to me as if your father and David were the two people who had a relationship, and you were just caught in the middle. I'm sure they'll get on very well on their own,'' he said dryly.

Kate laughed ruefully. ''I suppose you're right. I've been trying to work out how and why I fell in love with David. I'm not sure I know what that means anymore.''

''Of course you do. You just tried to convince yourself

that what you felt for David was love. I don't know, he sounds rather like a carbon copy of your father, and you never got much love or attention from him, from what you've said. It only makes sense to look for it in a similar man. Unfortunately that rarely works, because naturally you're looking for the wrong thing."

"I'm not sure I know how to look for the right thing, or even if I'd recognize it if it stared me in the face!"

"I very much doubt you've ever had it stare you in the face before. Love is only real when it's freely given, Kate, given for its own sake with no expectations or conditions attached. You can't own somebody's love, in fact as far as I'm concerned, the opposite is true. If you truly love someone, you encourage change and growth, for the sheer joy of seeing that person happy, even if it sometimes separates you. And that is true whether it is child, parent, friend, or lover. Although," he added lightly, "speaking for myself, the latter is a good deal more interesting."

"I'm sure it is, Sebastian, knowing you," said Kate with a smile. "But I can't imagine anyone ever loving me so forgivingly; I'm far too impossible."

"Sweetheart, we are all imperfect, believe me, and it's something to be thankful for. It's those people who think they aren't who are insufferable. However, you're right, you may well be one of the more impossible creatures I know, and as I believe I told you once, utterly adorable." He kissed her nose, his eyes dancing.

"You're no less impossible yourself, Sebastian, not to mention implausible," she replied tartly.

"Oh, how I've missed my little shrew, and ripe she is for the taming."

" 'Oh vile, intolerable, not to be endured!' " she pulled from the play, doing her best to look outraged.

" 'Kiss me, Kate,' " he quoted back with a grin and she did, laughing against his mouth. He suddenly pulled away and looked down at her, cupping her chin for a moment, his eyes puzzled.

"What is it, Sebastian? Why are you looking at me like

that?" Kate could no longer read his mood, but she sensed a sudden shift in the direction of his thoughts.

"I was thinking about what you said a few moments ago."

"About what in particular?"

"About love."

"Oh, that. Not my forte, I'm afraid. But tell me something, Sebastian—was that story you told me in Jamaica about the woman you'd once loved true?"

"That was true. I never deliberately lied to you if I could help it, Kate. Her name was Lady Anne Hodges-Trent. Of course now she's the Countess of Dortley. She was very beautiful indeed, and I thought . . . Well, to hurt so much one assumes one's in love. But I realized much later that what I felt for Anne had very little to do with love. Infatuation, certainly, and a great deal of young passion, but not love. We had nothing in common aside from the superficial things. She made that abundantly clear."

"And is she the reason why you never get involved?"

"Did I say that?"

"'Never, never, never.' Simon Dristoll, Act Two, the patio scene."

"Did I," he mused.

"Yes, you did. After Anne you never fell in love again?"

"Oh, it took me a very long time, and I certainly had my fair share of flings, but yes, I finally did." He smiled at her, a soft, gentle smile that touched his eyes, and then he looked away.

"But not the real thing?"

"Very much the real thing."

"Then what happened?" Her question hung for a moment in the stillness of the night, and then he turned back to her and fixed her with a steady gaze that somehow made her heart begin to race.

"I don't know yet." And he took her face between his strong, capable hands and lowered his mouth onto hers in an achingly tender kiss.

* * *

Kate woke the next morning horrified to discover that it was coming up on noon, and she dressed in a tearing hurry. Elizabeth was reading the Sunday *Times*, her reading glasses perched on the end of her nose, and she looked up over them as Kate came bursting into the sitting room.

"Why there you are, dear. I was wondering when you'd surface."

"I'm sorry, Elizabeth, you should have woken me!"

"Nonsense. You needed your sleep, you came in very late last night. Did you enjoy yourself?"

"Yes, it was lovely. But listen, I have something exciting to tell you. The person I went out with last night is from Christie's. I gave him the watch to have him trace its origins, and he found a photograph in it between the cases. Look!"

Elizabeth took the proffered photograph and examined it carefully. "My goodness, this could well be Susanna's mother! Imagine it sitting inside the watch for all these years and none of us knowing. It must have been intended as some kind of memento. Well done, Kate. Now what are you going to do?"

"I'm going to find out where a little town called St. Mouton is. After that, I don't know. I suppose I'll wait until Sebastian finds out more."

"Sebastian?"

"Sebastian Dunn, the man from Christie's. I hope you don't mind, he's been kind enough to offer to drive me up to London today, and I've invited him for tea."

"Not at all. I'll enjoy meeting him. You didn't tell him anything else about the watch, did you?"

"Of course not, Elizabeth. It's our secret. Stephanie knows, but she's like a sister and won't tell another soul."

"No, of course not. I can see it's something you might want to share with her. But I do think it's best if we keep it from anyone else. Good then, if we're to have a proper tea, I'd better start baking."

* * *

Sebastian arrived at four o'clock and Kate met him at the door. "Hello, Sebastian," she said, feeling suddenly shy.

"Good afternoon, Miss Soames," he teased, leaning down to kiss her. "You made quite an impression on Geoffrey, you know. He hasn't stopped talking about you and I had to make it quite clear to him that you were most definitely spoken for."

"You're awfully sure of yourself, Sebastian Dunn," she said with a light laugh. "You have no idea how I feel about you. I thought I made it perfectly clear last night that I wasn't prepared to rush into anything."

"Oh yes, you made everything perfectly clear." He smiled. "Now, what about that tea?"

She took him through to the garden and introduced him to Elizabeth.

Elizabeth had outdone herself, and there was an array of everything from plum cake to tiny cucumber and watercress sandwiches, and a pot each of Indian and China tea. They chattered away for the next hour, Elizabeth questioning Sebastian about the inner workings of Christie's with which she had always been fascinated.

"Now, young man," she said when they had finally finished and only crumbs were left on the plates. "Tell me where your family hails from."

"Leicestershire, Miss Forrest."

"And where exactly in Leicestershire would that be?"

"A small village called Whitworth."

"I thought as much," she said victoriously. "Whitworth Hall, isn't it?"

"Well, actually, yes." Sebastian looked quite surprised.

"And your father is Lord Dunn. I knew your grandfather quite well. I thought you had a look of him with that hawk nose of yours. The last time I saw your father he was a very naughty child tormenting his poor nanny."

"I can well imagine he was," said Sebastian with a smile. "But he seems to have settled down somewhat."

"Now let's see, he married that nice Joanna Yardley,

didn't he. Yes, that's right. And how many children did they have in the end?''

"There are just the two of us, my younger sister Lucy and I,'' said Sebastian, clearly amused by this trotting out of his family tree.

"How nice. Kate dear, would you please take the tea things in? I'm going to take Mr. Dunn for a walk around the garden.''

Kate opened her mouth to object, but then thought better of it and obediently began piling things on the tray, looking suspiciously after Elizabeth as she led Sebastian off.

"Now, Mr. Dunn,'' Elizabeth said after he had dutifully admired her horticultural efforts. "I hope you don't think me premature, but just what are your intentions toward Kate?''

"Please, Miss Forrest, call me Sebastian. And as for Kate, I intend to marry her, although she doesn't know it yet.''

"I thought as much,'' said Elizabeth with satisfaction. "What a splendid idea.''

"All right, Sebastian, give up. What was Elizabeth after?''

He pulled his attention from the busy M40 for a moment and looked at her impassively. "What do you mean, Kate?''

"She's a nosy old biddy and knows *Debrett's Peerage* inside out—and it came as quite a surprise to hear your name is emblazoned on its rarified paper—but she isn't usually quite so blunt. So what was she up to?''

"I haven't the faintest idea. Maybe she just wanted to know if I was next in line, heir to the throne, so to speak. How should I know? You know her far better than I.''

But Kate wasn't about to give up. "Exactly. And what were you two having such a long and cozy chat about in the garden?''

"Flowers, Kate, what else?''

"I don't believe you for a moment, but I see you're not

going to tell me. I just hope you weren't dissecting me like some poor insect."

"Kate, I assure you that you have nothing in common with an insect as far as I can see. You have nothing to worry about." He looked over at her with laughing eyes.

"I don't trust you. And speaking of that, you might have told me about your illustrious background instead of leaving it to Elizabeth."

"And what would you have had me say? 'Kate, my darling, I love you and by the way, my father's Lord Toad of Toad Hall'? It was no secret, it just didn't come up. Anyway, I want you to love me for myself, not my future title."

"You are an impossible man! You know, you're awfully good about weasling things out of me, and I know very little about you. In fact, it occurs to me that a good deal of what I do know belongs to Simon, and not you at all!"

He grinned. "There's not so much difference between us, you know. But fire away, what do you want to know?"

"I don't know, lots of things—for example, what made you want to become an expert in *objets de vertu*?"

"Oh, I've always been very keen on small important pieces. From the time I was a little boy, instead of playing outside with the other baby honorables, you'd find me at the tea table examining Lady Snydley's fan, saying, "You simply must tell me, Lady Snydley—"

"You see, that's exactly what I mean! You always make a joke out of everything and then I end up knowing nothing."

"Poor Kate, I apologize. You have every right to know anything you want about the man you love."

"I never said I loved you, Sebastian, so stop putting words in my mouth."

"But they're in there, sweetheart, you just refuse to let them out. They won't bite, you know."

"No, I mean it. Listen, Sebastian, this is important. I really don't know how I feel about you. It's all happening so quickly, and I need time to put it into perspective. First it was just going to be dinner, then there was after dinner—stop laughing, Sebastian, I'm serious. And then we had tea today, and now this. It's not that I haven't enjoyed it; but I don't know where it's all going, and I'm just not ready to get involved.''

His smile faded and he turned the wheel sharply and pulled the Jaguar off the road onto the verge. He switched the engine off, then turned to look at her fully, his face very serious. ''I'm going to explain this to you very carefully, Kate, and I'm only going to say it once. I know perfectly well this is happening quickly. There's very little I can do about that. I told you last night that I was falling in love with you and I meant it. We don't know each other that well, and that I can do something about—but in the meantime, the only thing I can ask of you is simply to take me on faith.''

''But Sebastian—''

''Hush. Look, Kate, I understand completely. You're scared, and have every right to be coming out of that bloody awful relationship with David, and so recently. But I'm not David, you know; I'm nothing like him. And what you had with him I'm fully convinced has nothing to do with being in love. I don't think I've ever been there myself, but damn it, I'm not so stupid that I don't know what's happening to me. And we don't have that much time. You're off to France in three short weeks. I can be just as persistent as you can be stubborn, and I have every intention of seeing you as much as humanly possible in that time, starting with dinner tonight. I don't intend to frighten you off, and I promise not to rush you into anything you're not ready for; but I've waited this long for you to come along, and I'll be damned if I let you slip away now.'' He ran a hand through his hair and sighed.

''Look, I'm not in the habit of giving speeches, and I hope to hell you don't think this is easy for me either, because it's not. Words of love don't come tripping easily off my tongue—I haven't had a reason to speak them for a very long time, as you well know. But if there's one thing I've ever had going for me, it's knowing what I want. And I know I want you. And I'm not going to say another word on the subject until you're damned good and ready to hear me." He turned the engine back on and eased the car out onto the road.

Kate stared at him in complete astonishment. "How can you be so sure about it?"

Sebastian shook his head in exasperation. "You really are an impossible creature, my love. You're just going to have to trust me." And he reached out a hand and stroked her cheek.

"Mr. Soames, sir! How nice to hear from you." David pulled the telephone around his desk and sat down. "Have you heard anything from Kate?"

"Not a word, but that comes as no surprise. I was going to ask you the same thing."

"Nothing yet. It's going to take her awhile to cool down, I'm afraid, but don't worry. By the time she returns, everything will have been forgiven. I think I may have pushed her too hard, but I can't believe she won't realize that's no reason to break off a perfectly good engagement."

"I hope you're right, David. She never did have much common sense. Well, never mind all that, I have some good news for you."

"Oh?" David pulled the telephone closer. "What's that, sir?"

"I've arranged an appointment for you with Sevronsen in the State Department. He's very interested in you and your ideas, and he's looking for a good assistant. This might just be the stepping-stone you were looking for."

"Thank you, sir! That's wonderful news! I haven't declared my candidacy yet, and if I could just skip the Congress altogether . . ." He listened carefully. "Yes, sir. I'll see you next week in Washington." He cut the connection, then dialed again.

"Operator, I'd like to place an overseas call to Germany. Yes, to a Mr. Wilhelm Schumann."

CHAPTER
Seven

Kate and Sebastian had dinner three times that week, attended the Royal Academy art exhibition during a lunch break, and had breakfast in the park on one rare, sunny day. That weekend, Sebastian had a client in Devon who needed a consultation, and Kate went up to Henley. Elizabeth asked casually after Sebastian, and just as casually Kate mentioned that she'd seen him and he was perfectly well.

Sebastian set the tone of their meetings; although he teased her often, he listened seriously to what she had to say, and as he'd promised he mentioned not a word about the future or his feelings toward her. There was certainly no more talk of love. He'd kiss her a light good night outside the mews house and leave quickly, and she found herself wishing he'd stay longer. His casual behavior was almost frustrating, but at the same time it gave her the distance she needed to see him clearly, and from that distance it was very clear to her that she had become alarmingly fond of him.

The following week they managed dinner only twice early on, and by the end of the week Kate found herself missing Sebastian acutely. She hadn't heard from him, and wondered where he was and why he hadn't called. The last time she'd seen him, Tuesday evening, everything had been fine between them. In fact, Sebastian had spent the evening in some hilarity. They'd been to the theater and were having a late supper at a small but fashionable restaurant in Chelsea, talking quietly about the play they'd just seen, when Kate realized that Sebastian's attention was not fully on her.

"Sebastian?"

"Kate, sweetheart, I think I ought to tell you that an extraordinary-looking chap off to the side there is staring at you very hard. Do you know him, or is he just admiring the cut of that smart black dress you're wearing?"

Kate looked over and the gentleman in question smiled coolly and inclined his oh-so-perfect head. He was dressed in a most interesting fashion—tight leather trousers and jacket with a T-shirt underneath, and a flowing paisley scarf wrapped around his neck. He was with another man, more conservatively dressed, who turned and looked at her, smiling shyly.

"Oh, no," whispered Kate, suddenly realizing who it was, and shrinking as they rose and approached the table. Sebastian raised his eyebrow at her in silent, amused question.

"Kate, my dear," said the second gentleman. "How very nice to see you again after all this time. May I introduce my friend, Lord Humbert?"

"How do you do. Sebastian, this is Peter Fulford. Peter, Lord Humbert, this is Sebastian Dunn. How are you?" She was quite scarlet.

"Never better, Kate. What are you doing with yourself these days?"

"I'm in the wine industry in the United States. At the moment I'm over here studying up on ports."

"Ports, is it?" drawled Lord Humbert in terribly refined accents. "I keep a large cellar of port myself at each of my estates. Wonderful stuff. Couldn't do without it."

"Quite," said Sebastian dryly.

"Ah, do you keep ports, Mr. ah—"

"Dunn," said Sebastian.

"Of yes, of course. Well as I was saying, marvelous stuff. Of course, one must keep a close eye on the crust, very fragile it is, don't you agree, Miss Soames?'' He fixed his eye on her.

''Oh yes. . .'' Kate was at a complete loss.

''I do try not to disturb my bottles,'' carried on Lord Humbert blithely. ''But of course, one can't help picking one up occasionally to admire the color. So very pleasing, the ruby red, don't you think?''

''Absolutely exquisite,'' agreed Sebastian dangerously, eyeing the paisley scarf.

''I'm afraid we must be on our way,'' said Peter nervously, sensing an uncomfortable situation arising. ''Lovely seeing you, Kate. Good-bye, Mr. Dunn.'' Lord Humbert graciously inclined his head once more and they swept out.

Sebastian was very quiet for a moment, his eyes on the door, then he looked at Kate, his face perfectly straight. ''An old friend, Mr. Fulford?''

''I suppose you might say that. I knew him years ago, when I was still in school.''

''Oh yes?'' he asked politely, thoroughly enjoying her discomfiture.

''Well, the truth of the matter is. . .'' She avoided Sebastian's eyes.

''And what is the truth of the matter, dear Kate?'' His lips began to quiver.

''Look, this is going to sound really stupid, but the truth is that he was my first boyfriend. We went out for a year during school holidays, and he really was a very nice person; but things weren't going the way they should have gone, and then he finally confessed that he didn't, well—oh, you know! I thought it was all my fault until Stephanie set me straight.'' She stopped abruptly, feeling ridiculous.

''Oh, dear God,'' said Sebastian, staring at her disbelievingly, then burst into hysterical laughter. ''Oh, Kate, only you can pick them. No wonder I haven't had any luck!''

She couldn't get a serious word out of him for the rest of the evening.

* * *

At eleven o'clock on Friday morning, a very casually dressed Sebastian burst into Kate's office. He was wearing jeans and a T-shirt and had a red silk scarf wrapped around his neck and trailing down his back. "Is Miss Soames in?" he asked the secretary in his most pompous tone. "I'm Lord Humboxer and I simply must see her at once. It's about a case of very valuable port, you understand. It's in my cellars and I've had a good look at it—I fear there's something dreadfully wrong!"

Kate came through the door, wondering what all the noise was about. "What—" She stared at Sebastian who was mincing around fretfully.

"This is Lord Humboxer, Miss Soames. He's here to see you about some port." The secretary rolled her eyes at Kate.

"Oh, thank goodness, Miss Soames, you're here! You must come at once. My port is dreadfully off-color. I fear the upper crust has been disturbed!"

"Why, certainly Lord ah—" She choked back her laughter.

"Lord Humboxer. Your reputation precedes you, Miss Soames. That smashing man in Oxford told me where to find you. Will you come?"

"Certainly, Lord . . . Humboxer," said Kate, trying terribly hard to keep a straight face and only succeeded in looking as if she were about to sneeze. Collecting her handbag she managed to say, "I'll be back later, Rebecca."

"Oh, no, I'm afraid that's quite impossible," interrupted Sebastian. "You see, we have to drive out to my vast estates. We'll be hours; I'm afraid you won't be coming back to the office today. Good-bye, dear." He waved a vague hand at Rebecca, who was looking at him as if he were quite mad, and pulled Kate out the door. Laughing uncontrollably, she couldn't pull herself together to speak until they got to the street.

"Sebastian, what *are* you up to? Are you out of your mind? And where did you find that ghastly red scarf you're wearing?" She started to laugh again.

"Darling, don't you like it? It took me hours to choose. I

thought it matched my off-color port." He pulled her, still laughing, into the Jaguar. "Come on, we're off."

"But where? Sebastian, what have you plotted?" Kate fixed a mistrustful eye on him.

"Aha . . . First to your house where you're going to pack a case and leave a note for Stephanie. Then to parts unknown."

"Seriously, Sebastian, what do you have in mind?"

"We're going up to the wilds of Leicestershire for the weekend, and no arguments, my lady."

"Where in Leicestershire?" she asked suspiciously.

"I'm taking you to meet the folks, sugar," he drawled.

The meadow was warm and the grass sweetly fragrant and woven with buttercups and daises. Sebastian had spread a blanket and laid it with things for a late lunch. They'd eaten all the French bread and cheeses, most of the Westphalian ham, peeled the last boiled shrimp, and finished the bottle of red wine. Kate, thoroughly satiated, lay back on the blanket and looked up at the blue sky and billowing white clouds.

"Oh, Sebastian, how glorious. I'm so glad you abducted me, although the way you did it was outrageous! But where have you been all week?"

"All week? I was gone only Wednesday and Thursday, Kate. Does this mean you missed me?" He looked down at her, his eyebrow raised.

"Maybe just a little."

"That's the best you can do? I'd far rather hear that you were languishing in abject misery."

"Well . . . I thought maybe after Tuesday night you'd given up on me completely."

"Oh, sweetheart, to the contrary. You really are the most unexpected woman; I live in constant anticipation of what you're going to drop on me next." Sebastian cleared away the basket and lay down on his back, his hands behind his head. " 'Learn all we lacked before; hear, know, and say what this tumultuous body now denies; and feel, who have laid our groping hands away; and see, no longer blinded by our eyes.' " He glanced over at Kate.

"What's that from?" asked Kate.

"My dear girl, don't tell me you don't recognize the immortal words of Rupert Brooke?"

"Oh, the First World War poet? Not particularly. He's too modern for me."

"It's what comes of having gone to Oxford," he said superciliously.

"Fiend," she said with a smile. "How is it you are so familiar with him, may I ask? He wasn't exactly your generation."

"No, but he is much admired by someone I know quite well. Thanks to him I know more Brooke than is probably good for me. He also said, 'For Cambridge people rarely smile, being urban, squat and packed with guile.' What do you think, Kate? Do you agree with him?" He rolled over onto his stomach and regarded her lazily.

Kate plucked a piece of grass and looked at him. His chin was propped up on his hand, and his back arched up in a long, smooth line. His T-shirt pulled up from his jeans, exposing a patch of skin. She had an impulse to reach out and stroke the bare flesh, but she quickly looked away, her cheeks going hot. "Not knowing the poet, I have no opinion on the matter," she finally said.

A little smile played on Sebastian's mouth as he watched her. "Ah. How very scholarly. By the way, I heard from the clock department this week, Kate. Apparently the reason that your watch doesn't work is because the tooth-slide is missing. Would you like it repaired?"

"What?" She risked a glance at him.

"I said, would you like the tooth-slide in your watch replaced?" His smile grew broader.

"Oh. Whatever you think, Sebastian . . ." Distractedly, she watched a pair of kestrals wheeling high above and her eyes followed them as they veered off toward the dark ridge of wood that bordered the east side of the meadow. "Oh, no—Sebastian, look what's coming!" She pointed to the enormous bank of storm clouds that was sweeping in on them. Within moments the sun had been blotted out, and a cold wind blew up.

"Here, give me your hand." He pulled her to her feet, and had everything put away in seconds. "You take the blanket. We'll never make it back to the car before it hits. There's a barn fairly close by."

But they were only halfway across the meadow when the sky opened up and the rain came lashing down in thick cold sheets. Sebastian pulled Kate along, but by the time they reached the shelter of the barn, they were both soaked to the skin.

"Oh, lord," said Sebastian, laughing as he looked Kate over. "You are one bedraggled thing, my love. Here, follow me." He led her past the empty stalls, picking up a pile of blankets as he went, and guided her up the stairs into the hayloft. Bales were piled high, warm and dry, giving off a comforting scent and there was a thick bed of loose hay everywhere.

"What a haven! How did you know it was here?" Kate asked, shivering.

"I used to play here as a boy. This is part of Whitworth. Here, Kate, get those wet things off before you catch your death." He pulled off his T-shirt and began to unzip the jeans that were plastered wetly to his thighs.

Kate didn't move. She couldn't have if she'd tried.

Sebastian had wrapped a blanket around his waist and was busy laying out his clothes on top of a bale. He looked around with a grin. "Oh, Kate, I should have known." He started toward her.

"Sebastian, what are you doing?" she said, shivering helplessly with something other than just the cold.

"Since you have no sense of self-preservation, I'm taking off your very wet jersey," he said softly, pulling it over her head, and down off her arms. "And your soaking shirt, too," and peeled that off her skin, leaving her sensitive breasts exposed to the cold air, but she didn't feel it; in fact, her skin felt on fire. "And all the rest of it," he continued almost inaudibly, doing exactly that.

She stood as if in a trance, unresisting as her clothes fell one piece after another into a sodden pile on the hay until there was nothing more. Then Sebastian handed her a blanket and stepped back, looking at her in a perplexed sort of way, almost as if he were at a loss, but his eyes never left hers, holding her in a relentless grip.

The silence between them swelled and seemed to pound in waves until Kate realized it was the sound of her own heartbeat in her ears. "Sebastian," she heard herself say, and he was there, pulling her into his arms, his breath coming in quick gasps, and he lowered his head and kissed her hungrily, the raindrops on his face mingling with hers.

And then he pulled away from her and took the unused blanket from her hand, spreading it out onto the hay and lowering her onto it, and came down to her.

"Kate, my sweet Kate, I don't know if I have the control left to wait anymore. This is killing me," he said hoarsely against her hair.

"No more waiting," murmured Kate, drawing his face down to hers.

He loved her then as if he'd been doing it all his life, as if he knew all the secret places that would give her the most pleasure, taking his time as he stroked and kissed her neck, her breasts, her hips, her thighs, and the hot, wet, ready place between them. "Sweetheart—ah, God, Kate my love," he whispered as he opened her to him and slid his full, taut shaft into her and she took him willingly, more willingly than she'd ever thought possible.

He moved slowly within her, teasing her until she wanted all of him, and he gave it to her then, even deeper and faster until her every muscle tensed in unbearable anticipation and then broke into unbelievable waves of pleasure as she cried out over and over. And then he rose up and called her name as he shuddered deep inside of her and pulled her even closer, impossibly close to him.

Kate opened her eyes and looked over at Sebastian. His face was still, the delicate white of his eyelids shutting out the incredible blue beneath, the dark lashes lying fanned out on his cheek. She realized with a little stab that she had never seen his face in sleep before; he looked so defenseless, so very dear. Her eyes traced the contours of his strongly sculpted face, the thin, hawked nose with the high bridge, the little indentation just above his upper lip and the full and well-shaped mouth, the mouth with the slight creases on either side that deepened just so when he smiled—and then that wonderful little cleft in the center of his square chin. She smiled and touched it with her finger, remembering how it had felt beneath her lips.

She'd never been loved like that in her life, with such generosity and tenderness, coupled with strength and carefully controlled passion. She should have known, really, from that first kiss on the boat, how it would be.

Sebastian stirred and opening his eyes, he smiled drowsily at her. "Hello, my love." He pulled her toward him and kissed her softly. "Did I fall asleep? How rude of me."

"Absolutely. But at least you had the good manners to pick up my wet clothes from where you'd tossed them and put them out to dry before you went out."

"Ever the gentleman, except for nodding off. It was all that exertion. I promise it won't happen again."

"I hope you don't mean the exertion part," said Kate with a smile.

"Do I detect a note of enthusiasm in your voice, ma'am?"

"How very perceptive of you. What a pity it's stopped raining."

"Who said the rain had anything to do with it?" Sebastian stroked her back in little circles, sending delicious tingles down her spine. "But we should be on our way. I booked us into a small inn for tonight where we'll be a bit more comfortable. We're not expected at home until tomorrow, you know."

"How stupid of me. And I thought it was the rainstorm that brought all this about."

"Well . . ." said Sebastian slowly, "I have to admit it helped things along, but I did have plans for you. You couldn't expect me to endure that kind of agony forever, could you? You know what Romeo said: 'Tempt not a desperate man.' Of course, that was under slightly different circumstances."

"And you know what happened to him."

"I reckon he thought it was well worth his while."

"You're a wicked man, Sebastian Dunn," she said and stroked the hay out of his hair, which only delayed them another hour.

They finally checked in and ate a leisurely supper, but the air was sharp with expectancy, and their appetites had little to do with food. Something indefinable had shifted between them; there was an intimacy that needed no words, an aura that surrounded them and excluded the rest of the world.

Sebastian smiled at Kate in a way that made her blush hotly. "Are you finished, my love? Shall we go upstairs now, or would you rather have a game of darts first?"

"No, I think we can skip the darts, you odious man."

Sebastian laughed, his teeth flashing whitely. "Oh, good. You're such a sensible woman."

"And you were such a sensible man, booking two rooms."

"Yes, but did you notice the connecting door?"

"How could I miss it? You were sensible but optimistic."

"I have already learned that you are a thoroughly unpredictable woman. I was simply hedging my bet."

"I should throw you right through that connecting door into the other room just to teach you a lesson."

"You don't have the strength of will," said Sebastian with a grin.

"What's that supposed to mean?"

"Come with me and I'll show you."

The late morning sun filtered through the curtains and Sebastian stretched his free arm and shifted Kate where she lay curled around his side. He dropped a kiss on the top of her head and then nuzzled the nape of her neck. " 'My lady sweet, arise.' Morning's nearly gone."

She opened her eyes and looked up at him. " 'To dance

attendance on their lordships' pleasures,' " she murmured sleepily.

Sebastian laughed. "How am I to take that, I wonder? But it sounds a most interesting idea. Did you sleep well?"

"What little sleep you allowed me was wonderful." She smiled and closed her eyes again.

"Oh, you little vixen! What little sleep *I* allowed you? As I remember . . ."

"Sebastian, you're wonderful," she said, slipping her arms around his back and pulling him closer.

"Am I, sweetheart? You're so easy to convince. I think I've finally found the way to your heart, and it isn't food." He kissed her ear, then the corner of her mouth and then his golden head moved down toward her breast.

Kate sighed contentedly. "Food enough for me."

Whitworth Hall stood on a hill, an Elizabethan masterpiece, surrounded by wide sweeps of lawn and garden. It could be seen from a distance, but it came into close view only as they rounded the final curve of the driveway. It was shaped in the traditional E, the shorter middle section being the main entrance. The whole impression was of sunlight, warmth, and peace.

"Oh, Sebastian," gasped Kate, "it's so beautiful!"

"It's home," said Sebastian simply, covering her hand. He parked the car on the far end of the gravel and helped her out.

She stood very still for a moment, a thousand thoughts, a thousand doubts and hesitations crowding at her.

"Kate?"

"Oh! Yes?"

He smiled, his eyes far too knowing. "Come in and meet my family. Amazingly enough they don't bite, either."

* * *

"Kate, we're so glad you could come. Hello, darling." Lady Dunn embraced her son warmly. "Why don't you show Kate upstairs to her room, then you can both come down and have some tea."

"Sounds marvelous. I say, you're looking very well."

"Am I, darling boy? How very gallant of you." She vaguely touched her beautifully set gray hair. "Do make yourself comfortable, won't you, Kate. Except for dinner, I'm afraid we have no need for formality," she added obscurely, indicating the stairway, and then disappeared in the opposite direction.

"It takes some time, but one eventually learns to interpret." Sebastian smiled. "My mother's appeared to have been slightly dotty all her life, but there's a very acute mind behind it, so don't let her fool you."

"No, indeed. You inherited more than your blue eyes from her, I suspect."

"Did I? Come along, follow me."

Tea was an extremely relaxed affair, if relaxed meant Sebastian's sister Lucy talking to him in a nonstop stream, Lady Dunn absently waving a hand in invitation toward the tea tray and wandering off with a cup "to check the alcea roseas which I've been meaning to get to all day. I fear they may need restaking after yesterday's storm" (hollyhocks, explained Sebastian), and five-year-old William dashing about the table in a frenzy of excitement. Lucy finally tore her attention away from Sebastian long enough to coerce William into sitting down and eating his tea, which was all the dinner he would have, and then informed him she was taking him off to his bath so that the rest of the world could have some peace and quiet.

"But Mummy!" he piped with great objection when he was finished with his boiled egg, toast, and cake. "If I have to have my bath now, then I miss my chance to play with Uncle Sebastian! It's not fair," he wailed.

"Darling, you'll see Uncle Sebastian tomorrow. There'll be lots of time to play, you'll see. Now hop to."

His small face crumpled in disappointment and Sebastian, who sympathized profusely with William, remembering well the same sort of unfair dictates, intervened. "All right then, monster, one fast trot around the garden and then you're off to your bath with no arguments." He scooped the little boy up and deposited him on his shoulders. "Off we go, and don't abuse the horse," and he loped off the terrace and down the lawn as Kate watched with a grin.

"Why, hello, you must be Kate." She looked up with a start to see a good-looking, weathered man, slightly balding, wearing work clothes and Wellington boots. "I'm Sebastian's father. How very nice to meet you."

"Oh, how do you do, Lord Dunn. Of course, I should have known immediately by the nose!"

He roared with laughter. "I'm delighted you noticed, my dear. We'll all very proud of our beaks. Very inbred I'm afraid."

Kate was about to reply when Sebastian appeared at her shoulder.

"Hello, Fa," he said, depositing William on his mother's lap and giving his father a hug. "I see you've met Kate."

"That I have, and I noticed immediately that she has very discerning taste."

Sebastian smiled. "So I hope. How are you, Fa?"

"Fit as a horse. Now, my boy, give me your filial report and get it over with."

"No overdrafts, no gambling debts, no ladies of the evening."

"Excellent. Anything else I should know?"

"Not a thing, sir. I have been an exemplary son since I last saw you."

"Oh, Sebastian, how dull!" said Lucy, laughing. "Wait 'til Fa leaves and then you can tell me the truth."

"How is a man to trust his children with the likes of these two?" said Lord Dunn to Kate. "It's nothing but a conspiracy, I tell you. Lucy, remove that child to his nursery. It must be hours past his bedtime." He spoke gruffly but gave William an affectionate pat on his little bottom.

William was duly removed by his mother, Lord Dunn went off to find his wife, and Sebastian and Kate were left by themselves.

"Your family's wonderful, Sebastian."

"It's the one thing you never had, isn't it, sweetheart? Never mind, you can share mine. There's always room for one more."

Kate changed the subject. "Where does Lucy live? She's married, isn't she?"

"Yes, she is, to a very nice chap called Neil Forsythe. He's the estate manager for Whitworth, handles all the farming and so on. They have a house of their own about ten minutes away."

"It must be nice for her to be so close to your parents."

"I think so, and especially nice for them to be able to see their grandson so often, although the way my father carries on you'd think he was a child eater. He was exactly like that with us, and there was never a more loving father although he'd hate for anyone to know it."

"I think he's very sweet."

"Kate, if he ever heard you say such a thing, he'd never speak to you again. He has spent most of his adult life trying to convince the world that he's an old curmudgeon, and despite the fact that not a soul has ever believed it, we all go along with his act to make him feel better. Even William's caught on."

"William is quite a handful; you're so good with him."

"I adore him; he's a sweet little soul, much like his mother."

"You adore her, too, don't you, Sebastian?"

"We've always been very close. You'll come to love her, Kate, when you get to know her. She's funny and caring and a little unconventional. Neil steadies her; they're good together."

"She sounds a lot like her big brother."

Sebastian was silent for a long moment. Then he said only, "How interesting you should think so." He took her hand and stood. "Let's go upstairs. It's time to change for dinner."

* * *

Dinner, although formal, was relaxed and filled with light conversation and laughter. Another older couple, Major and Mrs. Monmouth, had been invited from a neighboring estate, and a great deal of joking went on between them and the family as to the various superiorities of certain fields, livestock, and piles of mortar. Kate was made to feel comfortable in the group, and found the conversation easy and enjoyable, but she was content largely to watch and listen, drinking in the environment in which Sebastian had grown up. She was seated next to Lucy's husband, Neil Forsythe, a thoroughly pleasant and interesting man, and she could see what Sebastian had meant about his being a good balance for Lucy, who was chattering away as usual with a great deal of animation.

The ladies left the men at the table and retired to the drawing room, where Kate had the opportunity to talk with Sebastian's mother and sister, and they had the chance to find out more about the intriguing American woman Sebastian had produced.

"Now you must tell us how you met Sebastian, Kate," said Lady Dunn, handing her a demitasse of coffee.

"I met him at Christie's, actually." It was partially true, she thought. It was, after all, where Sebastian Dunn had come into her life.

"And did you go to Christie's to see Sebastian specifically? He has such a fine reputation, you know."

"Not exactly. I had a watch whose history I wanted to learn about, and I was referred to him."

"Oh, how very interesting. He's always loved things like that, tracking down history, objects, that sort of thing. He's always been so good at it, where the rest of us are hopelessly absentminded. Such a curse, isn't it, Lucy darling? Now I understand you're involved in the wine trade. I think it sounds fascinating. You must tell us all about yourself . . ."

Kate gracefully underwent the charming interrogation, thinking with amusement how well the Dunns had cultivated the art of effortlessly acquiring information.

After a time the gentlemen reappeared, and Sebastian went straight to Kate's side. "Did you confess to the murder?'' he whispered in her ear, and she laughed, once again amazed at how well he'd read her mind. He raised his voice and addressed his mother. "I've been meaning to ask you what happened with the church fete? How much did you manage to bring in this year?''

Kate was taken off by Lord Dunn and the major who engaged her in lengthy conversation, first on Chaucer, Lord Dunn's favorite author, and then on the subject of fine wines and their storage. And when Sebastian drifted over to her side half an hour later, he could clearly see that his father thoroughly approved of Kate.

"Kate, would you like to take a walk? Father, Major, would you excuse us for a few minutes?''

He drew her out onto the terrace and down to the lawn, slipping his arm around her waist when he felt they were out of sight. "They're quite something when they team up on you, aren't they?''

"Amazing! And they're all so sweet, Sebastian. I like your family tremendously, but I can't help but wonder what's going through their minds.''

"Nothing but sheer curiosity as to how their poor, bumbling son managed to convince such a beautiful, intelligent woman to accompany him up here. Quite beyond understanding.''

"Then there's a great deal they don't know about their poor, bumbling son, and thank you for the compliment.''

"Would you like to hear some more? I have a fine collection of sweet nothings.'' He cupped her face, his eyes full of unspoken things. Slowly he kissed her parted lips, his warm mouth lingering on hers. Then he smiled and said, "I think you're enough to do permanent damage to my heart muscle, Kate. When I'm aound you it does outrageous and unnatural things that can't be good for my health.''

"To the contrary, stimulation keeps the heart fit—anyway, think how boring it is to go the same old pace, day in, day out for all those years. It deserves a little excitement.''

Sebastian grinned broadly. "You have an answer for everything, don't you, Miss Soames? One day that's going to get you into trouble—for example, if you think it's so good for my heart muscle to be regularly exercised,'' and he pulled her into his arms, ''then I have an excellent suggestion.'' And this time he kissed her without restraint until she felt quite weak.

''Oh yes, that was an excellent workout,'' he said with satisfaction when he had finally finished. ''You'd better collect yourself, sweetheart. We should probably go back in, and we don't want my parents to think we've been doing anything improper.''

''You're a beast, Sebastian Dunn, and I shall get you when you least expect it.''

''Of that I have no doubt.'' He led her back inside.

CHAPTER Eight

"*Sebastian*, what are you doing in here? What about the burglar alarm?" whispered Kate, sitting up in the four-poster bed and peering through the dark.

"Not to worry, it's still on." He made his way across the room and sat down on the bed.

"But your father said once it was on, not to leave the room or it would go off!"

"Yes, quite. He always turns it on when he goes to bed and that's that for the night. It's his cunning device to keep us all in line, but as you can see by my very presence here, Lucy and I learned when young to circumvent it."

"But how, Sebastian?"

"You have to walk very carefully along the extreme edge of the floorboards, sort of sidling along with your back plastered against the wall, without at any point touching the carpet. The wires run under that, you see. Clever, eh? Of course, we figured out how to do it by trial and error, and more than once my father appeared with his shotgun."

"Oh, no! That must have scared you half to death!"

"Not in the least. By the time he'd managed to get into his dressing gown and slippers and actually fetch his gun, I was long gone. After a few of these episodes he was convinced that the system was defective and called in the repair person. Neither of us ever cared to enlighten him."

"You really were a dreadful child."

"Absolutely appalling," he agreed.

"You haven't changed much."

"Not very much, no."

"And you really shouldn't be in here."

"I know," said Sebastian, slipping Kate's nightdress off her shoulders.

The next day started with a pounding on the door at eight o'clock, and Lucy carrying in a tray of coffee, toast, and two cups that she placed on the bed.

"Wake up, Kate, I'm going to drag you down to the stables and haul you off around Whitworth. You do ride, don't you?" she thought to ask as she poured coffee for them both.

"Yes, I do, thank heaven," said Kate with a little laugh. "But I get the feeling that it wouldn't much matter whether I did or not."

"Exactly. Sebastian and Neil disappeared awhile ago—estate business—but I told them to meet us at the stables in an hour. Sebbie and I learned to ride practically before we could walk. Fa is a rabid horseman, of course, and riding is de rigueur around here. William's already jumping. So tell me, Kate, are you in love with my brother?"

Kate choked on her coffee. "I—what?"

"Oh, sorry, I'm afraid I'm terminally blunt. I think it's because my mother is so vague, you know. I'm like my father—we both just blurt out whatever's on our minds." She shook her mop of blond hair in despair. "Neil is forever telling me that I must think before I speak, but it's hopeless. I was just wondering about you and Sebastian because he hasn't brought a woman up here in years. I think it's absolutely marvelous, and it's quite clear he adores you. So it's only fair that you adore him, if you see what I mean."

"Yes, perfectly," said Kate, very amused.

"So are you?"

"I'm very fond of your brother, Lucy, and that's all you're going to get out of me. You and your mother did such a thorough job last night I'm amazed there's anything left to ask!"

"We are a meddlesome lot, aren't we? Oh, well, it can't be helped. I'd lay money that Sebastian cross-examined you too, only he's much more subtle than we are, isn't he? You don't even know he's digging out your life secrets."

"It's true! I only realize it after the fact."

"I'm awfully glad he's found you; he looks happier than he has in quite awhile. He went through such a terrible time when Tony died, you know, and for a long time I thought we'd lost the old Sebastian."

"Who was Tony?"

"Oh, he hasn't told you? That's like him; he keeps things very close to the chest, especially when they matter a lot to him."

"Lucy, we really haven't known each other very long, less than a month. There's a great deal I don't know about your brother."

"Oh, really? Somehow it seemed as if you're old friends. Well, Tony Morris was Sebbie's best mate. They grew up in each other's pockets and were at Cambridge together. I used to be jealous; they were like brothers and I felt left out, but then of course I grew up and saw it all quite differently. I had quite a thing for Tony—that was before Neil came along. Anyway, he and Sebastian went to Germany on holiday three years ago, but Tony never came home. He was killed outside a café in West Berlin. It was terrible, and Sebbie, well, he blamed himself."

"How awful! But what happened?"

"It turned out to be some East–West German confrontation. Someone tried to escape or something and Sebastian and Tony were in the wrong place. There was shooting, and fortunately Sebastian was across the street when it happened. Tony was shot in the chest. Sebbie ran over and dragged him away and Tony died in his arms in an alley."

"Oh, poor Sebastian!"

"It was quite grim. We were all so fond of Tony, and then the light seemed to go out of Sebastian. But I've talked too long. Anyway, I shouldn't mention it unless he does. He'd probably kill me if he knew I'd told you. I'll leave you to get dressed and meet you downstairs when you're ready. I'm just going to go see to William. Daddy gets foul tempered if naughty little boys disturb his breakfast. He's all right once he's eaten, though, his breakfast, I mean." Lucy rose. "Well, I'm off," she said, and was gone, leaving Kate to ponder yet another facet of the complex man called Sebastian.

With Kate astride an even-tempered but enthusiastic hunter she, Sebastian, Lucy, and Neil started off sedately enough; but after two hours of touring Whitworth, Lucy instigated a mad gallop through the woods and across three fields, which included their jumping all obstacles in the way as if they were covering some kind of unruly point-to-point race. Kate thanked the goddess of the hunt that she'd spent so many childhood hours on a horse as she hurled over yet another hedge. When they finally pulled up, Kate's face was flushed and her eyes were sparkling with exhilaration. "Remind me the next time I have a glass of wine in my hand to pour a libation to Diana!"

"You ride well, Kate," said Lucy with a grin, so like her brother's.

Her husband fixed her with a quelling eye. "And you, my darling, should be taken over my knee and spanked until you repent of your sins. You had no way of knowing whether Kate could sit a horse at that pace!"

"Nonsense," sniffed Lucy. "Stop being such an old stuffed shirt, Neil."But her eyes teased him and he smiled in reply.

Kate laughed at their exchange and looked around at Sebastian, to find him watching her with an unfathomable expression and the breath caught in her throat as he slowly smiled at her.

Then after an animated Sunday dinner he piled her first into the Jaguar and then into a pair of enormous hip boots and announced that he was going to teach her how to cast. Kate ended up in the river soaking wet, tied up in fishing line, and throroughly entertained. Sebastian finally conceded defeat, caught two trout to have something to show for his efforts, and took Kate home for a steaming-hot bath before tea.

She was sorry to leave, having vastly enjoyed the somewhat eccentric company of his family, who treated her exactly as one of their own. That in itself was an experience, but she came away from it feeling that somehow she'd been tested by each one of them.

Stephanie met them at the door. "Hello, Kate and Simon—although as you pointed out on the phone, it's now Sebastian?"

"I'm afraid so. I hope you can adjust to the change."

"Your name isn't the only thing you've changed. It's so nice not to see you floundering in poverty." But then the laughter faded from her face. "Oh—Kate, I almost forgot! Your father rang twice this weekend. He wants you to call him right away."

"Did he say what it was? Not Granny, I hope."

"No, he didn't say. Why don't you try to reach him now, and I'll take Sebastian upstairs and entertain him."

"Oh, thanks, Steph," said Kate in a distracted fashion. "If you don't mind, Sebastian?"

"Not at all. Take your time." He followed Stephanie up the stairs but gave Kate a backward smile of encouragement.

It steadied her and she took a deep breath, then dialed.

"Did you have a nice weekend? Kate's note was a little vague," said Stephanie, digging not very subtly. Her curiosity had been driving her wild and she knew she'd get nothing out of Kate.

"Yes, it was very pleasant, thank you." Sebastian sat down, crossing one leg over the other and managed to give an impression of immaculate grace. Stephanie was just waiting for him to take out a snuffbox.

"How nice. Where did you go?"

"Up to the country. How did you spend yours?" Sebastian looked politely interested.

Stephanie laughed. "Check to Mr. Dunn. So you're the man from Christie's. Have you got anywhere with Kate's watch?"

"No, not yet. These things take time. One wants to be very accurate when dealing with family heirlooms."

"Oh yes, of course," said Stephanie, feeling that she had somehow lost control of the conversation.

"While we're on the subject, tell me, Stephanie, you've known Kate for years; have you spent much time with her family?"

"I've stayed with her father on a few rare occasions, but usually if I've visited it's been at Elizabeth Forrest's. I believe you met her?"

"Yes, a very pleasant woman, but then she's not actually related, is she? Has Kate no other family, no aunts or uncles or cousins?"

"Just her grandmother. Why do you ask?"

"Simple curiosity. I had wondered why Kate had stayed with Elizabeth rather than with relatives, but I didn't want to ask. These things are sometimes delicate, and her father doesn't sound the most sympathetic of men. I gather her mother died when Kate was quite young."

"Yes, she died of cancer when Kate was twelve. It was very sad. Kate's father had a hard time coping; he'd been quite dotty about Susanna."

"What happened to Kate?"

"After that he decided it would be best if she spent school holidays with Elizabeth. He traveled a lot, although when she got a little older, he would call her to wherever he was, and she'd stand in as hostess for diplomatic receptions and so forth. It seemed that the older she became, the more he wanted her there, until he finally persuaded her to move back to New York."

"I see. How very interesting. But enough about Kate, let's talk about you. Tell me how your work is going."

"It's fine, the same old thing. Every now and then somebody declares war and I just keep to my cubicle and write myself into oblivion. Then when I look up again, there's been a change of staff."

"That seems a very sensible way of dealing with the situation."

"That's me. I make a policy of never getting involved."

"Famous last words," said Sebastian with a smile.

"Really?" said Stephanie, laughing, but she abruptly sobered as Kate appeared in the doorway looking pale and strained about the mouth. "Did you get through? What was it?"

Sebastian stood up and went over to her. "Are you all right, Kate?" he asked softly.

She nodded. "Everything's fine. He just read me a transatlantic lecture."

"Come sit down and tell us about it." He drew her over to the sofa.

"He was calling about David. It seems that David's accepted a job with Alec Sevronsen in the State Department. He's giving up his position with his law firm and giving up his bid for a congressional seat and is moving to Washington."

"So what?" said Stephanie. "I can't see why that has anything to do with you anymore."

"It hasn't, but Daddy doesn't see it that way."

"And how does your father see it, Kate?" Sebastian's eyes had gone quite cold.

"He wants me to come home and stop 'this foolishness.' He says I've done enough of running away and not facing up to reality, and I can't behave like a child forever."

"And of course all this is tied into David and his new position? I assume that your father intends to marry you into the State Department, and the sooner the better,'' said Sebastian.

''Yes, exactly.'' Kate nodded miserably. ''He wouldn't listen to a word I said. He kept repeating that David was waiting for me very patiently, and that's why Daddy felt he had to call me himself, to knock some sense into me. I said I was going to France in a week and would ring him when I got back. He exploded and said a few choice things, and then informed me that it was Granny's birthday yesterday and wasn't surprised that I hadn't remembered, I was obviously too busy being flighty and selfish and swanning all over the English countryside thinking of no one but myself. Damn!''

''Oh, Kate,'' said Stephanie simply.

Sebastian got up and paced the room, his hands in his pockets, a frown creasing his forehead. Then he stopped and gave Kate a long, appraising look. ''Stephanie, would you mind giving Kate and me a few moments alone?''

''No, of course not. I'm going to bed, anyway. It was—interesting seeing you again, Sebastian.''

''How kind,'' said Sebastian with a smile as she left. Then he turned back to Kate. ''All right, sweetheart. You and I need to have a talk.''

''What about?''

''To start with, you and David. Why are you so upset about what your father said to you?''

''Oh, Sebastian, wouldn't you be upset if your father spoke to you that way?''

''In the first place, my father's not a tyrant, much as he tries to pretend he is. In the second place, he would never begin to attempt to tell me how to live my life. It's becoming perfectly clear to me that's precisely what your father has done to you all your life, and the only use he has for you as a daughter is to marry you in a way that will continue his illustrious career.''

''That's not true! He may be domineering, but you make him sound cold and calculating!'' Her voice was hot with anger.

"Think about it, Kate. In any case, I'm not convinced that your father is the whole issue here. What about David?"

"What about him?"

"Are you really over him? Perhaps he has more of a hold over you than you're willing to admit."

Kate's eyes flashed but now she spoke coldly. "Don't you presume to analyze my feelings, Sebastian. You don't know what I feel."

"You're right about that," he said curtly.

"I—look, I'm sorry. It's just that this is still a sensitive area." Kate was suddenly acutely uncomfortable.

"Of course it is, and that's perfectly natural. You spent over a year with David. But it's important to me, Kate—I need to know. And there's something else. Don't you think it's a little strange for David to suddenly give up everything and head straight for the State Department?"

"A little, maybe, but that's where he's always wanted to be."

"It's not that easy to get in, Kate, there are tight security clearances, and so on. This happened very quickly, didn't it?"

"My father recommended him. He made sure I knew that."

"That's in character." He frowned again. "Something's bothering me, Kate, and I can't put my finger on it."

"Let's just forget about David and my father, Sebastian. I don't want them to ruin the end to a wonderful weekend. I haven't really thanked you, you know."

He looked at her intently. the finest of lines still marking his brow, then his face cleared as if what he saw in her face eased his mind. "I've always loved the way you thank me for things. Come here, you ridiculous girl." He pulled her into his arms and fitted his lips to hers in a long kiss that made Kate forget everything but the hammering of her heart and the heat of his body pressed against hers.

Eventually he said, "I must go, sweetheart. I'll ring you tomorrow and we'll make some plans."

She walked him to the door regretfully. "Thanks again, Sebastian."

"Now don't start that again or I'll never be out of here. Good night, my love, and think about what I said, will you?" And he was gone.

The next morning Sebastian sat behind his desk, a pile of untouched work sitting in front of him. He rubbed his forehead with his fingertips as if to smooth out the creases, and then finally reached for the telephone, waiting impatiently for the code he gave to clear.

"Yes, Dunn, what is it?" said Colonel Harrington on a note of surprise.

"It's David Russell, sir, the man who was watching the fishing boat. I may have made a mistake. He's accepted a job with Sevronsen, State Department, quite suddenly through the good offices of Peter Soames. Russell gave up a run for Congress. I have a bad feeling about this change of direction, and if he's in any way connected to the Group we've got serious trouble; Sevronsen may not live to know about it if the usual infiltration scheme works. There are just too many pieces here that are bothering me."

"I'll start a check on him at once. Thank you, Dunn." The line went dead.

Kate put the finishing touches on the beef Stroganoff and brought it into the dining room with a flourish. "Gosh, it's good to finally have an evening together. Dig in, Steph."

"This looks fabulous. Lucky me that Mr. Dunn couldn't manage dinner tonight. I suppose he's got you booked for the weekend as well? Come on, Kate, I've waited long enough without asking any probing questions, and it's only fair you reward my good behavior."

"You've hardly been around to badger me, Steph! Between your work, my work, and that new friend of yours, I've seen next to nothing of you."

"And what about all the time you've been spending with

Sebastian Dunn, including your disappearing act last Friday—about which you've said not one word except that it was very pleasant. You haven't told me anything!"

"All right, all right, I give in." Kate laughed. "It turns out that Sebastian's father is Lord Dunn of Whitworth Hall in Leicestershire. That's where we were, and his whole family is absolute heaven, and mad as hatters, which explains a good deal about Sebastian."

"You're joking!"

"No, and furthermore, Elizabeth knows the family well. Quite a long shot from our Simon Dristoll."

"Oh, this is too much! No wonder he was playing up the suave aristocrat. But what was the reason he was pretending to be someone else in Jamaica?"

"I can't really tell you, it has something to do with his work, but it was a reasonable explanation. And you mustn't tell anyone about it."

"Oh, another mystery? Really, Kate, you're beginning to remind me of someone out of a Dorothy Sayers novel! Oops, wrong thing to say. Never mind, what I really want to know is where you and Sebastian stand. I could have sworn from his behavior last Sunday that there was nothing really going on until he asked me to leave you alone, with that—that *look* in his eyes."

"I don't know where we stand, Steph, I honestly don't. I know I have very strong feelings about him, but I don't know how much of it is physical, because that's certainly a powerful thing between us."

"That answers one question I had. So much for Sebastian's circumspect behavior."

"Oh, you can forget circumspect altogether except when we're around other people. Then he's the model of the word, your perfect British gentleman. He's a chameleon, and there's a lot more of Simon Dristoll lurking behind that well-bred demeanor he puts on—not that it isn't a part of him; I just sometimes think that he's laughing behind it the whole time."

"That's how it seemed the other night, as if he were quietly having me on, playing me for a reaction, but there was nothing concrete to get hold of. I think he must have been doing the flip side of Simon for my benefit. It must be difficult having a relationship with a chameleon."

"It's funny; sometimes I feel as if he knows me far better than I know myself and there are no words necessary between us, but then there are times that I feel as if I don't know him at all. One minute he goes from an incredible intensity that makes me quite weak at the knees, and then he suddenly shifts into his cool and collected persona and I don't know what he's thinking. This week he's been on about David in his very subtle way, digging around in the past. I think he believes that I'm still in love with David, even though I've told him I'm not. It's maddening; and then he goes all quiet and reserved and you'd think we were strangers."

"Have you told him how you feel about him? Maybe that has something to do with it."

"No, not exactly. I'm scared, Steph, scared of making another mistake, scared of not knowing him well enough, scared of not knowing myself well enough to trust my feelings. He's so sure of himself, but I don't know where I'm going with this. I'm not ready for more heartbreak, but on the other hand, I can't seem to imagine my life without Sebastian in it."

"Oh, dear, this does sound serious. What are you going to do?"

"Bolt, what else?" She grinned.

"No—Kate, you're not!"

"No, not really, only for a few days. I'm going to take the free week at the end of my wine-buying trip and go to St. Mouton, the place in the photograph, do some digging around."

"You've found it? That's fantastic! Where is it?"

"It's a little village in the Dordogne. It couldn't be more convenient, since I'll be in the Bordeaux area at the end of my business trip and St. Mouton is only a couple of hours from there. Anyway, whether I turn up anything on my grandparents or not, I'll have some time to be on my own and do some serious thinking about where I'm going with my life. When I came over here the last thing I expected to do was to fall in love with Sebastian Dunn.''

''Maybe you should spend more time listening to yourself, and less time trying to analyze your feelings.''

Kate flushed. ''You're probably right.''

Sunday came much too quickly. Sebastian kissed her gently at the door and helped her into the Jaguar, saying very little as he wove through the London traffic. And he was unusually quiet throughout dinner, without any of his usual lighthearted banter. Kate was not in a particularly talkative mood in any case, feeling suddenly quite miserable about having to be away from Sebastian for three whole weeks. Even the excitement of her vacation and search for the past began to pale.

''Let's go somewhere we can be alone, Kate. You haven't been to my house yet. Would you like that?''

''Yes, please, Sebastian, I'd like that very much.''

The house was a tall, white Georgian-fronted structure. He turned the key in the lock and switched on the lights. They were standing in a large marble-floored hallway from which opened two large rooms, one apparently a dining room and kitchen, and the other a drawing room. ''Come upstairs, Kate,'' Sebastian said, taking her coat from her and draping it over a chair.

The house gleamed with an assortment of beautiful antiques, a reflection of Sebastian's keen eye and taste. The upstairs sitting room was comfortable and masculine but they bypassed that and climbed yet another flight of stairs. He drew her into his bedroom, a spacious area with long windows.

Without a word he slipped off his jacket and tugged at his tie, his eyes never leaving her. There was something in them she had never seen before and it almost frightened her. Then he was standing in front of her, his chest bare, and he turned her around and unzipped her dress, pulling it off her shoulders and letting it fall to the floor. His arms went around her and he held her like that for a moment. She could feel his heart pounding violently against her back, and she felt she surely could not stand if he let her go. And then he picked her up in his arms and carried her to the bed, discarding the rest of her clothes and his as he laid her down. Her eyes drank in his fine, hard physique, the broad, well-muscled shoulders, the powerful chest and flat, ridged belly, and she reached for him with a sigh, pulling him close, murmuring his name.

He held her to him for a long moment, then raised his head and kissed her softly again and again, playing with her lips, and then again, so deeply this time that she moaned with pleasure. Only then did his hands begin to move over her slowly, caressingly, until she forgot everything but the touch of his mouth and his sensitive fingers on her, the feel of him hot and alive under her hands, the pounding of blood in her veins.

"Kate—sweet, sweet Kate," he whispered. His voice was raw, his breath warm and vibrant against her cheek and he covered her mouth with his own and kissed her until she cried out for him. Sebastian slid into her. He was still for a moment, his eyes closed, his breath coming in rough pants, and then his lids opened and his eyes looked deeply into hers. The expression there sent a stab of something almost painful through her, and she gasped, it was so strong. Then very, very slowly he began to move his hips, and each stroke within her was a caress. His eyes never left hers, his pupils huge and black, the blue so incredibly deep, and behind them the never-wavering expression, so fierce, so tender, so full of what lay between them, almost as if he were drinking her in, memorizing her. And then he quickened his stroke, sensing Kate's need, as her hips moved in rhythm with his, rising, falling, like breathing, like the movement of the ocean, caught up in the very essence of life, a yearning beyond description. Sebastian's taut muscles worked under her fingers, his skin slick with sweat. And then everything within her coiled itself into an unbearably pleasurable knot at the core of her being and Sebastian pushed into it and held as she crested and broke, over and over until she thought she would die, contracting around Sebastian as if she were embracing him from within. Sebastian groaned and his muscles bunched and then released in a violent surge, and they came together as if their bodies were one.

Afterward, Sebastian kissed her gently and rolled onto his back, pulling her close to his side and he lightly stroked her arms, her back, her hair, not saying a word. Then after a long time he said, "Let's get dressed and go downstairs. I need to talk to you, and I can't do it here, like this."

"Sebastian, what is it? You've been so quiet all night, and then just now. . . What's wrong?" She felt a little thrill of fear.

"Please, Kate." He slid out of bed and pulled on his trousers and shirt. "Come down to the sitting room when you're ready."

She dressed quickly, truly concerned now and completely baffled. Was she about to confront Sebastian the stranger after what they had just shared? Her body felt unaccountably shaky and she sat down on the bed, steadying herself, trying to work out what had happened to change him so suddenly. After a few minutes she decided there was no point putting off whatever it was, and went downstairs.

"All right, I'm quite collected now. Whatever is going on?" Kate sat down in an armchair and looked at him in puzzlement.

Sebastian walked over to the fireplace and leaned on the mantelpiece for a moment. Then he turned around and looked at her with an unreadable expression. "How did you come by your watch, Kate?"

"What—my watch? *That's* what this is all about?"

"That's exactly what this is all about. Where did you get it, Kate?" He watched her carefully.

"I—I told you. My aunt gave it to me." There was something very wrong, she thought with alarm.

"I don't think so. The truth this time, Kate."

"I don't understand—have you discovered something about it you haven't told me?"

"Yes, I have, this Friday as a matter of fact. But first you're going to tell me who gave it to you. Was it David?"

"Damn it, Sebastian, will you stop dragging David into everything? This is growing tedious!"

"Tedious or not, did he give it to you?"

"No! No, he didn't give it to me, for heaven's sake. I told you—"

"You told me a lie. You don't have an aunt. This is important, Kate, and a lot rests on your answer aside from our relationship."

"Don't be ridiculous! What does our relationship have to do with my watch?" She glared at him.

"A small matter of trust, for one thing," he said coolly.

"Sebastian, this is absurd! All right, I don't have an aunt, but I'll be damned if I tell you anything more. It's none of your business in the first place!"

"That's where you're very wrong."

"Look, Sebastian, I gave you the blasted thing to have you trace its previous owners, not to have you interrogate me like some kind of criminal. Just because we have a friendship—although right at this moment you make me wonder—it doesn't mean you own me or have any right to anything other than what I choose to tell you! I'm quite sure you don't treat your other clients like this, or you'd be out of a job. Just tell me what you found out!" Her cheeks flamed with color.

"Certainly, Kate," he said with infuriating calm. "That watch once happened to belong to a man called Ernst von Fiedler. He was a high-ranking member of the Nazi party, the SS—the SD, to be more exact. But he was associated with a certain Gestapo major, Karl Erharder. It was a very interesting relationship. There was a certain amount of —drama surrounding his death. His watch hasn't surfaced again until now. Now would you like to tell me about it?"

The color had drained out of Kate's face. She could hardly think through her shock. "I . . . No, damn you, I'm not, I'm not going to tell you a blessed thing. It's my business, and my business alone, and I wish you'd stop bullying me!"

"So, it was David, then, wasn't it." Sebastian's voice was grim.

"No! And what if it was? I can't see why David would have anything to do with it!"

"Kate, that watch was a von Fiedler family heirloom. Now, suddenly it surfaces with you? I think that's very strange, considering your acute interest in having it traced, and your reluctance to tell me how and why you have it. If David gave you the watch I want to know about it."

"Don't be ridiculous, Sebastian! This has nothing to do with David! I think you're out of your mind with some misguided jealousy, and I'm beginning to thoroughly resent it."

"Resent away, I assure you that isn't the case."

"Oh, I've had enough of this, I'm leaving." She stood, angry and confused, wanting nothing more than to be away from this ceaseless questioning.

"Go then, Kate, but if you leave, we're finished." His eyes were steel, biting into her.

Kate's fury spilled over. "Oh, that's a nice easy way to manipulate me into telling you what you want to know, isn't it? Damn you to hell, Sebastian Dunn, I don't care if I never see you again! This has been a one-sided relationship all along with you calling all the shots."

"That's not true, and you know it. And that's not the issue."

"Isn't it? You were the one who pursued me, remember? But you stayed the man of mystery, didn't you, finding out everything you wanted to know, telling me next to nothing. For all I know this whole thing has been about David!"

"Just exactly what do you mean by that?"

"You know just what I mean. You've done nothing but ask about David from the very beginning—I think you're more interested in him than you are in me!"

"They're two separate issues, Kate, or at least so I thought."

"Don't try to make me believe that, Sebastian. I think it's extremely odd that you've devoted so much time to interrogating me on the subject of David if you didn't have an ulterior motive—is that why you went after me with such determination, to find out more about him? I'd believe it, the way you've harassed me. And you really started in this week when you found out he was going into the State Department, didn't you? God, what are you up to, anyway?"

"Stop it, Kate. You don't know what you're talking about."

She stared at him. "Jamaica! It's why you were there—there was no forgery! You were after David, weren't you?"

Sebastian's eyes had narrowed. "What would make you think that?"

"And Berlin . . . the shooting. It was you, wasn't it? It was you!" She looked at him in horror.

It took him two long strides and he was in front of her, gripping her painfully by the shoulders. "What do you know about Berlin—tell me, damn you!" He shook her hard.

"Let go of me!" She wrenched away from him, her eyes fierce. "So it's true . . . I can't believe how stupid I've been! Why didn't I see it—it was staring me in the face this entire time!" She backed off, terrified by the expression on his face.

"You bloody little—" He turned away from her, fighting for control. "By God, if you treasure your life, get out of here or I swear I'll do something I'll regret." He spoke between clenched teeth, his fingers bloodlessly gripping the mantelpiece.

"I'm going—my God, I'm going, Sebastian. Just stay away from me, and stay away from David or I swear I'll see you dead!" And she turned and ran out of the room and down the stairs. She paused only to grab her coat and then tore out of Sebastian's house, tears blinding her as she reached the street.

CHAPTER Nine

Kate paid the taxi driver and walked slowly up the steps to the mews house, the tears still wet on her cheeks. She was in a dream, she told herself, a nightmare, and she'd wake up and everything would be normal. But it was real, horribly real . . . She fumbled with the keys, pulling at the lock that wouldn't open. "Oh, damn!" she cried. And then the lock mercifully turned and she was inside, leaning against the door, the panic lashing through her veins refusing to quiet itself.

"Kate?" Stephanie's sleepy head appeared from the stairs, and then Kate found herself being held in warm comforting arms.

"What's happened? Look, never mind, come upstairs with me, and we'll have some cocoa and you can tell me all about it." She led Kate up the stairs and into the kitchen, putting on the kettle.

Kate leaned against the wall, trembling violently. "Oh, Steph . . ." She couldn't seem to stop shaking.

"Here, sit down and drink this. Now tell me what's happened. Is it Sebastian?"

"Sebastian? Yes—yes, it's Sebastian and David and a man called Ernst von Fiedler. Oh, Steph, it's a horror story." And slowly, in fits and starts, she managed to pour out the whole ghastly tale.

"So you see, Sebastian's obviously been working for some terrible organization or something, and David was his target all along. And thinking about it, aside from David, I'll bet his interest in me also has something to do with my father's connections to the State Department. He asked a lot of questions about him, too, and would always go all cool when Daddy's name came up. And if that isn't enough, I think he killed his best friend a few years ago in Berlin!"

"What! What are you talking about?"

"His friend Tony Morris—he died three years ago supposedly in an accidental shooting in West Berlin. Sebastian told everyone it was an East–West incident and they just happened to be there, and Tony was caught in the cross fire. But he never talks about it, and when I mentioned it tonight, he looked as if he were going to kill me next."

"Kate—my God!"

"And now it could be that my grandfather was some awful war criminal! And Sebastian's interested in him, too."

"I can't imagine what a watch belonging to a long-dead Nazi would have to do with anything."

"He said there was a drama or something surrounding his death, and the watch disappeared. You and I know why, but he doesn't. It was obvious that it worried him, and he was furious when I wouldn't tell him any more. He didn't bother to deny any of the things I accused him of, and he didn't try to stop me when I left."

"Oh, Kate! This is too terrible for words! But I think you should just let the whole thing lie—you can't possibly go digging things up knowing what you do." Stephanie's face was as pale as Kate's.

"I have to, don't you see? I can't leave it here, with everything Sebastian said. I should have seen it long ago—in Jamaica he was talking about the rot under jolly old England, and leaving it for more important things, or something like that. I remember wondering at the time what he was talking about, but then I thought he was a fisherman, and anyway, it didn't really matter. And later I even fell for his story about why he was in Jamaica in the first place! He's lied to me all along, used me, damn him."

"No wonder he came across like a chameleon."

"Exactly. He certainly knew exactly how to play me and gave me just enough rope to hang myself with. All that talk about love—"

"What talk about love? You never mentioned that."

"Oh, never mind, just forget it," she said, her eyes welling with tears again. "What about David—what am I going to do about that? If Sebastian's after him, I have to tell him!"

"No, Kate! You can't get any more involved, it's too dangerous!" Listen, you don't really know anything about this. Please, I beg you, stay out of it."

"No, Steph, I can't."

"Well, at least wait until you get back from France, okay? There's nothing you can do about it now, and if you tried to call David in the state you're in, he'd think you were crazy. Anyway, I think you should cool down and get some perspective on the thing before you go flying off half-cocked and get the State Department into an uproar."

"Yes, you're probably right. I should find out more, or at least check my facts first. But in the meantime, I'm going to find out the truth, about the watch anyway. I don't want to go through the rest of my life with this Nazi thing hanging over my head. I'm going to St. Mouton and somehow I'm going to find out what really happened. The truth has to be there, locked in that photograph."

"All right, if you're going to be so bloody stubborn, then I'm coming with you. You can't do this on your own, that's obvious. I'll take some holiday time and meet you in St. Mouton in two weeks."

"Oh, Steph, would you, really? You're such an angel. It would help. And I'm sorry I cried all over you."

"Sometimes you're such an idiot, Kate."

"I know. Don't think I don't know it."

* * *

Sebastian didn't move for a long time after Kate had left. He stared out the window, his eyes unseeing, trying to still his raging emotions, trying to make sense out of Kate's words, out of all the tangled pieces. That night after lying awake for hours, he finally fell into a troubled sleep. Images flashed in and out of his mind, fragments of dreams, then Kate, standing there pointing a gun at him and pulling the trigger, as he turned into Tony and fell, then back to himself, lying broken, bleeding, on the cold streets of Berlin.

He woke up in a cold sweat, the light of early morning streaming through the window, bringing him back to harsh reality, a reality that seemed no saner than his dream. He dressed slowly, thinking hard, trying to find some way out, but there was nothing, nothing but this void in him that felt like death. "Oh, God, Kate, why?" he whispered. Then he went to the telephone and dialed.

"Good morning, Dunn. What do you have for us?"

"Run a thorough check on Kate Soames. She could be part of the Group."

He put the telephone down carefully and ran shaking hands through his hair, his eyes blurred with tears.

Kate spent one night in Paris, then hired a car, a Peugeot 505, and drove down to the Loire Valley. From there she made her way slowly down to Bordeaux. For the next two weeks she was wined and dined by the proprietors of vineyards eager to conduct business with Rosterman and Marsh. She stayed at various châteaux, made many profitable contacts, and should have enjoyed herself thoroughly. But she went through her business like a sleepwalker, laughing at the appropriate moments, making negotiating calls to London and New York (and sometimes to blessed James in Oxford for advice), and charming her hosts with her good manners and flawless French. She had to be ever alert, ever on her guard, for the French were wily businessmen, and she was young, female, and untried.

She couldn't wait for her escape to St. Mouton, to have some time to be on her own, to allow herself to let go. The strain of keeping Sebastian out of her thoughts was exhausting her. And the terrible thing was that although she made every effort to do that, he was there with her at the most unexpected moments. Something foolish said to her would suddenly make her think of how Sebastian would have kept silent, but the laugh would have lurked in his eyes. Or suddenly the memory of the look in his eyes that last night of lovemaking would come stabbing back to her. Her body betrayed her at night, remembering his touch during those last few unguarded moments before sleep, and then sleep, the worst of all, where Sebastian had free reign.

There her dream was always the same; he would love her, with his words, with his body, with his incredible eyes, and then the dream would shift and Sebastian was chasing her, shouting something dreadful that she could not hear, and she could not run, she was frozen, and she looked back over her shoulder and it was not Sebastian at all, it was the hideous fish head with the huge mouth, chasing her down the streets of St. Mouton. And then she would wake up with a start, shaking with terror.

Whatever she might find buried in the little town of St. Mouton, no matter how awful, it surely couldn't be as bad as the dream.

"Stephanie, thank heaven you're finally here! I was beginning to think I'd never make it through the trip." Kate picked up her case and led her through the airport to the waiting Peugeot.

"You look tired, Kate. Are you all right?" Stephanie looked at her with concern, not liking the pallor of complexion and the dark circles under her eyes.

"I'm okay, I guess. It was quite a grueling fourteen days, nonstop, and I haven't been sleeping well. I feel better already just seeing your face."

"Are you sure you want to go on with this?"

"Absolutely positive. Now let's figure out the best route to get to St. Mouton. Here's the map. Oh, these French motorways terrify me! We take this thing, the N89, northeast as far as Montpon, then get onto a smaller road, thank goodness. It weaves through Riberac, then up between Brantôme and Périgueux. Do you see? The village is only a small dot, but it should be easy enough to find."

"Yes, I've found it—here. You know, Kate, I'm half-terrified, but half-excited, too."

"I know exactly what you mean."

They finally got off the motorway and into the country proper. For another two hours they passed collections of villages sitting on top of hills or nestled down into the valleys, uniform in their stone walls and tiled roofs and the shutters fit to every window and door. Haystacks glowed softly yellow in the early evening light, light that fell hazy and sleepy around them. It backlit the vineyards that stretched everywhere, some more elegant, boasting a higher appellation with their little posies neatly planted in front of every row, others a farmer's simple crop for his own consumption. The river Dronne sparkled as if a handful of jewels had been carelessly scattered on its surface, and sunflowers, millions of sunflowers, planted in fields that burst with their brilliant yellow, nodded their heads lazily in the soft breeze. They passed an old, bent woman dressed in black, leading her herd of cows home for the night, her dog bringing up the rear, guarding against strays.

"Here's the turning, Kate!"

The Peugeot slowed at the sign, pointed like an arrow to the west, old, its paint beginning to peel: St. Mouton. Kate shifted into second gear and turned. "Here we go, Steph." She found that her heart was hammering.

The Hôtel Périgord sat directly in the middle of the village, forming part of one side of the village square. Kate and Stephanie had no trouble getting rooms, although their passports were examined and noted carefully by the concierge, a Monsieur Barbier. This was a village accustomed to occasional tourists passing through, now that the beauty and charm of the Dordogne had been discovered by sophisticated travelers, although it certainly wasn't in the main line of traffic.

The rooms in the hotel were small but clean and simply furnished, and each contained its own sink and, of course, a bidet. The communal bathroom and W.C. were down the hall. As soon as they'd unpacked, they headed downstairs and out to explore the village.

It was not as small as Kate had first anticipated. The square contained a bakery, one restaurant, not including the Hôtel Périgord's own, and a handful of other businesses. The streets extending off the square all had their share of shops and residences.

"What do you say we go back to the square and eat. I'm starved!" Kate dragged Stephanie away from the window of a dress shop. They settled on the café across from the hotel.

"*Vin blanc cassis, s'il vous plaît*, monsieur. Kate?"

"*La même, s'il vous plaît.*" She waited for the waiter to leave and summoned up her courage. "Steph, there's something I've been meaning to ask you." She bit on her lip nervously.

"What is it? Trouble?"

"I don't know. This is going to sound foolish, but I was just wondering. Sebastian didn't try to get in touch while I was gone, did he?"

"Oh, Kate. No, not a word. I'd have told you first thing. I'm sorry, I really am. Have you been able to figure out what happened now that you've had awhile to think about it?"

"Not really, I haven't allowed myself to dwell on it. When I do it terrifies me. I kept hoping the whole thing was just some dreadful mistake, or that I heard it wrong. But if he were innocent he would never have left it like that. But you see, there were just so many things that didn't seem to fit, so I thought I might have been mistaken."

"Like what, for example?"

"Oh, just little things; things Sebastian said or did." Her cheeks flamed, remembering.

"Oh, I see. But couldn't he have been stringing you along, using those things to make you confide in him?"

"I suppose so. It just didn't seem like that sort of thing; it was too genuine. Of course, then again, I suppose that even spies have their normal moments. I mean, they can't be evil all the time, can they? They must eat and sleep and love just like everyone else."

"Apparently," said Stephanie wryly.

"And it's just when their political ideology gets crossed, or they're on the job or something, that they become dangerous."

"What are you saying, that you're going to go running back to Sebastian but you're going to try to stay out of his ideological warpath?"

"No, of course not. I just can't believe that I could fall in love with someone so wicked."

"As you just pointed out, he's only partly wicked and that's not the part you fell in love with."

"Oh, stop confusing me. I can't believe my instincts were so wrong—it just shows you what an emotional idiot I am, making mistakes with both David and Sebastian. Oh, let's not talk about it anymore, I'll just start blubbering"

"For heaven's sake, don't do that. Let's order," said Stephanie sensibly.

When they had finished their dinner of soup, grenouille in brown butter sauce, a pork roast, salad, and cheeses, and poured out the last glass of local red wine, rich and mellow, Stephanie pushed back her chair. "All right, what's the plan?"

"To tell you the truth, I don't know. I have the photograph here." She pulled it out and unfolded it. "But it was so many years ago, and who's going to remember now? Then there's this Ernst von Fiedler. We know he was an SS officer, and we know it was his watch that traveled with my mother to England but how do we know if there's any connection to St. Mouton?"

"That shouldn't be too hard to find out. If he hung around here and was SS, then I doubt he'd be easily forgotten. He'll probably turn out to be a dwarf in the bargain. Who could forget a Nazi dwarf?"

Kate laughed. "You are appalling, Steph."

"Just optimistic. We have the photograph, why not simply start with that, show it around to people."

"Yes, I suppose that's the only thing to do. Well, I'm exhausted and more than ready for my bed, but I want to make one phone call to Elizabeth to tell her I'm here. There's a booth on the corner. You go ahead back."

Kate managed to get through without too much trouble and Elizabeth professed herself very glad to hear her voice. "Is it all going well, darling?"

"Everything's fine, so far. Stephanie and I made it to St. Mouton today. It's a quiet, pretty sort of town. I don't know how much luck we're going to have, but I do have the photograph. Anyway, I just wanted to let you know where I am. We're staying at the Hôtel Périgord if you need to reach me for any reason. Have there been any calls?"

"Not a one. Whom were you expecting, Sebastian Dunn?" she asked teasingly.

"He'd be the last person in the world to call, believe me, so you can drop his name from your roster, Elizabeth. No, actually I thought Daddy might try to get through. He was none too pleased with me the last time we talked. If he does call, let him know where I am, will you?"

"Of course I will, Kate, although I don't see any reason he constantly needs to know where you are and what you're doing."

"I know, but it helps avoid arguments. I'll ring off now, Elizabeth. See you in a week."

"Good-bye, Kate, and let me know if you discover anything, won't you."

"Of course. Good night." She left the booth and made her way down the west side of the square, wondering why she had chosen not to tell Elizabeth about von Fiedler. If anyone would be interested, she would. But then again, maybe it would be better if Kate knew the whole story before she told Elizabeth anything, before Elizabeth began to regret giving her the watch at all. A bronze plaque fastened against the wall glinted in the dim light, and curious, she walked over to it, trying to make out its wording.

> On the night of June 14th, 1944, sixty men,
> women and children were shot against this
> wall by the Nazis.

And then there followed a long list of names, many grouped in families. Kate held her breath for a moment, swallowing against the horror that rose up in her. She wondered if this might have something to do with the infamous von Fiedler. A shiver ran through her and she hurried off across the square, pulling her jacket more tightly around her.

The next morning, after a fortifying breakfast of café au lait and croissants, Kate and Stephanie set out, stopping first to look at the plaque on the wall.

"Oh, it's awful, Kate. It's hard to believe that such a monstrous thing happened here—look at all these names! But it's one more thing to find out about. I suppose we'll have to tread very carefully."

"Yes." Kate shuddered. "I hope to God this has nothing to do with me or my heritage."

"Even if it does, Kate, no blame lies with you. Come on, stop being morbid, and let's get started."

The first few places they showed the photograph in drew no response at all, and even less interest. "I think we're going to have to start being more blunt about the slaughter, don't you?" asked Stephanie.

"I don't know. I hate to have to ask these people about something they must consider so deeply personal, but I can't see any other way of finding out what we need to know. Why don't we just start with von Fiedler's name? If he's the butcher, then we're likely to hear about it. But maybe it's best if we split up. You take the photograph and I'll ask about von Fiedler, since it's bound to draw an unpleasant response, and I'm responsible for this whole thing. I'll meet you back at the hotel at lunchtime."

"If you say so. I'll take the north side of the village, you go south."

Again, Kate had no luck. She brought up von Fiedler's name to a number of people, but it only evoked a vague response. The name that burned on the village lips was that of Karl Erharder, the man Sebastian had mentioned in connection with von Fiedler, and apparently the man responsible for the reprisal. But nobody seemed to want to talk about what had happened. The most she was told was that it was a matter of record, and although she could perhaps find something helpful in the church, or maybe the town hall, for the public records she would have to go to Périgueux.

On her way back to the hotel, she made one last stop in a *boulangerie*. An old woman with an angular face, dark, shoe-button eyes, and dressed in the inevitable black shuffled out. "*Bonjour*, mademoiselle."

"*Bonjour*, madame. *Une baguette, s'il vous plaît.*" She already had a basket filled with various tidbits from the different places she'd made inquiries. The woman handed her the long, crusty loaf.

Kate counted out one franc, twenty centimes and handed them to her. "Madame, I was wondering if you were familiar with a German, a Nazi, who was in this area during the war."

The woman shrugged. "There were many Nazis here during the war." She turned to put the money away.

"I do know about Karl Erharder. But this man's name was Ernst von Fiedler. I'm trying to discover—"

The woman did not turn around. "I cannot help you. I have never heard of such a man. The past is dead and buried and you'd be wise to leave it that way. Tourists!" she spat. "They always want to know about our tragedies. Good day, mademoiselle."

"Good day." Kate hurried out into the sunshine. She'd obviously offended the woman. Perhaps she had lost someone in the reprisal. It was becoming quite clear this was not going to be easy.

The storekeeper locked the door and went into the back of the shop. She pulled a box from the top of the closet and rifled through it, finally locating an old, grimy piece of paper. Then she sat down at the telephone and dialed a series of numbers. "Get me Herr Schumann," she said into the receiver. Tell him it's Madame Celeste Chabot, and hurry, it's urgent!"

"I came up more or less empty-handed. It seems Karl Erharder is the local man to hate—he's the one who killed half the village. But von Fiedler got me absolutely nowhere. I don't suppose you came up with anything?" Kate asked, judging by the expression on Stephanie's face that she hadn't.

"Nothing at all," said Stephanie regretfully. "I have a suggestion, though. Here we have all this food we've both managed to collect. Why don't we get our bathing suits and go down to the river somewhere. We can spend the afternoon in delicious idleness while we come up with another plan."

"That's a fantastic idea. We have the whole week, after all."

They quickly changed and threw their clothes back over their suits; then they were off, following the road that ran by the river until they found a little dirt turnoff and a sign that said "Pêche." Where there was fishing, there was surely the Dronne, and they took the road that wound through a thick tangle of trees. It opened onto a cow pasture bordered on the far side by the river. The bank was hugged by thick bushes and trees that bent out over the water, dappling the sunlight and shading the shoreline. The water was deep green and crystal clear and it smelled fresh and mossy and good.

They spread themselves out on a blanket in the sun, and laid the picnic out around them: first, the fresh bread, hard and crusty on the outside, light as air within; then the cheeses, a lovely ripe brie, a tart chèvre, and a rich, earthy pâté de campagne. And Kate had found the most glorious peaches, sweet and warm from the sun. All of this they washed down with white wine kept cold in the river. Filled to the brim, they packed the leftovers away and lay down in the sun, drowsy and content, the world silent except for the sound of the wind in the trees, the lowing of cows far off in the pasture and the gentle singing of the river.

"Steph? Wake up, you lazy old heifer. You're going to burn yourself to a frazzle unless you turn over or do something sensible like go for a swim."

"I never burn," murmured Stephanie without opening her eyes.

"Oh, really? I remember just exactly what shade of magenta you were after your first day of Jamaican sunshine."

"Oh, all right." Stephanie dragged herself to her feet and looked down into the water. "Have you been in?"

"Not yet. You can do the honors," she said and unceremoniously pushed Stephanie over the edge.

There was a scream and then an enormous splash, and when Stephanie's blond head emerged from the surface she was gasping. "Oh, my God, it's freezing! I'm going to murder you, and believe me, it'll be in cold blood!" She quickly swam to the side and managing to get a foothold on a tree stump, she pulled herself out of the water to find Kate doubled over, helpless with laughter. "It's curtains for you, my friend," she crowed victoriously, grabbing Kate's arms and hauling her over to the bank.

Kate was no match for Stephanie's superior size and

despite the fact that she planted her heels in the grass and resisted with all her weight, still laughing uncontrollably, she found herself dragged inch by inch to the edge of the water. "No!" she cried, but too late, as she found herself falling, but she kept her grip on Stephanie's arm, pulling her along over the edge.

The water was ice cold and the shock took her breath away for a moment; but once the initial plunge was over, her skin began to tingle deliciously, as if it had been mentholated. She looked over at Stephanie and grinned. "You're a wretch and a bully."

"You started it, and don't you dare try to use your diminutive size as ammunition!"

"I'm not diminutive, you're a giant. And just remember the story of David and Goliath." She rolled onto her back and floated contentedly.

"And you just remember the story of the Tailor and the Flies."

"*What*?" Kate started laughing again.

"Or was it the Cobbler and the Forty Blows?"

"Stop it, Steph," gasped Kate. "I'm going to drown!"

"It will serve you right, and don't think I'm going to rescue you."

"Oh, God, for someone who writes, you really know how to twist literature."

"It wasn't literature, it was a story about—"

"I know, I know." She shook her head with a broad smile.

They paddled around for a while, letting the river carry them downstream; but then enough was enough, and when their bodies started to become numb, they climbed out and walked back to their towels, letting the sun warm them on the way.

They stayed the rest of the afternoon, reading, idly chatting, and when the light began to deepen into gold and the shadows fell more steeply, they finally pulled themselves up and put on their clothes, agreeing that it had been a most gratifying way to spend the day. Then, reluctant to go back to St. Mouton and the problems that it held, they decided to drive farther afield. They found a wonderful little town in which to have dinner and a simple family restaurant, one room with a set menu and oilcloth on the wooden tables. But the food was delicious, the proprietors friendly, and the handsome young son more than happy to have them linger over their meal. Finally, having whiled away the evening entirely to their satisfaction, they headed sun-soaked and sleepy back to St. Mouton.

The next day dawned clear and bright, promising to remain that way and this time they had a more cohesive plan.

"Now," said Kate. "While you finish your coffee I'm going to write down all the names on that plaque, and then check them against the phone book. There's got to be someone still living here who had a relative killed." She hurried off and came back to find Stephanie still lazily sipping her coffee.

"Well, did any of the names match up?"

"As a matter of fact, eight surnames. That's not bad. Come on, Steph, will you drink that up and let's get going? I have the addresses, too, and we'll just have to start knocking on doors."

"Where to begin?"

"I don't know. We might as well do it alphabetically."

Madame Chabot watched from the door of her boulangerie with beady black eyes narrowed and a decidedly sour expression on her sharp face. She very much wanted to know what that girl intended to do with the names she had taken down. More worried than ever, she rushed to make another telephone call.

Kate and Stephanie started with Pierre Anjou, a middle-aged man who regretted that although he had an uncle who had been killed in the terrible reprisal, he had been only a young child at the time, and both his parents, who might have known more, were dead. Yes, the name von Fiedler was familiar, he allowed, but the photograph was not.

It was the same story at the next place they tried, but the second person, a Madame Dumielle, suggested they try the third person on their list, old Monsieur Jumeau. He could be found at the camera shop just down the street and might be more helpful. She believed that his family had all been destroyed by the filthy Boche, and since he had been a young man during those years, he might remember the face. As for her, well, her family had moved to St. Mouton after the war, to take on their cousin's house. So many houses had stood vacant then.

With renewed hope Kate and Stephanie entered the little shop that advertised Kodak film outside. A bell tinkled their arrival, and a slight, dark-haired man Kate judged to be somewhere in his very early twenties appeared from the back.

"Mesdemoiselles?" he asked politely.

"Excuse us, monsieur, we are looking for a Monsieur Jumeau."

"I am Monsieur Jumeau. How may I help you?"

"Oh, I beg your pardon," said Kate. "It is an elderly Monsieur Jumeau I'm looking for."

"Ah, that would be my grandfather, Henri Jumeau. If you will just wait here, I shall bring him."

Kate exchanged an apprehensive look with Stephanie, and a moment later an older gentleman stepped through the curtain. "Bonjour, mesdemoiselles. You asked to see me?" The eyes behind the thick spectacles flickered for a moment as they took in Kate, but then they returned to puzzlement.

"Monsieur Jumeau, I am trying to identify a woman who was in this village in 1943. I have a photograph of her, and I was hoping you might able to help me." Kate placed it on the counter.

"I was not here at the time, mademoiselle, but I can certainly look at it." He picked it up and held it up to the light coming in through the window. For a long moment he was silent, then with slightly trembling hands he placed it down again. "How do you happen to have this?" he asked in a shaking voice, his skin suddenly quite ashen.

"Then you knew her, monsieur?"

"Yes, I knew her well. She was my sister. I ask you again, how is it you have this?"

For a moment Kate could not speak. Then she cleared her throat and said, "I have reason to believe she was my grandmother."

"No. No and no." Henri Jumeau shook his head to emphasize his words. "That is quite impossible. My sister died in 1944. She was killed in the reprisal, and her only child had died days before. How did you come by such a fantastic idea?"

"Monsieur, I think we need to talk. Is there somewhere we can go?"

"Certainly, mademoiselle, but I assure you it will be fruitless." He lifted up the partition in the counter and led them through the back of the shop to the kitchen, gesturing to his grandson to follow.

"I should introduce myself," said Kate, suddenly feeling nervous. "I am Kate Soames, from America, and this is my friend Stephanie Matthison, who is from England."

"My grandson, Pierre." They all shook hands, and Monsieur Jumeau indicated seats around the table.

"I have a story to tell you, monsieur, and it will sound outrageous, I'm sure, but perhaps somewhere in this is an answer for all of us." She looked over at Stephanie who nodded encouragingly. "Not long ago, I discovered that my mother had been adopted as an infant during the war. She had been smuggled out of France by the Resistance. Her adoption by my grandparents was kept a secret from everyone with the exception of a particular friend. My mother arrived in England with nothing but a watch, which has been locked away for all this time. It was given to me recently by the friend, and I desired to trace my true grandparents. Inside the watch was this photograph, the photograph of your sister."

"Giselle," he whispered.

"Your sister Giselle. I took the watch to—to an expert,

and he discovered it had once belonged to a man, an SS officer called Ernst von Fiedler—"

"Von Fiedler!" Monsieur Jumeau jumped to his feet. "It is not possible!"

"Why not, monsieur?"

"He was responsible for what happened to my sister! If Giselle had not killed him herself, I would have killed him with my own hands!"

"But I thought Karl Erharder—"

"He was bad enough, but it was von Fiedler who—"

"*Pépé*, please, you must calm yourself." Pierre gently sat him down again.

He took a deep breath. "I will tell you the story so that you will see how this cannot be true. I was in Germany at the time, a prisoner of war, but I heard later, from others. You see, my family was involved in the Resistance through Giselle, who ran her own escape line. She was only eighteen when she started. She was captured once and interrogated by Major Erharder, but she made an escape. Eventually, many months later, she was taken in again and brought to Gestapo headquarters in Paris. There she was given back to Major Erharder. He—he beat her terribly, leaving her chest covered with scars. And then she was mysteriously released by Colonel von Fiedler of the SD. His reasons became apparent when he followed her to her house and raped her. He then released her to the shame of bearing his bastard child." His eyes filled with tears and he paused to wipe them away with shaking hands.

"Please, monsieur, if this is too painful for you—" Kate wasn't even sure she wanted to know more. She was fighting back her own tears.

Henri Jumeau made a visible effort to collect himself. "No—no, I must continue. It is a story that must not be forgotten." He took a deep breath. "Colonel von Fiedler came to our village with Major Erharder, just before the birth of the child. Major Erharder had not been able to learn anything from Giselle, even with the torture. Colonel von Fiedler had different methods. He knew her role in the Resistance movement but he waited, weaving the net around her. Giselle gave birth to her daughter in the second week of June, but the poor baby—Hélène was her name—was born two months too early, and she died after only one day. The Gestapo came for Giselle the next night, but she had buried her child that day and had gone off to grieve privately. My family was taken instead. Major Erharder posted a notice in the square saying that if Giselle did not turn herself in, her family would be shot along with five other innocents from the village. Giselle heard of it the next day, and she gave herself up to Major Erharder and Colonel von Fiedler. Somehow during the course of the interrogation, she managed to get hold of Major Erharder's gun and she shot Colonel von Fiedler in revenge for what he had done to her. She tried to kill Major Erharder as well.'' He paused for a moment, then swallowed hard and continued, his voice tight. ''Erharder ordered the reprisal. It was the night of the fourteenth of June. A night pouring with rain, I was told. Random members of the village, including all of my own family, even the village priest, they were all taken and they were shot. Shot in cold blood, against the wall of the village square . . .'' He fell silent.

Kate, stunned, finally found her voice. ''I am so terribly sorry, monsieur! I—I did not mean to intrude.''

''It is long in the past. I came home after the war to find my family gone. I swore revenge, but Major Erharder had disappeared without a trace, and so he was never punished for what had been done.''

''But I don't understand. How did Colonel von Fiedler's watch and your sister's photograph end up in England with an infant?''

''It is a mystery, mademoiselle. I wish I knew myself.'' He shrugged helplessly. ''But as you must see, it could not be the infant Hélène.''

''Yes, of course, I can see that. I apologize, monsieur, for having troubled you, and I apologize for having brought back such painful memories. Thank you for your time.'' Kate rose to leave.

''I wish I could have helped you, mademoiselle. Perhaps if you discover the truth you could let me know? I would be very interested to know how you came to have the photograph and the watch."

"Most certainly—"

"Kate—Kate, wait..." interrupted Stephanie, putting a hand on her arm. "Perhaps we are all being too hasty. It seems too much of a coincidence that there should be an orphaned child, a girl of the same approximate age as Hélène would have been, who just happened to have arrived in England with Giselle's photograph inside Colonel von Fiedler's watch. There has to be some reasonable explanation. Now bear me out for just a moment. As you were talking, I was thinking. Suppose, just for a moment, that Giselle's child was perfectly healthy, that she didn't die."

"But I tell you, mademoiselle, she did! She is buried in the churchyard," said Henri Jumeau as patiently as he could manage.

"What are you getting at?" Kate could hardly miss the note of excitement in Stephanie's voice.

"Well, suppose that Giselle suspected Colonel von Fiedler might have been planning some harm against Hélène. After all, she would have been his illegitimate child and evidence against the terrible thing he had done. Given the fact that he was the inhuman brute Monsieur Jumeau has described, why would he have hesitated?"

"All right," said Kate slowly. "And so?"

"And so Giselle was in the perfect position to protect her child. How many people in France ran their own escape line? It might seem drastic, but wouldn't sending your child out of the country be the most sensible solution if you thought her life was in danger?"

"Yes... Yes, it would be! And to cover up the escape, she invented the child's death?" asked Kate, picking up Stephanie's train of thought.

"Exactly. Then somehow she got hold of von Fiedler's watch and hid her photograph inside, so if it was ever necessary, her baby's identity could be proved—I would assume that she intended to come for her, but then she was killed."

"Steph, you're brilliant! Your script-writing career hasn't

been a waste after all! It does tie in with my mother arriving in England through the French underground, and why Guy Jessop would say that nothing must connect her with her past. We know that's why the watch was hidden for all these years. But what do you think, monsieur? Is it possible?"

The older Monsieur Jumeau, who had been carefully absorbing the exchange, rose to his feet. He walked over to Kate and took her face between his wrinkled hands and looked at her very closely for a long moment. Then saying nothing, he went to the bureau against the wall. He pulled out a picture frame, and brought it over to Kate.

It was a formal photograph of a seated man and woman, obviously taken in the earlier part of the century, judging by the clothes they were wearing. Three children of varying ages were seated at their feet, and the woman was holding a baby in her arms.

"My parents," said Monsieur Jumeau simply. "The baby is Nicole, and from left to right are myself, my sister Giselle, and my brother Christian."

Stephanie rose and went to look over Kate's shoulder. "It's amazing, Kate," she said softly. "There is a resemblance between you and the mother. Can you see it? She would be your great-grandmother."

Kate nodded speechlessly. "Then you think it might be true?" she finally said to Monsieur Jumeau.

"It is something that must be thought over carefully, but at this moment I can see no other explanation. It is the sort of thing that Giselle would have done: She was a courageous woman. And I thought there was something familiar about you when I first saw you. As impossible as it seems, it appears our Giselle's granddaughter has come home to us." His eyes again filling with tears, he bent down and kissed her softly on both cheeks.

CHAPTER
Ten

S*ebastian* walked into Colonel Harrington's office, reminding himself once again, as he had done repeatedly since Kate had walked out that terrible night, that he was a professional with a job; there was no room for personal feelings. Yet despite his resolution, it took more strength of will than he had to keep Kate from haunting his days and nights. He had prayed for her innocence harder than he'd prayed for anything in his life.

"Thank you for coming so quickly, Dunn. Please sit down, we have a great deal of talking to do." The colonel immediately noted Sebastian's drawn face and tired eyes, showing the strain of these last weeks, and he strongly suspected he knew the cause. It reminded him too clearly of the days after Tony Morris had been killed. For a brief moment he reconsidered his decision, but then discarded his doubts. Sebastian Dunn was the best they had for this job.

"Did you turn up anything on Russell, sir?"

"Yes, we certainly did and you were quite right. It was not easy to uncover, but there's no doubt that he is part of the Group and has been for some time."

"And Kate Soames? What is her involvement?" He steeled himself.

"That is the principal reason you're here. Tell me, Dunn,

just exactly what is your relationship with her? I understand you've spent a good deal of time in her company."

"I no longer have a relationship with her, sir. We had started one, but then her probable connection with Russell and the Group put an end to that. She put an end to it, I should say, when she realized who I was."

"Yes, I see. And how was it you made this connection with Miss Soames and the Group?"

"Primarily through an old watch she had given me to discover its provenance. I traced it directly back to Ernst von Fiedler. The night before I called you, I confronted her about it. She refused to tell me where she'd gotten it, and the link had to be obvious, with my suspicions about Russell; that, and the fact that she'd figured out that I was the second, unnamed agent in Berlin. Nobody could know about that except for the Group or this department."

"Yes, I see. As far as hard facts are concerned, I haven't been able to find anything incriminating in her background, and I combed it very thoroughly."

"Nothing?" said Sebastian, leaning forward in his chair.

"No, but I have to agree with you that her connection with Russell and the other things you've mentioned don't look very good. There's also the fact that she's spent the last two years in New York, associating with her father's friends. It's highly probable that she was recruited by Russell for her political connections. Still, up until now it's been coincidental, but your Miss Soames is not only in France, she's also in St. Mouton at the moment."

Sebastian shrugged. "St. Mouton? Yes?"

"St. Mouton just happens to be the little town in the Dordogne where von Fiedler was killed and those blasted documents disappeared. We know for certain that they were never recovered. Erharder would do anything to get his hands on them. Naturally, so would we, for as I have often said, I am quite certain that the information we would find in them would put an end to the Group. The point is that Erharder is not going to risk having them discovered now and leading us directly to him and his friends. If for some reason he has a key to where they were hidden, he is going to retrieve them. One coincidence too many for Miss Soames, don't you agree? This wine-buying trip of hers was a perfect cover if she is in St. Mouton on Erharder's behalf. Furthermore, David Russell took a flight from Kennedy to Bordeaux an hour ago." Colonel Harrington watched Sebastian's reaction carefully. There was no change in the impassive expression, but his face had drained of color.

"I see." Sebastian sat back, feeling as if he had just had the wind knocked out of him, the bile rising in his throat. He struggled for composure. David and Kate, together in St. Mouton—lovers all this time, working together with Erharder. There could no longer be any doubt about Kate's complicity. He somehow managed to speak, his words sounding oddly calm and distant to him, surely spoken by someone else. "Yes, of course; there was a photograph of a woman sandwiched between the pair cases of the watch. On the back was an inscription: St. Mouton, 1943—how stupid of me not to have made the connection! That could have been the thing she was looking for, the key to the puzzle of the missing intelligence."

"Just a minute. You said there was a photograph of a woman inside the watch that belonged to von Fiedler? This could be very important! Do you have either?"

"We have the watch, but I gave the photograph to Kate when I found it. She seemed quite excited. Then later, I told her that the watch had belonged to Ernst von Fiedler. I asked her to tell me how she had gotten it, whether David Russell had given it to her. I think that's when she put the pieces together about me. There was no mistaking her shock. Then she closed up and refused to say another word."

"I wonder. I do wonder. Perhaps the watch turned up somewhere recently. Erharder might have seen it, thought he recognized it, and given it to Kate to have its ownership confirmed. The photograph must have been of Giselle, but I can't see why—"

"You know who this woman might be, sir?"

"Oh, yes, I certainly believe so—there was a woman

from St. Mouton, Giselle Jumeau. She was an important member of the Resistance, working with MI-9."

Sebastian was surprised by the unusually heated tone of the colonel's voice and wondered what the importance of this Jumeau woman could be. But instead of continuing, the colonel stopped talking altogether and stared down at the file in front of him, his fingertips pressed hard together, his brow drawn down in heavy concentration. Finally he looked up at Sebastian, studying him as if he expected to find some kind of answer in his face, and apparently he was satisfied with what he saw, for he finally spoke.

"I'm going to tell you a story that few people know about. You will understand why this has been kept secret for so long when I have finished, and why it is so deeply personal to me. The story is bizarre but quite true, like so many other stories that came out of the war, and I think at this point you need to know everything."

"Yes, sir." Sebastian's curiosity was colored with a good deal of puzzlement.

Colonel Harrington cleared his throat and began. "Giselle Jumeau gave birth to a daughter in St. Mouton in June of 1944. It was general knowledge that Ernst von Fiedler had fathered her. Within only days the child had been orphaned, and was delivered to us in England. She died shortly thereafter. But to start in the proper place, we must go back a bit . . ."

He talked for the better part of an hour eloquently weaving a story that gripped Sebastian in its twists and turns and left him quite shaken by the time the colonel had finished. Silence filled the room, heavy with the ghosts of people long dead. Sebastian shook his head, bringing himself back to the present. "Unbelievable. The whole damned thing is unbelievable."

"But as I say, quite true. There are still so many gaps, so many things we don't know. And now you can see why they think the photograph is so important. There has to be something in it that gives them a clue to where the information is."

"I can't believe how stupid I've been," said Sebastian,

trying to keep his rage in check. "I gave it to her, just put the blasted thing right into her hands. Well, it can't be helped now. What is it you'd like me to do?"

"I'd like you to get down there immediately and discover what they're up to."

"I'd be happy to for quite a few reasons, Colonel Harrington, but I can't see how I can possibly be effective. For one, Kate no longer trusts me. She knows I suspect Russell, that I'm on to Erharder and know the association with von Fiedler. She obviously has made the connection with Berlin, and although she has no concrete proof I can think of, she knows that I work for you. She's not going to be very happy to see me."

"True, but there might be a way you can get her back into your confidence."

"I'm not sure I ever had it. Damn it, I can't work the thing out. I'd have sworn she'd finished with Russell, and I'd have sworn she didn't have a clue about me from Jamaica on."

"That's another one of those coincidences that seems too implausible. I think we'd better go through it from the beginning. You said you used her as your cover, originally when the boat was being watched by a man we now know to be Group, also her fiancé. Then you used her as cover again when you found her in the same restaurant as Erharder and the others. It was only because of a telephone call that you went up there. Suppose a meeting had been arranged. Your arrival might have given her cause to think."

"Yes, she did look very surprised to see me, I must admit; in fact, flustered would be a better word."

"And then you went to a club."

"Yes, and Kate couldn't have been more obvious about staring Erharder down . . . Yes, I see. Then she told me she'd had trouble with her fiancé, later told me that she hadn't even known he was on the island until that last night—but only after she knew I'd seen them having dinner together. What else could she say? Her assignment must have been to keep an eye on me, just in case I was trouble."

"Was she ever alone on the boat or out of sight long enough to have found the radio equipment?"

"No . . . Wait. Christ, she was, now that I think about it. She was violently seasick that first day. I put her down below with some tablets that made her sleep. I waited for the day's transmission to come through, then covered everything up and left for maybe half an hour. She was out like a light, and I had some questions I wanted to ask the other girl, Stephanie Matthison. When I came back, Kate was up and about. I didn't think anything of it at the time."

"Could she have faked the sickness to get down below?"

"No. That was real, believe me. That's what initially made me relax my guard."

"But she could have taken something to make her sick in the first place."

"Yes." Sebastian frowned. "I should have thought of that. Apparently I haven't been doing very much thinking all around, have I? We were in the middle of a tropical storm; the whole damned thing seemed so plausible."

"All right. Let's suppose that the presence of the boat and your activities caused some suspicion. Miss Soames was put on to check you out. Let's also assume that she found nothing too definite, or they would have come after you, certainly after you'd seen Erharder. What about this trip of hers to England, and bringing the watch directly to you?"

"I'm convinced that was coincidence. She was definitely surprised to see me. She ran like a frightened rabbit and wanted to have nothing more to do with me. If she'd been following me as Simon Dristoll, I can imagine just how thrown she was. I suppose she went off to find out what she should do next."

"Yes, that would make sense, and was told to discover all she could about you, develop a relationship if necessary. And then? Surely she asked you about your alias. Did you make the next contact or did she?"

"I did. I brought her the photograph. She was not very pleased to see me, but then when I told her it concerned the watch, she changed her tune. That's when she relented and agreed to have dinner. I fed her the story about the forgery and she appeared to believe me."

"With reservations?" The colonel raised an eyebrow.

"I honestly don't know, sir. I don't think so. After that we saw each other—often. Nothing odd came up that I can think of, until she got a call from her father. He and Russell are as thick as thieves, and I suppose we should be wondering about him, too, with Kate's connection as good as confirmed. He wanted Kate to know immediately that David had been given the job with Sevronsen. When I questioned her about it, she became hostile. At the time, I thought it was because she still had something for Russell."

"I see. Is there anything else?"

Sebastian sighed. "No, sir. I think I must have allayed any suspicions she had early on, because she became much more—relaxed. Then the last night, she was genuinely horrified when she realized who I was, and I think shaken out of caution, or she never would have revealed how much she knew."

"And her feelings for you?"

"I don't know. I suppose I ought to tell you that I was in love with her. Love appears to be quite a distorter of judgment. It's a good thing I haven't made a habit of it." He smiled bitterly. "As for Kate, I believed she felt the same way, but—let's just say certain things now make sense . . . Still, I suppose there's a possibility that she felt something for me, enough to keep her from turning me in, which could be why I'm still drawing breath. I can't imagine my life is worth anything at the moment if she's passed the information on to Russell or Erharder. Perhaps it wouldn't hurt to discover exactly where she stands, twist her arm a little to find out what she's up to."

"Do you think you can be objective, given the circumstances?"

"I hope so, sir; I intend to try. Let me put it this way—after this rather revealing interview, there's little love lost between Kate Soames and me. If anything, I'll be hard pushed to keep from strangling her."

The colonel smiled. "I can understand that, but I'm

trusting you to keep your head. If she is down there looking for the documents, you must get to them first. I can't stress how important that is. Use your judgment once you're there as to how to proceed, but I want you to leave immediately. Here are the files on Russell and Soames; your ticket is waiting at the Air France counter. Take the next flight."

"Yes, sir. Damn, this is a mess, and all of it my fault. She's good, Kate Soames, very good, and she played me for the fool I was. It's ironic; this time I'm the one who drew the mole directly on to myself." He laughed harshly, and when he left, a cold, hard anger had fastened itself around his heart.

"Oh, Steph, I can't believe it! It's really incredible." Kate's emotions were in shreds. The row of Jumeau headstones stretched bleakly gray across the graveyard, one of the few in France to be attached to the church. The inscriptions were already slightly worn. There Giselle, and next to her, supposedly the infant Hélène, June 11th–June 12th, 1944. And Nicole, Christian, and the parents, Marie-Claire and Michel, they were all here too, each stone engraved with the infamous date: June 14th, 1944.

"Now you know. I don't think there can be any other explanation, Kate." She looked at her friend with sympathy, having some idea of what she was suffering.

"That poor old man, what a terrible thing to have happen to him—his entire family killed like that in one round of bullets."

"And you have a new great-uncle," added Stephanie lightly, trying to ease Kate's misery. "He seemed terribly pleased and touched once he'd gotten over the shock. I think it was awfully nice of him to invite us for dinner, but I think you should go on your own, don't you? I don't really have anything to do with it, and I'd be just as happy at the hotel with a book."

"Yes, you may be right." Kate's voice was small and choked. She looked up at the church spire that stretched high above, fighting back tears. "Steph, I'm going to stay here for a while. I'll meet you back at the Périgord. We'll have another picnic, take a swim, and maybe go exploring somewhere."

Stephanie nodded her head, quietly appraising Kate's mood and deciding that it was safe to leave her. "As you like. See you soon." She walked away and Kate was left alone.

She let herself into the church, and slipped into a pew. It was cool and dark and very peaceful and she let the tears come as they would, pouring silently down her cheeks in a release of grief too profound to formulate into coherent thought. She wept for the tragedy of St. Mouton, for so many people senselessly killed at a single command from Major Erharder. And there was the horror of Colonel von Fiedler and what he had done to Giselle, and the fact that she was in part a product of that. She wept for the lies and deceptions, the dark secrets so solemnly kept and for the two mothers whose infants had been taken from them. And in the end and perhaps most of all she wept for what might have been with Sebastian, for that grief was hers alone; the time had come to probe it. She finally understood what Sebastian had told her about love given freely and for its own sake, the love it had taken her so long to admit, the love that still was there, despite what had come later. What she'd had for David paled beside this, could not even be called by the same name. It could make no difference that Sebastian had not loved her in return—although somehow she still could not truly believe that. Whatever evil he was involved in, whatever reason he had pursued her for, there was still the Sebastian she had come to know so well. Sebastian. Once again the memory of the way he had looked at her that night flashed vividly into her mind and she rocked soundlessly with pain.

But finally her tears were spent, and shaky but better, she went outside into the sunshine and drank in the warm, fresh air. She was Kate Soames and alive, the sum of many parts, and although one of those parts labeled her as the granddaughter of Ernst von Fiedler, his dark burden was not hers to carry. Nor was Sebastian's. She was strong in her recognition that it was time for her to release the past and let it rest in its rightful place.

She wandered back to the hotel, collected her key from Monsieur Barbier, and went upstairs to change, contemplating how different her life seemed since she had walked out of her room only hours before. She looked in the drawer for her bathing suit, but it wasn't there. Perplexed, she tried to think where she might have put it. She finally found it in the back of the drawer where she kept her shirts. Kate straightened up slowly and looked around her. She walked over to the desk where she kept her books and notes, and opened the drawer to make sure her passport holder and everything it contained was still there. It was, but her notes weren't in the same order she'd left them and the books had been rearranged. She checked the rest of her things. It was the same story; nothing was missing, but things were slightly out of place. Someone had taken great care to find out all about her and leave no trace, although he hadn't done a very good job. Then looking around her one last time, worry pricking at her, she locked the door, checked the handle, and went to see if Stephanie had been given the same treatment.

"I still don't understand. Who would bother to break in, go through all my things, and not take anything? And your room wasn't touched." They had driven up to Brantôme, a medieval town split by the Dronne, crowned by an abbey, full of charm and history.

"I've been thinking about that, Kate. I know this sounds a little strange, but do you think it has something to do with all the questions we've been asking? Maybe somebody's wondering what it's all about."

"That could be. You don't think it was one of the Jumeaus, do you?"

"But they wouldn't have any reason that I can think of. You were honest with them, and they seemed to believe you. No, it must have been someone you talked to on your own, when you were asking about Colonel von Fiedler."

"I think that's quite odd, really. After all, we're clearly together. Why shouldn't you appear to be just as worthy of suspicion as I am?"

"Actually, it could have happened in the time that you were at the church by yourself. I was in my room, so maybe that's why it wasn't touched."

"All I can say is that I hope whoever it was satisfied his curiosity."

"So do I," said Stephanie with feeling.

She stood outside the Jumeau house, around the corner from the camera shop but connected to it through the kitchen. The *crépisage* was gray with age, but the white shutters had been recently repainted and a tub of fresh pink geraniums brightened the door. She felt absurdly nervous, an intruder in their private world, an impostor with an unsubstantiated claim, and she had to force herself to knock.

"Welcome, Mademoiselle Kate, come in, don't stand outside like a stranger!" Pierre Jumeau opened the door to her and pulled her directly into the midst of the family who were all in a great state of excitement. The room was large but simple, dominated by an enormous oak dining table, behind which were arranged some old armchairs and a sofa that had seen better days. But the armchairs were brightened by cushions, and carefully embroidered linen squares covered the worn places on the sofa. Kate felt even more an outsider and ill at ease. But Henri Jumeau stepped forward quickly and kissed her on both her cheeks, then he stepped back and cleared his throat, preparing his speech to her.

"Mademoiselle, we have had time to talk among ourselves about these extraordinary events, and have come to the conclusion that you surely must be our beloved Giselle's granddaughter. The coincidences are too many and the explanation too likely. Therefore, we welcome you into our family. What we have is yours, and anything we can do for you we shall. And so now we drop all formality and I introduce you to your family. My wife, Nadia.'' Kate was kissed again. ''And my eldest son Giles and his wife Jeanette, and of course their son Pierre.'' More kissing and hand-shaking. ''And over here we have my younger son Marcel and his wife Trista, and their two children Jean and Marie-Joseph.''

Kate laughed as everyone talked at once, asking questions, exclaiming over the incredible circumstances that had returned Giselle's granddaughter to them. They seemed to have accepted her completely, and any doubts that Henri initially might have harbored had clearly dissipated. Kate forgot that she had ever been an outsider under the onslaught of their affectionate enthusiasm.

She was cajoled into telling her life story over dinner, and that of her mother, whose early death was a source of great sadness and disappointment to them. How they would have liked to meet the heroic Giselle's child, they exclaimed, but quickly reassured her that she would certainly do. They were intrigued and astonished by her unusual background and the places she had been, places they had only read of. And then after the meal was finished (a meal so typical of the region with vegetable soup, rich and creamy, and crusty bread, a veal roast, salad and cheeses, and an unlimited quantity of *vin de pays),* Henri asked Kate for Giselle's photograph. As it was passed carefully, reverently, from hand to hand, he clapped his hands to gather all attention to him.

''It is now time for us to tell you of your grandmother, Kate. Still people speak of her all over the area, those of us who were fortunate enough to know her, although there are not many of us left, and those who have only heard tell of her extraordinary courage. She hated the Boche, and swore from the day the war began that she would fight them in any way she could. She had her first chance when she discovered two British airmen hiding in Madame Girisse's cow barn where she did chores. With only the help of a Basque guide, she took them over the Pyrenées. That was the beginning . . ."

He talked for some time, explaining how Giselle had built up her network. "But you said she was caught and taken to Erharder, and she escaped?" said Kate, utterly fascinated. "When did that happen?"

"Ah yes," replied Henri, his eyes twinkling. "My wife must tell this part, for Nadia heard it from Giselle herself when she came from her family's village to help with the birth."

Nadia laughed. "Henri loves a romance, but in truth I cannot be sure it was so. But I shall tell you what I know. It begins when Giselle was taken to Gestapo headquarters in Paris in connection with an important escaper. I do not know the details, only that it was urgent that he leave the country. There Major Erharder interrogated her, and getting nothing, he had her sent on the next transport to Ravensbrück concentration camp. Giselle was terrified, for she had heard stories, and knew her chances of survival there were next to nothing. Imagine her surprise when the transport was stopped! She heard shooting. The Gestapo in the car ahead and the transport driver and guards were killed. And then the door to the transport was opened and a solitary man dressed all in black stood there, his face covered with dirt. 'Get out!' he said to the prisoners. 'Hurry!' he said. But he took Giselle to one side. 'Are you Marie Burrell?' he asked. That was the name Giselle used, you see. This man, Jacques was his name, was a Resistant working for S.O.E. They were involved with the English. He knew all about the important escaper and promised to help Giselle get him out of the country. He had to rescue Giselle, you understand, because only Giselle knew where the escaper was hiding. After that they worked together on and off. And then on the very day when Giselle was having her baby, he walked into St. Mouton in the broad daylight when the town was full of Gestapo and came straight to the house! I opened the door myself. He was very handsome—blond hair, blue eyes, tall, dressed as a *maquisard*—a fighting soldier of the Resistance, you understand." She giggled and looked over at her husband. "It is a good thing I was married to my Henri or I might have run off with him then and there! 'I must see Giselle immediately,' he said. 'It is of vital importance. Is she here?' I said, 'Yes, but you cannot see her, she is in labor.' He did not even reply, he just pushed past me and ran up the stairs two at a time and straight into Giselle's bedroom!"

"Goodness," said Kate with a laugh. "The message must have been important!"

"I don't know," said Nadia, shrugging. "I ran up after him, but Giselle only smiled and said he was an old friend and could stay. He did, too, helping when the baby was born. 'You poor girl,' he said as Giselle took little Hélène in her arms. 'You poor, dear girl that this should have to happen to you.' He looked so unhappy. We all were, of course, but no one wanted to say anything to Giselle about the child's origins. And then Giselle asked us to leave and he gave her the message, whatever it was. Not an hour after the birth and she was back at work! He stayed with us that night—in and out he went, but we all knew better than to ask questions. At dawn he asked to borrow our transmitter, which was buried in the basement. It was very dangerous to let him do that, but Giselle said it was that important. He left not long after. I never saw him again. After, Giselle told me the story of how they had met. She laughed a great deal over it. But you can see why I don't know whether it was a romance or only a close friendship."

"What a lovely story!" said Kate. "I do hope they were in love. It would be nice to think that she had some happiness in the middle of all the other terrible things."

"Yes," said Nadia with a sigh. "It was the last time I saw Giselle, too, for I had to go back to my children in my family's village."

"And thank the good Lord for that," said Henri, "or I would have come home to nothing. But this is not a night for sadness, it is a time for celebration!" And he launched back into tales of the Resistance as everyone began to talk at the same time, arguing over details of who had said what, and when, exactly, such and such a thing had happened.

Her head filled with stories, her heart with affection for this simple and amazing newfound part of her family, Kate took her leave with many thanks and walked back toward the square, their return invitations ringing in her ears. The moon was waning in its last quarter, and the light was dim, but Kate didn't have far to go. She walked slowly, savoring the evening, turning the events over in her mind and smiling at the many poignant moments, the easy laughter, the closeness of the Jumeau family. She was just approaching the square when the sound of a car traveling very fast toward her made her turn in alarm. She had no time to think. The headlights flashed up and pinned her in their glare. They didn't waver for an instance, came straight at her and she jumped frantically to the side, tripping and falling to the sidewalk as the roar of the car went past her. It turned abruptly, sharply, as it approached the square and its tires squealed around the corner, the black body swallowed up into the black night.

For a moment Kate could not move at all—she felt frozen. But after a few seconds that seemed an eternity, she was able to pull herself up to a sitting position and she huddled there taking stock of herself. Her knees were grazed and her elbow bruised and bloodied, but aside from that and a tear in her dress, she seemed to be all right, just badly shaken. She listened with all her nerves on edge for the sound of the car returning, but finally, realizing that she could not stay there all night, and convincing herself that the driver must have been drunk and not deliberately trying to kill her, she cautiously made her way back to the hotel. As she passed the plaque she paused, and she reached her hand out and touched the cool surface with her fingertips as if she could somehow summon up the lives beneath the names, names that had taken on all too much significance. And then she sighed and dropped her hand, and crossed the square.

Stephanie had left a note at the desk, saying that she'd decided to take the car and return to the little restaurant they'd so enjoyed. She probably wouldn't be back until late. Kate gave a little smile, remembering the attractive and attentive son and wondered when she would next see Stephanie.

She suddenly felt very much alone and, more shaken than she cared to admit, she stiffly climbed the stairs to her room. Her hand, infuriatingly shaky, fumbled with the key. She finally managed to turn the lock, and closed the door behind her, groping for the light. As it snapped on, a tall figure stepped from the shadows of the window.

"Hello, Kate."

CHAPTER
Eleven

Kate smothered a scream and backed up against the door, her eyes wide with terror, a cold sweat washing over her.

"What's the matter, Kate, were you expecting someone else? David, perhaps?" Sebastian folded his arms and leaned against the wall, regarding her cynically, a Beretta gripped in his right hand.

"You bastard!" she finally managed to whisper above the painful hammering of her heart. "What do you want from me? Get out—get out of here now!" Her hand reached behind for the door handle, searching frantically to find it.

Sebastian was at her side in a moment, moving her away from the door and taking the key easily from her clenched fist. "What's your hurry? I'm not going anywhere and neither are you until you and I have had a little talk." He locked the door and pocketed the key, and picking up her dropped purse, he looked quickly through it for a weapon. "Well, well, empty," he said sardonically. "Imagine that. Now why don't you sit down." He gestured with the gun toward the bed.

"I—" Kate tried to think, to make sense out of what Sebastian was doing. It must have been Sebastian who'd tried to run her over, and his attempt failing, he was going to shoot her—but why? She forced the words out of her dry throat. "Please, Sebastian, don't do this. Just go!"

"What are you so afraid of, Kate? Are you worried I might hurt you? I won't touch a hair on your head if you tell me what I want to know. Why don't we start with what you're doing in St. Mouton." He forcibly sat her down on the bed, although her body was too weak from shock to protest, and pulled up a chair opposite, the gun still pointing at her. "Well?"

His face was not that of Sebastian, the man she'd loved, had cried for so bitterly that very morning. This was a stranger, someone she'd never seen before, someone stony and desperately threatening, his eyes as blue and cold as ice. It somehow made it easier to spit her words at him. "It's none of your business what I do or where, Sebastian. I thought I'd made that perfectly clear. I don't want anything more to do with you."

"That's too bad, because I haven't finished with you by a long shot. You have a lot of explaining to do from the moment you first placed that slender little foot of yours aboard my boat."

"I don't know what you're talking about!"

"Don't you? Give it up, Kate, your blood is out. I know all about your involvement here."

"How could you know about that..." She looked as though she'd been slapped.

"I assume that's an admission of sorts? The light finally dawned, although it took me long enough. You must have thought you were being very clever giving me von Fiedler's watch, letting me find the photograph for you. In fact you did a brilliant job altogether of leading me down the garden path, but it's finished, my dear. You finally gave yourself away."

Sebastian's eyes, needle-sharp, bore into her. She felt as if she were suffocating in her fright and confusion, her mind refusing to work with any semblance of clarity. "Sebastian, I don't understand—I, if you know about my connection with von Fiedler, then why are you interrogating me like this? Oh, God, what do you want from me!"

"You're a bright girl, Kate; you know exactly what I'm after. I must say, you play a good game, right up there with the best of them. I should congratulate you. You had me right where you wanted me and that's not so easy to forgive. No man likes being made a fool of." His voice was brittle.

"It's not I who plays games, Sebastian! I don't know what sort of hideous scheme you're involved in, but don't you presume to drag me into it! You've got something very wrong and I can't even begin to imagine what it is, but believe me, I don't want any part of it. Why don't you just tell me what it is you want from me instead of speaking in riddles and then leave me alone. It obviously has something to do with von Fiedler, although I can't imagine that my blood, as you call it, is worth killing me for."

"I have no intention of killing you, believe me, although I'm sorely tempted to throttle you and will if you tempt me any further, Kate."

"Then I suppose when you tried to run me down it was just a scare tactic?"

"Come now, Kate. I attempted to run you down, did I? And when was this?" He leaned back in the chair, sarcasm heavy in his face.

"Just now, as you know perfectly well! Stop toying with me, Sebastian. You've already frightened me half out of my mind, and having a gun pointing in my face doesn't help." Her voice caught on a sob.

Sebastian for the first time took in her grazed knees and elbow and the tear in her dress. He looked at her face again, hard. "All right then, my proficient little liar, why don't you tell me exactly what happened?"

"Oh, are you trying to tell me there's somebody else trying to kill me? Lucky me, two men chasing me at once." She tried to look defiant but the attempt failed miserably.

Sebastian hesitated, wondering if the Group had turned on her and were out to eliminate her. It had certainly been known to happen, and it could have something to do with her association with him. At this very moment she looked so much like a frightened child, it was almost impossible to believe she was a hardened agent. "Kate, I'm not prepared to trust you for an instant, but I did not attempt to run you down; however it certainly looks as if someone did, so if you value your neck, tell me what happened!"

"I don't know why I should believe anything you say, but right now I'm so scared I'll tell you anything to get you out of here." She ran a trembling hand through her disheveled hair and in halting tones described the incident.

When she had finished Sebastian was silent, assessing what she had told him. His eyes raked her face looking for some sign of dissemblance, doing his best to remain professionally detached, but he could find nothing in her haunted expression save naked fear. "Kate, I want you to start at the very beginning of the story, from the day you met David and how you got involved, to the moment you walked in here tonight. Leave nothing out, and tell no lies, because I can verify every part of your story."

"Why should I, damn you? You dog me halfway around the world, lie to me, use me, play with my feelings, then you come in here waving that gun of yours and accuse me of God knows what—and now you expect me to drop into the palm of your hand just because you claim *not* to have attempted to kill me? I think you're out of your mind!"

"Listen, you silly girl, you've involved yourself in a very dangerous thing, and obviously you've put a foot wrong somewhere if someone's trying to run you down. You could be in a great deal of trouble, and unfortunately, I am the only one around here who might be able to bail you out. So as you can see, it's to your advantage to cooperate with me."

"Oh, I see, now it's Sebastian, the hero, the knight in shining armor. Just who in hell do you think you are?"

"British Intelligence, as you well know. Now talk."

Kate stared at him. "You're *what*?" The room seemed to tip over and she fell with it, thinking inconsequentially of how Alice must have felt going down the rabbit hole. The words echoed inside her head and she felt stupid for not being able to understand them. British Intelligence? Not the enemy? She suddenly realized how ridiculous she must appear, how ridiculous the entire situation was. "Oh, dear lord." She covered her face with her hands, trying to work out where the confusion had started, and then after a long moment muffled laughter escaped from between her fingers. She finally looked up at him. "You mean you're not Sebastian, the terrorist?" she gasped. "And, and you thought *I* was the villain of the piece? Oh, Sebastian, I don't believe it! And put that ridiculous gun away." She fell onto her side, laughing uncontrollably.

A treacherous flicker of doubt ran through him that he quickly stifled. This hysteria was the last reaction he'd expected. He looked for the trick in it, but as Kate's laughter turned into sobs, he moved to the bed and pulled her up, holding her with one hand against his chest until she had quieted. The Beretta stayed at the ready in the other.

"Better now," she said after a few minutes, taking the handkerchief he offered. "Oh, Sebastian, how did we get into such a mess? I—I thought you were one of them, a Fascist, or something. You had me so scared!"

"*Me* a Fascist? My God, Kate, you can't be serious? Where did you come up with that idea?" He was utterly confused.

"It all made sense, you see."

"Kate, for the love of God I don't know why I'm doing this, but I'm going to give you a chance. Why don't you explain it to me. What are you doing in St. Mouton, and what is your connection with von Fiedler and the Group?"

"What group?" She raised puzzled eyes to him. "I thought you knew. Ernst von Fiedler was my grandfather."

"*What* did you say!" It was his turn to stare. "Kate—" Sebastian's mind raced, putting the puzzle together. The infant who had been smuggled to England supposedly had died—but was it possible, just possible that there had been some mistake? Kate would be the right age for a grandchild, he quickly calculated, and how else would she know the story—unless Erharder had somehow discovered the deception and was now masquerading Kate in the role. He tempered his elation with caution. "What would make you think such a thing?"

Kate launched into the story, her words tumbling over each other, finishing up with her dinner with the Jumeaus. "And the car tried to run me down, and here you were with a gun. Of course I thought you were a Facist, or terrorist or something, especially after the way you behaved in London about the watch, and David and Tony and everything else. You were extremely sinister. How was I to know you worked for British Intelligence?"

Sebastian walked over to the window, one last question burning in his mind. "And how did you know about Tony and what happened in Berlin?"

"Lucy told me. How else?"

"Lucy! Oh, sweet Christ, of course she would—but surely not the truth? How did you know about that?"

"I don't know the truth. I just surmised from everything that night that you hadn't told the full story about it, like everything else—and by that time you were sounding very much the enemy agent, and then you jumped all over me when I mentioned it. I—I thought you'd killed him, you see."

He stared at her. "You thought I—Christ, never mind. I can see we were both thinking at cross purposes." He ran a hand through his hair, still balancing on a knife's edge and praying for her to prove herself. "Kate, do you have the photograph?"

"Yes, right here." She pulled it from her bag and gave it to him, and he breathed a silent thanks. "But Sebastian, I still don't understand what all of this is about. Why are you skulking around playing James Bond and frightening harmless women to death? And I wish you'd put that gun away!"

He looked at her again, then opened his jacket and slipped the Beretta into the holster strapped under his arm. "It's a long story but I'll make it short. Years ago, not all that long after the war, a Fascist group was formed in Germany, very secretly. It was headed by Karl Erharder of St. Mouton fame. Over the years they've been up to a lot of skulduggery, terrorist operations, that sort of thing, but more important, they have been very successful in infiltrating various governments. They recruit bright young men of impeccable backgrounds, who place themselves in a position of trust with important government officials, and not only pass on highly classified information but also eventually eliminate the official in question and take his place, having made themselves invaluable."

"David?" asked Kate, her voice almost inaudible.

"Exactly, using your father as his dupe, and you as bait."

"Oh, Sebastian! That's why you were following him and asking all those questions?"

"That's why."

"But what did I do to make you come in here looking like murder itself?"

"I'll explain all that later. It started with Jamaica and your connection with David, and finished this afternoon when I learned you were in St. Mouton, and David was on his way."

"What! I can't believe it!" Her face blanched even whiter.

"Believe it."

"Here to St. Mouton? But why?"

"Some very important documents were hidden during the war that could destroy the Group as it is today. Somehow David knows you're here asking questions and probably thinks you accidentally stumbled across something through him. In any case, I suspect because of your past relationship he's been sent to find out what you're up to. If, that is, your story is true and you're not working with them."

"Sebastian, how can you doubt me?" Kate looked at him helplessly, not knowing what more she could say to convince him of her innocence.

"Either you're the greatest Mata Hari that ever lived, or you've managed to get yourself entangled in the middle of a highly dangerous situation. God help me, but I'm inclined to think the latter. But there's one thing I must do, Kate, before I go any further."

"What's that?"

"I have to verify your story."

"But how?" She was puzzled.

"The only way I can think of with any speed. I'm going to ring Elizabeth."

"It's far too late at night, Sebastian!"

"Are you hedging, Kate?" he asked coolly, once again assessing.

"No, of course not, I want you to believe me." Her eyes pleaded with him.

"Then give me the number."

They walked together down to the telephone booth. "If David should be here and watching, or be foolish enough to expose himself, I'm good old Simon, and we're here together on a little holiday. That's all you need for now. We'll come up with something more interesting later." He listened to the phone ringing on the other end. "Hello, Miss Forrest? Sebastian Dunn. I'm sorry to be calling you at such a late hour, but I'm afraid it's terribly important and can't wait. I'm in St. Mouton with Kate. She's gotten herself into a little difficulty, nothing we can't work out, but I need you to confirm what she's told me."

"It's extremely late and this sounds very strange, Mr. Dunn. Just what is it you need to know?" Elizabeth's voice was chilly but edged with fear.

"Could you please tell me exactly what happened in late June of 1944 at your house in Henley?"

The wire went silent and Sebastian held his breath, praying that Kate had told the truth. Then it came singing alive again. "I don't know that I can do that without Kate's permission."

"She's standing right here. I'll put her on." He turned to Kate. "She wants your permission. Give her just that, nothing more.

Kate nodded her understanding and took the receiver. "Elizabeth? I'm fine, really I am. It's all right, tell him *everything* he wants to know. I can't explain now, but don't worry." She gave the telephone back to Sebastian who then closed the door of the booth.

"Miss Forrest?"

"I must say I think this is quite peculiar and I don't like it. The last I heard from Kate the two of you were on the outs with each other. Now you're down there talking of trouble. For all I know that trouble is you, Mr. Dunn."

"Would it help at all if I told you that I'm with British Intelligence and that I'm trying to protect Kate?"

"Good lord! What on earth is going on!" Elizabeth's horror transmitted itself very clearly over all the miles between Henley and St. Mouton.

"I'm afraid I can't tell you that just now, Miss Forrest; I'm sure you understand. However, I do very much need that information I asked for, directly from you."

"Oh yes, yes of course." Elizabeth pulled herself together and recited the story clearly and concisely, ending with why she'd given the watch to Kate. "Now what's all this about, and what sort of difficulty is Kate in?"

"Miss Forrest, I really can't tell you, at least not just yet, I'm sorry. I can't thank you enough for your cooperation. You've made all the difference in the world. Try not to worry, and Kate will be in touch with you soon."

"Wait—tell her that her father called last night and wanted her address. She can probably expect to hear from him. She wanted to know."

"Yes, I'll tell her," said Sebastian, frowning.

"And please, look after her, won't you, Sebastian?"

"I promise. Good-bye, Miss Forrest." He put the receiver down and stepped out of the booth, taking a deep breath.

"Am I cleared?" said Kate anxiously.

"Come with me," said Sebastian.

He led her back to the hotel and into her room, shutting the door and once again locking it behind him. He took off his jacket and undid the shoulder holster, placing it on the dresser, but the Beretta he put on the bedside table, along with the photograph. Kate watched him with worry, wondering whether Elizabeth had said the right things, or enough things, to convince him.

Then he walked over to her and took her by the shoulders. "Kate Soames, you have led me a merry dance indeed, and given me more trouble than any man has a reason to expect. And you're absolutely right, I must be out of my mind." He bent his head down toward hers and covered her lips with his own, kissing her with a hunger and relief and love too intense to be expressed in words, but perfectly conveyed to her.

"Oh, Sebastian," cried Kate when he had finally released her. "I thought I'd been so wrong about you, that I'd lost you forever, and there were these terrible nightmares when you chased me and turned into that awful fish—"

"Wait, slow down, Kate. I strongly object to being turned into a fish, even in your dreams. I was none too happy myself, my love, but I did one worse that you; I turned you in to MI-6."

"You did what! Sebastian, how could you!"

"Fascinating things I learned; what an interesting little girl you were—no, don't glare at me like that, Kate, you came up quite clean. I had to, you see; there was too much riding against you. In the end the only thing I could get you on was circumstantial evidence, but there was plenty of that. Why the hell didn't you just tell me about von Fiedler's watch when I asked? It would have saved us both a lot of misery."

"I couldn't. I'd promised Elizabeth that I'd only tell Stephanie."

"Oh, Kate, sweet Kate. There's so much we need to talk about, but I'm afraid it's going to have to wait. There is something much, much more important that I have to do." He unceremoniously started removing her clothes, dropping them piece by piece, and then did the same with his, and scooped her into his arms and fell with her onto the bed, kissing every inch of skin immediately available to him. They were caught up in laughter and teasing, a lightheartedness that came with deliverance from their fears of each other, filled with the simple joy of being back in each other's arms. But then Sebastian's face grew serious and he took her face into his hands, stilling her. His eyes burned into hers and very slowly he lowered his mouth, possessing her lips with his own, opening her with his tongue in a prelude of what was to come.

She melted into him, her body suddenly on fire, her heart threatening to burst from her chest, its wild beating matching his own. His hands were everywhere, stroking, kneading, memorizing the feel of her under his fingertips, on her breasts, up her thighs and between her legs, his mouth hot on her flesh. And Kate, too, ran her hands over his body, the skin smooth over hard, delineated planes, and where her mouth touched, his own particular taste, strong, salty, and male. She was lost in heightened sensation, making up for all the time of being without him. And then when neither of them could wait any longer, he buried himself inside her as if thrusting his very soul into her, their hearts and minds joining in the physical union until there was no separation and they came together in a shattering climax.

Kate finally opened her eyes, and her breath caught as she took in Sebastian's naked expression, his eyes studying her face. "Sebastian? Sebastian, what is it?"

He took her hand and kissed it. "I'm sorry if it sends you into a blind panic, sweetheart, but I'm afraid I have to say this, despite my vow of silence."

She looked at him cautiously. "What vow of silence?"

"I swore I wouldn't speak until you were ready to listen, and I can only hope you're ready now because it won't wait. I love you, Kate—and when I thought I'd been wrong about you, it nearly killed me."

Kate thought her heart would break. "Oh, Sebastian—forgive me, I've been such a fool! I know how much I've hurt you, and I could kill myself for it. I was just so frightened, and too stupid to see things for what they were. If anything, I was terrified of how I felt about you. I don't think I really knew until I'd lost you."

"And how do you feel, Kate?" he asked softly.

"You know how I feel. And the hell of it is that you've known all along."

"No more doubts?"

"No more doubts. I've been so unhappy," she said simply.

He pulled her close with a deep sigh of relief. And then, very quietly, he began to speak to her of things he had held in for far too long.

Later, after they had talked at length, Kate asked,

"Sebastian? How did you get mixed up with British Intelligence? It's what you were really doing in Jamaica, wasn't it?"

"Yes. I was on Erharder's trail, and I found him. Do you remember Mr. Schumann to whom you took such a great disliking?"

"Oh, Sebastian, was that him? No wonder he gave me the shivers."

"It was, and you were a very helpful cover indeed. I'd been working on finding him for years."

"How did you get involved in the first place?"

"Tony and I were recruited at Cambridge. Don't look so surprised, it's not that uncommon," he said with a little laugh. "I was just coming out of the disaster with Anne, and was feeling particularly disillusioned with the world, ripe for recruitment. I was responsible for getting Tony involved. I'll never forgive myself for that." His eyes darkened.

"What happened, Sebastian?" asked Kate softly.

He looked over at her, then up at the ceiling, his eyes haunted with memory. He could still see it as vividly as the day it had happened, feel the bitter cold of the bleak winter day, see the cathedral where he stood, watching Tony cross the street to his death. He heard the whine of the bullets, saw Tony jerk back and fall, his chest spreading red with blood as he ran to him, heedless of his own safety. But it was too late, too late for Tony, too late to do anything about the men who apparently had vanished into thin air. A shudder ran through him and he felt Kate's warm hand on his face, pulling him back from his private hell.

"Sebastian? Please, I'm sorry, I shouldn't have reminded you."

"No, my love, it's all right, I want to tell you. It's strange, even after all these years it's still a raw place." His face was stark as he stroked her hair. "Our special department had always been centered on tracking down the Group and their activities. We were getting close, very close indeed. One day a call came in with a possible sighting of Erharder in West Berlin. We assumed our cover identities and went. What we didn't know was that there was a mole in our department. He didn't know our physical descriptions, but he had access to our covers, our movements using those covers, and our information. It all went straight to Erharder. Tony and I followed him and another man, Anton Schwab, to a café. Schwab was the blond man with Erharder in Jamaica. Anyway, we marked them from across the street and Tony moved in to take a photograph. I was supposed to provide diversion if anything went wrong, but we had no reason to believe it would. Naturally, since they had lured us in, they were quite ready for anything that looked suspicious. Schwab riddled him with bullets and they were gone. There was nothing I could do for Tony but pull him away where he could die in peace without the benefit of a crowd."

"Oh, Sebastian, I'm so sorry. But what about you—why didn't they go after you?"

"Believe me, they tried. But as I later discovered, they never saw my face, and didn't have my actual identity, so there was nothing they could do. I left the Department, having lost my taste for espionage. There was little they could use me for after that, anyway; as far as anyone knew I had been marked. A marked man is as good as dead and can only endanger others. The mole was eventually uncovered, and as a result of that and the Berlin fiasco the Group went farther underground and we lost all track of them."

"But then why were you in Jamaica, if you had left the Department?"

"They had a strong lead that Erharder would be there holding some sort of meeting, and there was no one else who could positively identify him. So I went. That night up at Joe's was when I finally found out that my face was in the clear."

"So that's why you were wearing the gun."

"That's right. Fortunately, I didn't have to use it."

"Sebastian! You might have been killed!"

"I might have been. But I wasn't. I did my job, then I went home. Enter Kate. And here we are."

"Yes . . . Here we are. I'm sorry, Sebastian. This is all my fault."

"Not at all. As I said, it would have helped if you had told me the truth when I asked, but you had no way of knowing that. My God, you did put things together upside down, though! I can't take kindly to being thought a terrorist, Kate," he said with a smile.

"I know. I'm sorry about that, too. But if it helps at all, I've loved you from the beginning."

"It helps. Believe me, it helps. But Kate, there's something else I have to tell you, something that directly concerns you. It's something that I've always known, but only a handful of other people have, and it should make you very happy. Ernst von Fiedler was no Nazi. He was a deep-cover agent for Britain."

CHAPTER
Twelve

Stephanie parked the Peugeot outside the little restaurant and went inside. She was greeted kindly by monsieur and madame, but the son was nowhere in sight, and she shortly learned that it was his evening off and he had taken his sister to a fete. With a little sigh at her misfortune, she decided to make the best of the evening and ordered the set menu. But her luck seemed to be holding after all, because not five minutes later, a dark-haired, attractive man close to her own age walked in the door, very much on his own, and it immediately became clear that he was an American.

His French was less than adequate and he struggled valiantly to make himself understood to madame. "Pardon, madame. Ah, *parlez-vous Anglais*, American? No? Oh, hell." He lifted his hand to his mouth and pretended to drink. "*Vin?*" he asked hopefully. "*Et*, some *manger*," and rubbed his stomach. Madame caught Stephanie's eye and smiled broadly.

"*Je ne comprends pas*, monsieur. *Qu'est-ce que vous voulez?*" she shot back.

"*Je um . . .*" He looked thoroughly lost and desperate and both Stephanie and madame burst into laughter.

Stephanie decided to put him out of his misery and

appeared at his elbow. "D'you think I might be able to help?" she said, still laughing. "I hope you won't be offended, but even I couldn't understand a word you said!"

"To the contrary, I would be everlastingly grateful. I was trying to get a glass of wine and something to eat."

"And here I was thinking you were having a good scratch." Her eyes danced. "Your problem is easy enough to solve. There's only one menu, and tonight it's soup, steak, fried potatoes, salad, and cheese. And you get a half liter of wine with your meal so that takes care of everything, all for forty francs."

"It sounds perfect." He grinned in relief as she ordered for him. "Ah, I was wondering, if you're eating alone, may I join you?" His deep brown eyes looked pleadingly into hers.

"That would be nice! I'm Stephanie." She led him to her table.

"And I'm David, a very hungry American who was beginning to think he'd starve in this country." He pulled out her chair for her.

"Thank you. How long have you been here?"

"Long enough to miss two meals, although a nice touch of jet lag makes me unsure which two they were supposed to have been. I thought since it was dark, I might as well make this dinner."

"A very wise decision. Are you on holiday?"

"Yes, although it didn't occur to me that I'd need the language to enjoy myself. I guess I'm one of those disgusting Americans who assumes everybody speaks English."

"Not down here in the very little towns like this one. In fact when they learn you're American, they're just as likely to throw their arms around you as if it's still the liberation. Time has stood still in this part of the world."

"That sounds great! None of the fighting, all of the glory. But don't quite a few Americans come through here? I can't believe our reputations haven't preceded us."

"There are quite a few British who travel in the area, and a good many more who have settled here, but Americans seem few and far between. Actually the friend I'm with is

American, but then her French is so good that she'd have to announce her nationality to have it known."

"So nobody has grabbed her yet and kissed her as a liberating soldier?"

"Heaven forbid! They'd find themselves knocked down and tied up in a matter of seconds." Stephanie laughed at the picture it conjured up.

"I see. Your friend sounds a little unsettling."

"She's just not in a kissing frame of mind at the moment."

"What a pity for her. Why's that?" His eyes flickered with interest.

Stephanie shrugged. "She's recovering from a broken heart."

"Really? How very dramatic, but I'll bet it's not a lot of fun for you. You should have gone somewhere like Cannes."

"Not at all. I detest Cannes."

"But why would a single, attractive girl like yourself choose such a remote part of the world as this to take a vacation in?"

"And why would a single, attractive man like yourself choose such a remote part of the world to take a vacation in? Assuming you're single."

"Unfortunately, I am. But I came to look up an old friend, and see a part of the world I'd never visited. Now your reason."

Madame put the steaming tureen of soup on the table and Stephanie ladled it out into two wide bowls. "My friend wanted to do some digging around in her family tree, and I came along to accompany her. Would you desert someone with a broken heart?" She handed him a bowl.

"Certainly not." He took a sip. "This is delicious soup! What is it?"

"All sorts of puréed vegetables, primarily carrot and potatoes today, I would think. Whatever's around goes into the soup pot."

"Fabulous stuff. So your friend's half American and half French?" He looked puzzled.

"Oh, no, it's a distant French connection, but it's a

diverting pastime for a holiday—in between eating and baking in the sun."

"How do you dig up a family tree in this part of the world?" He watched her face intently.

"Just as you would anywhere else, if you have the language. You ask around, look up old records, that sort of thing. Of course, over here, with so many people killed during the war, a lot of the links are lost. Have you ever tried to trace a remote branch of your family?"

"No, I can't say that I have."

"I understood it was a big American craze, genealogy. Personally, I think it comes from being such a young country. You all have inferiority complexes. You wouldn't believe how many Americans want to acquire a family crest," she teased.

"And all you British stand around on your family crests becoming more inbred by the generation, and waffling away about tradition while the mind becomes progressively more stale."

Stephanie burst into laughter. "I think you're still throwing tea into the Boston harbor!"

"And it's exactly where it belongs."

The steaks arrived, each on its own platter, gently sizzling and nestled in rich juices. A separate plate of golden *pommes frîtes* was placed down and all conversation halted while they ate with total dedication to the excellence of madame's cooking. A light salad of lettuce and tomatoes dressed with walnut oil followed, and finally the cheeses, laid out on a basket woven of grapevines.

"That has to be the best meal I've eaten in years," he said, offering her a cigarette and lighting it, then taking one for himself. "It's a pity your poor friend wasn't here to enjoy it—or is she crying herself to sleep?"

"Oh, no. She met some very pleasant people who invited her to dinner. I thought I'd pass. I enjoy doing things on my own."

"Good for you. I do too, but I'm afraid I've made things a little difficult on myself this trip. You should hear my Spanish, though. Fabulous."

"Poor old thing, you should have kept going south a few hundred miles. Still, it shouldn't really be that difficult for you. You need to pick up a good dictionary or phrase book, and you'll be able to find one of those in Périgueux, I'm sure. Then, with a guide book, you can go and see some of those places I was telling you about."

"You do make it sound easy. I'm sure I'll do fine."

"I'm sure you will. It's been lovely meeting you, but I'm afraid I'm going to have to leave you to your own devices and get home. You are staying here, aren't you?"

"Yes, I checked into a little pension. That was easy enough, I just handed over some money and received a key. Thanks, Stephanie, I've really enjoyed the evening, and the company."

"So have I." They walked outside together and Stephanie got into the Peugeot. "Good night, David, I hope you enjoy your holiday."

"Good night." He watched her drive off, then walked to his car, parked a block away.

Sebastian smiled as Kate abruptly sat up in bed and stared at him in complete disbelief.

"Von Fiedler was a British agent! *Not* a Nazi? How is that possible? Are you sure?"

"Quite sure. Jock Harrington, the man I work for, and Ernst von Fiedler had been close friends for years. They'd been at Cambridge together, and when Ernst began to express his disquiet at the direction Hitler was taking Germany, Harrington persuaded Ernst to join the SS as an Intelligence agent for Britain. That was back in 1936, and he was convinced that war was inevitable and they would need all the inside help they could get. Ernst quickly became one of Himmler's golden boys, and was set up in the SD, Counter-intelligence, supposedly turning captured Allied agents for Germany. He played a very tricky double game."

"I can't believe it! But how does Giselle come into the

story? If this is true then surely he couldn't have raped her?''

''That's where it becomes even more interesting. But are you sure you wouldn't rather wait and hear it in the morning? It's late and you must be exhausted.''

''I couldn't sleep if my life depended on it!'' She hugged her knees to her chest. ''Please, Sebastian, if you don't mind?''

''Of course not. How can I resist when you look at me that way? But just give me a moment to pull my thoughts together.'' He swung his legs over the side of the bed and wrapping a towel around his waist, he crossed over to the sink to splash some water on his face.

''Okay,'' he said, wiping his face dry with a hand towel and tossing it on the chair. ''To begin with, this is a story I only just heard myself this morning, so you'll have to be patient. But I'll tell you everything I know, and maybe we'll be able to put some of the missing pieces together. Now Giselle, as you know, ran an escape line. It was code-named the Swallow line, and was highly successful, unlike most of them which were usually broken in a matter of months. The Swallow line had been in operation for three years. Despite how careful Giselle was, it was inevitable that her luck would run out.''

''This is when she was first arrested, then?''

''Yes. It was 1943. She was meant to be taking out a certain Captain Stade of the Abwehr, also a double agent, who had been compromised, but she was seen sitting next to him in a Paris park. In fact, she was passing him the key to a safe house taped inside a newspaper. Stade escaped, but Giselle was taken into Gestapo headquarters. Erharder was her interrogator.'' Sebastian sat down on the edge of the bed. ''It was said that he gave the word Gestapo new meaning. But he had nothing concrete on her, and she wouldn't talk, so he sent her to Ravensbrück concentration camp. I suppose he thought that would break her if nothing else would.''

''But then she was rescued by a man named Jacques. He was a Resistant the Jumeaus told me about.''

"Exactly," said Sebastian with a smile. "You already seem to know a good deal of this story."

"Yes, but only about Giselle. What about von Fiedler?"

"I'm getting there. Jacques was well known to Special Operations. He knew how important it was for Max Stade to be taken out immediately. He and Giselle managed to get him on a Lysander flying out at night from a little clearing much farther north. Jacques sent with him some very important information of his own. Then they stayed the rest of the night in the attic of a little farmhouse Giselle knew to be safe. I suppose that is where it all began."

"Then they *were* lovers!" said Kate with delight. "The Jumeaus were not sure on that point."

"Oh yes, they were lovers. They met as often as possible throughout the summer and autumn, which wasn't as often as they might have liked, given that they were both heavily involved in their work."

"But Sebastian, *what* about von Fiedler?"

"My God, you're impatient. I'm just coming to that. It's important you know that as a result of this relationship between Giselle and Jacques, Giselle became pregnant. I imagine they must both have been very upset, given the circumstances they were in. But much worse was to come. Giselle was taken in again. This time she'd been in a train station, sending an escaper up the next leg of the line. The Gestapo showed up and checked all the identity cards. They recognized the name on hers, Marie Burrell, as the girl Erharder had been seeking for months. Back to Erharder she went, and this time he was not prepared to let her get away. He used torture."

Kate shuddered, thinking of Giselle's scarred chest.

"Erharder did not take it well when his superior from the SD interrupted him. There was no love lost between Colonel von Fiedler and Major Erharder. Von Fiedler insisted on taking over the interrogation on the basis that Giselle had possibly been connected with Max Stade's escape, which was his department. He then managed to 'prove' in front of Erharder that Giselle could not possibly have been involved. He let her go, to Erharder's fury. Because as you might have guessed, Erharder had developed an obsession about Giselle, or Marie Burrell as he knew her. Before he started the torture, he had apparently offered her an arrangement—sexual favors in exchange for leniency."

"I don't believe it! God, how twisted!"

"Oh, he is indeed twisted. I believe when she refused he was particularly brutal in the sort of torture he used. In any case, Colonel von Fiedler saw that Giselle was released."

"I suppose he knew how important she was to the Resistance."

"He most certainly did. He was confident that Erharder would not immediately bring her in again as there was no correct information on her, where she lived, any of it, but he knew that Erharder would immediately start to hunt her down."

"So Colonel von Fiedler, knowing her to be Giselle Jumeau, discovered where she really lived and went to her house to warn her?"

"He certainly went to her house, although he knew the address quite well. He had been there often."

"*What*?" said Kate in confusion.

Sebastian laughed. "Haven't you guessed, Kate? You know him to be your grandfather, after all."

Kate stared at him. "Surely not—Jacques?"

"The very same. I cannot imagine what Giselle's reaction could have been when Jacques walked into the interrogation room, dressed as a colonel in the SD and known to Erharder as Ernst von Fiedler. But she was clever enough not to give anything away. Ernst really put himself on the line over that one."

"Dear God," said Kate, slumping back against the pillows. "I can't believe this. I just can't believe it."

"I do understand. I had a hard time believing it myself. But it's true, every word of it. Jacques was well known in the Resistance and considered slightly mysterious for he operated completely on his own. He reported directly to Colonel Harrington. In this way, Ernst managed to be sure his friend Jock knew the full story of what happened between himself and Giselle."

"He must have had nerves of steel!"

"I would imagine so. But then he believed very deeply in his cause. Falling in love with Giselle was a complication he hadn't counted on. Now that she knew who he really was, he obviously had to explain the circumstances to her. So, as Jacques, he went straight after her. But now there were big problems to be dealt with. First there was the problem of Erharder and his troublesome obsession. Ernst tried to persuade Giselle to use her own escape line to go to England. She refused, insisting that she could not leave her work. So they compromised, and Giselle agreed to go home to St. Mouton. Then there was the problem of the baby. Ernst insisted that Giselle put the story out that he had released her only to rape her. It would protect his cover as the filthy Nazi he was supposed to be, but more important, the child's parentage would not be questioned. The truth could come out after the war. He also made Giselle promise that when the baby was born, she would send the child up the escape line to England until after it was all over. And there was a third problem. Do you remember the documents concerning the Group I mentioned that had been hidden during the war?"

"Yes, of course."

"Good, because this is crucial. The fact that two identical sets of those documents existed was the very important information that Max Stade carried with him when he was smuggled out."

"But what was in them that was so important?"

"Erharder apparently was not very confident that the Third Reich would outlast the war. He had made contingency plans for his own personal Reich, and had arranged escape routes, new identities for himself and his friends. If we had had access to that information back then, we would have been able to prevent the development of the Group. But since the Group is still functioning today, the information remains extremely vital. But to get back to the story, Ernst was charged by Colonel Harrington with finding one of the sets, not such an easy task. In the end he managed to steal them and reported that he was sure that Erharder would not suspect him to be the thief or the real reason the papers had been stolen. We don't know the details. But however he did it, it was at great cost."

Kate sighed. "We're getting close to the end, aren't we?"

"Yes, we are. Here, sweetheart, put my shirt on. You look cold. I know it's not pleasant having to hear about this, especially when we know how it finishes."

"No, it's not pleasant," she said, slipping into the shirt he held out to her. "But I'm glad to know the truth, especially after everything else I heard today. I don't think anything could be worse than thinking one's grandfather was a rapist, not to mention an elite member of the SS. To hear that he was a man like this is a great comfort. But it still breaks my heart."

"I can imagine," said Sebastian sympathetically. "Then I'll go on, for despite the tragic ending, there is much for you to be proud of. Where were we? Oh yes. Giselle was now running the Swallow line from St. Mouton with the help of her family. The war was reaching a critical point. Erharder was posted down to the Dordogne to quell the heavy Resistance activities in the region after D day."

"And he stumbled across Giselle there," Kate interjected. Tense with the inevitability of what Sebastian was now to tell, she slipped out of bed and padded over to the window, pulling his shirt more closely around her. A street lamp slanted a thin, hazy column of light across the carpet toward where Sebastian sat.

"He did," said Sebastian, watching Kate carefully. "Imagine his delight. First he established his headquarters in St. Mouton, right here in this hotel, and he watched her. Then he had his thugs arrest her. But apparently he must have believed her story about von Fiedler raping her, because he let her go. I imagine it's just the sort of thing he might have done to her himself. But he was none too happy that his bitter enemy had taken his pleasure with her. To see her so obviously near the end of her pregnancy must really have galled him."

Kate leaned her forehead against the cool windowpane.

"We know very little after this, Kate. There was only one last transmission from Ernst, from St. Mouton the morning of June the twelfth. He notified the colonel that Hélène had been born and she was being sent directly to Jock in England. Giselle, in great danger now herself, would follow the baby as soon as she had arranged for her family's safety. She also wanted to make sure that Erharder believed the child had died. Tony, like everyone else, thought the child to be two months early since the 'rape' had taken place just seven months before. Ernst also said that he had the copy of the documents with him in St. Mouton. He was going to place them somewhere safe and send the colonel word of their location in case something happened to him. But he was killed before he could manage it. The papers have never been found."

Kate wrapped her arms around herself. "And now, all these years later, we're back to Erharder and the missing documents."

"Yes, not to mention having Ernst and Giselle's grandchild in St. Mouton."

She turned to look at him. "Did you know that Jacques attended Hélène's birth?"

Sebastian's eyes sharpened. "No . . . I didn't know. How very interesting. There must have been a reason, given the circumstances. What else did you learn?"

"Only that he arrived that day bringing with him important information for Giselle. Since he was unaware that she had gone into labor, he hadn't come just to be at her side. He took a tremendous risk by showing up as a *maquisard* in a village crawling with Gestapo, any number of whom might have recognized him had they seen him."

"Yes. It does seem a big risk to take."

Kate managed to smile. "So big a risk that when I heard the story I even wondered if Jacques hadn't been the natural father. I was probably doing some wishful thinking, but I was closer than I thought."

"Hmm. What do you suppose was the information he was bringing? Damn! This could be important!"

"I don't know. But it seems to me that if Ernst had heard

that Erharder had suddenly landed in St. Mouton, he'd want to get Giselle away as fast as possible. Couldn't he have gone to St. Mouton to try to take her out, and then been unable to because she was in the middle of having the baby?"

"It's a good theory, Kate. In fact it makes a great deal of sense. But what about the bloody documents? He indicated he had them in St. Mouton. And then there's something else. Colonel Harrington knew that Ernst—as Colonel von Fiedler—left St. Mouton early on the morning of the thirteenth of June, in response to an urgent summons. A British agent had been captured in Bordeaux, and he could have compromised the entire network if Ernst hadn't gotten to him first. He did, we know that for certain. The agent was 'turned' and sent back into the field by afternoon of the following day. Then we know that Ernst must have returned to St. Mouton in early evening. His name was on the Gestapo headquarters log, pinpointing his arrival there at eight o'clock. He must have known that Giselle and the Jumeau family had been arrested. Only ten minutes later he was dead."

"But *how*, Sebastian? Everyone believes that Giselle shot him, but we know that can't be true!"

"I wish I could tell you. We have absolutely no idea what actually happened. It's as frustrating to me as it is to you. The only thing that seems certain is that Giselle couldn't have shot Ernst. But to go any further than that is pure speculation. I'm sorry. That's the story as we've pieced it together from what Ernst told Colonel Harrington over the course of that year, and up until that last transmission." Sebastian's last words fell softly into the deep silence.

Kate turned back to the window and looked out into the dark square. The execution had happened here on these same streets over forty years ago, against that rough stone wall, where now hung a simple plaque, so simple, leaving the unspeakable horror of that night to the imagination. Time seemed to wind down to nothing... She could see Giselle standing against the wall, hear the shots ring out, see her fall. What could she have been feeling at that moment? She and Ernst had sacrificed so much—in the end had sacrificed everything. Kate closed her eyes, swallowing against the hard, hot knot in her throat.

Sebastian's arms came around her, drawing her back into the present, and he kissed the tears from her cheek, resting his head on her hair.

"Kate, my love, don't be too upset. This story isn't yours, as much as you're a result of it. I know it's tragic, but we can only be grateful for Ernst and Giselle's courage and convictions. The war would have been lost without people like them, people who were willing to put everything on the line for their beliefs." She was shivering, and he led her back to the bed, pulling the covers up around her and holding her close against his chest. "All right, sweetheart?" he asked gently.

"Oh, Sebastian, I'm an idiot. Here I am crying, and I'm safe and warm and dry, and very much alive." Kate wiped her eyes and tried to smile. "They were so brave, so courageous in the face of everything, Sebastian. I don't know how I would have reacted in their situation, although I strongly suspect you would have found me hiding under the bed."

"Somehow I doubt that."

"No, even you, look at the strength of your convictions and how you've acted on them—you're an agent for MI-6, for heaven's sake. I've never had to have the courage of my convictions except in little things, things important only to me."

"Kate, you silly girl, you do underestimate yourself." Sebastian kissed her hair. "One never knows one's strength until tried. As far as I'm concerned, you have plenty. Perhaps one day you'll come to see it for yourself, but believe me when I say that Giselle and Ernst would have been very proud of you, sweetheart. Can you understand that and not diminish yourself too much, needlessly?"

"Sebastian, you're very kind, but I'm afraid there are lots of things I've been cowardly about, and you're a perfect example—I was far more interested in protecting myself from being hurt that I was in caring about what your feelings might be."

Sebastian chuckled. "I remember, in what seems a lifetime ago on a certain beach, hearing you say very much the same thing, and I told you then that you judged yourself too harshly. But then, you grew up with a harsh master, Kate. Your father never gave you any room to be yourself, and when you tried to be, you received no praise, just criticism. The harm done to your self-confidence isn't your fault—and I hope to God you haven't swallowed his myopic version of Kate Soames too completely."

"To tell you the truth, I don't know anymore which is which."

"I can imagine it must be hell to get out from under such a dictatorship. But you know, Kate, he had no right to treat you as he has. No human being should feel justified in trampling another underfoot. Between him and David, they really had you down on the ground, didn't they? God, you looked miserable in Jamaica."

"I was. You know, I look back and I can't believe how stupid I've been."

"No, not stupid. Life never deals out its lessons easily, and it's only those who aren't cowards who are willing to face them. It's what makes you a fighter, Kate—even though sometimes you fight the wrong things," he finished with a smile. "But I love you all the more for it."

"You're an amazingly forgiving man."

"No, not really. We all struggle and we all make mistakes, sweetheart. I'd be a fool if I let your past—or mine, for that matter—get in the way of our future. The only thing I ask is that you be honest with both of us."

She slipped her arms around his neck and drew him close. "I'll do my best, I can only promise you that. You know, yesterday in the church, I realized how much I loved you, really loved you. I thought you were a traitor, and I certainly never thought I'd see you again; but no matter how much that hurt, I couldn't be sorry for what time we'd had. I knew that I'd never be the same again; I'd changed because of you, Sebastian, and despite what I thought of your politics, I couldn't deny how I felt. Do you understand?''

''Only too well, believe me. And let that stand as your own special brand of bravery. Now sleep, my love, and don't worry about anything. We'll sort the rest of it out in the morning.'' He curled her body against him, holding her protectively, and when her breathing finally deepened and he knew her to be asleep, his own eyes finally closed in exhaustion.

CHAPTER
Thirteen

The next morning Kate awoke cradled in the security of Sebastian's arms. She smiled sleepily, drinking in the warm fragrance of his sleeping body. Pure, undistilled Sebastian, she thought, nuzzling the strong line of his jaw, the tender, vulnerable flesh just underneath and moving up to kiss the corner of his mouth with warm, exploring lips.

His eyes opened, swimming into focus, soft and liquid, and they found her face and became clear. "Kate," he murmured, slipping his arm about her waist, then more strongly as he rose to full consciousness. "Kate, my love," and he pulled her into a tight embrace full length against his taut body and took her in the filtered light, a reaffirmation, a renewal.

"Do you know when I first started loving you?" He stroked her hair back off her face.

"No, when?"

"That very first day when you'd finished being sick all over me and then grinned like an idiot."

"Oh, Sebastian, you fiend! What a ghastly thing to say."

"It's true. And someday you're going to have to explain to me exactly what you meant by, 'Apollo, the lamb.' That had me perplexed for days."

"Oh! I meant—nothing, it's too complicated to explain."

"Kate, my love, you're blushing," he said, laughing softly. "Anyway, by the time you left Jamaica, I was very sadly regretting the circumstances under which we'd met. All of them, including your engagement to that bastard."

"You were? Is that why you were so persistent after I was so rude to you at Christie's?"

"My love, when you walked in the door, I couldn't believe what fate had laid at my feet. Naturally it helped to speed things along when I reasoned that I had to protect my cover, but that was the least of it. I was already halfway in love with you, and the field was clear. I was my true self, you were a free woman. By the time dinner at Geoffrey's was finished, my fate was sealed."

"So you said at the time. I'm afraid I wasn't very forthcoming."

"I think you were a little more forthcoming than you realize. Shall we say you gave me reason to hope?"

"And then you completely confused me by backing off, until—Sebastian, why did you take me up to Whitworth that weekend?" Kate looked at him curiously.

"Why do you think?"

"Probably to seduce me," she said with a grin.

"Good heavens, no! I could have done that anywhere."

"You are a low creature!"

"Well, my God, you made me wait long enough," he said, rolling on to his side and regarding her lazily.

"How much longer would you have waited?" she asked, remembering the rainstorm and how, even then, he had watched her for a reaction.

"I honestly don't know. But that night when Peter waltzed over with Lord Humbert, I began to doubt your instincts. I decided it was time I took matters into my own hands and taught you a few things. And I also decided it was time I introduced you to my family."

"Do you think they knew?"

"Good heavens, yes! They're no fools. The last person I'd taken there had been Anne, all those years ago."

"Sebastian, you might have told me!"

"Kate, darling, they'd have known anyway, believe me. I knew, they knew, even Elizabeth knew. The only person who was oblivious was you."

"Elizabeth? Whatever do you mean?"

"She has a good nose, that woman. She wanted to know what my intentions were that first day at tea."

"No! Did you tell her?"

Sebastian looked very surprised. "Naturally. Why wouldn't I? I said, 'I intend to seduce Kate, Miss Forrest, although I don't think she knows it yet.' And she said, and I quote, 'What a splendid idea!' Naturally I was very gratified."

Kate was laughing helplessly. "You really are a very dreadful man, Sebastian."

"I know, but just think what wonderful stories we'll have to pass down to our grandchildren. 'Tommy, my boy, did I ever tell you about the time I had my way with your grandmother in the old hay barn?' "

"You would, too! And who said anything about grandchildren?"

"Silly girl. Of course we have to produce the first generation, but I can't see any difficulty in that, can you?"

"Have a heart! I've never been spoken to like a brood mare before."

"Sweetheart, I'm not asking for a racing stable, just a few grandchildren to dandle on my knee in my dotage. Hmm. Speaking of dotage, there is one small matter of business my father would insist I take care of."

"Business, now? Sebastian, your sense of timing is definitely off."

"There's nothing wrong with my timing and this is serious business. After all, I gave Elizabeth my word." His face was grave.

"What about, Sebastian?" She was suddenly worried, remembering the telephone call.

"That I'd make an honest woman of you." He burst into laughter.

"Oh, you beast!" She grabbed a pillow and whacked him over the head, and still laughing, he rolled her over and pinned her underneath him, looking down at her with a grin.

"Kate, my love, will you marry me?"

She stared at him in amazement. "My God, you do pick your moments, don't you?"

He smiled. "Are you hedging?"

"No, but the least you could do would be to remove yourself from bed and get down on one knee."

"Oh, is that how David did it?" he said, starting to laugh again.

"Sebastian! As a matter of fact, David proposed in a very proper manner, over dinner."

"And did you take this long to give David an answer?"

"Longer."

"Longer? How much longer?"

"Two weeks," said Kate with a grin.

Sebastian groaned. "Two *weeks*? How can anyone be so indecisive?"

"David didn't mind. He thought I was being sensible."

"What a steamy romance," said Sebastian dryly.

"And furthermore, David had a ring."

"How could I forget that great winking thing? He probably bought it with the proceeds of Erharder's fat paycheck. Tell me, did he put it in the bottom of the champagne glass and wait for you to discover it?"

"No, over coffee he gave me a box from Harry Winston, and waited for me to see what was inside before he—"

"I'll bet he did!" interrupted Sebastian gleefully. "Now there's a man who really knows how to hedge his bet. Well, my love, I'm sorry to be caught empty-handed, but I came down here to thump the truth out of a black-hearted spy, not to propose to my future wife. Anyway, I'm afraid you're stuck with the family jewels." He shifted onto his elbow and looked down at her. "Now, let's try this again. Miss bloody impossible Soames, will you marry me?"

"Yes, Mr. Dunn, I will." Kate's eyes danced with laughter.

"Thank God for that. That's the most sensible thing you've said all morning. And it took you only two minutes to make up your mind—I'd say you were improving." His last words were whispered into her neck, and after that, Kate was unable to speak for a very long time.

"Come now, sweetheart," said Sebastian, sitting Kate firmly up in bed. "We have to stop this shameless behavior and get on with the day at hand. I have a plan."

"Oh, good, I think we definitely could use a plan."

"I think I'd like you to take me to meet the Jumeaus. We all have a good deal of talking to do, and if anyone can help us figure out why the photograph might be important, Henri can."

"And just think how thrilled they'll be to know about Ernst and Giselle!"

"Yes—I think they must be told. I'm going to get in touch with Colonel Harrington first thing and let him know what's been going on. I'm sure he'll clear the information."

"There are so many things that I don't understand. You said the colonel believed that Hélène had died, but I'm living proof that she didn't. What made him think that?"

"I have no idea."

"But Guy Jessop obviously knew the truth. He was involved in Special Operations, too, you know. I wonder why he would have lied to Colonel Harrington about such an important thing?"

"Maybe he thought he was doing the best possible thing for Hélène. If no one knew of her existence, she could never be in danger. One could never be certain there weren't spies in the Resistance, or any of the Intelligence departments, for that matter. Hélène's parents were dead, and so there was then no reason that she should not permanently become Susanna."

"I think I see. How incredible! It worked, too, and nobody else ever would have known the truth if Elizabeth hadn't given me the watch."

"Yes, the watch with that hidden photograph. I can't help but wonder what the significance of that is. You know, it's a great pity the check on you didn't go back one more generation, or we might have put things together about Jessop and you and avoided some unpleasantness. I think the colonel is going to be extremely pleased with this turn of events for more than one reason."

"What do you mean?"

"Aside from the fact that his old friend Ernst has a granddaughter, and the infamous Kate Soames is not attached to the Group and digging up trouble, I think he'll be quite happy for me. I told him how I felt about you."

"Oh! How embarrassing to have him aware of all the stupid things I've done—David being a shining example. And Sebastian, that's something else—what about David? What are we going to do about him?"

"Yes, our fine friend David. He's bound to be showing up shortly, and I think it's best if he makes no connection between us, sweetheart. I'm going to be keeping a very low profile. I have no way of knowing how he intends to play this, but if I were in his position, I think I'd probably play to your vulnerability. And the safest thing for you to do is play back to his weakness. He may well believe you're still in love with him."

"But what about the reason I'm in St. Mouton?" Her eyes searched his face.

"I think a scaled-down version of the truth might do nicely. Let him believe you're here to rethink your decision about him—" He was interrupted by a knock on the door and immediately reached for the Beretta, then nodded at Kate.

"Who is it?" she called, her eyes fixed on Sebastian.

"Stephanie, you idiot! Who else would it be!" Her voice was muffled through the door.

Kate breathed again. Sebastian gestured at the door. "I'll be right there." She found her dressing gown, opening the door just enough to slip out into the hall. "Hi! Did you have a good time last night?"

"Fabulous—I met the most interesting American—but Kate, what's the mystery in your room?" Her eyes lit up in speculation. "You haven't got a man in there, have you?"

"Stephanie, honestly! Give me ten minutes and I'll meet you downstairs."

"All right, I can wait ten minutes." She gave Kate a long look, and then went back down the hallway.

"Sebastian, what am I going to tell her? I never keep her out in the corridor!"

"Nothing. Let her stew for now, it's good for her. Seriously, Kate, the less she knows about this, the safer she'll be. She obviously isn't under any sort of suspicion if her room wasn't searched."

"Are you sure?"

"As sure as I can be. Now listen to me very carefully. You're going to have to convince Stephanie as surely as you convince David that what you're saying is true. Otherwise she might give you away unwittingly and put you both in danger. Can you do that?"

"I'll hate it with all my heart, but I'll do it."

"Good girl. I assume you told Stephanie all about what a filthy, treacherous soul I am?"

Kate flushed. "Yes, I did."

"Wonderful! Oh, I do love situations like this."

"Sebastian, how can you be so unfeeling?"

"Never unfeeling, Kate, but I must confess I do love a good bit of sport." He kissed her soundly. "Hurry up now, sweetheart. I'll slip out the back way, and I'll meet you at the Jumeaus' camera shop at noon. That should give me enough time to get things moving."

"But where are you going?"

"Oh yes, last night a certain Simon Dristoll booked into the Hôtel de Ville at the back of the village. But I don't want you going there under any circumstances. If David sees us together, his nasty little brain is going to begin spinning. But if by any chance that should happen, you're going to have to conjure up a quick affair between us. That could be a little sticky, and I'd rather not risk it. Ah, sweetheart, 'we that are true lovers run into strange capers.'" He grinned and pulled on his trousers.

Sebastian had made it all sound like a diversion, but Kate was brought back to the seriousness of the situation as she watched him buckle on the shoulder holster and slide the gun into it.

* * *

"Do tell, Kate! What have you been up to?" Stephanie poured Kate a cup of steaming coffee and handed it to her, expectation written all over her face.

"Nothing, Steph! You're always jumping to the worst of conclusions." Kate smiled, doing her best to look innocent.

"Then why didn't you want to let me into your room?" asked Stephanie, persistent to the end.

"No reason—where do you think I'd come up with a man on such short notice, anyway? In any case, as you well know, I spent the evening with the Jumeaus."

"Oh, all right. I suppose you're not exactly in the right frame of mind for it, anyway. How did everything go last night?"

"It was terrific." Kate launched into a rendition of the dinner. "What about you? Who was this American you met?"

"Oh, a sweet, helpless tourist who wandered into the restaurant, and his French was practically nonexistent, so I helped him out."

"I'm sure you did, you little conniver! I can imagine the ending."

"Never, Kate! It was all innocent, I swear it. Who am I to let a fellow-traveler flounder in the intricacies of a foreign language? Anyway, he was decently good looking and longing for company, and since I was alone, I thought, why not?"

"Are you going to see him again?"

"No. I don't know, I just didn't feel like mixing anything else up in this, d'you know what I mean?"

"Perfectly. Do you have any special plans for today?"

"No, nothing in particular. I'd love nothing more than going down to that place by the river, maybe doing some writing. What about you?"

"I have to go over to the Jumeaus a little later, and I'm not sure after that. I'll tell you what, why don't you take the car and go on, and I'll walk down there when I can get away."

"You're ever a sweetheart." Stephanie grinned, well pleased with the turn of events.

* * *

David Russell furiously paced the floor of Madame Chabot's kitchen. Then he turned to glare at Brecht. "What the hell got into you to try to run Kate down! You were supposed to follow her, not kill her, you fool." He spoke in French.

"I wasn't trying to kill her, just scare her off," said Brecht defensively. "May I remind you that you didn't do a very good job of following her yourself? I was lucky to have picked up her trail at all!"

"How was I to know she wasn't in the car with her friend? I tried to make the best out of a bad situation. At least now I have a decent cover set up to get to her. The Matthison girl will back up my story completely. This time you stay with Katie—find out where she goes and who she sees, is that understood? But for God's sake don't let her see you. She knows your face from Jamaica, and I don't want any unnecessary connections made. We could still be safe, if Matthison's story of some long-lost relative is true."

"But monsieur, she was asking about von Fiedler, and writing down names!" cried Celeste Chabot, extremely agitated.

"If you'd think for a moment instead of trying to save your own collaborating skin, madame, there's a perfectly good explanation for that. If she's trying to trace a relative, she could believe he was killed in the reprisals. Barbier found nothing in her room to indicate anything else. Use your head, woman, instead of flying into a panic. Herr Schumann isn't going to be very pleased if we accidentally put her onto him by your foolish actions."

Madame Chabot pulled herself up. "Herr Schumann has been very good to me over the years, monsieur. And the very reason he pays me is to keep him informed of anything, *anything* that might be suspicious, so I would thank you to keep a civil tongue in your head."

"We will get nowhere by arguing," said David. "I'm simply trying to say that we might cause more trouble by jumping to the wrong conclusion and acting hastily. Let me handle Katie Soames. Anyway, I know her. She's not the type to go off involving herself in this sort of thing, believe me. Personally, I think this entire affair is ridiculous."

"We cannot be too careful, especially with the connections she has," Brecht said firmly.

"Don't worry about that, I have her father in my back pocket. And you were the one who flew off the handle about that stupid fisherman in Jamaica, if you remember. I could have wasted a great deal of valuable time if I'd listened to you. He was after Katie, no more, no less. I think you're all too jumpy for your own good. Oh, well, I suppose it won't be a wasted trip if I can get Katie back. I'd better get started."

Kate entered the camera shop and was instantly relieved to find Sebastian already there, his head bent over an assortment of postcards, a cap pulled low over his forehead.

"Kate!" cried Pierre, coming around the counter to kiss her soundly on both cheeks. "It is a fine thing that you stopped by to see us so soon."

"I must first thank you for the most wonderful evening, Pierre. But I also want you to meet a very dear and trusted friend." Sebastian came over to the counter. "Pierre, this is Sebastian Dunn. Sebastian, Pierre Jumeau."

They shook hands formally. "Monsieur, it is a pleasure to meet any friend of my cousin."

"Thank you. Kate has told me how welcoming your family has been to her. I must tell you now that Kate, because of her connection with your family, is in no little danger. Is it possible that we might talk somewhere more private?" Kate was staring at him in astonishment. She had fully expected to be the interpreter, but Sebastian's French was as fluent as her own.

"But what is this you say, monsieur! Kate, in danger? We must indeed talk. I shall close the shop for the lunch hour. It is time, in any case." He did just that and led them both back through the kitchen where Henri and Nadia were just sitting down for the midday meal. There were general exclamations of welcome, and quick explanations made by Pierre, and in moments two extra places were laid and three solemn faces were regarding Sebastian.

He explained everything to them, quickly and clearly, his words punctuated by their expressions of amazement as the story of Giselle and Ernst unfolded. At the end there were tears of happiness in the eyes of the three Jumeaus, but then as Sebastian went on to explain the present problem, they sobered.

"But this is incredible!" cried Henri. "It is a terrible thing indeed. I knew nothing of any of this, but if there is information hidden somewhere that these people are willing to kill for, then we must certainly protect Kate. What can we do?"

"I think that the clue to the information must lie within the photograph. Is there anything you can recognize in it, or anything out of the ordinary, that might give us an indication?" He handed the photograph to Henri, who examined it once again.

He finally looked up and passed the photograph to his wife. "I see nothing, monsieur. I believe it was taken on the wall that leads out of the village toward the west, but I can see nothing else. I am sorry." Nadia and Pierre concurred with his statement.

"I see," said Sebastian. "Never mind. We'll just have to find something else to go on. As you were not here at the time, Monsieur Jumeau, can you think of anyone who might have worked with Giselle, someone whom she might have confided in?"

Henri's brow wrinkled in concentration, then his face lightened. "There is a man in Angoulême, but it is a fair distance. His name is Louis Villers, a carpenter. Pierre can take you to him this afternoon. He was one leg of the Swallow line to Paris. Giselle might have told him something."

"Excellent," said Sebastian with satisfaction. "You can spare your grandson?"

"Easily. He will be glad to accompany you."

"Indeed, monsieur," said Pierre, his young face lighting with pleasure. "We shall go as soon as you like."

"Kate, a word with you. If you'll excuse us, madame, messieurs?"

He took her through into the living area. "Listen, sweetheart, I don't want you coming with me. You mustn't be seen with me; if I'm followed, it could be dangerous. Best if you carry on as you have. You needn't lock yourself in your hotel room; that would look too odd. Just stay close to Stephanie, and for God's sake don't go far. Will you do that for me? I'll be back as soon as I can. I'll look for you at your hotel tonight. Watch for a man lurking in your curtains." He grinned at her.

"Please, Sebastian, let me go with you. I don't think I can bear the suspense of waiting. And although I'm sure you find it impossible to believe, I might be able to help."

"Kate, I know it makes little sense to you, but you're far safer here, doing what you've been doing all along, and I'm better off without you on this."

"All right, then I'll call on your protective instincts—remember the car last night? Suppose David was driving it."

"Yes, I've given that a good bit of thought. In the first place, David would be crazy to try such a thing. If he were caught, he'd be in big trouble with the authorities and the State Department. Originally, when I thought you were mixed up with them, I thought that the Group might have turned against you for your involvement with me, but that's clearly not the case. No, they wouldn't send David to kill you. First he has to find out what you know. It would be sheer idiocy for him to do anything before he determines that. I think it must have been an accident. The French are renowned for drinking and driving."

"Do you really think that's it, or are you just trying to squirm out of taking me with you?"

Sebastian smiled. "I wouldn't swear to anything considering what's been going on and the stakes involved; but if they were planning on killing you, they could easily have done it before now, and before you could stir up too much curiosity in the village. But we take no chances. Don't go out after dark, and as I said, stick with Stephanie. All right, my love? Will you wait for me to come to you?'"

"I suppose it's pointless to argue. Just be careful."

"Ever careful. I don't really think there's going to be any problem. In fact, right now the biggest problem I have is you, stubborn woman. Promise me you won't set out on your own and try to do any investigating."

"I promise," she said reluctantly.

He looked at her skeptically. "Why don't I believe you?"

"Really, Sebastian, when have I ever given you cause to doubt me?" She smiled innocently.

Sebastian burst into laughter. "Oh, Christ, and I'm going to be shackled to you for life. Remember what I said. Stay close, and stay with Stephanie. And this is very important. If David does show up, relax. Do exactly as I told you, and you should be in no danger. I'm afraid this is something you're going to have to do on your own in any case. Remember, he knows nothing except that you're asking some questions. If you have to, weave him a story—but follow his lead. Let him tell you what he thinks you're up to, and stick as closely to the truth as you judge safe. I wouldn't leave you, sweetheart, I really wouldn't, but I've got to track down this lead. It could be important, and we can use all the help we can get. All right?"

"Yes, all right. I suppose I can see the sense in that."

"Good. Now I want you to leave by the front door here, in case the shop's being watched, and take a roundabout route back to the hotel." He kissed her quickly, and he was gone.

CHAPTER Fourteen

The sunlight dazzled down onto the meadow, warming the cow-cropped grass and dancing like a million stars on the surface of the river. Billowing clouds, nearly motionless in the hot, lazy afternoon, hung in the deep blue sky. The scene was quiet, pastoral, and blissfully normal, thought Kate, as she came through the cool, shady avenue of trees and broke onto the pasture to find Stephanie sitting at the edge of the river, her back against the trunk of a tree, a notebook in her lap.

"Don't scream, it's only me." She threw herself down on the grass.

Stephanie glanced up casually, then took a more careful look at Kate's face. "Are you okay?"

"What do you mean? Of course I am."

"I must say, you look awfully worn out. Are you sure you're okay?"

"Fine, really. It's just been a bit of a strain the last few days." She pulled her knees up to her chin and stared down into the green, gently flowing water, wishing she could tell Stephanie everything but not wanting to involve her in any more danger.

"You want to know what I think? I think you've been under a strain since Sebastian revealed his rotten core, and I don't think you're going to be better until you've worked him out of your system."

"Please, Steph, let's not—"

"No, I'm sorry, my girl, no more evasions. I've kept out of it for too long as it is, and I'm beginning to worry about you. You know I try not to meddle in your affairs, Kate, but this has been eating away at you and I can't bear to see you hurting so badly."

"What is it that you want me to say?" Kate stood up and turned away, trying hard not to smile.

"I want you to tell me what's going on inside that convoluted head of yours. Come on, Kate, stop being so damned stubborn!"

"All right, Stephanie. I'll tell you exactly what's going on, and it's as convoluted as you could possibly wish. I love him. I love him with every fiber of my being. How's that?"

Stephanie stared at her, quite astonished. "What's that supposed to mean?"

"Just that." She turned around and met Stephanie's eyes squarely.

"But Kate, how can you love someone who treated you like that, who's a bloody spy or something!"

"That's a very good question, and someday maybe I'll be able to explain it to you, but for now let's just assume I'm out of my mind."

"You must be. Don't you have any sense of self-preservation?"

"Look, Steph, this is very complicated, but despite everything that happened, there were moments, wonderful moments that had nothing to do with his other life. So no matter what else was going on, I had something very special for a short while, and I'd be a bigger fool to ignore that. I suppose I'll get over the worst of it, but there'll always be a part of me that loves him. Now can we drop it?"

"Oh, absolutely, you bet we can. I'm checking you into the nearest asylum when we get home." She shook her head. "Maybe David wasn't as bad for you as I thought."

Kate had a few choice things she would have loved to say on the matter, but she'd already gone too far. "Maybe he wasn't. Maybe I just needed to go out and get clobbered over the head to realize how good he was to me."

"I don't mind admitting that I'm baffled. You love Sebastian, but you've changed your mind about David?"

"Haven't you ever been so infatuated with someone that he's like a poison in your blood? Passion's a heady thing, I discovered. But you can't live a steady diet of it, and I suppose eventually you have to return to earth. At least I hope so. And when you come down, there are all the normal things, the things that seemed commonplace, that you suddenly realize are the things of value. It's like a married woman having an affair, do you know? She goes temporarily out of her mind, and when it's all over, she realizes how much she loves her stable old husband. I'm not saying I'm going back to David, but I need to think it over again. I could use some of that steadiness in my life, and maybe I discarded it too quickly and for the wrong reasons, if you see what I mean."

"I suppose so. I guess that makes sense, but I'm confused as hell. Never mind, I asked for it, didn't I? It seems as if you've thought it through. Well, as long as you don't go tearing back into Sebastian's arms and bed—which sounds rather fascinating, by the way—maybe I'll reconsider committing you."

"Gosh, that's big of you, Steph," said Kate with a laugh. "Don't worry about me, okay? I swear to you, I'm fine. Now be quiet. I'm going to take a nap."

"Good idea." Stephanie looked one last time at Kate, who had already stretched out on the blanket and closed her eyes, then shrugged and went back to her writing.

Sebastian pulled into the dirt courtyard as Pierre directed and turned the engine off. "Let's get to work." He got out of the car and picked his way around the chickens that ran scatterbrained about his feet.

Pierre led him into the old barn, which was evidently now used as a carpentry shop. It was crowded with bits and pieces of furniture, some half-completed, others newly finished and neatly stacked. A round, red-cheeked old man in blue coveralls worked in the back where the light spilled through a large window. He looked up without surprise, apparently accustomed to having customers stop in.

"Good day, messieurs." Then he frowned as they came into the light. "Pierre Jumeau, isn't, Henri's grandson?"

"Good day, Monsieur Villers. It is indeed, and this is Monsieur Dunn, a friend."

"How may I help you? You're out of your way, Pierre, my boy. Have you come to commission a piece?"

"No, monsieur. My grandfather has sent us to you on an urgent matter."

"Yes? An urgent matter? And what could that be, I wonder." He smiled at the impetuousness of youth.

"Monsieur Villers, he speaks the truth. This concerns your work with Giselle Jumeau during the war." Sebastian's face was grave.

The carpenter immediately sobered and put down his awl. "And who might you be to come asking questions like this?"

"I'm with British Intelligence, monsieur. Giselle Jumeau was connected with some information that disappeared during the war, and we are trying to get to it before Herr Karl Erharder does."

"That filthy Boche! I had hoped he was dead. Bah!" He spat into the dirt, then looked Sebastian up and down assessingly. "British Intelligence, is it? Yes, all right then, monsieur, I will tell you whatever I can, but we will not talk of such things here. You will come to my house. It is only a short distance."

His house was up on a hill, overlooking a series of undulating fields that alternated sunflowers and maize. The house was beautiful in its simplicity and the carpenter welcomed them to it graciously, pouring out three glasses of his own wine, young and earthy, still tasting of the fresh grape. Only then did he speak.

"This is a serious matter to be bringing me. I, like so many others, have a special reason to hate Major Erharder.

He ordered my brother killed, a brave *maquisard*, not three months before the end of the war, and had his body left in the street for three days as an example before we were permitted to take it away and give him a decent burial. I would have seen the Boche dead myself but Erharder has not been heard of all these years. Now you say he is looking for this information? It must be important to bring him out into the open. How is it I can help?''

Sebastian once again laid down the basic facts, then waited quietly. These were steady country people whose values lay as deep as their roots, and judgments were made with care.

Monsieur Villers was quiet for a long moment after Sebastian has finished. Then he shook his head. ''I didn't know. All these years and I didn't know.''

''Almost no one did, monsieur, don't let it trouble you. Ernst von Fiedler never expected anyone to know the truth.''

''No. No, that is true, but not what I meant. You see, I saw Giselle for the last time two days before her death. It was the twelfth of June. She came to me with a newborn infant, to be sent on. She said it was a Jewish orphan—its parents had been taken but the mother had managed to hide the baby in the cellar. It was not an unusual thing to have happen. We passed quite a few children on. But Giselle was adamant about one thing. She pressed a watch into my hand—she said it must stay with the child at all cost, and I must be certain to pass the word.''

''Did she say anything else about the watch, anything at all?'' Sebastian's face was alive with excitement. Here, at last, there might be something.

''No, monsieur, nothing I can remember. And I never thought to put it together. The word about her little Hélène's death came with the news of her own in the reprisal. Poor Giselle, she was a brave one. They all were, those Jumeaus. The Gestapo never did find out about the rest of our line.''

''Look at the photograph, monsieur. This is the only thing we have to go on. Perhaps there is something in it that you might understand? A clue of some kind?''

His faded eyes filled with tears as he looked on the face

of the young Giselle, Giselle who had not lived to age with the rest of them . . . "There is nothing I can see, monsieur," he said in a choked voice.

"No, I'm not surprised," said Sebastian gently. "Is there anything else you can tell me about that day?"

"Nothing, monsieur, except that at the same time she arranged for a group of four to be taken up the line to the Swiss border at Lyon. I sent a contact to Verteillac the night of the thirteenth, but the people never appeared. He waited from ten o'clock until two in the morning, and then left. It was dangerous to stay any longer. That is all, monsieur."

"I see. That doesn't tell me much. I don't suppose you know of anyone else in whom Giselle might have confided."

"I don't know, monsieur. I can understand why she told no one about the true identity of the child—one could never be too careful—but information of that sort, so important to the future? Surely Colonel von Fiedler would not have been so careless to secret it away with no way we might find it later?"

"My thoughts exactly, monsieur. The question is, did Giselle know what von Fiedler did with the information?"

"I have no idea. Normally I would think not—we did not exchange information. That was the rule we all lived by in case of capture, but in this case . . ."

"And Giselle knew how important it was that the watch stay with the child."

"But she would have to know that much, would she not? How else could I pass the word on?"

"Is there anyone else you know of whom Giselle contacted around that time?"

"I gave her some important information that needed to get to a courier in Charroux. She was going to go directly there after leaving me that day. I discovered after the war that the courier was a Madame Elise Mauriac. Most of us never knew each other. Giselle was the only mutual contact. It was to protect us. But Madame Mauriac never mentioned anything to me that Giselle said, nothing that would give a clue of any kind."

"I can't believe von Fiedler left nothing more to help us.

I'm sure it's just staring me in the face. Damn! I feel as if I'm so close to whatever it is.'' Sebastian pushed his fingers through his hair in a gesture of frustration.

''We shall go to Charroux. When Madame Mauriac hears the story, she might realize that Giselle said something to her that she didn't understand at the time.''

Stephanie knocked on Kate's door. ''I'm going out to buy some postcards, not that they'll arrive before I get home, but goodwill and all that. Do you want me to get you some?''

''No, thanks anyway, Steph,'' called Kate. ''I sent all mine last week. Come and get me when you want dinner. I'm going to take a bath.''

''Right. See you later.'' She ran down the stairs and across the square to the little shop that sold newspapers and such. Leaving with an assortment of postcards that largely featured flocks of geese, and women selling plucked chickens at market, she walked back toward the hotel. The quickly deepening light poured down the face of the stone walls and caught on the leaves, outlining their delicate veins.

''Stephanie! Gosh, what a surprise running into you like this!'' David walked up to her with a broad, slightly lopsided smile that made him look very young.

''Hello! I never expected to see you here—how are you surviving?''

''Two square meals so far. I got a guide book, and it's been really helpful, but I decided it was time to find another English-speaking person. Anyway, it's why I'm really here, to look up that friend, but it took me a little while to work up my courage. So here I am.''

''Your friend lives in St. Mouton? You're joking!''

''Well, she doesn't live here, she's just visiting. What about you—what are you doing here?''

''I'm staying here, just across the street.''

David's eyes suddenly narrowed and he looked at her

closely. Then he laughed. ‘‘No, it couldn't be, it's too ridiculous.’’

‘‘What's too ridiculous?’’

‘‘You're not, by any chance, Stephanie *Matthison*, are you?’’

She stared at him for a long moment, the impossible suddenly hitting her. ‘‘And you're not Kate's David—Oh, lord! What in heaven's name are you doing here? I don't believe this.’’ She sat down on the nearby bench, thoroughly discomposed.

‘‘Stephanie, listen, I'm sorry if I've startled you. It's a shock to me too, but this is really important and maybe you can help. It's about Kate—I came all this way to see her, to see if maybe she won't forgive me. What do you think? Last night didn't you say she had a broken heart?’’ His face was eager.

‘‘I don't know what to tell you, David. You're going to have to give me a minute.’’ She stood up and walked away from him in agitation.

‘‘Of course. I do understand that this must be awkward for you.’’ But the eyes that watched her back were not kind.

She turned around abruptly. ‘‘This is awfully difficult, David. You took a hell of a chance coming all this way, and I don't know how Kate's going to take it. Look, I think it's best if I break this to her myself. Then if she wants to see you, you could meet her someplace for dinner. How does that sound?’’

He pushed the fallen lock of hair off his forehead. ‘‘Okay, if you think that's the best way. I thought maybe the element of surprise would help.’’

‘‘No, David, that would definitely be a mistake. She's fragile enough as it is. Just let me talk to her first. I'll tell you what. Why don't you be in the hotel bar at eight o'clock. If she wants to see you, she'll meet you there, and if not, I'll come instead and explain everything. Agreed?’’

‘‘Yes, okay. I hope to hell you're convincing. I know I made a lot of mistakes with her, and I want to explain that. I could kick myself for being so stupid.’’

‘‘Don't worry about that now, just find a way to make it

up to her. And don't push the issue! That's what got you into trouble in the first place.'' She hurried away.

''Kate, may I come in?'' Stephanie was breathless, having flown up the two flights of stairs.

''Coming.'' Kate opened the door, one hand rubbing her wet hair with a towel, but her arm dropped as she took in Stephanie's expression, and she pulled her into the room. ''Steph! What's wrong—what's happened?''

''I don't know how to tell you this; you're never going to believe it!''

''What? Believe what, for pity's sake?'' Kate went cold with foreboding.

''You know the person I had dinner with last night?''

''Yes? What about him?''

''It was David, your David! I don't know how I could've been such an idiot not to have realized it, but it was the last thing I would have expected. Anyway, I just ran into him outside, and he was on his way to see you. That's why he's here, in France, I mean.''

''Dear God,'' said Kate, sitting down slowly. ''What did you tell him?''

''I told him I'd talk to you, and that if you agreed to see him, you'd meet him downstairs at eight for dinner. I hope that was all right. I didn't know what else to say, and I couldn't let him just appear on your doorstep.''

Kate was silent.

''What are you going to do?'' Stephanie sat down beside her and looked at her with concern, aching for her.

''I don't know. I have to think.''

''It can't hurt to see him, can it? I mean, after what you said this afternoon, it could be the best thing. He looked so lost, Kate, and he did come all this way.''

''Yes, you're right, of course, I have to see him. But listen, Steph, first I have to know what you told him. Did he ask anything about me or why we're here?''

''I feel awfully foolish. Last night I told him I was here with a friend who was nursing a broken heart, but you see, I never mentioned your name, and neither did he. Naturally when he put it together, he assumed you were heartbroken over him.''

''Thank heaven for that, anyway! What about our being here? Did he ask about that?''

''Yes, casually. He wanted to know why we'd choose such a tiny place to holiday in. I said you were tracing a remote branch of your family, just for a lark, and that's all I said. I led the conversation onto genealogy, I think.''

''Good, that's all right then. Look, don't worry, you did the right thing. I'm not going to accomplish anything by running away again. Oh, damn! I'm just not ready for this.''

''You'll do all right, Kate. I know this is a miserable thing to have sprung on you, but maybe it'll all work out. This could be just what you need to forget about Sebastian.''

Kate smiled. ''That would take a miracle. I mean, could you forget about Sebastian? He is something of an unorthodox character, you must admit.''

''No argument, but here you have safe old David to bring you back to earth, remember? Faith, constancy, and stability, all the things you were pining for earlier this afternoon.''

''Oh, Steph, if you only knew how much. But never mind about me, what about you? I feel terrible deserting you again.''

''Don't be silly, I don't mind at all. I think maybe I'll drive into Périgueux and scout around. The Michelin has some good listings for restaurants, and you know me, I'm always happy to be left to my own devices.'' She smiled. ''Who knows, perhaps tonight I'll run into Sebastian—at least I'll know him before I put my foot in my mouth—or better, in his face!''

The whole situation suddenly struck Kate as terribly funny. Stephanie had no idea how close to the truth she was, and here they all were, playing at cross-purposes like some awful comedy of errors. She grinned. ''Well, if you do run into him, for God's sake don't bring him here. We could end up with a battle between my former lovers on our hands!''

''Can you imagine? What a lark that would be. Whose side would you take?''

"What a question! Suffice it to say, 'there's small choice in rotten apples.' "

"Oh, God, you and your Shakespeare. You always throw a quote at me to get out of answering a question."

"I have to use all those years of education for something, don't I?"

"Yes, well I have one for you. 'How camest thou in this pickle?' "

Kate burst into laughter. "Steph, that's good—*The Tempest*, yet!"

Stephanie sniffled. "You're not the only person who can throw quotes around, you know. I have one coined specifically for you. 'Some, for renown, on scraps of learning dote, and think they grow immortal as they quote.' Edward Young." She grinned.

"I should have expected no less from you. Anyway, you should hear Sebastian—" She stopped abruptly.

"Never mind. As you said, you'll get over it. Why don't you concentrate on what you're going to say to David tonight. Think up some good quotes to stop him dead."

" 'At lovers' perjuries, they say Jove laughs,' " said Kate very softly.

"Quite," said Stephanie. "I'll tell you what. I'll come and check up on how it went when I get back. If it went *extremely* well, just leave the 'Do Not Disturb' sign outside, and I won't bother you. Otherwise, leave your door unlocked in case I'm late, and I'll wake you. It'll do you good to talk about it, and quite honestly, I wouldn't be able to sleep without knowing one way or the other."

Kate smiled, thinking of Sebastian lurking in the curtains, and somehow, the thought cheered her. When Stephanie saw the sign hanging outside, she would jump to all the desired conclusions. "All right," she said. "That sounds fair enough."

"Good. Not to worry, you're going to get through this fine."

"I'm counting on it." But her eyes belied the easy words.

* * *

Sebastian drove as quickly as he could through the dark night, the headlights of the car flashing over the small winding roads, but he still couldn't be in St. Mouton before midnight. Still, the trip to Charroux had been well worth his while, despite the hours he had had to wait for Madame Mauriac's return from a visit to her niece. His mind was working keenly, playing with all the new pieces of information, trying to put them into some semblance of order. Madame Mauriac had been as helpful as she could, and what she had said gave Sebastian cause to reconsider.

"She talked about a deception, monsieur, one that would have us all laughing when the war was finished, but she would say no more. She was like a child with a secret. I didn't understand her, and put it down to high spirits. Never did I think it was anything like this. I asked her to tell me what she meant, but she just laughed and said she could say nothing more, it was all in the hands of time. It was the same day that you say she delivered the child to Louis Villers. She must have been overwrought. And she kissed me and thanked me for my work."

Sebastian pressed harder on the accelerator, urging the car faster toward St. Mouton.

Kate stood at the door to the bar, watching David's back, fighting down the anger that had risen so unexpectedly at the sight of him. She had not expected this lashing rage, in fact had prepared herself for a conflict of emotions. But instead, she had to suppress a strong urge to strangle him, and the rage had the wonderful effect of dissipating the fear that had been preying on her since Stephanie's announcement.

She bit her lip in silent resolution then forced herself forward. "Hello, David."

"Katie!" He stood up quickly, anxiously it seemed, then took her shoulder and kissed her cheek. She flinched at his touch and he must have felt it for he released her quickly and pulled out a chair for her. She would have to stop this, she told herself firmly, sitting down. And she would have to take control and keep it. The only hope she had of success was to keep him off guard.

"Needless to say this is quite a surprise, David." Her voice was cold.

"Yes, I know. I'm sorry, but I couldn't think of any other way. I wasn't sure you'd meet me. Would you like some wine?" He smiled at her, that crooked, boyish grin.

"White, please. How did you know where to find me?" She had the satisfaction of seeing him hesitate for a split second.

"Your father found you for me. I explained that I had to see you, and he was eager to help." He watched for her reaction.

"Yes, I'm sure he was." Kate kept her face noncommittal, but beneath its bland exterior she was seething. Her father had interfered once again, with all good intentions, she was sure, but it made no difference. And he had given David the perfect alibi to come after her. The waiter approached and David ordered, fumbling with the language, but she didn't offer to help. Instead she said, "And what was so urgent that you had to see me?"

"I—look, Katie, can we wait a few minutes before we get to the heart of the matter? It isn't easy for me, either."

"No? I didn't ask for this, you know. I came down here for a holiday, not a confrontation. You might have written."

"I'm sorry about that, too. I was very upset after you left, and it took awhile for my anger to cool down. Once it did, I saw things in a different light. Here, drink your wine and relax a little. You look terrific tonight! That red dress really suits you; it shows off your tan."

"Thank you. How amazing that you should run into Stephanie like that."

"It was a little embarrassing after the fact, having dinner with her and neither of us having any idea who the other was. She tells me you're down here looking for some long-lost branch of your family?" He pulled a cigarette from the pack on the table and lit it, watching her over the flame.

Here it was, then. "Yes. I thought it would be fun tracking it down since I was going to be so close."

"Close?" asked David casually, leaning back in his chair.

"I was in Bordeaux for the firm. I wouldn't have thought you'd forget so easily, David."

"No, of course not. I just hadn't put it together," he said quickly. "So where does this branch of the family fit in?"

"They're cousins of my grandmother. Elizabeth mentioned them a few weeks ago and they were as good an excuse as any to use for my week off. I haven't had time to draw breath since I left New York, and I badly needed to get away. A distraction seemed like a good idea."

"Your break's been successful, then?"

"I think so. I won't know until I get back to New York and we see how well this trip has done. As for the port aspect—"

"No, I meant your ancestral hunt. Did you find the family?"

"They were wiped out during the war. There was a terrible massacre in the village; a good many families were destroyed. It's a touching story, and a tragic one."

"That's a shame," said David. "How much longer are you staying?"

"I have to be back in London Monday morning. I think we should order." She relaxed, relieved to have cleared the biggest hurdle at the beginning. David certainly hadn't wasted any time getting to the heart of his matter. Now she could throw herself into the emotional scene without too much worry. She was as certain as she could be that she'd convinced him of her innocence; the wary look was gone from his face.

They talked of neutral things during dinner, and David seemed to have lost interest in her presence in St. Mouton, for he didn't mention it again. He told her of the post he was taking up with Sevronsen, spoke to her of her father in glowing terms (all of which tightened the cord around the knot in Kate's stomach), and caught her up on friends.

But when dinner was finished, so was the unspoken

truce. "Can we talk now, Katie, really talk? We're very good at skirting around the issues, aren't we."

"Aren't we," she said sweetly. 'What would you like to talk about?"

"I want to talk about us, our future."

She examined his face, the contours softened by candlelight. The long, narrow planes hadn't changed, nor had the shape of his slightly tilted mouth, but it was a foreign face, belonging to someone she didn't know at all. And now his brown eyes were earnest, the dark brows arched over them, and she wondered what he was really thinking behind the mask. Most likely something along the lines that she was a recalcitrant bitch. Improbably, she wanted to laugh.

"Katie?"

"What makes you think we have a future, David?"

"I know we do—I've had a lot of time to think about what went wrong between us, and I'm prepared to take a hefty share of the blame. You were right, I tried too hard to control you, and I expected too much of you."

"And now?" She looked down into her glass.

"And now I'm prepared to do anything I can to make it up to you. I've been in hell since you left." He rubbed his forehead, then looked up at her with a combination of frustration, longing, and despair, perfectly calculated to melt the heart of any sane woman, "Katie, dear Katie, do you think maybe you still love me a little?" He reached for her hand and she let him have it.

"I don't know, David." He was working hard for it, she thought with a vengeful pleasure.

"Feelings don't just disappear, not the kind of feelings that we had."

"No, they don't disappear, but they can change, David." She met his eye.

"Have yours changed, then?"

"Look, isn't it enough to tell you that I've been desperately unhappy? I don't want to go through that all over again!"

"But do you love me?" he persisted.

"Yes! All right, yes I do, but that doesn't mean I'm going to go running back to you—oh, David, can't you understand? It's not that easy! I've been in torment, trying to forget about you, and after all this time you suddenly show up and my legs turn to water and I want to throw myself into your arms, and it's just not fair!"

She jumped up from the table and walked quickly through the hall and out the door to the square. Her shoulders started shaking with suppressed laughter, and she covered her face trying to regain control. This was too close to the emotional borderline of last night, and she couldn't afford to lose her grip.

She heard him coming up behind her and she spun around and buried her face in his jacket before he could see her condition had nothing to do with anguish. "I'm sorry, David, I didn't mean to create a scene," she managed to mumble against his chest.

He slipped his arms around her and held her close. "Katie, my little Katie, don't cry now. Everything's okay, it's going to be just fine, you'll see. I'm going to take care of you, honey." He kissed the top of her head, and Kate suddenly realized with amazement that David had always been slightly condescending to her. She'd never noticed it before, but it was so clear now after being with Sebastian, who always treated her as an equal, never as a child, even when comforting her. At those times he offered simple solace and support, but never condescension. The thought of Sebastian mercifully sobered her, and she pulled away from David and looked up at him in the faint light.

It was a mistake. He took it as an invitation and bent his head, kissing her slowly, parting her lips. It was the last fence and the most difficult of all. She forced herself to respond, loathing every minute of it, but telling herself with a bleak inward smile that Sebastian, with that laugh in his eyes, would have told her to think of God and England, and it helped to get her through. Finally it was over, and David smiled down at her, still holding her closely.

"Oh, God, Katie, I feel so much better! You have no idea what that kiss did for me. I've really missed you, you know."

"I've missed you too, David." She tried to smile back.

"So what do we do now, Katie? Where do we go? I'm feeling at a loss—there's nothing more I can say, except I love you and I want you back more than anything, but it's your call now."

"I don't have an answer yet, David," she said helplessly. "This is too important a decision to make impulsively, especially after being kissed like that." She moved away from him, but had not missed the flicker of satisfaction in his eye. "I'm going to bed, and I'm going to think everything through very carefully before I say anything else."

"Do you want some company? I'm great at thinking." He grinned hopefully.

"No, thanks—it's best if I do this kind of thinking on my own. Look, I'm exhausted, David. Why don't we talk again tomorrow? Come by the hotel, or if I'm not there, leave a note where you want to meet. All right?"

"Okay, if you're sure," he said reluctantly, and bent to give her another kiss, but this time it was quick.

"Good night, David."

He lit a cigarette as he watched her go back to the hotel and through the door. Drawing in the smoke, he mulled the situation over and decided he was thoroughly satisfied on all counts; her presence in St. Mouton was clearly harmless, and as for the other, well, he really couldn't have expected her to take him to her bed quite so soon. But it was only a matter of time before Kate capitulated. He knew the pattern well, and had always tried to give her enough room to think that the decision was hers. He threw the cigarette into the gutter and walked away.

David halted abruptly in Madame Chabot's doorway, then quickly cleared his throat and managed to walk casually into the room. "Herr Schumann! This is a surprise! But why are you here? I'd have thought this town was very dangerous for you."

Karl Erharder rose slowly from his chair, where he had been impatiently awaiting David's return, Schwab at his side. His light blue eyes glittered coldly in the lamplight, and every inch of him breathed menace.

"Never mind the danger," he said in chilling tones. "I

came to hear your report personally. I don't like the way things have been going. What do you have to tell me about the girl?"

"I've just come from her." He gave a quick account of what he had learned. "So you see, she's quite innocent, and virtually back under my control."

"And you are a fool, Herr Russell. Do you know where she went today?"

"Yes, I had all her movements traced by Brecht. She did nothing in the least bit suspicious." David was quite puzzled by the cold fury in Erharder's eyes.

"She went into a camera shop, is that correct?"

"I believe so, yes."

"And she did not reappear until two hours later."

"Brecht did not see her until she entered her hotel, no. He thought he must have missed her when she'd left the shop."

"My dear Herr Russell. It just happens that the shop in question is owned by a certain Henri Jumeau. Do you have any idea what that means?"

"No, sir. What's the harm in that? I told you she was tracing a branch of her family, asking questions—"

"Henri Jumeau just happens to be the brother of Giselle Jumeau, the brave little Resistance heroine. I had thought all the scum of that family dead, but it appears I was wrong. Now does that mean something, you idiot?"

David blanched. "I can't believe it was anything but coincidence, sir—she's not the sort of girl to get involved—"

"No? And I suppose it was just coincidence that she was in a remote restaurant in the mountains of Jamaica at the same time I was there, and later at the same club? Just coincidence that she became your fiancée and then later broke it off, just coincidence that her father worked in the State Department for so many years? Do you realize what sort of connections that gave her into the CIA? And finally, just coincidence that she is in this little village, of no interest to a tourist, nosing around with questions about von Fiedler and consorting with the Jumeaus when it was Giselle who stole my documents in the first place?"

"Herr Schumann, I assure you—if you knew the girl, you would never question her!"

"So, you're even more of an idiot than I thought. Get her, Russell. Get her and bring her to me. I shall find out myself exactly what I want to know." His lips curved upward in a small, malicious smile.

After trying her own room and discovering that Sebastian was not there, Kate went to Stephanie's door and knocked, but there was no answer. Sighing, she returned to her room and sat down in the armchair, determined to wait up for Sebastian. She could hardly believe the insanity of what was going around her. It had shaken her up a good deal more than she'd first realized to spend three hours in David's company, and the relief of being able to let down her guard was enormous.

At times it had seemed almost impossible to believe that David was an enemy, a spy against her government. Their conversation throughout dinner had been so normal, so like the conversations they used to have, and yet every now and then the calculating expression in his eyes had reminded her of exactly who she was dealing with. When had it started? He had obviously gone after her from their very first meeting with a purpose in mind, to get to her father through her. In a way it was a balm to her soul to know that in the end, her instincts about their relationship had been dead accurate. But it didn't help to know how thoroughly she'd been taken in. Sebastian had been right; she had chosen David because her father approved of him, because the two were in many ways alike. She went over to the window and looked out over the dark square, pushing the hair hard off her face as if it would help to clear her thoughts, hardly noticing the black Renault that had pulled up to the sidewalk.

Why, damn it? Why had it been so necessary to have her father's acceptance? He hadn't wanted her around until she was old enough to be of use to him, and even then he had managed to make her feel as if any form of dissent was rebellion. And once he had talked her into returning to America, she'd been trapped, had fallen into the pattern he'd set for her, met his friends, been his hostess, the perfect daughter. And ultimately he had chosen her future husband, encouraged her to spend time with him, had showered her with praise when she'd become engaged. He had, in fact, dictated the circumstances to suit himself.

Anger stabbed at her. That was another thing Sebastian had been right about; no human being had a right to trample another underfoot . . .

Impatiently, she turned from the window, wondering what was taking him so long, and on that thought a knock came at the door. She leapt across the room. "Who is it?" she asked softly through the door.

"It is Monsieur Barbier, mademoiselle. There is an urgent message for you."

Alarmed, she opened the door to the concierge. "Yes, monsieur?"

He regarded her sadly, apologetically. "It is not good news, mademoiselle. Your friend, Mademoiselle Matthison, has met with an accident in her car. They have asked for you to be brought to the hospital in Périgueux. I shall drive you, yes?"

The color drained from Kate's face. "Oh, God, no! What happened! Is it serious, do you know?"

"I do not know, mademoiselle. The police called with the news, and did not say, simply asked for you to be taken to her."

"Yes, of course! Give me just a moment and I'll be with you." She closed the door, her mind racing, panic for Stephanie obliterating thought. She had to force herself to concentrate. Sebastian first. Quickly she jotted a note for him and left it on the pillow, then collecting her handbag, she went downstairs with Monsieur Barbier.

"My car is just outside, mademoiselle."

"Thank you so much, monsieur, this is very kind. Please hurry!"

"It is nothing." He led her to the black car and opened the curbside door for her. She quickly got in and shut the door, her fingers fumbling nervously with the catch on her bag, silently urging him to be faster as he went around to the driver's side.

"How long will it take to—" Her words were cut short by a sudden blow to the back of her head, and she was aware only of a sense of surprise at her own stupidity as she slipped into blackness.

CHAPTER Fifteen

Sebastian took Pierre to his house and stayed only long enough to briefly tell Henri (who had waited up to hear the news) about the two interviews. He then drove to his hotel and had a quick wash, changed into jeans and black polo-necked jersey, and fastened on the inevitable gun holster, covering it with his suede jacket. After feeling around in the back of the closet, he removed the watch from where he'd hidden it from prying eyes. He looked at it for a long moment, his eyes slightly narrowed, then gripped it hard as if he'd made a decision and slipped it into his pocket. He left the room as quietly as he'd entered and headed for Kate.

Careful to take the back streets, alert for any sign of being followed, he slipped through the service entrance of the Hôtel Périgord and made his way noiselessly up the back stairs. The light was still on under Kate's door and he knocked softly. There was no answer and he tried the handle; the door swung open easily. He frowned. There was no sign of Kate.

Sebastian shut the door quietly behind him, and puzzled, he looked around the room, wondering if she wasn't down the hall. But then his eye caught the piece of paper on top of the pillow, and he read the hurriedly scrawled writing.

Sebastian, Stephanie's had a car accident and I've gone to the Périgueux hospital. Meet me there as soon as you can. I don't know how bad it is, but the police called for me to come. Please hurry—I'm so worried. Kate.

He stood very still, absorbing the shock, a thousand possibilities twisting at him all at once. But there was no time for thought. He'd first call the hospital from the square and try to reach Kate, find out how Stephanie was, then work out the implications later. Christ—poor Stephanie, he thought as he turned off the light.

A knock came at the door, then another. He flattened himself against the wall, his hand going to his gun as the handle turned and the door slowly opened. A silhouette very cautiously stepped over the sill. Sebastian kicked the door shut with his foot and jumped, going for the chest, pinning the arms down.

"What—let me go, damn you!"

He felt a sick jolt of recognition and immediately released the very healthy, struggling body of Stephanie, reaching over and snapping the light on.

Stephanie had been scared out of her wits being grabbed like that out of nowhere, and it took her a moment before she could control the frantic beating of her heart. "You!" she gasped, blinking at him. "What are you—oh, my God—" She took in the significance of the empty room. "Where's Kate? What have you done with her, you monster?"

Sebastian looked at her blankly. "Stephanie . . . Is Kate not with you?"

"Of course not! What in God's name are you doing here, skulking about in her room in the dark?" She stared at the gun.

"Stephanie, hush for a moment and let me think." He finally realized what she was gaping at and slipped the gun away. "Have you just come from the Périgueux hospital?"

"I—I don't know what you're talking about! I've just come back from Périgueux, and certainly not from the hospital—now tell me what's going on! What are you doing here, and where's Kate? If you've hurt her, I'll kill you!" She backed away, looking very unlike a would-be murderess.

"Oh, for Christ's sake, Stephanie, be still! Listen to me—Kate's supposed to have gone to the Périgueux hospital for you. She got a message saying you'd had an accident with the car. Do you know anything at all about this?" His eyes bit into her, demanding an answer.

"No . . ." She glared at him. "Why should I think for a minute you're telling the truth? Maybe you've taken Kate, done something awful to her, and you're just covering up for yourself. What are you doing with that gun!"

"Stephanie, don't be an idiot. Kate's in trouble, serious trouble; she's obviously been led into a trap. There's no time for a lot of nonsense—you're going to tell me everything that happened today, where you went and what you did. But first, when's the last time you saw her?"

"I'm not telling you anything. I know all about you and your filthy activities, Mr. Dunn, and you're not going to get away with this, I swear it."

Sebastian fingered his brow in frustration, then threw his hand out at her. "Look, I know what Kate told you, but none of it's true, and she knows that as of yesterday. She just couldn't tell you what was really going on. For God's sake, what do I have to do to convince you!"

"I don't believe a word of what you're saying. I'm calling the police!"

"Who the hell do you think she was in bed with this morning?"

Stephanie's eyes widened. For the first time it occurred to her that there might be some truth in Sebastian's story. "What?" she said idiotically.

"Look, I'm sorry, I'm not thinking very coherently at the moment. Of course you have good reason to doubt me." He impatiently dug in his pocket for Kate's note and handed it to her. "Here. Read this, it should convince you."

"Oh . . . Yes, I see." She looked up at him, confused and bewildered. "But I don't understand! What about David? She was going out to dinner with him tonight, to talk things over; she said you were finished and—"

Sebastian had gone white about the mouth, and he sank down on the bed. "She went out to dinner with David Russell tonight?" he said in carefully measured tones. "When did David appear on the scene, if you don't mind my asking?"

For a moment, Stephanie felt a throb of sympathy for him, he looked so shaken. "He came around this afternoon. Look, I'm sorry if you're hurt, or Kate's playing you and David off against each other—" She was stunned when Sebastian gave a short, harsh bark of laughter.

"No, my dear girl, believe me I'm not hurt, although it's very kind of you to worry about my feelings. No, I've got quite a separate bone to pick with Mr. Russell." His mouth was grim and tight.

"I don't understand any of this."

"No, of course you wouldn't. We tried to keep you out of it, but it's too late for that now. I'm going to need your help, Stephanie, if Kate's going to survive this." His words were spoken in a flat, neutral tone, and their very lack of emphasis served to underline the message behind them.

"What on earth do you mean?" Stephanie was thoroughly frightened now, if she hadn't been before, a chilling fear that went clear through her bones.

"David Russell works for a neo-Nazi organization that thinks Kate has access to some very dangerous information. He came down here to find out what she knows. It's all connected with von Fiedler."

"And you, what do you have to do with all this?"

For what seemed like the hundredth time that day, he said, "I work for MI-6. That's where the confusion came. I thought for a time that Kate was mixed up in David's dirty business. I discovered last night I was wrong. And Kate learned the truth."

Stephanie stared hard at him. Then she finally managed to say, "I don't believe this."

"Understandably. Unfortunately you're going to have to believe it, as unlikely as it may seem. The basic, damnable fact is that Kate had dinner with Russell, and sometime between then and now she was lured away with this story of you and an accident. She must have said something at dinner to make him doubt her. Stephanie, if we're going to help Kate, we're going to have to put our heads together. Look, you need to know what's happened so far..." In a flash he outlined the old story and the events, and when he'd finished, Stephanie looked at him helplessly.

"Sebastian—what are we going to do?"

"We're damned well going to find Kate if it kills me. Now here's where we start..."

Kate opened her eyes, wincing against the blinding pain in her head. The faint light, gray and too sharp, came through the filmy window and she realized that she must have been unconscious for hours. Gingerly she felt the lump on the back of her skull and had to fight against the sudden nausea that rose in her throat.

She was on a narrow bed, covered by a thin blanket. The room was empty save for an armoire against the wall and a straight, lattice-backed chair. She struggled to sit up but only made herself dizzy with the effort, and her body sank back down onto the mattress. David—it could only be David who'd done this to her. How could she have been such a fool? By now Sebastian would be terribly worried, she thought with a little stab. Sebastian... Hot tears stung unbidden in her eyes and she tried to think what to do, but her weak attempt at logic was blotted out as darkness closed over her again.

"No matter how many times we've been over it, I can't make any more sense out of what happened. Damn!" Sebastian ran a hand through his hair, then clenched it into a fist, banging the table. His face was white and strained, and seemed much older, as if lines had been drawn on it that had not been there only hours before.

They sat around the Jumeau table, Pierre, Henri, Nadia, and Stephanie, shadows of worry carved under their eyes.

The night was running down to nothing and they were no further than where they had started. The police had been called, but obviously had received no report of a car accident in the area, and had issued no summons. Therefore it was apparent that someone had given Kate a false message from the police. But who? It would have to be someone she would have no reason to doubt.

"It can't have been David," said Sebastian again. "We know that she went back to her room, she wrote the note, and she'd never have opened her door to him, knowing what she did."

"Unless she wrote the note under duress," said Pierre.

"If that had been the case, they would have come up with a far more reasonable explanation for where she'd gone, something that wouldn't have Stephanie raising the alarm when she got back. They can't have known where Stephanie had gone, must have simply made sure she wasn't back, and used that as the lure," said Sebastian tersely. "In the first place, David knew Stephanie would think Kate was with him when she found her gone. No, they can't have known that she left a note. But there are still too many loose ends. Something, *something* Kate said to David must have tipped him off. I should never have left her, but I never thought he'd take such a risk as this. Damn and blast my stupidity!"

"You must not blame yourself, monsieur," said Henri gently. "None of us could have known such a thing would happen. No, we must try again to piece things together. There has to be reason in this somewhere."

"Reason. Oh yes, you can depend that there's reason, cold and calculating. I'll lay money that Kate's somewhere close by, and safe—for now. The only reason they'd take her would be to interrogate her, find out what she knows—or try to recover the photograph. The question is, who did she go with? It must be someone connected with the Group, but she'd know better than to trust David for an instant."

"You don't think that maybe he persuaded her back to him? She was engaged to him, after all, and at one time he had quite a hold over her."

"Stephanie," Sebastian sighed. "Believe me when I tell you that's not possible."

"I'm sorry, Sebastian, but how can you be so sure?"

He spoke very quietly and in English. "Because Kate and I love each other very much and we're going to be married as soon as this whole mess is over with."

For the third time that night Stephanie stared at him. "I . . . see. Yes, I can understand why you'd be sure." She smiled at him then. "Congratulations."

"Thanks. But if this wedding's to come off, we'd better get back to the business of finding the bride."

"Wake up, mademoiselle. I have brought you coffee and bread. Wake up, now."

Kate heard the voice coming from a long way off, and struggled against it, but it was persistent, droning in her ear. She reluctantly opened her eyes, and then memory came flooding back to her, all of it, black and heavy. And leaning over her was a vaguely familiar face, old, harsh—of course, the woman from the *boulangerie*. She put her in mind of the wicked witch of the west with that long narrow nose, beady eyes, and sharp chin. Where were the mole and hair, she wondered rudely.

"Here, I have brought you a cloth for your face and a brush." She put the items down with, incongruously it seemed, a mirror.

"How very hospitable of you, madame," said Kate wryly, sitting up. Her head still ached, but the nausea seemed to have abated. "I don't suppose you run to a change of clothes?"

Madame Chabot regarded her acidly. "There are gentlemen waiting to see you. I will give you a few minutes to arrange yourself." She gestured to the tray and left Kate alone.

Kate now had time to take stock of the situation. Gentlemen—that meant David and at least one other person. But who? That at least she would find out in no short order. Where had she slipped up last night—there had to be something she'd said that had given her away, but hard as she tried, she could think of nothing incriminating. And David had seemed so convinced . . .

She ran the cloth over her face, and cautiously brushed her hair, staying away from the area behind her right ear. The coffee and bread she ignored. Not three minutes later, the door opened and David walked in.

"My, isn't this is a surprise," said Kate nastily.

David ignored the comment. "So, Katie. I'm sorry about the knock to your head. How are you feeling?"

"You can take your pick of angry, confused, frightened, and indignant. This is a fine way to persuade me to marry you."

"I'm afraid it wasn't I who arranged for your abduction, Katie. There's a man here who's very interested in talking to you."

"He might have gone about it in a normal manner," she said dryly. "Does this have anything to do with the State Department, David? Is this their way of checking out my credentials for wife material, or have you hired some thug to bully me into submission?"

"Not exactly. What have you been doing, Katie, I wonder, to bring you to this?"

"I can't think what you mean. God, I've got a headache, and I don't mind telling you that I'm absolutely furious with you and will probably never speak to you again."

"That's really not my concern right now. Pull yourself together, Katie. I suggest you tell this gentleman everything he wants to know as truthfully as you know how."

She looked up. There, standing in the doorway, was the old, scar-necked man from Jamaica. A little thrill of shock ran through her—the infamous Erharder, of course. This was a great deal worse than she'd anticipated. She was thankful there was no color in her face to start with, or he'd have seen it all drain away. She bit back her fear and spoke boldly. "Why, if it isn't Mr. Schumann from Port Antonio. Have you left your tropical paradise to come and effect a formal introduction?"

"You may think yourself very clever and courageous,

Miss Soames, but that shall not last for long, I assure you. You may either answer my questions of your own volition, or I shall have to find other ways to discover what I want to know.''

''Oh, my, you do have charming friends, David. Just what the hell is going on here!''

''You appear to know Mr. Schumann, Kate. How is that?''

''For heaven's sake, David. I saw him one evening in Port Antonio. He was rude enough to stare me up and down, and I asked someone his name. Is that some kind of offense?''

''Mr. Schumann believes you are trying to avail yourself of some information that belongs to him.''

''Don't be absurd! This is beginning to frighten me, David. Please, tell me what this is all about—what have you gotten yourself involved with?''

''Mr. Schumann would like to know what you were doing with Henri Jumeau yesterday at noon, and for two hours thereafter.''

She felt as if he'd hit her. ''Monsieur Jumeau?'' she said as blankly as she could manage. ''I had lunch with him and his wife and grandson—why ever would you be interested in that?''

''And why were you suddenly invited into his house, Miss Soames? These people do not instantly take tourists into the bosom of their family.''

''As I told David, I've been trying to trace a distant branch of my family—they were acquainted, and they offered to tell me a little about them.''

''The name of your family, Miss Soames?''

''Oh, this is ridiculous!'' She thought furiously. She had to say something, anything to divert attention from the Jumeaus. ''Why do you want to know all this?''

''I shall ask the questions. The name of your family?'' His little eyes glittered at her.

''Lambourte,'' she said, pulling a name from the plaque. She knew for certain from the phone book that there were none left in the village.

He looked at her coldly. "And what would be your interest in Ernst von Fiedler?"

Her heart kicked, hard. Now, Kate, she told herself. Now or never. "In case you're not aware of it, Mr. Schumann, half this village was annihilated during the war, my family being only a few of the unfortunate victims. A man called Karl Erharder gunned them down in cold blood in reprisal for Resistance activities. I understood that von Fiedler was Erharder's superior. Naturally I would be interested in learning more about the people who were responsible for such an appalling thing." She could see with great satisfaction that he hadn't expected this. He hesitated for a fraction of a second, then jerked his head at David.

"I shall be back later, Miss Soames. Please, do not allow yourself to become too confident in my absence." He strode out, and Kate wondered even if he decided to believe her story, whether she'd be allowed to live.

By mid-morning, Pierre had been sent to bring Monsieur Villers down to St. Mouton. The other Jumeau children and grandchildren Sebastian had organized to spread out around the village, looking for any sign of anything unusual and to ask subtle questions of the villagers, trying to determine if anyone might have seen Kate being taken, and where.

Sebastian was not accustomed to working with his hands tied, having to use other people to be his eyes and ears, but he couldn't take the risk that David might see him, recognize his face and put the two things together. He could only pray that David still had no idea he existed.

As the sky had lightened he'd sent a gray and obviously exhausted Stephanie back to the hotel to sleep, telling her she'd be useless to him without it, and in the meantime it was imperative that she not raise the alarm just yet. If she were to discover Kate missing, it would only be natural that it happen when Kate usually rose. They had to do everything possible to keep Kate's innocence unquestionable to the people who had taken her. Without a doubt they would be watching carefully. Stephanie reluctantly agreed, and used the back entrance to the hotel as Sebastian had insisted.

He then called Colonel Harrington and they spoke for a long time. When Sebastian emerged from the tiny closet the Jumeaus kept the phone in, although tense and drawn, he looked slightly relieved. The Jumeaus persuaded him to take a couple of hours of sleep upstairs, giving him the same argument as he'd handed Stephanie, and he agreed, surprised to find that his eyes closed immediately and he slept deeply. In this one thing, his training had served him well, he reflected bitterly, as he rose to start the hunt again.

"Monsieur Barbier, I was wondering if you'd seen my friend Mademoiselle Soames. She did not sleep in her room last night, and I'm concerned about her." Stephanie had somehow managed to sleep until noon, and now felt much more competent to deal with the task at hand.

"Mademoiselle Soames?" He shrugged. "Perhaps she spent the night elsewhere? It is not an uncommon thing these days."

"No, monsieur, she left a note, you see."

A flicker of surprise came and went in his eyes. "A note? And what did it say, mademoiselle?" He assumed a bored expression.

"She'd mistakenly received a message that I'd been injured and taken to the Périgueux hospital. It must have been someone playing a nasty joke, but she left for the hospital and never arrived there. I'm terribly concerned. I mean, I'm sure there's a reasonable explanation for all this, a mix-up of some sort, but I thought I'd ask, just in case."

"I see . . . Well, since you ask and are concerned, no message came in for her, but there was a young man, an American, mademoiselle. I didn't want to mention it for fear of being indelicate, but she left with him, quite happily. She must have written this note so that you wouldn't know of it."

"But monsieur, that's ridiculous. I knew perfectly well I

hadn't been in an accident.'' Stephanie's mind was elsewhere—so Kate had left with David, and willingly! But then why wouldn't she have said so?

''Then she wrote it for someone else, perhaps another young man?''

''What? No—no, of course not,'' said Stephanie, flustered. That aspect of the situation hadn't occurred to her. Sebastian's presence was not to be known about, he'd made that quite clear. ''No, you've cleared up the problem for me, monsieur. I think she was just playing a little joke on me and I failed to see it. Thank you so much.''

He waited until she was out of sight, then called for the chambermaid. After a quick conversation with her, he pulled on his hat and hurried off.

''Katie, listen, I'm sorry about all that earlier business. Did it upset you?'' It had taken him two hours, but in the end, Erharder had been convinced and was willing to let her go, if David could persuade her his story was true.

''What do you think, David? You knock me out and kidnap me, then throw that monster at me with no explanation, frighten me half to death, and refuse to tell me what's going on. Of course I'm upset!''

''I'm really very sorry, honey. I couldn't do anything to help you until you were cleared. You see, you got youself entangled in a bizarre set of coincidences, and Mr. Schumann had to be very sure you were not involved.''

Kate couldn't figure out what he was up to. ''Involved in what, David?''

''Mr. Schumann is with the State Department, Katie. He's involved in very high-level, classified information.''

She choked on the enormity of the lie. ''Oh, I see,'' she said faintly. ''But what does that have to do with me?''

''He thought you might have stumbled on something you shouldn't have through me, you see, and that you were stirring up trouble. I can't really explain any more than that. But he's convinced now that you're clean, so you have nothing more to worry about.''

"His methods are a bit rough, don't you think?"

"I'm sorry, but that's the way things work. He can't afford to take chances."

"What do you have to do with all this, David? Isn't this a little bit too much like cloak-and-dagger for your line of work?"

"Well . . ." He had the grace to look away for a moment, but then his eyes met hers again. "I never intended for you to know about it, but I've been involved in this sort of thing for quite awhile. Mr. Schumann and I have been working together on a highly classified project involving von Fiedler, you see. That's why I had to go down to Jamaica, to meet with him there. I couldn't tell you at the time, which made it all the more difficult when you were so angry with me. I'd arranged the trip for that very purpose, and then when you—well. Anyway, I began to wonder about you myself when you broke things off so abruptly and suddenly went to London. I thought maybe you'd come across something in my papers you shouldn't have. And then I heard you were in St. Mouton—that's when Mr. Schumann decided something needed to be done."

"Yes—yes, I do see," she said slowly. "I suppose this was necessary, if it's that important to the government. Oh, David, and here I thought you were mixed up in something terrible!"

"Never mind, honey, it was natural you should think that." He kissed her hair. "As I said, you're in the clear, and everything's okay now."

You're very good at this, David, thought Kate. *Very good indeed, you lying bastard, but I can match you.* "Then last night, the things you said to me, you didn't mean them?"

"No! I meant every word, I swear it. Look, I believed you, but Schumann wasn't convinced. He insisted you be brought here, and I hated it, but I had to put the country's security over us. Do you understand?"

"Yes, of course. Poor David, it must have been terrible for you." She bit her lip, overcome with a terrible, treacherous impulse to laugh.

"Yes, it was. But it's all over now. We can go home and forget all about it."

"I don't think so, Herr Russell." Erharder advanced slowly and silently into the room like an animal coming in for the kill. He pushed David to one side and looked down at Kate with a small, nasty sneer. Then his hand lashed out and grabbed her arm, his fingers biting into her flesh. "You're very clever, Miss Soames, but nowhere near clever enough. And now you shall tell me the truth."

"I don't understand," cried Kate, struggling against the merciless grip, her pupils dilated with fear. "Take your hand off me! I swear, I'll scream this house down!"

"That would do you no good at all, Miss Soames, for there would be no one to hear. There isn't another house around within screaming distance." His fingers squeezed even harder and she let out a little cry at the pain.

"David! Please! Tell him—"

David was looking extremely alarmed. "Mr. Schumann, I don't understand—I thought we'd agreed Kate was no threat!"

"You're a fool, Russell. Your little friend here managed to deceive you very nicely. I don't suppose you know she wrote a note to someone telling him she'd gone to Périgueux hospital for the Matthison girl?"

"No, I—"

"So now there shall be a hue and cry, looking for her. You assured me that Miss Matthison would believe the girl was safely with you." He turned his glittering eyes back to Kate. "And who is this someone, Miss Soames, that you would be writing a note for?" There was no doubt about the menace in his tone.

Kate's body seemed to turn to ice, the only heat left coming from the pain in her arm. They'd found the note, and knew about Sebastian . . . "I—"

He reached out with his free hand and slapped her, hard. "And now, Miss Soames, now you shall tell us everything."

CHAPTER
Sixteen

Sebastian paced up and down the Jumeaus' living area like a caged beast. Nothing had come in, no sign, no indication of where Kate might be. The immobility was killing him, but he daren't risk Kate's safety by putting his face out on the streets. Not just yet . . .

"Sebastian!" Stephanie hurried in the door.

He turned and gave her a long, assessing look. "I'm glad to see you're looking better."

"I slept far too late, but I feel a hundred percent better, you were quite right. But you'll never guess—I've just talked to the concierge at the hotel—he says he saw Kate leave willingly with David late last night!"

"Did he, now." There was no obvious change in Sebastian's expression, but the chill in his voice sent a shudder through her. "And how was it he happened to volunteer that information?"

"Well, it was quite simple, really. I told him that Kate hadn't slept in her room last night, and that I was concerned about her, because she was supposed to have gone to Périgueux hospital after me, but obviously someone had played a—"

"What!" roared Sebastian. "Jesus, Stephanie, you told him about the note?"

"Why, yes . . . I couldn't see the harm, and it worked, because he said he hadn't been going to mention Kate's leaving for fear of being indelicate, you see. But when he thought Kate had left a note to put me off what she was really up to . . . or someone else . . . Oh, my God, I do see."

"Yes, exactly. This could have torn it, Stephanie—no, don't look like that, it's done now. Maybe it'll go no further, but one can never count on that. Look, let me think for a moment." He ran his hand through his hair, concentration narrowing his eyes, then after a minute or two he looked over at her. "Was there any indication from the concierge, anything at all that might make you think he knows more than he's telling? Think very carefully."

"I don't know. He did seem a bit cagey, especially when I first asked, but then, maybe he was embarrassed. And I suppose he did look a little surprised when I mentioned the note—but maybe I'm making that up. God, I just don't know," she said helplessly.

"Now listen. I have an idea, Stephanie. Suppose the concierge is in on this? It would explain two things. First, how her room was so easily accessed and searched—"

"But you got in that night with a locked door," she interrupted.

"A trained professional in the dead of night. David wouldn't have had time to arrive in St. Mouton and it was blazing midday. An amateur would have to be out of his mind to try it. And the concierge would know whether you were in or out. Yes, it's possible—just possible. In fact, the more I think about it, the more I wonder why it didn't occur to me earlier. If I'm right, he might well lead us straight to Kate. And if I'm wrong, then it will only be a matter of slight embarrassment."

"What d'you mean by that?"

"Never mind—you'll see. Suffice it to say that one of the elementary rules of espionage is one must always cover one's backside."

Stephanie laughed. "Well, then what's the other thing it would explain?"

"Kate would never—but never—have willingly left the

hotel with David, no matter what he told her. But if the concierge came to her with a message from the police, she'd have no reason to distrust him, would she? In which case, he was lying through his teeth about her leaving with David. I'll lay money he offered to take her to Périgueux himself. After all, she had no car."

"No, of course she didn't. Oh, Sebastian—you could be right! But how do we find out for certain? And how do we find out where Kate is?"

Sebastian smiled with satisfaction. "A simple matter of friendly persuasion, my dear. You may have done us a good turn today after all. Now listen: Here's what I want you to do."

Kate's face was white, save for the red imprint of a hand on her cheek and she looked at Erharder defiantly. "I'll tell you nothing, Mr. Schumann. Aside from the fact that there's nothing to tell, I don't speak to men who make a habit of brutalizing women."

Rage swelled and erupted in him. There was something about the girl's challenging look that reminded him of something . . . "You're as much a fool as your friend next to you, Miss Soames. You'll talk, all right. You'll be thankful to talk. Russell, bring in Schwab."

David blanched. "Please, sir. Why don't you leave her alone with me. I'll get her to tell me everything, I swear it."

"She could tell you the moon was made of green cheese, and you'd believe her. No. Go and get Schwab."

Kate's heart was pounding in her ears and she closed her eyes. Schwab, Tony's murderer. How much did they already know? How much could she give away without letting on about Sebastian—somehow they knew there'd been a note, but they didn't know about Sebastian—thank God, they didn't know about Sebastian. She opened her eyes to find Erharder glaring at her and she glared back.

"Now, Miss Soames." David came back in with Schwab,

and she recognized him immediately as one of Erharder's two Jamaican companions.

"Yes, sir?" His face was quite bland, but there was an unmistakable glint in his eyes.

"Tie her to the chair," he commanded shortly.

Kate found herself roughly dragged to the straight-backed chair and bound, her hands tied tightly behind her back, her feet lashed together. She still said nothing, continuing to glare at Erharder.

"Now, you little bitch, you will tell me to whom you wrote the note."

"No one. There was no note." This time she saw it coming and pulled her head away, but the back of his hand caught her high on the cheekbone and the force snapped her neck back.

"Who was it?"

"There was no one."

"You're lying. The chambermaid said there'd been a man in your bed the night before last."

"What?" she whispered in confusion. She vaguely heard David's sharp intake of breath.

"That didn't occur to you, did it, you stupid girl. The French are a very practical race of people. And who was this man?"

"No one—it was nobody important—please, I just didn't want David to know."

Erharder laughed at that. "That's the first thing you've said that I believe. So it was a nobody, but an important enough nobody to leave him a note?"

"Yes—I, we'd arranged to meet in my room, but then David showed up, and naturally it changed everything. I, I was going to tell him, my friend I mean, but then I got called away, so I left him the note. I didn't want him to wait."

"You're still lying. Where did you meet this man?"

"At a restaurant. I met him at a restaurant when we first arrived. Please . . . I don't understand." They really didn't know it was Sebastian, she thought over the pounding in her head.

"His name, Miss Soames?"

"What?"

"Your lover's name. Come now."

"Oh. Yes, of course. Georges, his name is Georges."

"Georges? He has no surname?"

"I can't remember; du Maurier, like Daphne, something like that." The pounding was growing stronger, like waves smashing incessantly on rock, wearing it away.

"Ha!" He laughed. "Your woman is a slut as well as a liar, Russell, what do you make of that?"

David's face was white with rage. "Leave her alone, Schumann. You've got what you wanted out of her, isn't it enough?"

"Oh, no, my good friend, not nearly enough. She knows a good deal more than she's telling, don't you, my angel."

"I know nothing, nothing at all," she whispered, her eyes closing. The inevitable blow came again, and a trickle of blood appeared at the corner of her mouth, but this time she scarcely felt it as she fell into blessed unconsciousness.

"Monsieur Barbier, I was wondering if I could have a private word with you?" Stephanie looked at him anxiously.

"But what is it, mademoiselle? I am very busy, as you can see."

What she could see was that he was doing absolutely nothing. "Yes, monsieur, but this is very important. It is about my friend, and I think we must speak in private. If you don't mind, we can go to her room. There's something I must show to you."

That did the trick. Curiosity gleamed in his eye. "Yes; yes, I suppose I can leave for a short while, mademoiselle." He came around the desk and followed her up the stairs.

"I've been so worried, monsieur, even after what you told me, and now with this—" She opened the door and he walked in after her, closing it behind them.

"Now, mademoiselle, what is it you wanted to show to me?" he said eagerly.

"This," said Sebastian, stepping from behind him, the Beretta pointing at his chest. "Please, monsieur, won't you sit down?" he asked coolly.

"But—but I, I don't understand! What is this nonsense, monsieur!"

"Nonsense?" said Sebastian, smiling lazily. "I shouldn't call it nonsense, monsieur, if you value your life. You Frenchmen understand about matters of the heart, do you not? Mademoiselle Soames is affianced to me. Now do you understand a little better?"

"Ah yes, monsieur," he said, relaxing. "You are jealous of the man she left with last night, and hope I can tell you where they went."

"Ah, no, monsieur. I know you will tell me where they went."

"But how should I know?" He shrugged gallically.

"Because I believe that you took her there yourself, Barbier. Tell me, is it really necessary that I shatter your kneecap before you tell me what Russell did with her?"

The little man's eyes grew impossibly wide. "You are crazy, monsieur!"

"Perhaps," said Sebastian. "But suppositions about the state of my mind will not help your kneecap one bit. Stephanie? I think it's time for you to leave."

She nodded and went out quietly, closing the door firmly behind her. Sebastian locked it without taking his eyes off the concierge. A fine film of sweat had broken out on the man's brow.

"Now, Barbier, suppose you sing for me."

He swallowed, his larynx bobbing violently in his throat. "I do not know, monsieur, I swear it!"

Sebastian took aim at his right leg.

"NO!" he screamed. "All right, I'll tell you—anything you want to know! Please, put the gun down." He held his shaking hands out in front of him imploringly, as if to ward off the bullet.

Sebastian lowered Barbier. "So, Barbier, how very reasonable a man you've turned out to be. Where is she?"

"Five kilometers outside the village to the north. My aunt

has a house there, it's the only one, white with blue shutters, on the hill.'' He licked his dry lips.

''I see. And who else is staying at your aunt's house?''

''Three others, with my aunt and Monsieur Russell.''

''The names of the others?''

''I don't know, monsieur, I don't. They are Germans, not from around here. I have never seen them before.''

''Then you will have to describe them, won't you.''

''There are two, one with dark hair, one with light, in their early middle years. Then the old man, silver hair, light blue eyes.'' The words could not come out fast enough.

Sebastian's eyes were narrowed. ''This old man—he has a scar on his neck?''

''Why yes, monsieur,'' said the concierge in some surprise. He was beginning to lose the purpose of this line of questioning. What would a jealous lover want with this information?

''Very good, Monsieur Barbier. And did you go running to this man to repeat the conversation you had with Mademoiselle Matthison this morning?''

He blanched. ''No, I—''

Sebastian raised the gun again. ''Such a pity. We were doing so well.''

''Yes,'' he whispered, ''I did.''

''I assume Mademoiselle Soames was quite all right at that time?''

''Yes, monsieur. She was closeted with Monsieur Russell, but I was assured that she was.'' He knew now without a doubt that this had nothing to do with a jealous lover and a great deal to do with what was going on in that house.

''And just what did you tell our good friend?''

''I told him about the note she'd left—and, and that she had entertained a lover in her bed the night before.''

''I should cripple you for that alone,'' said Sebastian tightly. ''There's one more thing. How did you persuade Kate—Mademoiselle Soames—into your car?''

''No, it was not my car, it was a black Renault belonging to the other man, the one with dark hair. I told her about an accident, that I would take her to Périgueux. It is what I was paid to do."

"And once she was in the car?" Sebastian's voice had gone very, very quiet.

Monsieur Barbier looked away. "Monsieur Russell hit her head from behind with the handle of his gun."

"I see," said Sebastian. "Like this, perhaps?" And he raised the butt of the Beretta and brought it down with a sharp crack. Monsieur Barbier slumped to the floor.

"That's one to your account, Kate," Sebastian said tersely and started to tie him with the curtain cord.

Schwab threw some cold water in Kate's face and she came to with a gasp, still tied to the chair. The light still came through the window, but more steeply, and foggily she thought that it must be coming up to early evening.

"You have been sleeping long enough. Mr. Schumann has more he wants to say to you. You will wake up now."

She looked up at him and spoke quite deliberately through her sore lip. "You're a big bully, just like your master."

He stared at her for a fraction of a second, then his brow came snapping down. "And you are a stupid girl who is more than dispensable."

She thought how odd he looked trying to frown. His eyebrows were so fair that they didn't glower the least bit effectively. He was the perfect Aryan type, could have been straight out of Hitler's breeding program. She shrugged. "Show the lions in."

Erharder came back in, but this time he had Brecht in tow. David had apparently been judged too squeamish, she thought mockingly. "Mr. Schumann. How kind of you to come and visit me. You'll have to excuse the state I'm in."

"So, Miss Soames. I see you have recovered your spirit. I hope you have also recovered your common sense. You and I both know there's a great deal more going on here than meets the eye. You will have to tell me eventually, and

I'd rather it be before I have to do anything more severe to you. Do you understand?"

"Quite well. Beat away."

"I must say that I admire your obstinacy. It reminds me of someone I once knew, long ago."

Kate smiled tightly. "Really. I wonder who that could be."

"It was a young woman named Giselle Jumeau. She was a member of the French Resistance, and sister to the man you were talking with yesterday. I'm sure her name was mentioned if you were asking about the war."

"Yes, as a matter of fact it was. And given what I heard, I should be quite pleased that I remind you of her."

"Ah yes, but then she had a great deal at stake. You have only your own life, and what a pity it would be to waste it, don't you agree?"

"That depends entirely on what you want from me, Mr. Schumann."

"I think by now you've figured out that I'm not with the State Department, haven't you, Miss Soames? You're a great deal more clever than I'd originally thought, and far too clever for your own good."

She was silent.

"And I think you know much more than you're letting on. Just what was it you stumbled across that led you to us?"

Kate sighed. "Mr. Schumann, why don't you beat me, or shoot me, or whatever you're going to do, and get it over with? I have nothing to tell you. As David pointed out, it's been a series of coincidences from start to finish, so this interrogation is pointless. So if you don't mind, I'd rather avoid a lot of unnecessary nonsense. I doubt very much you plan on keeping me around after this, anyway, so I'd like to get the nasty stuff over with as soon as possible."

He laughed then, loud and long. "Very good, Miss Soames! I like your style. You don't mind if I call you Kate, do you? No? Good, good. Now then Kate, we start at the very beginning. You fabricated your little argument with David just before the Jamaican holiday. Was it so you could come down and watch us surreptitiously?"

Kate wearily shook her head. "Believe it or not, I was genuinely furious with your golden boy."

"Yes, yes indeed. Now, who was the man you spent so much time with while you were there, the fisherman?"

At that her heart kicked. She had to protect Sebastian at all cost. "What does he have to do with anything? He was just someone I picked up. As you said so succinctly, I'm a slut."

He laughed again. "I begin to wonder if I was not mistaken. A girl with your spirit and intelligence—she wouldn't go with just anyone."

"My dear Mr. Schumann, you're a little out of date, aren't you? A girl with my spirit and intelligence, as you call it, would do precisely as she pleases. And don't tell me that's not what you were thinking the first time you laid eyes on me. Now do you mind keeping my sexual activities out of the conversation?" She chafed at the rope behind her back. Her arms had long since gone numb, but where the rope bit at her wrists she could still feel pain.

"I like you, Kate. It's such a pity we had to meet this way. You know, I think your life might just be salvageable. Can I not persuade you to come over to my side? We could work well together, and I could use another good double agent."

"Oh, for pity's sake, Mr. Schumann, what does it take to convince you I know nothing about agenting, double or otherwise?"

"Untie her, Schwab."

Kate looked at him in blank amazement. This she was not prepared for; it almost frightened her more. But the blood came mercifully rushing back into her limbs as she was loosed, and painfully she moved her arms. She watched Erharder warily.

"Now then, Kate. I give you a last chance to come clean. If you choose not to, then your friends the Jumeaus shall pay the consequences. Do I make myself very clear?"

She went deathly cold. "But they're innocent! They have nothing to do with any of this!" she blurted out in the first real fear she'd felt from the time she'd been tied and given up her life as lost.

"Yes, I thought as much. Now we're getting somewhere. You came to find certain documents, did you not, Kate? It is why you were questioning the Jumeaus, for you have somehow learned that Giselle stole them. You think they know something about where she hid them, do you not?" he asked gently.

"No!" How could she possibly keep the Jumeaus safe now? And then Sebastian's words, spoken in what seemed a century ago, came faintly back to her. 'Stay as close to the truth . . .' They poured through her, giving her a quiet strength, and she knew now what she had to do. Her voice came very calm and soft. "No. I came to find my grandmother."

"What's this?" The defiance had fled from her face and he sensed the truth. "Your grandmother? And who would that be?"

"You should know. I remind you of her."

For the first time she'd truly caught him off his guard. "I don't understand," he said, staring at her blankly.

"Don't you? Giselle Jumeau was my grandmother, Herr Erharder. You killed her."

Stephanie left her vigil over the unconscious concierge and opened Kate's door to the soft prearranged knock. "Sebastian?" Then she stopped dead in amazement at the sight of Sebastian's companion. "Not from Jamaica? On the boat!" The two of them were standing in the doorway, Eustice's black face split by a broad grin.

Sebastian laughed as they walked in. "We MI-6 blokes hang together, Stephanie. Still out? Good, it serves him bloody right, the swine."

"I don't believe it!" cried Stephanie. "Eustice, of all people!"

"Bouge would have sent his regards, but he's on another assignment." Eustice laughed in his soft, lilting accent.

"Okay, we've got work to do." Sebastian checked the knots holding Monsieur Barbier one last time and stuffed his handkerchief into the man's mouth, dragging him over to the closet and depositing him neatly inside. "Let's go." He hung the "Do Not Disturb" sign outside the locked door as they left.

They went out the back way and carefully made their way to the Peugeot. "Right, now, Stephanie. We're taking your car, I hope you don't mind. I gave Marcel and Jean mine." The engine roared into life. "I was only waiting for Eustice's arrival before we moved. Pierre and the rest of the younger male Jumeau clan have gone ahead. They're waiting for us down the road. It's dark, so we'll have cover. Henri is with Louis Villers at the house; he had some interesting things to add. It seems that Monsieur Barbier's aunt is a certain Madame Chabot, who very cleverly avoided collaboration charges at the end of the war. She disappeared for a period of time, then came back to the village, claiming to have been sent to a concentration camp near the close of things—for conspiring against the Germans, naturally. However, Monsieur Villers tells me that she was suspected of shacking up with Erharder during his stay in St. Mouton. He's fairly certain that Erharder's kept her in his pay all these years to keep her nose to the ground. How else would a widow woman who supposedly lost it all in the war be able to afford a large house? She couldn't be doing that well out of her *boulangerie*. Anyway, it explains a good deal about how Erharder was tipped off. Kate obviously must have gone into her *boulangerie* asking uncomfortable questions."

"Oh . . . of course," breathed Stephanie softly. "And she found out that Kate was staying at the Périgord. So she engaged her nephew to do her dirty work for her, discover what Kate was up to."

"Exactly, and once he'd proved so convenient they used him again."

"Yes, it all makes perfect sense. But what do we do now?"

"We go and get Kate, of course."

* * *

"Giselle Jumeau?" Karl Erharder's voice came out on a whisper like dried leaves. "No, it is not possible. Not possible!"

"Oh yes, Herr Erharder. Not only is it possible, it is also true."

"And—and your grandfather?"

"Ernst von Fiedler." Kate spoke calmly as she sat there facing her enemy, Giselle and Ernst's enemy.

Erharder gazed at her with a stunned expression. Her eyes . . . Of course, the expression in them was Giselle's. It was what she had said to him as she'd faced the firing squad, watching him with her clear gray eyes—he had never forgotten it: "This is not an end to it, Major Erharder. I'll be back to haunt you, depend on it." And she had come back just as she'd said she would. He cleared his head from the old, familiar vision. "But I saw the child buried in the churchyard. How?"

"Giselle knew what you would do. She smuggled my mother out of France under your very nose."

Unexpectedly Erharder began to laugh, a harsh, grating sound. "I should have known. So she staged her grief and the funeral, all that ceremony. And I watched her do it, lower that little casket ino the ground while the churchbells tolled, with that beautiful face of hers so solemn. She must have been laughing behind it the whole time. Ah, Giselle—she was my Nemesis, my Niniane. I loved her, you know."

"You're sick!" spat Kate. "You murdered her in cold blood!"

"No, not in cold blood, exactly. I was forced to kill her. The illustrious Baron von Fiedler was another matter, too good for anyone. *Lieber Gott*, they even made him colonel three years before the permissible age! Believe me, it was a pleasure to put the bullet through his brain. But Giselle, no."

"*You* shot him! And you blamed it on Giselle? How low could you stoop?"

"But she couldn't be allowed to live, knowing what she did. I would have been shot myself. It wasn't the proper thing to kill one's fellow officer. But you see, von Fiedler tried to take her from me one time too many, and that night was the last straw. He walked in on my interrogation and took her by the arm, daring me to stop him. He only wanted her for himself, the swine! So I shot him in the back of the head as he was walking out with her. And to be fair, she did try to kill me after that. She gave me this, my little Giselle, with a paper knife from my own desk." He laughed and touched the jagged scar on his neck. "I have always looked upon it as something of a memento. I did do her the honor of shooting her with my own pistol rather than let the firing squad mow her down like the others. Yes, and she stood against that wall and looked at me as you do now, like the young Joan of Arc with a little smile on her lips as I pointed my pistol at her head."

"Now you know why."

"Yes, now I know why. And you, Kate. It's as if she's come back to me. She said she would, you know. One of life's little ironies. It will be such a pity if I have to kill you, too."

"There's no reason to kill me, Herr Erharder. You know the reason now that I'm here. I came to meet my great-uncle and cousins. They're as little danger to you as I am."

"Sadly, very sadly, Kate, I cannot believe you. You see, you're more like her than you realize. I cannot help but wonder how you knew my true name, for example, and the story."

Kate shrugged but her mind raced. "Giselle sent a letter out with my mother, telling the truth about her birth and her parentage and about you, Herr Erharder, and how she feared for her child's life at your hands. That was all, but I found the letter recently and thought I'd come down to see what more I could discover about her. It wasn't too difficult to work out that you were the infamous Erharder when you started to interrogate me, with your curiosity about the Jumeaus and von Fiedler. I can't say the knowledge filled me with confidence."

"She admitted to giving birth to von Fiedler's child? I don't believe it. Why would she want to admit her disgrace?"

"It was no disgrace. And there had been no rape. She loved him. And he loved her."

"They *loved* each other?" He stiffened but then he seemed to relax. "No, never—never! Giselle was nothing to von Fiedler but an object of his lust! And she despised him! Everyone knew it. Where did you get this nonsense?"

"From Giselle's letter. Why else would Colonel von Fiedler have tried to take her away from you—not once, but twice?"

Erharder's eyes hardened to stone. "I don't believe you. Where is the proof?"

"I haven't proof, but then I don't need it."

He smiled. "Of course you would like to think it, and I suppose it is exactly what Giselle would have wished. Yes, I can see that you have put it together carefully. But not quite carefully enough, Kate. My God, if Himmler had found out von Fiedler had fathered a love child by a little Resistance worker, do you know what that would have done to his illustrious career? He would never have considered it! He had as much intention of seeing his bastard daughter dead as I did. And furthermore, before the birth Giselle signed papers I drew up, stating he had raped her. I intended to use them to bring him down, but she stole them back from me, and now I know why. She didn't love von Fiedler. She just didn't want her daughter to have to grow up under the stigma of bastard when the information came out later. No wonder she sent her to England." He started laughing on a high, disturbing note. Then he sobered and gave her an appraising look.

"So, Giselle and Ernst's grandchild. Both of them in one—how very convenient. You must be hungry. I shall bring you something to eat." He left the room, and she heard the key turn in the lock.

Shakily she got to her feet and went over to the bed, standing on it to try to see out the window. The shutters were closed and locked although the slats were open, letting in the very last of the light. It was useless; she could see nothing through the spaces but the silhouette of treetops, which gave her no indication of where she might be. She sat down on the bed and huddled there, her back against the wall. If nothing else Sebastian was safe, the thought coming as if from a distance. And the Jumeaus too, as far as she could tell. But her heart was oddly numb; she didn't seem to be able to feel anything at all. The mirror was cold and sharp under her knee and she picked it up, examining her face. A large bruise was coming out on her cheekbone and her cut lip was swollen at the corner. Her face, Kate Soames's, but not. It was strange. She knew perfectly well she had next to no chance of getting out of this alive, yet she felt that somehow it was right that she be here with Erharder. He'd said that Giselle was his Nemesis; there was some kind of divine retribution to come. The past and present had blurred at the edges, run together to become one. Giselle and Kate, here, now.

The lock turned again and Erharder came in with a tray. "Here, my dear. You need nourishment." He set the tray on he floor and pulled the chair up to the bed. "Have some wine. It will warm you." He poured out two glasses and handed her one. Then he offered her a piece of bread covered with a thick slab of cheese.

"No, I really couldn't—"

"Eat!" he said, his chilly blue eyes commanding it.

She took a small bite, her cheekbone aching horribly, but she dared not disobey him. It tasted of sawdust, and she gulped the wine to try to wash it down. The liquid burned at her throat, but then after a minute it sent a warm glow through her body, relieving the cold she hadn't even realized she felt.

"That's better. Have some more. I want to see you finish it."

He spoke to her cajolingly, as if she were a small child. It came to her then that he was quite insane. She choked down the rest of the bread and cheese, and he poured her some more wine. Then, when she had finished that, he took the glass from her hand and put it down on the tray, which he carried over to the side of the door as if it were the most normal thing in the world to be locked in a bare room with a young woman he'd recently finished beating. And then he returned to her, sitting down on the bed and softly stroking her hair. She cringed from him, horror crawling down her spine at his touch.

"Don't be afraid, Kate. Can't you see that I want you?" His voice came soft and sibilant, like a snake.

She froze in terror at his words. This wasn't possible, this was worse than any form of torture she'd imagined. She squeezed her eyes shut and shook her head blindly. And then his lips, hard and cold, were on hers, savaging her mouth and she pushed at his shoulders, then pounded her fists when he didn't give way. She twisted her head away. "No—No! Let me go!"

But it was as if he hadn't heard her. "Kate, dearest Kate," he said, groping at her breast through the thin material of her dress. "Come now, you want it as much as I do, you know you do."

"Take your filthy hands off me!" She twisted under him, but was pinned, couldn't seem to move and he ripped her dress, pawing at her naked skin. She bit his shoulder and tasted blood.

"Ah, you little bitch!" he cried. He hit her face then, catching her jaw so hard that she thought she was going to faint with the pain. He looked down at her with the most hideous grin she'd ever seen.

"You're more like Giselle than I'd even imagined. She struggled against me, too, that last night. I called her in to force her to return my documents, you see. She refused me that—and she refused me this, Kate."

He pulled at the skirt of her dress and Kate spat in his face.

"That's it, Kate. I like a woman with fight in her—it excites me. And you'll give me what I never got from Giselle, thanks to von Fiedler's untimely arrival." He pulled at his zipper and she closed her eyes in mute dread.

His hand plunged under the flimsy material, grabbing at her tender, private flesh and she writhed away from him, trying desperately to get away. "No, oh, God—NO!" she screamed, a piercing cry that split the air with its terror, and with the adrenalin of fear she found the strength to get her leg from under her and brought her knee up, crashing into his groin. He groaned and doubled over, suddenly ashen and limp, and she fled across the room, tripping over the tray. The glasses crashed and the bottle of wine tipped over and splashed a puddle of deep red onto the floor, but she was oblivious; she pulled at the door frantically and it wouldn't budge. Tears were streaming down her cheek, blinding her as she pounded on the wood and as if by magic, it lurched open, and there was David. He didn't hesitate, grabbing her by the arm and pulling her out of the room, locking the door behind him.

"Come on, Katie, move!" She was frozen, shaking with terror from danger gone, this new danger unknown. "There's no time for hysterics now. I'm taking you out of here." He dragged her down the stairs. She could hear the voices of Schwab and Brecht talking casually in the front room as if nothing were happening in that little room upstairs, but he pulled her the other way, through the empty kitchen toward the back door, just as she heard the roar of Erharder's voice, shouting something in German. Then came the heavy fall of the henchmen's feet, tearing up the stairs. And at the very same time, the front door burst open and she heard a dear familiar voice.

"Sebastian!" she cried, but David had pulled her through the door, his hand immediately covering her mouth. She bit it and he softly swore, then threw her into the Renault with such force that she fell across the other seat. And then somehow he was around the other side before she could move and the black car had leapt to life. He gunned the accelerator and the tires spun, throwing up gravel as they bit into the road and screeched away from the house.

Sebastian had heard Kate's scream from where he was cautiously hugging the trees that bordered the road. It put an end to all stealth. He exploded into a flat-out run up the hill, Eustice racing beside him, Pierre and his father Giles close behind, Marcel and his son Jean closing in from the other direction. Without pausing he pulled the Beretta from its holster, and then they were at the door. Eustice stood to one side, his gun also at the ready, and with one mighty kick, Sebastian was in. ''Eustice, upstairs with me. Pierre, Giles, cover the back.''

And then he heard Kate crying his name and everything was forgotten as he tore toward the kitchen, reaching the back door only in time to see the big black car hurtling away. ''Damn!'' he cried.

Eustice was at his shoulder. ''Go,'' he said. ''Take the car and go after her. I have enough help here to put this lot away. Run, man!'' There was a sudden commotion behind him and Sebastian was gone into the night.

CHAPTER

Seventeen

S*ebastian* reached the car and wrenched the door open. Stephanie had been waiting impatiently, chafing against the order she'd been given to stay. When Sebastian burst out of the dark she sat up with a stiff spine, a silent, fearful question in her eyes. She too had heard the scream rending the night.

"Sebastian—where's Kate? What's happened! For God's sake, why do you look like that?"

"Someone's taken Kate off." Sebastian's breath came in fast, hard pants. "We're going after her." Savagely he turned the key in the ignition and pulled the Peugeot off the road, gunning the engine. They were already minutes behind, but he'd seen the direction the black Renault had taken and as luck would have it, there were no turn-offs for at least ten kilometers.

"Put your seat belt on, Stephanie—it's going to be a rather fast ride," he said curtly as he pointed the car toward Brantôme and leapt onto the road in an explosive burst of power.

She obeyed instantly, then clenched her hands in her lap and stole a glance at Sebastian. His face was set in fierce concentration as he maneuvered the car at lightning speed. She would not interrupt by asking any pointless questions.

The road was narrow and winding but the Peugeot held to it well as Sebastian expertly negotiated the curves. The tiny flicker of headlights wove in the distance and he downshifted to take the small hill ahead.

Eustice had spun around to find Pierre wrestling desperately with Schwab who was trying to get to the back door. Giles lay out cold on the floor behind them, blood trickling down his forehead where Schwab had hit him with something. In the split second of taking all this in, it became immediately clear to Eustice that Schwab had no gun on him, or he would certainly have used it. Without another instant's delay he jammed his gun into Schwab's back. Schwab froze and Pierre fell away, gasping.

"It would be my pleasure to kill you here and now, Herr Schwab, but there's another who would like to claim the privilege. However, I won't hesitate if you press the issue." He jerked his head at Pierre who had dropped to his knees next to his father.

"He will be all right," said Pierre shortly.

"Then find out what's happened to the others and get some rope." Eustice turned back to Schwab. "Who took Kate and where are they going?"

There was no answer. Eustice placed the cold metal of the gun barrel against the skin behind Schwab's ear. He felt him shudder, could smell his fear. "Talk, man," he said softly.

The words burst out of him. "I don't know, I swear it! It was Russell, he took the girl—Herr Erharder was—was going to kill her and he knew it. He made him stand guard outside the door. Russell couldn't take it, the fool. He got her away without our hearing anything. I don't know any more."

"Don't you now, my fine friend. And where are your other two mates?"

"I don't know that, either—we all ran when we heard the break-in. The Soames girl had—had hurt Herr Erharder, and then locked him in, and we were up there dealing with him.

I came out this way. The others must have gone to the front."

"Thank you." Eustice removed the gun, and pressed gently on Schwab's neck, and the large body gave a little sigh, went limp, and sank to the floor.

He left him there where he'd fallen and ran outside. Pierre was helping Marcel into the house, and Jean, steady Jean who had been the wrestling champion of the region, had tackled Brecht, pinned him down and stunned him with a blow to the throat. And all this without a shot being fired, thought Eustice in amazement.

"Erharder?" he asked with a frown, as he helped Jean pull a white-faced Brecht to his feet.

"He got away. I'm sorry. We were behind you and they came rushing out of the house. I jumped this one, but the old man hit my father in the stomach and winded him. He took off in Monsieur Sebastian's car, the one we came in. There was nothing I could do to go after him. What happened to Monsieur Sebastian and Kate?"

"Russell took her. Dunn's gone after them. Come, let's get this scum into the house and tie him up with the other one. Then he's got some talking to do."

"David, where are you taking me! Please, please David, you don't need me for your dirty business—for the love of God, will you let me go?"

"Shut up, Katie," said David in a voice about as warm and comforting as slate.

"But then why did you take me away? Why did you rescue me from Erharder?"

"Who's Sebastian, Katie?" The Renault hurled down the road like a bullet, the headlights flashing up and down on the asphalt, picking out the row of trees bordering the river below on one side, the wall of rock on the other.

"What?" she asked stupidly.

"Damn it, you heard me. Who is Sebastian?" He jerked

the wheel around the corner, and she was flung back against the seat.

"Please, David, slow down! You'll kill us both—" Her words were cut off as he took the next corner even faster and she was thrown against his arm.

"A more pleasant death than the one that was coming your way, I can promise you."

"David, I don't understand any of this!"

"For the last time, who is Sebastian? He's your lover, isn't he? Answer me!"

She looked over at him in the flickering light. His jaw was tight, his mouth set in a tight line. "Yes, he is," she said quietly.

"Damn!" spat David. "So Erharder was right about that. I didn't believe it, fool that I was. What is he to you, Katie?"

There was no point in holding anything back. It was over, whatever happened. "I'm going to marry him."

"You're going to do what!" His hands tightened on the wheel.

"I love him and I'm going to marry him, David."

"Over my dead body you are!" His fury was palpable in the charged air.

"What difference could it possibly make to you? You've thrown your lot in with that despicable Nazi. It's quite clear to me that you used me from the very beginning, so let's not play any more games."

"That's not entirely true, Katie. In the beginning, yes. You had the right connections. But I grew to love you. I never wanted to see you hurt." He said it flatly.

"David, do you take me for an idiot? You kidnapped me, damn you, put me straight into Erharder's hands!" Her voice was sharp and bitter.

"I got you away from him, didn't I?"

"You also stood by while he tied me up and hit me and did nothing. And then—then afterwards. You must have known what he was going to do!"

"I had no idea how far he was prepared to go. I thought you were innocent! Then he told me all about your confession. I have quite a few questions to ask you myself. My tactics may not be as brutal as Erharder's but I'm just as sure going to get the answers from you." The tires squealed around another corner.

"And then you'll finish off Erharder's dirty work?" The words were heavy with contempt.

"Look, goddamn it. I never meant any harm to come to you, you're just going to have to believe that. I gave up a lot, everything in fact, when I pulled you out of that room."

"And now you expect me to go running back to you out of gratitude? You're as sick as Erharder is." Kate suddenly saw the yellow gleam of lights catch and hold for a moment in the rearview mirror. She turned around. A car was on the far stretch of road behind them, going very fast. Please God, let it be Sebastian, she prayed silently.

David had seen them too, and accelerated yet again. The car swung violently around the hairpin curve, the rear swaying alarmingly, then mercifully it gripped the road again. Kate's fingers clutched at the dashboard and she choked back the nausea that had been rising for the last fifteen minutes. "Not now, Kate" she whispered to herself, desperately trying to regain control of her treacherous stomach.

"What did you say?" David risked a quick glance over at her.

"Nothing—nothing. Please, slow down, David; I'm feeling awfully queasy."

"Hell, I'll slow down. That car behind us is either Erharder or your darling Sebastian, and I have a lot to lose on both accounts. Who is he, Kate? What does he have to do with this?" He said it coldly.

It hadn't occurred to her that it could be Erharder, and the possibility made her swallow hard against sudden panic.

"What does he have to do with this, damn it?"

She forced the panic down along with the nausea. "A great deal, as it happens. He works for British Intelligence, and he's on to the lot of you. Remember Simon, the fisherman?"

There was a long silence. "I see. You were two-timing

me even then, were you? Not very attractive of you, Katie.'' His voice sent a chill through her.

''Oh, and what you were doing was attractive? Please, David, don't be ridiculous.'' Her voice was faint and a film of cold sweat had broken out on her forehead. Her hand covered her mouth.

''Erharder told me all about you and I laughed at him. I vouched for your innocence even after I learned what you were. You made me look like a fool, didn't you, honey. Sweet, innocent Katie, playing both ends against the middle. You're a fucking agent, aren't you? I should have let him rape you, you goddamn bitch. Never mind, I'll just pick up where he left off.''

But Kate was beyond responding to the jibe. ''Please, David, stop the car! I'm going to be sick!''

''Nice try, Katie,'' said David with a hard, cynical laugh.

It was too late. The food she had so recently forced down her throat forced its way back up again in rebellion, and as the Renault swung around another corner to the left, she was violently sick, and David took the worst of it.

It was enough to startle him out of the rigid concentration he needed, and his hands jerked involuntarily at the wheel. The Renault skidded and he frantically tried to bring it back under his control, but the split second of lost command took its toll. The car veered wildly, then spun around, and the force of the spin threw Kate against the door. It couldn't have been latched properly, because as the weight of her body hit it, the door flew open and she was flung out into the night. Her body landed with a thud on the verge of the grassy bank that led down to the river and she saw the car turn over slowly, twice, and then she fainted.

''Dear God,'' whispered Sebastian, as he rounded the corner and saw the car ahead of him, dangling over the edge of the bank, its headlights still slashing through the night, but pointing obscenely down at the river.

He slammed on the brakes and Stephanie, who had not

spoken a word during the entire chase, gave a little cry of alarm at the sight. She was infinitely grateful for the seat belt Sebastian had insisted she wear as the brakes gripped and held with an ear-splitting scream, and the Peugeot came to a wrenching halt.

Sebastian was out in a flash and over to the Renault, taking in its caved-in roof as he ran. He tore the door open. David's inert body was resting against the steering wheel, his face and chest a mask of blood. Kate was nowhere to be seen. Reaching his hand in, he felt for a pulse. He heard Stephanie at his shoulder and turned.

"Oh, God—Kate?" she managed to whisper.

He shook his head. "She's not here—it looks as if it rolled. She must have been thrown clear. No, don't look in." He took her gently by the shoulders and turned her away.

"What is it, Sebastian? Who's in there?" Her eyes searched his face for the truth.

"David Russell."

"Is he—"

Sebastian nodded his head. "Forget him. Quickly, let's start looking for Kate. She can't have been thrown far."

She heard her name coming as if from a long distance and the first reaction that penetrated the mist in her head was fear. She couldn't remember where she was, then Erharder sprang into her mind and she knew it was him—he was coming after her. With a sob of fear, she got to her knees and tried to crawl away. And then she saw the figure looming, a huge black shadow coming toward her with a flickering light in front of it, and a tiny scream of sheer, helpless terror was torn from her throat as the light caught her eyes. She felt like a hunted animal trapped by its predator, and she wanted to sink into the earth and die rather than face any more. And then she heard the shout: "Over here, Stephanie!" and inexplicably she found herself cradled gently in strong, warm arms, and fierce words of love were being poured into her hair. She blinked, tears stinging at her eyes, and she managed to look up through them at the face above her.

She swallowed hard. "Sebastian?" she whispered through a dry throat.

"Kate, Kate, my love, are you all right, sweetheart, are you hurt?"

"No—no, I don't think so. Oh, God, I thought you were him! I thought it was Erh—harder." And then the tears came hot with the memory, and Sebastian held her and rocked her as she cried soundlessly with all of the fear and hopelessness of the last twenty-four hours.

"Is she okay, Sebastian?" Stephanie crouched down next to him, examining Kate's appearance anxiously.

"Yes, I think so. I don't know how, but there doesn't seem to be anything seriously wrong other than shock."

"Oh, thank God! Oh Sebastian, I thought—never mind, everything's all right. What can I do?"

"Steph, you're an angel. Thank you for not having hysterics all over me."

"That would be most unnatural behavior for me."

Sebastian managed to smile. "Kate's always said you were eminently sensible. Listen, Stephanie. Do you think you can drive into Brantôme? It's only a few more minutes down the road. Get the police, tell them there's been an accident. We'll need one of their cars out here, and another one sent on to the Chabot house, but I'll explain it to them when they arrive. I'm going to stay here with Kate."

"No problem—I'll be back as soon as I can." She squeezed his hand quickly and was gone.

Sebastian pulled off his jacket and wrapped it around Kate. She had quieted, but her eyes were too large and her skin too cold for his liking. The moon was but a slender crescent in the sky and gave off next to no light, and he turned the flashlight on her, looking for any sign of blood he might have missed, and it was then that he saw the bruises on her cheek and jaw. He drew his breath in between his teeth. "Kate . . ." Very, very softly he touched her face but his voice was hard as steel. "How did you get these?"

She shuddered. "I . . ."

"Who did this to you? Was it Erharder?"

She nodded.

He swore softly under his breath. "Can you tell me a little of what happened, my love? I don't mean to remind you of it, but I need to know before the police come."

She nodded again. The blood was beginning to run through her veins again, and she felt reality beginning to creep back into the world that had tilted out of control, beyond understanding. "David?" she asked in a little voice.

Sebastian gently shook his head and she immediately understood. "Oh . . . He tried to save me from Erharder in the end, Sebastian, but then—"

"Why don't you start at the beginning, my love. I know all about Monsieur Barbier and what they did to you in the car. I got him back for that. He's residing in a closet in your room at the moment with a very sore head, I'd imagine."

"Did you?" The glimmer of a smile touched Kate's eyes. "Is that how you knew where to find me? Oh, Sebastian, I'd given up all hope, and I was so scared they were going to find out about you!"

"Were you, sweetheart? So you were going to protect me from them? Kate, my brave little tigress." He laughed and kissed her hair. "How did you deal with the fact that they knew you'd spent the night with a healthy male?"

"Oh—I told them I'd picked up someone called Georges."

"Georges!" he said unsteadily. "*Georges*?"

"Well yes, it was the only thing I could think of. I said I'd left a note for him so he wouldn't wait for me. David wasn't very happy, but he was much unhappier when I told him in the car who you really were and that I was going to marry you. I think after that he was planning on killing me himself." And then the story came pouring out in fragmented pieces. Sebastian interrupted only to ask a few brief questions, but when Kate got to the part about Erharder's attempt at rape, he jumped to his feet and walked away a few paces with his back to her.

"And that's when you screamed?" His voice was tight.

"Yes. I thought—he came so close to it, and then I kicked him in his groin and that's when I got away."

"*Did* you!" Sebastian turned around. "Good for you!"

"It was very satisfying, but wouldn't have done me much good if David hadn't been outside. I guess he realized what was happening and finally decided to stop it."

"Thank God for that. So he unlocked the door and dragged you off."

"Yes. Oh, Sebastian, I couldn't believe it when I heard your voice. It was as if some form of sanity had been returned to the world."

"Where was he taking you?"

"I don't know. He was blazing furious with me for not being everlastingly grateful to him. We had something of a—bizarre conversation."

"It's no wonder he lost control of the car if he was holding a conversation at that speed," said Sebastian with disgust.

"No—he's usually a good driver. It was all the fast corners. I asked him to slow down, but he wouldn't listen."

"No, of course he wouldn't. It's a dangerous bit of road and that last corner is particularly bad. He must have taken it too fast."

"No, you don't understand—it was my stomach. I was sick on him. And then he jerked the wheel."

"You *what*!" It exploded out of him and, improbably, he began to laugh. He dropped to his knees and pulled her into his arms. "Kate, you should be a secret weapon. Honestly!" But then he sobered. "You might have been killed, too. Oh, God, Kate—if anything had happened to you—" He didn't finish. His mouth came down on hers and he kissed her with a violence that came out of the violence they had been wrapped in for two nights and a day, and the thought of David's body only a hunded feet from them that might so easily have been hers. He kissed her as if he were pouring his life into her and she clung to him returning his kiss in full measure, heedless of her sore lip and bruised face and body, heedless of everything but Sebastian and his touch and taste and feel.

And then car lights swept down on them, pulling them apart, and when Stephanie came over, Sebastian finally left her to go and deal with the police.

"Hi there, loyal friend." Kate gave her a shaky little smile. "I guess Sebastian's told you everything. What do you make of his line of work? You were closer than you thought with your mystery in Jamaica." She stopped abruptly. "I—I'm sorry about all this."

"Oh, Kate, you do make for an exciting holiday," said Stephanie with a laugh. "Next time remind me to pack a pistol and a first-aid kit, will you? Are you sure you're all right—no broken bones, internal bleeding or anything?"

"Really, Steph, I'm okay, just some bruised ribs, I think—and anyway, if there was internal bleeding or broken bones, what would you know about it?"

"Absolutely nothing. It just seemed the right thing to ask."

"Oh, Steph, you're a gem." Kate gave her a little hug.

"I know," said Stephanie, and then they were distracted by the wail of the ambulance arriving.

It seemed to take hours, but in reality, it was probably no more than thirty minutes before they were heading back to the Chabot house with a car of very interested gendarmes as escort. Kate had been thoroughly checked by the doctor who'd arrived separately in his car, and although he'd wanted to take her to Périgueux hospital for a more thorough exam, she'd flatly refused, and Sebastian hadn't forced the issue. He understood perfectly what drove her back toward St. Mouton.

The gendarmes had already gone inside, and they walked in to find all the Jumeau men talking at once and gesturing with great animation. Kate stood at the door, trying to take it all in. And then her eyes widened as she saw a dark figure detach himself from the group and walk toward them.

"Eustice!" she cried with delighted surprise. "I don't

believe it! 'Et tu, Brute!' Sebastian, why didn't you tell me?"

Eustice smiled with vast relief. "You're all right then. Kate's safe."

Sebastian laughed. Relief was no small thing in him at the moment. "As you can see, all rescued." He clasped an arm around Eustice's shoulder. "How many did we take in?"

"Only the two. Erharder got away in the melee."

"*Damn*! But never mind that now; were there any injuries?"

"No casualties other than bumps and bruises on all parts. You wouldn't have believed it—it was like some mad children's free-for-all. And Russell?"

"Dead," said Sebastian shortly. "Where are they? I have an old score to settle."

"I thought you might. They're in the kitchen, trussed for you like Christmas geese and just as ready for the carving."

"Thank you." The simple words carried worlds of meaning.

Sebastian went over to the policemen and said a few brief words and they nodded their understanding. Then he headed back for the kitchen. Kate bit her lip as she watched him go, and Eustice's hand gently touched her shoulder. He said nothing, but the look on his face told her all she needed to know. And then she was surrounded by Jumeaus who exclaimed over her, and insisted she be sat down with a glass of fortifying cognac. After that, things seemed to dissolve into a haze as the police took down her statement, then Stephanie's, constantly punctuated by Jumeau opinion. Every now and then Eustice stepped in to clarify or add some necessary history, but on the whole it was a fairly wild affair, bringing the Keystone Cops distinctly to Kate's mind.

And then a bloodcurdling scream came from the kitchen, and another, dissolving into a long moan and everything stopped dead. The men all exchanged significant glances and Stephanie paled. "My God . . . Kate?"

"A small matter of West Berlin, I believe," she said softly.

Eustice looked at her in surprise. And then Sebastian appeared, his mouth grim.

"They're all yours," he said to the gendarmes.

* * *

The gendarmes had taken a protesting Brecht and very subdued Schwab out the back way, and the Jumeau men had been dispatched back to Henri's house to give the good news. All was suddenly quiet. Sebastian had Kate tucked protectively in the crook of his arm and he looked down at her with a smile. "I want you and Stephanie at the Hôtel de Ville with me," he said firmly. "With Erharder on the loose, it's too dangerous to have you at the Périgord. Agreed?"

"Yes, of course, Sebastian. I'm not sure I want to go back there anyway. But what are we going to do about Monsieur Barbier in my closet?" she said with a little laugh.

"The gendarmes have taken care of that, and they know about Madame Chabot's role, so you're not to worry. But I still don't want to take any chances. This thing isn't over yet. Eustice, you'll stay in Stephanie's room."

"Naturally," said Eustice. Stephanie started and opened her mouth, then shut it again firmly.

"Kate will be with me."

"Naturally," said Eustice again, grinning.

"Are you implying that this is anything but business as usual?"

"Would I dare?"

Sebastian laughed. "Probably not, but you'd be right if you did. You're looking at my future wife. Smashing, isn't she?"

"Smashing—and pretty damn tough," said Eustice, throwing Kate a broad smile. "Well, I can't say it comes as a surprise, although someday you're going to have to fill in the blanks between Jamaica and here."

"You have quite a few blanks to fill in yourself, Eustice," said Kate. "Are you from Jamaica?"

"Originally, yes. I haven't lived there for a number of years."

"Oh, I see—but your name *is* Eustice?"

"Sometimes." He laughed. "But you may call me Brutus."

Sebastian smiled. " 'For Brutus is an honorable man.' "

" 'So are they all, all honorable men,' " finished Eustice.

Kate shot him a look of surprise and Sebastian burst into laughter. "I'll put you out of your misery, my love. Cambridge. And I reckon that's the most you'll ever know about our friend here."

"Never mind, I'm adjusting to the vagaries of you Intelligence types. I'm even growing accustomed to snuggling up against a gun." She looked at Sebastian's shoulder holster with a smile.

" 'Necessity's sharp pinch.' It gives one a certain sense of security."

"I should think so, with the people you seem to mix with."

"Speaking of that, what about Erharder?" interrupted Stephanie.

"I don't know," said Sebastian honestly. "There's nothing to be done about him tonight. He'll have made himself very scarce indeed. But I have a feeling that he's not going anywhere. We still have a job to do and I reckon he thinks he does, too."

"What job?" asked Stephanie, puzzled.

"To try to recover the lost documents. I doubt Erharder knows Eustice and I are here, considering he was tackled by a mob of incensed Frenchmen, who he's likely to assume were the Jumeaus. Therefore that puts us at a slight advantage. However, if he does in fact believe that Kate's an agent, then he's not going to let it go easily. Do you see what I mean?"

"He's not going to let it go easily anyway, Sebastian," said Kate with a little shudder. "You were right; he does have a weird obsession about Giselle, a violent love-hate sort of thing. But what's stranger is that as far as he's concerned, she's embodied in me. I can't really explain it; it's just a feeling that I got, some things he said, and—and what he did."

Sebastian gave her a long, appraising look. "Give Kate and me a few minutes, will you Eustice, Stephanie?" he asked, looking over at them. "Thanks. We'll meet you at the car." He turned back to Kate as soon as they had left the room. "Do you want to talk about this now?"

"No. I'm fine, Sebastian, really I am. But you need to know something else. It's important. Erharder told me that he shot Ernst. Through the back of his head, when he was trying to take Giselle away."

"Sweet Christ," said Sebastian. "He *admitted* that?"

Kate nodded. "He was proud of it. And then Giselle went after him with a paper knife. He said he couldn't let her live, not with what she had seen. Then he described how he shot her in front of the firing squad—with his own pistol. Sebastian, he killed them both, by his own hand—with the same gun."

Sebastian pulled her close. "I'm sorry, Kate. I'm so sorry."

"Thank you. But I'm all right. There's more. At some point before, he had made Giselle sign some papers . . ." She quickly related what Erharder had told her. "He obviously thinks she was the one who stole his documents and hid them because of the confession."

"You're a marvel, my love!" said Sebastian, sitting forward and thinking for a moment. Then he looked up. "It all begins to come together. I think I'm beginning to see it. There are still some bits missing, but I do begin to see . . ."

"See what, exactly, Sebastian?"

"Hmm? Oh—sorry. To begin with, Giselle would have signed those papers very happily, given that they would have had exactly the effect that she and Ernst were looking for. She must have seen him put them away and somehow realized that it was the file Ernst had been looking for. That would be the information Giselle gave him when he came to St. Mouton."

Kate considered. "Nadia Jumeau said that he was in and out of the house at strange hours that night of the eleventh of June, and at dawn he sent the transmission to Colonel Harrington, the one that said he was in possession of the documents. The timing's right. But then what?"

"I'm not sure. But Ernst knew that Erharder would think

Giselle had taken them when he discovered his papers missing. We know that from what he told Colonel Harrington, and he was quite correct. Ernst must have been hoping that Erharder would discover the theft later rather than sooner, for he had to get Giselle, who would be the target, away. We know from Louis Villers that Hélène was sent away on the twelfth. At the same time she arranged for a group of four to go up the Swallow line on the night of the thirteenth. They were supposed to have met with a contact in Verteillac who was to take them out but they never showed up. It must have been the Jumeau family, because Giselle would never have left them behind in St. Mouton, but the Gestapo took them before they could leave. As for Giselle, she would have gone on her own. It has to be why she was not at the house that night. But I'll lay money that she was hiding out, waiting to meet with Ernst somewhere, because remember, he'd been called away. She might well have had something important to tell him about the documents, her escape route, who knows? In any case, we know that, somehow, the next day Giselle heard the news of her family and turned herself in. From there we mostly have the rest of it. It doesn't tell us a damn thing about where the documents are, but we're getting closer. We're definitely getting closer."

Kate looked at Sebastian in amazement. "You do know how to reconstruct a story, don't you?"

"Not well enough, I'm afraid. Maybe if I sleep on it, something will come to me. Are you ready to go, sweetheart?" He rose and reached a hand out to her.

"Very ready." She cast a last look heavy with memory up the stairs as they went out the door.

Sebastian insisted she bathe her sore, stiff body before she even considered sleep. "I swear, it will make all the difference in the morning. Take it from an expert," he said, drawing the bath.

"I know you, Sebastian Dunn. This has nothing to do with stiffness. You just like your women clean."

"Really, Kate, you are the end," he said, standing up and putting a clean towel next to the tub. "I rescue the damsel in distress, and all she does in gratitude is attribute the lowest of motives in my chivalry. Now into the bath with you."

"You might very well have to haul me out again," she said, taking his hand and gingerly slipping into the water. "Oh, but that does feel good. Perhaps I'll just stay here all night."

"Just don't drown. Oh, and here's the soap." He tossed it to her with a grin. "I'm going to have a quick word with Eustice." He closed the door behind him, still smiling.

"Eustice, here—take one of my shirts for Stephanie. No doubt she'll appreciate it for tonight."

"I've already given her one of mine," said Eustice.

"Did you now." He smiled broadly. "Oh, they do turn us into gentlemen, don't they? All right, quickly, let's compare notes. There's a good bit you need to know—and tomorrow, first thing, I'd like you to take Stephanie over to the Périgord and pack up their things. Have Stephanie check them out—she might as well plant the story that they're going back to England. You can meet us at the Jumeaus." He carried on talking for another fifteen minutes, and by the time Kate had finished soaking, Eustice was long gone. Sebastian saw her into bed and kissed her forehead.

"My turn," he said, heading for the bathroom. "I won't be a minute."

"You mean I get a clean hero thrown into the bargain?" said Kate, but her voice was faint and sleepy, and her eyes had already closed. Sebastian looked at her for a long moment, then disappeared through the door, and by the time he slipped into bed next to her, she was fast asleep. He gently pulled her close to him and dropped a tender kiss on her hair, and then he, too, was asleep.

CHAPTER Eighteen

Morning touched Kate's lids and she slowly opened her eyes, starting at the unfamiliar room. But then she remembered—the nightmare was over, and she was safe, safe with Sebastian. She cautiously rolled over, tender, but less so than she'd expected, and looked at his sleeping face. The lines of fatigue had been erased along with the tight, careworn expression. Here was no skilled and deadly Intelligence agent, simply Sebastian.

She understood him now as she hadn't before, had seen him in a situation that most people never come to. He was a man, a complex man to be sure, but a man complete with his own set of flaws. The difference between him and so many was that he'd come to terms with himself, and there lay his strength. There was no pretense in Sebastian; he was not a hero, merely a person with strong principles, a man who felt deeply about things. He was as equally capable of violence as he was of gentleness. And where she'd always seen him as someone in complete control, it was more that he kept a tight check on the emotions that blazed beneath the surface.

He was proud, and when he hurt, he hurt deeply. It must have tortured him far more than she'd realized to wait for her, chafed at his pride and his patience, but he'd never let on for an instant. Sebastian did not love easily, she knew that now, but when he did, his love was given completely and without hesitation. She had behaved like the worst sort of fool, yet he didn't hold it against her. Instead he had forced her to grow up—he had silently insisted that she come to terms with herself, just as he had with himself, and he had not begrudged her that growth. He had no illusions about her, had had none from the first, had no expectations other than that she be true to herself, and to him. Dear, sweet, vulnerable Sebastian . . .

And then his eyes opened and he came immediately awake. He smiled as he found her watching him. "What's the scrutiny all about, sweetheart?"

"Oh, nothing. I was just thinking that James Bond must look quite different when he's asleep. You know, sort of harmless."

Sebastian laughed at that. "I see, you think I look harmless, do you?" He pulled her head down and kissed her. Then he looked at her again and sighed. "Do you still think I'm harmless?"

"Thoroughly."

"Do you." He gently rolled her onto her back and pulled the sheet down, kissing her neck, then her breast. "And now?"

"As a baby," she said somewhat breathlessly, and then she was unable to speak at all as Sebastian kissed her again, this time in the way he had that left her thoroughly shaken and her blood pounding. She was ready for him and he knew it, and he shifted his body and pushed into her, careful not to move her, supporting the weight of his torso on his hands. But she was oblivious to her bruises, every fiber of feeling concentrated on the way he moved in her. "Oh, God, I love you, Sebastian!" she cried softly, her hands in his hair, her eyes looking into his.

"As I love you, Kate," he said thickly, and the truth of it was written on his naked face. And then the explosion of sensation took her by surprise and she gasped, lifting up to him, pulling him deep into her, and the last thread of Sebastian's control was stripped away. He groaned, his eyes closing and his face contorting as he thrust even deeper and poured himself into her in spasms that racked his body. Then he collapsed on his side, breathing heavily.

"Christ, Kate," he finally managed to say. "That's a hell of a way to wake a man up." But then in a few minutes when he'd recovered himself, he propped himself up on his elbow and looked down at her with a smile. "And now? How harmless am I now?"

"Harmless as ever." Her eyes danced.

"I can't take it," he said. "Come here."

"Sebastian, there's still so much we have to get straight—"

"I know, I do know, my love. But we have time later for sorting it all out. There are a good many things I'm going to need to know, but not now. You've been through too much already."

"I'm fine, truly I am. I want to tell you this now; it's important, too."

He sighed in resignation. "All right then; I can tell I'm not going to get any peace until you've said your bit. Out with it."

"I discovered that it's my story after all."

"How do you mean, my love?" He looked at her curiously.

"It was the strangest thing, and I don't know if I'll ever be able to explain it, but it was as if I were Giselle, and not just for Erharder—for me, too, as if the two of us were one. It was eerie, Sebastian, but it was right, as if in some way time had ceased to matter, and I was there to finish something. I know that doesn't make any sense, but did you know that he'd tried to rape her, too? That's when Ernst came in, you see. And when she attacked him with the knife after he'd shot Ernst, it was to slash his neck."

"*Did* she, by God! I'd always wondered why he'd never had such an identifying scar removed."

"He considers it a trophy. Oh, and he had no idea that she and Ernst had loved each other and it absolutely infuriated him, although he said he didn't believe it. I think—well, in the end I think that's what set him off, as if he were taking it out on me, and—"

A shudder ran through Sebastian and he placed a finger over her lips. "Please, Kate, don't."

"No, listen." She smiled softly. "Nothing Erharder could do to me made any difference. All that mattered was that you and the Jumeaus be kept safe. I began to understand how Giselle and Ernst must have felt."

"Christ, every time I look at your poor face, Kate—"

"Shh. It doesn't matter. It really doesn't."

"It matters to me," he said very quietly. "And you thought you hadn't the courage of your convictions. My God, Kate, when I said you were strong, I never thought you'd find out like this."

"Ever stubborn," said Kate, laughing. "Poor Erharder was quite upset with me. And you should have seen David's face—" She stopped abruptly.

Sebastian stroked her forehead. "Sweetheart, I'm sorry it had to end like that."

"I'm not. I know that sounds heartless, but in the end, I think it was for the best."

"I have to agree. David would have labored under a heavy load of disgrace and might easily have ended up with a treason charge against him. And it also saved me the trouble of setting him straight on a few things."

"Sebastian . . . Speaking of setting things straight, I was wondering. What did you do to Schwab in the kitchen?"

He drew in a sharp little breath. "How did you know it was Schwab?"

"Tony," she said simply.

"Yes, exactly. Tony." He looked at her carefully. "I made quite sure Schwab would never fire a gun again."

"Good," she said quietly.

He took her in his arms with a smile.

The Jumeaus were waiting for them, and naturally there was a great hue and outcry and Kate was kissed a hundred times—the only modulation of Jumeau enthusiasm in that they stayed away from her bruised cheek. She was patted by the women and sat down with a large cup of coffee and a thousand questions. Sebastian was sequestered by the men, Monsieur Villers included, who delved into all the details of yesterday's affair with relish. He thought with an inward laugh that they would be living off the pickings of this for years to come. And then Eustice and Stephanie arrived and there were more exclamations and kisses. The Jumeaus—one big happy family and growing bigger by the minute.

Finally Sebastian managed to calm them all down and they crowded around the table, those who could not fit standing behind.

"Now," said Sebastian decisively, "we still have work to do." But the telephone rang and Henri disappeared into the closet to answer it and when he reappeared he solemnly announced that it had been the police on the telephone.

"Madame Chabot was nowhere to be found last night, although her nephew was taken into custody with great protestation, claiming that a mad, blond Englishman had tried to kill him and was to be arrested immediately."

Sebastian grinned. "Poor Monsieur Barbier. How sad his fondest wish won't be realized."

"No, indeed. Apparently he was greatly saddened to learn your identity. However, Monsieur Sebastian, the police would like to see you as soon as possible. There are details that need clearing up."

"Yes," sighed Sebastian, "there would be. All right, then. Marcel, you and your family live in Montagrier, don't you? Good, I think it's best if all you Jumeaus go there until tomorrow, and Monsieur Villers as well. I don't want Erharder slipping back into town and taking out any of his venom on you. Eustice, I'd like you to stay with Stephanie. Keep an eye out for our man, won't you—you know what needs to be done. See if you can come up with any ideas in the meantime about the location of the documents. Kate, you'll come with me. And now, with your permission, Monsieur Henri, I'm going to call London and put them in the picture." He stood, and the roar of conversation started again.

When Sebastian came back out, an expectant silence

descended, but he only gestured to Eustice and disappeared with him for a few minutes. Then he excused himself and Kate and took her to the Peugeot.

The rest of the morning and the entire afternoon were taken up with bureaucratic police business. Sworn statements had to be taken, and London was on the telephone with Brantôme, giving Sebastian and Eustice clearance and deciding on the dispensation of Schwab and Brecht as well as countless other details. Kate was kept equally busy, once again grateful for her fluency, for she wondered how much longer the proceedings would have taken without her translating ability. In the end Brecht and Schwab (carefully holding a heavily bandanged hand) were taken out by heavy police escort to be transferred to Bordeaux, awaiting extradition to Britain. Sebastian quietly made arrangements to have David's body flown back to the United States, and called the Russell family himself to inform them only of an unfortunate car accident. There was no mention of Kate. Barbier, it was decided, was guilty of nothing worse than kidnapping and conspiracy and would be tried locally—with no problem about the outcome, the police assured an amused Kate. As for Madame Chabot, the consensus seemed to be that she would not likely be seen in those parts again.

And then it was over. Sebastian turned to Kate once they were in the car and said, "Did you think the espionage business smacked of romance and intrigue? It's three parts boredom and paperwork. What a bloody waste of a day."

Kate laughed. "I can tell you can't wait to get back to your beloved *objets*—although this side of you has a certain appeal, I must admit."

"Does it? Then perhaps I ought to consider staying in. I wouldn't want to disappoint you, now would I?"

"Darling, I loved you when you were a deboshed fish, and I'll love you when you're covered in antiquities, but I think we've had enough excitement for a lifetime. And I never want to see another French policeman as long as I live."

"Spare us the gendarmerie, God bless their bureaucratic souls," he said heatedly.

"Amen," said Kate. "You know, I thought they were so wonderful last night with everything, and they didn't question your authority or interfere with you at all."

"No, they were perfectly willing for me to exact my pound of flesh before they exacted theirs, if you see what I mean."

"Perfectly. God help us if Erharder shows up. There's going to be more exacting than I care to imagine."

"He'll rue the day he ever laid a finger on you."

"I think he will," she said with a little laugh. "And if it makes you happy, at this moment you don't look the least bit harmless."

He looked over at her with a grin. "Honor restored."

By the time they got back to St. Mouton, it was nearly dinnertime. "Tired, my love?" Sebastian took Kate's hand and examined her face.

"Not at all. Stop worrying about me, and for heaven's sake, let's find Stephanie and Eustice and get something to eat. I'm starved!"

"Sweetheart, you never fail to astonish me. I'm delighted that you're back to your normal raging appetite, but I must confess, I would have expected you to be done in by the last couple of days."

"Never! I kept praying that the gendarmes would have taken their usual two-hour lunch break, but no such luck. I think having a bona fide MI-6 agent in their midst had them more excited and swelled with importance than they've been in years."

"So it seems," said Sebastian wryly. "Well, I couldn't agree with your instincts more. Let's hunt down Eustice and Stephanie and get something to eat before we both expire."

Fortunately for all concerned, Eustice and Stephanie were waiting at the Hôtel de Ville, and just as ready to eat. They converged on the restaurant in the main square and ordered up a meal fit for kings, running the gamut from escargots to coq au vin, and finishing with a delectable glazed apple tart.

"Right," said Sebastian, when the last superb morsel had been devoured. "It's time to get back to the business at hand. It seems that none of us has managed to get much accomplished today, more's the pity. As I explained earlier to Eustice, it seems that London's not very interested in seeing us back until we've done something more useful about these documents. I don't have any better an idea where to start than I had two days ago, but I do think that Kate's watch has more to do with it than I'd originally thought."

"You mean you don't think the clue lies in the photograph?" said Kate slowly, putting down her coffee cup. "Sebastian, do you have my watch with you?"

"Never underestimate a spy," said Sebastian with a smile, pulling the watch from his pocket and placing it on the table. "I haven't had a chance to tell you, Kate, but Madame Mauriac from Charroux also worked on the Swallow line. Giselle had gone to her the day she delivered Hélène to Monsieur Villers." He summarized the pertinent details. "So you see, Giselle obviously knew what Ernst was trying to get across. She said it was 'all in the hands of time.' I've been racking my brains, trying to figure out what the hell she meant—if in fact she meant anything other than the obvious. But it seems to me that she might somehow have been referring to the watch. Do you remember, Kate, that I told you that the reason your watch didn't work was because the tooth-slide was missing?"

"What?" said Kate, bewildered.

Sebastian grinned. "Never mind. It was that picnic we had in the Whitworth field. I didn't think you were paying attention at the time."

"No—no, I don't suppose I was."

Sebastian threw his head back and laughed. "Oh, good. Well anyway, it had to have been deliberately removed. Why would someone do that unless it was for a reason?"

"I don't know," said Kate. "What are you getting at?"

"I think I see," said Stephanie slowly. "You think that the watch was deliberately stopped and that has something to do with its hands?"

''Exactly,'' said Sebastian. ''Suppose the position of the hands has something to do with the location of the documents—then that would be why it was so important to Giselle that the watch be delivered with the baby. Colonel Harrington had been expecting some important information from von Fiedler to arrive, and it never did. He assumed it was because of his death, but let's just say that the information was in the watch and not the picture—that was coincidental, a confirmation that Giselle was Hélène's mother. Do you see my train of thought?''

Eustice leaned forward, his elbows on the table. ''Then why didn't the watch end up with the colonel, if that had been Ernst and Giselle's intent?''

''Because the baby went straight to Guy Jessop,'' said Kate. ''She never went through Colonel Harrington; she was sent directly to Henley for some reason. And Guy then convinced the colonel that she had died. Then his wife hid the watch away with Elizabeth, afraid that if Guy knew about it he'd take it away because it connected Hélène, or rather Susanna, with her past. Special Operations never knew there'd been a watch!''

''I think that might be it,'' said Sebastian. ''Colonel Harrington certainly never knew about it. But that doesn't help us to figure out what the code is in the position of the hands—if, in fact, there is one. Going on the supposition, I think it might have something to do with latitude and longitude. Suppose von Fiedler decided to bury the documents. If you look at the way the hands are positioned, its set at two-fifty. Does that mean fifty degrees longitude and two degrees latitude, or the other way around? Or anyway, some combination of the two. It's only a shabby theory at best, but at least it's someplace to start.''

Eustice frowned. ''There are so many different combinations that are possible. It could be fifty-fifteen if you went by fives. Does he want us to look at it as two-fifty or ten to three? We can't go around digging up half the Dordogne unless we have more to go on.''

Sebastian picked up the watch again and looked at its

face. "'O! that a man might know the end of the day's business ere it come.' "

"Oh, for heaven's sake, not you, too," said Stephanie in disgust. "If I hear any more Shakespeare, I'm going to scream. Why don't you quote something appropriate and sensible like Brooke: 'Now God be thanked who has matched us with his Hour' or Dylan Thomas: 'The hands of the clock have stayed still at half past eleven for fifty years.' Keep it clean and contemporary. . . Sebastian, why are you staring at me as if I'd suddenly grown two heads?"

"Rupert Brooke . . ." said Sebastian slowly. "Colonel Harrington knows his poetry inside out. My God!"

"What is it, Sebastian?" Kate bit her lip against the excitement on his face.

"Ernst would have known that—they were at Cambridge together, after all—he'd have sent him the watch with the child as the confirmation, knowing that the colonel would have made the connection."

"*What* connection?" asked Stephanie impatiently.

"Brooke, as you said, Steph. Fancy your knowing Brooke!"

"I'm not a complete moron. But what on earth has that to do with anything?"

"It's so damnably clever!" said Sebastian, heedless of these remarks. Why the hell didn't I think of that before!"

Kate, after exhanging an amused look with Eustice who appearently was also accustomed to these leaps, leaned her chin on her fist and prepared to wait out the storm.

"What does Brooke have to do with the documents?" persisted Stephanie, not quite so familiar with Sebastian.

"What? Oh, the quotation, of course. 'Stands the Church clock at ten to three? And is there honey still for tea?' It's from 'The Old Vicarage' . . . Of course, *that's* why he would have removed the slide."

"Sebastian!" demanded Stephanie. "You are being impossible. Do you think the documents are inside the church clock?"

"Don't be absurd," said Sebastian. "Kate, you said that you'd been to the church?"

"Yes . . ."

"And surely you visited the Jumeau graves? Was there one for Hélène?"

"Why, yes . . ."

"Which is empty."

"Sebastian—of course—the coffin would be empty! And Erharder was right there at the baby's funeral, he told me so!"

"Was he? Invited by Ernst, no doubt. What better way to throw him off the fact Hélène had been smuggled away? And that his precious documents had been used to fill the child's coffin. Erharder would never have reason to look inside. Dear lord, how diabolical. He buried the things right under Erharder's nose."

Kate ran a hand back through her hair. "I think you must be right, Sebastian."

"I do think I must be. And of course, Ernst was in Bordeaux the day of Hélène's mock funeral, so he would have to have returned to Giselle after the fact to be certain that all had gone as planned. That explains why she was still in the area to hear about her family being taken. And Ernst must have meant to send the actual quote or whatever to Special Operations under separate cover, but he must have been fairly certain that Colonel Harrington would make the connection without it."

"Does this mean what I think it does?" asked Eustice dryly.

"Afraid so, Brutus. It means we're going to be doing a little graveyard scavenging tonight. Does anyone have any squeamish objections?"

"No, of course not," said Kate. "But there's one thing. I think we ought to ask Henri if it's all right with him. After all . . ."

"You're quite right. I like the way your mind works, Kate. Never mind getting permission from the authorities, just clear it through Jumeau."

"Don't tell me that's not exactly the way you operate, Sebastian Dunn." Kate looked at him and smiled.

"As it happens you have me pegged. Act first, pay the

consequences later. It sounds like a good plan to me. Do you agree, Eustice?"

"Agreed. Let's get ourselves to Montagrier and speak to Jumeau. Thank goodness there's no moon tonight. I don't relish the idea of the village converging on an exhumation."

"How did I ever get myself involved in this?" said Stephanie. "A nice cozy holiday full of sun, food, and relaxation, the epitome of normality . . ."

"Shut up, Steph," said Kate and Sebastian in unison.

"And a pack of lunatics thrown into the bargain."

"But it seems to make perfect sense," said Henri calmly. "Of course you must dig up the grave. After all, there cannot be anyone in it, can there?"

"I hope to hell not," said Sebastian with a frown. "We don't know if Giselle didn't substitute the body of another infant, just in case Erharder bothered to check. But the facts seem to fit together so well. Thank God for Stephanie and her Brooke—we could have wasted days on speculation. So, we go ahead then. Thank you, Monsieur Henri."

"Not at all—but Louis Villers and I would like very much to be there, Monsieur Sebastian."

"I'm afraid that's out of the question, although I completely understand your wish. I have enough on my hands than to worry about you on top of it. Surely you can understand? We'll let you know as soon as we have anything."

"Naturally, monsieur. It's only that it's very much my concern, with what happened to Giselle."

"Yes, but let us not forget what happened to Kate. That's very much my concern."

"Yes . . . I was wondering, Monsieur Sebastian, if it's not too much to ask?"

"What's that?" said Sebastian with a small laugh.

"We were all wondering. You and Mademoiselle Kate?"

"Yes, quite," said Sebastian. "Yes and yes and yes, if that answers your question. And that cancels out three nevers I seem to remember," he said, looking over at Kate with a grin. "Now that Kate's out of danger, it's only right that you should know."

Nadia smiled and said to Kate, "You have chosen well. He is just like Giselle's *maquisard* as he appeared that day. Tall, blond, blue eyes. Involved in danger all the time. It is good for romance, this."

Kate colored and shot a helpless look at Sebastian.

"So you will be married, *hein*?" Henri grinned broadly, nodding his head.

"We will be married shortly, God willing," said Sebastian, barely maintaining his composure. "And that is one more reason that we need to clear this business up as quickly as possible, and the less—help, the better. You can surely see the sense in that, monsieur?"

"Of course. The family will be so delighted to hear your good news. We had all thought this was the case. A grand passion, you see, will spur a man on against impossible odds."

At this Sebastian collapsed. "Indeed, Monsieur Henri, as you say," he managed to say. "Now, shall we be on our way? 'We have heard the chimes at midnight,' as we say in English. Thank you again." He rose.

Henri kissed Kate on both cheeks. "God keep you safe tonight," he said with tears in his eyes. "You are a fine woman."

Kate smiled. "Thank you, Henri. It must be the Giselle in me." And they left.

Sebastian parked the car in the little thicket down the road from the churchyard, wanting to be quite sure that there was nothing unusual in appearances. He'd borrowed shovels and flashlights from Marcel, and he and Eustice removed them from the back of the car. There was a distinct chill in the air, and Kate shivered as she got out.

"Look, Kate," said Sebastian, coming around to her. "I think it's better if you and Steph wait here."

"Oh, come on, Sebastian. This is as much to do with me as it is with you, if not more so. At least we can hold the lights while you dig. Anyway, darling, don't you think that there's something deliciously Hamlet-like about it all? You know, 'In the dead vast and middle of the night'?"

"Yes, well as far as I'm concerned, 'be somewhat scanter of your maiden presence.'" He laughed and caught her around the waist, kissing her with a certain degree of preoccupation.

"All right then, you and Eustice get to your skulduggery, but I'm going into the church. There's a certain point here where you have to give over to reason."

"Oh, for Christ's sake, 'give it an understanding but no tongue.' And enough said and quoted. You'll damned well do as you're told and stay here in the car. And keep the doors locked. Let's get to work, Eustice."

"Sebastian—"

"Kate, I'll take up this prenuptial argument with you later. In the meantime, you'll do as you're told. God keep us from disobedient women. Come along, Brutus." He fixed Kate with one last severe look and then he melted into the dark.

Kate turned to Stephanie who had been standing silently by. "Oh, honestly!"

"You don't give up easily, do you?"

"Nor do I intend to."

"Oh, no, Kate. You're not thinking of following them! Look, there's been enough trouble—"

"I know. I'm just going into the church, Steph. There's no harm in that, and Sebastian won't even know. I'll use the side door."

"Kate, be reasonable. Sebastian obviously has his reasons for wanting us to stay put."

"He's just being overprotective. Listen, there's no need for you to treat me like a hothouse plant, too."

"Don't you think after everything that's happened that maybe you need a little looking after? You've been through a tough time, Kate. Look at you!"

"Are you going to go on about it, too, Steph? Give me a little room, will you?"

Stephanie looked at her doubtfully. "I don't like it, Kate. Can't you wait until tomorrow?"

"I'd rather not. I'm here, and it's the right time. I can't really explain more than that, but I need this. Can you understand?"

"No. At least let me come with you."

"Thanks for that, anyway, but no. I really do need to be alone. God knows I haven't had much of that recently. I'll only be about ten minutes."

"Well, I still don't like it. But just bloody well be back here in ten minutes, all right?"

"I promise." Kate slipped off into the night.

The heavy oak door creaked very slightly as she pulled on it, its weight like stone in her hand, but then she was in. The interior of the church was very dark as she cautiously made her way to one of the pews and sat down. She had a good many thoughts to get in order, and the peace and privacy of the church were a balm to her bruised soul. This strange adventure she'd been thrown into was almost over, and amazingly enough she'd come through it virtually unscathed; in fact, she was more complete. Strange how things came to pass—and now after all these years, Giselle and Ernst's souls could finally be laid to rest. She bowed her head and said a silent little prayer for them.

She was pulled abruptly from her thoughts by the rustle of a cassock at the altar, and an icy fear washed through her veins.

"Who is there?" the voice said softly in French.

She breathed again. Of course, it was Saturday night and the priest would be making ready for the next morning's Mass. "It is only a visitor, Father," she called.

"And who would that be at the hour of midnight, my child? What trouble do you come to the church with that would not wait until morning?" The disembodied voice came distorted and hollow as if from a long distance.

"It is nothing, Father. I'm simply a visiting American who felt the need for a little solace."

"I see. Perhaps I can be of help." He left the altar and she heard the wooden gate squeak as he closed it after himself.

Kate rose to her feet, wishing she could see better. "It's

not necessary, really, Father. I'm sorry if I disturbed you in your work. I'll just be going." She turned to leave.

And then he was upon her, and he lashed out and grabbed her against him, crushing her bruised ribs, a hand coming violently over her nose and mouth.

"So, we meet again, my dear Kate," Erharder said softly into her ear.

CHAPTER
Nineteen

She was suffocating against his hand, struggling against his iron grip, but it was useless.

"How very convenient this turned out to be, Kate. I hadn't thought that sheltering in the church would bring me such a reward. I wasn't very pleased with the circumstances of our last parting, you know; I believe you have a little something to make up to me." His voice was almost a croon.

Kate's lungs burned horribly, starved for air. A ringing started in her ears and the world went red. And then she found herself suddenly released, and her breath came in great gasps, pulling painfully at her ribs. She collapsed onto the seat of the pew, her hands at her sides. She would have screamed if she'd been able but at the moment she was too concentrated on gulping the precious oxygen into her body.

"Don't even consider making a sound, dear Kate." A knife flashed cold steel in his hand. "I would be more than happy to gut you with this. Now, I think we have some talking to do. Where's Russell?"

Kate, still gasping, shook her head. She felt the point of the knife against her back. "Dead. He's dead," she managed to say.

"Dead? You expect me to believe that? Come now, Kate.

I thought we had gone beyond these silly little lies. Protecting him will get you nowhere. Where is he?''

She swallowed hard, trying to think. She had to keep Erharder distracted, keep him from discovering Sebastian and Eustice. ''I—I don't know. I got away. That's why I came to the church, to hide from him. He thought everything could be just the same as before, but I . . . I waited until he was asleep and then I ran.''

''Hmm. That's much better, Kate. And what of Schwab and Brecht? It wasn't very nice of the Jumeaus to break into the house like that.''

''I have no idea what happened. David took me off in his car.''

''And where did you leave him?''

''I—we were in the village. In the Hôtel de Ville. He's registered under another name, Dris—something.'' Maybe, she thought, just maybe Sebastian would look for her there. All she had to do was to delay Erharder in the room long enough for Sebastian to return.

''Very good, Kate. Very good indeed. You and I shall take ourselves over there, I think.'' He jerked her to her feet and dragged her over to the front door, opening it very quietly. Kate's heart fell as she heard the faint sound of Sebastian's voice from around the corner along with the sound of scraping. Erharder went very still, and then he pulled Kate back inside, pressing her against the wall. The stone was cold and hard against her back.

''What is this!'' he hissed. ''What do you know of this, you little bitch!''

Kate mutely shook her head and Erharder grabbed her by the shoulders and shook her until her teeth rattled.

''Tell me! What is happening in the churchyard? You will tell me—is it Russell?''

Kate said nothing, but she could just see his eyes narrow in a manner far too familiar to her. She flinched, waiting for the blow. To her surprise, he stepped away and regarded her with something akin to amazement.

''My God . . .'' he said very softly. ''How stupid of me not to have realized sooner! Clever, clever Giselle. And how appropriate that her granddaughter should lead me to the very thing she took such pains to hide. And what does Russell intend to do with my documents? Does he think he can blackmail me?''

''No. I don't know who it is out there! I told you, David's asleep in the hotel room!''

Erharder considered for a long moment. ''Yes . . . You have no more reason to lie. Perhaps it is one of the Jumeaus. They would know now that the grave is empty. Yes, that must be it. They look for Giselle's hidden secret. They can have no idea what else they will find. How very perfect; I do like neat endings. And much as I would like to exact a pretty revenge for what you did to me, Kate, I will use you as my leverage. They'll hand over my property soon enough when they see I will kill you if they don't. And I will, Kate, be quite sure that I will, so don't be foolish enough to try to alert them. Think of it like this: They'll all die if they see the contents of that little box.''

He yanked her against him and once again opened the door. He held the icy tip of the knife at Kate's throat and she dared not make a noise. Her heart pounded painfully in her chest, and in the drawn-out minutes that followed, she cursed herself silently for the stubborn fool she was. And then the sound of metal against wood rang out and there was more scraping, and finally the shuffling noise of the box being lifted out of its hole and placed down on the grass.

Erharder made his move. He urged her ahead of him down the wide, uneven stone steps that fronted the church, still holding her tightly, and now the blade of the knife lay across her throat. An owl hooted hollowly from somewhere in the distance like a portent; the sliver of moon hung sideways in the sky giving barely enough light to see by. Gravestones rose in uneven lines, eerie testaments to the past. Erharder pushed Kate around the corner of the building, their feet whispering across the grass damp with evening dew. Kate shivered involuntarily. Here was a scene from the worst of nightmares—she was trapped in a graveyard with evil incarnate and there was nothing she could do to warn Sebastian away. Two shadows moved like wraiths on the far end of the churchyard, pinpricks of light flickering around them as they bent over their ghostly work.

Erharder moved her closer to them, hugging the wall with his back, until they were only yards away. Some kind of sixth sense must have alerted Sebastian, for he stopped and lifted his head, listening like an animal interrupted in its forage. The light swung around and caught them in its beam, causing the knife blade to glint against the tender skin of Kate's throat. Sebastian rose cautiously to his feet and stood quite still.

"So you came after all, Erharder."

"Drop the light," commanded Erharder, his sharp voice tearing the night like a razor across velvet, and Sebastian immediately obeyed. "Now throw your guns at my feet or I'll use the knife."

A moment later the guns landed with a soft thud, just out of reach.

"Let the girl go, Erharder. She's nothing to do with this." Sebastian's voice was tight with control.

"She has more than enough to do with this—I'd be happy to slit her throat for what she has to do with this," he said nastily. "However, in light of the circumstances I'll let her go, but only when you push the box over here."

Sebastian nodded his head at Eustice, still crouched, who was watching warily, and he picked the box up, moving it toward them.

"There, that's close enough—not another step. Now back away."

"Now release Kate," said Sebastian quietly.

"Not so quickly," said Erharder. "First you'll leave. Then I'll release her."

"Not on your life. We fulfilled our part of the bargain. I go nowhere until I have Kate with me."

"Do you think I'm a fool!" Erharder's voice rose with anger. "Go!" The knife bit into Kate's throat.

"Sebastian? Kate's not in the church—is she with you?" Stephanie's voice came from across the churchyard and Erharder's head jerked around.

It gave Sebastian the split second of diversion he needed

and he leapt. He went straight for Erharder's knife hand and Kate was knocked violently aside as Sebastian struck. She was grabbed and pulled farther away by Eustice as Sebastian struggled with Erharder for the knife. There was a brief scuffle and then it was all over, the old man no match for Sebastian's youth and strength, and Erharder was pinned to the ground. Sebastian hovered over him, the knife in his hand pointed at Erharder's throat.

"By God, I should kill you here and now for what you've done."

Erharder stared at him through the dark, recognition sharp in his eyes. "You?" he whispered. "You, the fisherman, this entire time?"

"That's right. The fisherman, and once the closest friend of the man you had killed in Berlin. MI-6, Erharder. I trust you remember?"

Erharder's breath hissed in through his teeth.

"I see that bothers you. I wonder why. Could it be you're afraid I might be a little upset about your rather—brutal record?"

"You'll do nothing—you know how much Britain wants me," he said with a cold laugh.

"Won't I?" said Sebastian, and his hands flashed out, the knife drawing a line from jaw to collarbone. Erharder screamed and his hands flew to his neck as the blood welled up thickly.

"To match Giselle's on the other side. I imagine you know what it's for." He stood then, looking down at Erharder. "My God, you're a contemptible piece of filth. Eustice, take the box into the church." He pulled Erharder to his feet. Eustice handed Sebastian his gun, and he jabbed it into Erharder's back. "Inside."

"Sebastian—" Kate took a step forward.

He shot her a look of pure disgust. "You damned well stay out of my way." Without another word he walked past Kate and Stephanie who had come to stand behind her.

"Lord, he's a tough one, your Sebastian," said Stephanie on a long breath. "First Schwab, now this. You'd better behave yourself from now on or I wouldn't count on your chances.'' Stephanie watched them disappear and a moment later the church lights came blazing on. ''Kate?'' she asked, when there was no reply.

''I don't think it much matters,'' said Kate in a small, tight voice. ''I doubt if Sebastian will ever forgive me for what I did.''

''You'll be lucky if he does,'' she said brutally. ''I don't know how many times your stubbornness has gotten you in trouble, and this time there might have been some lives to your account, never mind your own. For heaven's sake, Kate, what happened?''

''Once again Kate Soames behaved like an unmitigated idiot. I should have listened to you. Erharder was hiding out in the church, and I realized a little after the fact that he wasn't the visiting priest.''

''Oh, Kate, you poor thing. He didn't hurt you, did he?''

''No, just scared the life out of me. Never mind that, it's exactly what I deserved. I'm afraid that what's coming is going to be much worse.''

''Here's your chance to find out, you flaming idiot.''

Sebastian's tall figure rounded the corner, silhouetted by the light blazing out of the windows. He came straight for them.

Kate winced as she saw his expression. He stopped abruptly in front of them.

''Stephanie, go inside with Eustice. Erharder's well restrained; you'll be perfectly safe. Kate, you'll stay here.'' His voice was barely controlled. Stephanie left without a word.

Kate's heart sank. ''Sebastian—''

''I don't want to hear a bloody word out of you.'' He took her by the shoulders, not gently, and pushed her over to the yawning hole in the earth. ''Hold the light.''

She did as she was told, more miserable than she'd ever thought possible. She had done the one thing Sebastian would never tolerate, and done it of her own volition like the spoiled, thoughtless fool she was. And this after all he had done for her.

Sebastian began to shovel earth back into the grave. He

worked quickly, with economical and rhythmic strokes, but there was something else about the way he moved that told Kate how very angry he was, more so than words ever could. Finally he was finished, and put the shovel down, placing the slab he'd earlier removed back over the top. The grave looked almost untouched.

"Sit down, Kate."

She obeyed cautiously, flinching as her ribs protested. Sebastian looked down at her, his arms folded across his chest. Still he didn't speak, and she didn't try. She couldn't see that it would make any difference in any case.

Finally he said, "I should take you over my knee and thrash you."

"Yes, you should." She wished he'd explode in rage—anything but this icy control.

"You didn't stay in the car, did you."

"No. I went in the side entrance of the church." She looked away.

"Where Erharder was waiting. And you provided a sitting target for him."

"Yes, I did."

"And put all of us in danger."

"Yes."

He suddenly banged his fist into his hand and then roared, "Damn it, Kate, how could you have been so bloody stupid? When the hell are you going to learn?"

She looked up at him then, only to see the fury blazing in his eyes. "I know it won't make it any better but just let me say I'm sorry, I really am, Sebastian. I only wanted to say good-bye to Ernst and Giselle, and I needed the peace. I didn't think there'd be any harm in it, although I see now what a fool I was, and you were right all along." Hot tears stung at her eyes. "I know you'll never forgive me, and you shouldn't—"

"No, you're damned right I shouldn't."

"But you see, I didn't think about—look, I'm just not used to mixing with the Gestapo, and Intelligence agents, and I know it's no excuse at all. I—I'd go, but there isn't another car . . ." She hung her head in misery, the hot, hard knot of unhappiness constricting her throat.

Then disbelievingly, she heard him give a short laugh, and he dropped to his knees beside her, taking her in his arms. "There are two words that will not be left out of our marriage vows and they are *to obey.*"

She looked up at him, the tears now falling freely. "Oh, Sebastian, I thought—" And her words were cut off by his mouth coming down hard on hers, leaving her in no doubt of his feelings toward her.

Then he put her away from him. "Now I have some things I want to say to you, and you're going to listen to me very carefully, because I have no intention of ever repeating them." He took her by the shoulders, and this time his hands were gentle as he looked into her face. "Kate, I *have* to know that I can trust you without fail. That goes above and beyond anything else, no matter what the circumstances. And the same goes for you—you're going to have to learn to trust me without question. Without that, we have nothing. Look, I understand completely why you wanted to go into the church. What makes me so blasted angry is that I couldn't count on you to do as I asked. I had a damned good reason for wanting you to stay put. Do you understand? It's taken us too much anguish to get to where we are, and I'm very well aware of what you've been through, as far as learning to trust people is concerned. But damn it, I'm not about to carry around David's legacy, or your father's for that matter. I love you, Kate, God knows I do, but love is a fragile thing that has to be nurtured, and it's built on the foundation of trust and honesty. I have every intention of living out the rest of my life with you, but I want to know here and now if you can live up to these principles. If you don't think you can, let me know right now, because when we marry, it's not going to be an experiment in joint living; it's for keeps." He examined her face intently. "Do you want some time to think about it?"

Kate took a deep, shaky breath. "No, Sebastian. I've been an idiot."

"I'm presuming we never have to have this conversation again?"

"Never. I'm so sorry, Sebastian."

"Hush, my love. We won't talk about it again. I imagine having a knife at your throat has taught you a thing or two. Come now; there are still a good many things to be done before the night is over."

She wiped her eyes with the back of her hand. "What are you going to do with Erharder?"

"I'm going to turn him over to the police. I don't trust myself with him. He'll be extradited to England and they can interrogate him there to their hearts' content."

"Sebastian . . ."

"Yes, sweetheart?"

"Aren't they going to be a little upset with you for what you did to him?"

"I couldn't give a damn. It's a pity he's not going to bleed to death." He stood and offered her his hand. "Now let's get inside and see what Eustice has discovered in the coffin. I imagine it's been killing Erharder to watch his precious secrets exposed after all these years."

Erharder had been lashed to the altar railing. His priest's collar was soaked a ruby red, but the slash hadn't been very deep and had now stopped bleeding. A gag was tied around his mouth. He looked like a victim of the Spanish Inquisition, Kate thought with satisfaction. Stephanie had Eustice's gun and casually sat in the front pew, taking great pleasure in holding it on the Nazi. Eustice had pried the top off the box and sorted through the papers. He looked up as Sebastian and Kate approached.

"London was right. It's a gold mine."

"Good. We'll run through it later."

"There's something I thought you might want to see . . ." Eustice handed him a yellowed slip of paper, and Sebastian took it and read it quickly. He shook his head, then smiled and looked over at Kate.

"Kate, I believe this belongs to you." He handed it to her.

Kate ran her eyes over the spindly writing. Giselle Marie Jumeau . . . Baron Ernst Marcus von Fiedler . . . It was their marriage certificate, signed by their hands on February the twenty-third, 1944, and also by Father Antoine Bordelet, village priest. She looked up at Sebastian, speechless.

He nodded his head, then stepped to one side. Kate walked up to Erharder and met his flickering eyes with a little smile. "The proof you wanted, Herr Erharder?" She held the marriage certificate up in front of him so that he could read it.

A muffled noise of fury came from Erharder and Sebastian untied his gag. "Was there something you wanted to say?"

"Fools!" spat Erharder. "Perhaps he was stupid enough to marry the girl, but if so, then your precious Giselle married a well-known colonel of the SS, a man who spent the war turning your agents for Germany. It doesn't speak well for her supposed Resistance record, does it? It makes her as good as a collaborator." He smiled sarcastically.

"Actually," said Sebastian easily, "if we're speaking of fools, it seems as if Ernst von Fiedler had the last laugh on you. He'd been working for Britain from the day he joined the SS, and Giselle was well aware of the fact."

"What is this?" Erharder ran a tongue over his lips, clearly shocked.

"It was von Fiedler who stole your documents, not Giselle. He'd been on to your conspiracy for a good year. And I might add that he not only supplied British Intelligence with a constant stream of German secrets, but also was responsible for a full network of our other agents—agents you thought had been turned by him."

Erharder's shoulders slumped. It was the final insult—an insult leveled after more than forty years, and leveled hard.

Kate smiled in satisfaction. "He was also the 'Resistant' who rescued Giselle from the transport on the way to Ravensbrück, who with her help saw Max Stade safely out of France. I don't know if you ever learned that Giselle was leader of the Swallow escape line? So although you never had any proof, you were right all along about Giselle's involvement as well as the other Jumeaus in the Resistance. Oh, and Herr Erharder, just to assure you that the wheel is come full circle, Sebastian and I are to be married."

Erharder stared.

Sebastian laughed, his arm going around Kate's waist. " 'A hit, a very palpable hit.' "

" 'This even-handed justice,' " replied Kate.

"Ah yes, how apt. Poor Herr Erharder. It's come to a crashing end, hasn't it, and all thanks to Ernst and Giselle."

"It's lies, all lies!" screamed Erharder.

"I'm sure that MI-6 will fill in the rest, but I believe you have the salient points. So Brutus, shall we cart our friend off to the police? I think I'd better bring the car from down the road. I'll just be a few minutes." He retied the gag and was gone.

Eustice started to gather all the papers and put them back into the box, and Kate went and sat in a pew, rereading the marriage certificate with a little smile. She felt eyes on her and glanced up; Erharder was staring at her with a singularly unpleasant expression. She looked away with a little shudder and her eye caught a movement by the side door that led into the chancel. Impossibly, Madame Chabot stood there, a gun pointed at Stephanie.

"Stephanie! Watch out!" cried Kate.

"Drop the gun or I will shoot," said Madame Chabot in a high, dry voice.

Eustice slowly straightened. "Do as she says, Stephanie. Throw it to the end of the pew and get down. You too, Kate," he said over his shoulder.

"Now let him go," said Madame Chabot. "Do it!" Her little black eyes burned like coals in her pinched face. Eustice slowly unlashed the ropes that held Erharder, thinking quickly, wishing he didn't have Stephanie and Kate to worry about.

"Stand back and let him through the gate to the altar. Quickly!" She waved the gun dangerously.

"Easy now," said Eustice. Then three things happened at once. Madame Chabot's gun went off, knocking the arm off the baby Jesus that graced the altar, and Eustice made a dive for her. She frantically threw the gun away and it went slithering along the stone floor. Erharder grabbed it up and at the same time the front door burst open and Erharder spun around, taking a wild shot.

Henri Jumeau never hesitated. The rifle came up to his shoulder and he fired, hitting Erharder squarely in the chest. A look of complete surprise came over Erharder's face as his hands went to the front of the cassock and came away covered in blood. He looked at them blankly as he sank slowly to the ground and then fell over on his side and was still. Madame Chabot screamed and threw herself on his body, and Eustice quickly picked up the gun that Erharder had dropped.

"Jesus Christ." Sebastian burst in behind Henri and Monsieur Villers, breathing hard, his gun outstretched in his hands. He pushed past them, looking quickly over to Kate and Stephanie to make sure they hadn't been caught in the cross fire, and satisfied that they were unharmed, strode up the aisle.

He went straight to Erharder's body, pulling a wailing Madame Chabot away and handing her to Eustice. He felt for the carotid artery. "He's dead. What the hell happened here?"

Kate couldn't bear the sound of Madame Chabot's hysterical crying, and she went to the altar and gently removed her from Eustice's restraining hands. "Come, madame," she said gently. "You need to sit down, I think. It's all over now." Madame Chabot nodded, still sobbing violently, but went unresistingly with Kate.

Sebastian looked at Kate curiously as she led the old woman away, then said, "Eustice?"

Eustice quickly and concisely told him what had happened.

"My God, who would have thought Madame Chabot would show up in the right place and the right time with a gun?" Sebastian shook his head. "All right. Monsieur Henri, Monsieur Villers, you have some explaining to do." He walked back down the aisle toward them. "I thought I told you to stay put in Montagrier. What the hell are you doing here with a rifle? You've just killed the biggest catch Britain has had in years! I'm going to have a hard time explaining this one."

Henri shrugged. "I received a call from Monsieur Truffaux in the village, saying the Madame Chabot had just been seen sneaking out of her *boulangerie* with a basket of food. I came here to tell you, as I did not know when you would come by again. Louis came to keep me company."

"And the rifle?" said Sebastian dryly.

"Protection. Naturally I did not hesitate to use it when the Boche fired at us. It was a lucky shot," he said with satisfaction.

"And what about 'Vengeance is mine; I will repay, saith the Lord'?"

"And there was that, too," agreed Henri.

Sebastian shook his head. "I now know where Kate gets it from. It comes straight down the genetic line." He sighed. "Eustice, go and call the police, get them out here right away. It's going to be another long night."

Morning broke through the windows of the church and still they hadn't finished. "Look, I think we've had enough of this," said Sebastian impatiently. "We could all use some sleep, and if there are anymore questions we'll answer them later."

"Yes, monsieur, I agree," said the chief gendarme, suddenly reasonable. "But you must not leave the *département* until we've finished everything."

"Of course," said Sebastian. But there then followed a long argument about who should have control over the documents. The gendarme seemed to feel that since they had been buried in French soil for all these years, they came under the category of antiquities and therefore belonged to the French. In complete frustration, Sebastian explained for the last time that the documents were the property of Britain since they had been specifically collected for that country, and they were not about to leave his sight if he had to be locked in a prison cell with them. At this final sally, the gendarme threw his hands up and conceded the point. He looked thoroughly invigorated as if he'd just completed a satisfying argument, and then gestured genially at everyone to go.

Henri and Monsieur Villers were sent off as heroes, and Madame Chabot was taken off by the police to be held until they had decided what to do with her. That alone could take months, thought Sebastian dryly as he watched her taken away.

"Kate, come here," he said in exhaustion after Eustice and Stephanie had gone out with the box, and drew her into his arms. "Promise me here and now that you have no more skeletons in your familial closet."

"None that I'm aware of." She relaxed against the familiar planes of his chest and closed her eyes. "What about you?"

"Oh, the usual mad uncle who reappears every other generation or so, but nothing else too alarming."

"How reassuring. I've had about as much alarm as I can take for a while."

He brushed her hair with his lips. "The most alarming thing that's going to happen to you is marriage to me, I promise."

She looked up. "That doesn't sound so bad."

He smiled down at her. "Good. But about that—I'd like to arrange it as soon as possible after we get home, all right?"

"Yes. Oh yes."

"You are becoming more decisive on the subject of marriage, aren't you?"

"I most certainly am, Mr. Dunn. I believe it has something to do with being terribly in love." She reached up and kissed him.

"Mmm. I think I like this terribly in love part." He looked up at the sound of a horn. "Listen, there's Eustice. Oh, Kate—before we go, there is something I wanted to ask you."

"What?"

"Madame Chabot. What suddenly moved your hardened little heart to take pity on her like that?"

"Oh, Sebastian, the poor woman. She's obviously been carrying a torch for Erharder all these years, and then to see him shot like that—I think she really loved him."

He smiled softly at her, and taking her hand, he kissed it. "Kate, you will never, ever cease to surprise me. Come, my love, let's get some sleep."

He led her from the church.

CHAPTER
Twenty

It was a warm, breezy afternoon, and for once that summer, the London streets were dry. Sebastian looked down at Kate and smiled. "Don't look so nervous, my love. He's perfectly harmless." He gave her hand a squeeze.

"Don't look nervous? Sebastian, I've never had to talk to a colonel in MI-6 before!"

"You've never had any trouble talking to me that I've ever noticed."

"No, you know what I mean. It's different. It's like walking into a spy novel or something."

Sebastian burst into laughter. "You're priceless, Kate. Just what do you think you've been living the last few months? Anyway, it's no different at all. I can't imagine what sort of image you've conjured up—he's a nice old man who wants very much to meet you. You should be complimented; this doesn't happen often."

"That's what worries me," she said wryly.

"Well, stop being worried. You are something of a special case, after all. He just wants to ask you a few questions. You were rather instrumental to this whole business, and you not only had direct access to Erharder but also to David. There could be things that you know without realizing their significance. But aside from that, I suspect he has a sentimental reason for wanting to meet you.''

''Sebastian . . . Does he know everything?''

''Yes he does, sweetheart, but don't be worried. He was quite impressed with the way you handled the situation. And I did leave out the parts that went like this.'' He stopped her in the middle of the street and pulled her into his arms kissing her very thoroughly, and completely ignoring the smiles and stares of passing people.

''Sebastian!'' said Kate when he finally released her. ''That was very nice, but what on earth came over you?''

''Sheer unmitigated lust, my love. Now stop dawdling, we're going to be late.''

''Utterly, hopelessly impossible,'' she sighed.

''And you couldn't do without me,'' said Sebastian with a grin.

''Miss Soames, I can't tell you how pleased I am to finally meet you,'' said Colonel Harrington, shaking her hand. ''I've heard a great deal about you.''

''So I gather, sir,'' said Kate with a little smile, immediately liking him and relaxing. ''And I should think you'd be extremely annoyed with me for having caused you so much trouble.''

''Not at all. If it hadn't been for you, Erharder would still be on the loose, and we wouldn't have these documents. We have nothing but thanks to offer.''

''That should go to Sebastian and Eustice. They had to chase all over the countryside because of me. I can't tell you how many times Sebastian was ready to murder me for some of the idiotic things I did, not the least of which was to accuse him of being a terrorist.''

''Really?'' said the colonel with interest, looking at Sebastian. ''It couldn't have upset him too badly. I understand felicitations are in order.''

Kate smiled, looking down at the sapphire on her left hand. ''It's quite beyond understanding, I know.''

"You're a lucky man, Dunn."

"I know, sir. And don't let Kate fool you—she's tough as nails under that modest demeanor."

"I suspect I know where it comes from. I knew your grandfather well, you know. He'd have been very proud of you, Miss Soames."

"Thank you, sir," said Kate, coloring. "I wish I'd known him. He must have been a fine man."

"He was indeed. And although I never met her, Giselle was well respected and liked by the people she worked with. She was a fine, brave woman. I was extremely surprised to learn of the existence of their grandchild. As you know, I had believed their daughter dead all these years."

"Yes, sir. But that's something I still don't understand. How did it happen that the baby went to Guy Jessop and not to you, as Giselle and Ernst must have intended?"

"It was an interesting set of circumstances. I had received the information that the child was on her way. But then only days later, I heard about the death of your grandparents. That changed my responsibility considerably. Originally, I was going to have the child placed in a temporary home, but once she'd been orphaned, I wanted to find a permanent family for her without the usual sort of delay. Guy Jessop worked with us, knew of the situation, and knew Ernst. He admired him greatly and wanted to help. He came to me with the solution: He had friends up north who were willing to adopt the infant immediately. I agreed, and had the child directed to Guy in Henley, where he had someone take her to her new family. A few days later, word came to me that she'd been killed in an air raid along with her courier on the journey up. I had no reason to believe otherwise. It was one more wartime tragedy."

"Sebastian and I thought that substituting the baby for his own was Guy's way of protecting her from any possible trouble."

"I would have to agree. It was a fine plan, except for the disappearance of the watch. Guy had no idea that Ernst might have been trying to get a message to us. As far as he knew, Ernst and Giselle were simply trying to get their child out of wartime France. We were very closemouthed about each other's work. Perhaps if he had known, he would have been on the alert for something. But then none of us expected Ernst's death when it came, and so we thought the secret of the documents' location had died with him . . . I wish we had thought of the empty coffin, though. A nice touch, I must say. But all that's in the past, and here you are now. It's certainly been a journey of ironies. Ernst would have found it most interesting. Another time I would be delighted to tell you all about him—the lighter side. He had a wonderful sense of humor. But now if you don't mind, I would like to ask you some questions about your adventure."

"I'd be happy to tell you anything you want to know."

"We'll start with your father. When did he first meet Mr. Russell . . ."

Kate stared for a long moment at the telephone receiver in her hand, then dialed. It rang four times, long hollow rings, then her father's voice came snapping over the line.

"Soames here."

"Hello, Daddy, it's Kate. How are you?"

"Katie! Good heavens, I've been trying to reach you for days!"

"Elizabeth told me. I've just returned and this is the first opportunity I've had to call. I have some news for you."

"My dear Katie—then you've heard after all."

"Heard what?" She fiddled with the cord, twisting it round and round her finger.

"Oh, my poor girl, you haven't heard? Katie, brace yourself; I have some very bad news for you. David was killed in France."

"David . . . In France?"

"Yes, he wanted to reconcile, Katie. I told him where he could find you."

"Did you?"

"Yes, my dear. He never reached you, then? He was

killed in a car accident five nights ago. The funeral is tomorrow. I'm so sorry, Katie. I think you'd better come home immediately. If you catch the next plane, you should be here in time for the service."

"No, I'm afraid that's impossible. It's why I'm calling. This probably sounds very sudden, but I'm getting married in three weeks."

"My God, Katie, what's the matter with you!" His voice thundered in her ear, and she held the receiver away. "Didn't you hear me? David's dead! How can you talk about marrying someone else in three weeks! I can't believe you're being so callous!"

"I heard you quite well—David's dead. I don't want to hear anymore. I was wondering if you could fly over for the wedding." The tip of her finger began to throb and she looked down to see that she'd cut off her circulation with the cord.

"How can you possibly contemplate some ridiculous wedding at a time like this? It's beyond comprehension that my own daughter could be so selfish! I want you home right away, Katie. The least you can do is pay your respects to David's family."

"No," said Kate softly. "I'm not coming home."

"Damn it, Katie! You'll do as you're told! And you might have the decency to show a little grief. Your attitude is despicable."

"I'm sorry if you don't like my attitude. Things have been a little rough around here, and I haven't got the patience to pretend to feel something I don't. I'd very much like you to be here when I'm married, but if you can't manage it, then I'll have to do without you."

"That's it!" he roared. "This is typical—*typical* of you. Why should I expect anything but to have you be willful and disobedient? I'm deeply disappointed in you, Katie—I can't tell you how much. I think you owe me an apology."

"I have nothing to apologize for. I broke it off with David well over two months ago, and I have no further obligation to him or his family. I don't love him, I love someone called Sebastian—"

"I'm not interested in anything about him, including his name, Katie! If you don't come home immediately, and you go through with this precipitous marriage in the face of everything that's happened, I will no longer recognize you as my daughter. Is that clearly understood?"

"It's understood. Good-bye." Kate carefully hung up the phone. She stood quite still, her eyes far away, and then she took a deep breath and went into the sitting room where Sebastian was talking to Elizabeth.

He rose as she came in. "I don't suppose I need to ask how it went," he said, looking at her face.

"No, you don't. It's what we both expected. As of this moment, I'm a fatherless child." She tried to laugh but failed.

Sebastian put his arms around her and held her close. "I know it doesn't help much, but you have my father. You know he adores you."

"Thank you, Sebastian. You're very generous with your family."

"They make it easy to be generous with them, and anyway, they're soon to be your family. What on earth did you do to your finger?"

"Oh. I strangled it with the telephone cord. A symbolic gesture, I suppose."

"I'm sorry, Kate. I know that can't have been easy."

"I just wish I could have told him the truth, although I don't know how much even that would have helped. He made the choice: himself or you. It wasn't a difficult decision to make." She pulled away from him. "I'm going for a walk. I'll be back later."

"Do you want company?" he asked gently.

"No, thanks. I have some thinking to do." She turned quickly and went out and Sebastian looked after her with concern.

Elizabeth scowled. "There are times when I'd like to do something uncivilized to that man," she said. "That poor child has taken nothing but abuse from him from the first day I can remember."

"She won't be taking any more. I'm going to see to that myself." His face was grim.

"What do you have in mind?" asked Elizabeth.

"I think it's time Peter Soames and I had a little chat."

"You don't know him, Sebastian. He'll never listen; he'll just disconnect you."

"I wasn't planning on using the telephone. Mr. Soames is going to be coming to England whether he likes it or not."

"Whatever do you mean?"

"I didn't want to tell Kate before the fact—she'd only worry and that's the last thing she needs right now. The Department very much wants to talk to him about his involvement with Russell."

"I see . . . Do you suspect him of being in on this business, whatever it is?"

"I doubt it. However, David had close access to Soames, and it's important to discover how much Soames might have confided in him."

"Surely that's a matter for the CIA?"

"I believe that if he is clean, Colonel Harrington would like to save him the embarrassment of being interrogated by the CIA."

"Nonsense. He deserves every difficult moment coming to him."

"I must confess, the thought had crossed my mind. But for a number of reasons it's best to keep this as quiet as possible. And I'm sure you agree that Kate needn't know anything until it's over and he's been cleared."

"Oh yes, indeed. She's endured so much, and come through so well. Thank goodness for you, Sebastian, or I can't think what might have happened."

"I was just doing my job, Elizabeth," he said with a smile.

"Well you could have knocked me over with a feather when you called from St. Mouton in the middle of the night and told me what that job was. Now why don't you go out and see to Kate, and I'll just get supper started. And Sebastian, thank you for telling me what you could, but above all for bringing Kate home safe and sound."

He laughed. "What else could I do? As my father pointed out, it's high time I was married."

Peter Soames was extremely shaken by the time Colonel Harrington had finished with him after three full hours of questioning. "You have to believe I had no idea . . ."

"I do understand, Mr. Soames. A man of your position is always vulnerable to this kind of infiltration. I don't believe this needs to go any further; however, I would caution you to keep this information to yourself. And may I remind you it was only good luck that kept Mr. Russell from commencing his position with Mr. Sevronsen and creating a major breach of security." A knock came at the door. "Yes, come in."

Sebastian entered the room. "Excuse me, sir. I didn't mean to interrupt."

"It's no interruption. I think we're finished here. Mr. Soames, this is Mr. Dunn, who conducted the investigation."

Sebastian shook his hand. "How do you do, sir." His face was void of expression but his eyes were very cold.

"Very pleased to meet you. You did a fine job as I understand it," said Soames gruffly.

"Thank you, sir. Colonel Harrington, I just stopped by to give you the final report." He placed the thick file on the desk.

"Thank you, Dunn. If you'll wait a moment, I'd like to have a word with you."

"Yes, sir."

"I think that will be all, Mr. Soames. Thank you. If I have any more questions, I'll be in touch. You'll be at the Dorchester?"

"Yes, for a few more days."

"I see. Business or pleasure?"

"Not exactly business, but certainly not pleasure. My daughter Kate is over here at the moment with some harebrained scheme for a sudden and unsuitable marriage and I plan on taking her home with me."

"How—interesting. Were you planning on telling her the truth about Mr. Russell? It's quite all right with this department."

"Good God, no!" He looked horrified.

"Don't you think she has a right to know?" asked the colonel quietly.

"You don't know my daughter. As you must have guessed from what I told you, she's stubborn and impulsive, but she's not a strong character. I don't think she could be trusted with this kind of information."

"Ah, I do think I see," said the colonel, standing. "Good day, Mr. Soames."

"Good day, Colonel Harrington. Mr. Dunn, my congratulations." He shook their hands.

"Good-bye, Mr. Soames," said Sebastian evenly, watching him leave.

"Why don't you sit down, Dunn, and take a few deep breaths. That must have cost you an enormous effort of self-control."

"It confirmed some things to me. Have you drawn any conclusions about him?"

"Aside from the fact that he's a pompous fool and a poor judge of character, I think he's guilty of nothing more than shortsightedness. No, he had no idea about Russell, and fortunately had the good sense to keep his mouth shut. He's been in politics too long and too high up to make that sort of mistake."

"That's a relief. How much does he know of the story?"

"I told him the facts only from the angle of the Group. He knows nothing at all of Kate's involvement. However, you have my permission to tell him anything you choose."

"Thank you, sir. It will be a pleasure, believe me."

"Yes, I can imagine. Now, about these identifications; I thought you might like to know what has happened before you leave us. It may have taken over forty years, but I think Ernst would have been pleased that his information proved so helpful. That's a fine granddaughter he has, incidentally. There's a certain something of Ernst about her. I don't suppose you'd consider having her come in with us?"

"Absolutely out of the question, sir," said Sebastian with a smile. "And don't you even think to ask her."

"No, but it is a pity," he said wistfully.

"I have every intention of living to a ripe old age alongside my wife, sir. Which reminds me—" He removed the Beretta from his holster and placed it on the desk. "I'm retiring this."

"I can't persuade you to reconsider?"

"No, sir," said Sebastian firmly.

"Ah, well. I must thank you for seeing this job to its conclusion. It's quite amazing how the story turned out. Ernst would have been highly amused."

"Colonel Harrington, I'm curious—would you have connected the Brooke quotation with the watch if it had been delivered to you?"

"I would certainly like to think so. But never mind, better late than never. As Brooke said in 'The Dead': 'And Nobleness walks in our ways again; and we have come into our heritage.' Very appropriate for Ernst and Kate, don't you think?"

"I might have expected that, sir. But for Kate and myself I would say 'in hearts at peace, under an English Heaven.' 'The Soldier.' "

"Very good, Dunn!" said the colonel with a chuckle. "And it's a good thing you know your Brooke or we might never have recovered the documents." He pushed a folder over to Sebastian. "So far we've located these surviving SS officers in these countries in their assumed identities. Those on the short list will be netted, but those who have smaller networks of young men in the Group will be watched and infiltrated with our own agents. I believe this man Maartin has been earmarked to take over for Erharder. Your Mr. Schwab was very helpful in updating us. Such an unfortunate accident with his fingers."

"Yes, sir. Such a pity it was the right hand . . ."

Kate was weeding Elizabeth's flower beds vigorously, thinking about the five hundred things that had to be done before the wedding less than a week away. Sebastian's family had been thrilled with their announcement and had insisted that they use the Whitworth chapel for the ceremony. They'd happily accepted the offer but constantly had to fight to keep the guest list small. Sebastian and Kate found the frantic proceedings very amusing and quite out of control, and in the end had given up and handed everything over to Elizabeth and Lady Dunn to get on with. Lady Dunn had produced her wedding dress, a beautiful concoction of ivory satin and lace with a train and intricate lace veil. Sebastian had produced the sapphire from the family vaults, a ring that traditionally went to the eldest son's wife and had been gathering dust for years, he'd said with a laugh. Kate had burst into tears, prompting him to ask unromantically if she was feeling overtired. Kate grinned as she remembered what had followed.

Footsteps sounded behind her and she looked up, still smiling, expecting Sebastian.

"Hello, Katie."

"Daddy!" She stared at him in shock. "What are you doing here! You've changed your mind?" She rose to her feet and slowly pulled off her gardening gloves, not taking her eyes off his face.

"No, I haven't changed my mind at all. I had to come to England on business, and I thought I'd knock some sense into your head while I was here."

"Oh. I should have known. Well, we might as well go inside and be comfortable while you do it." Kate sighed, knowing it was going to be an impossible conversation.

"Can I get you some tea?" she asked as he sat down.

"No thank you, Katie, I didn't come to drink tea. I came to talk. I'm still very upset with you, but I'm prepared to give you another chance. Now what's all this nonsense about your getting married? Have you considered what I said?"

"It's not nonsense, I haven't given another thought to what you said, and I'm going to be married on Saturday in Leicestershire." She regarded him calmly.

"Katie, be reasonable! You'd be a fool to marry on the rebound. How long have you known this man?"

"Long enough to know I want to spend the rest of my life with him, and nothing you can say will change my mind, so you might as well get used to the idea."

"If nothing else, it's clear that he's done nothing for your manners."

"My manners have nothing to do with this. I think it's time you listened to me for a change. I love Sebastian, and I'm not asking for your permission. I just want you to be happy for me. David and I—well, I don't want to go into it, but it was very wrong. This is right."

"All right, I'm prepared to accept that maybe David was wrong for you, Katie, but you can't go off three months later and marry some man you've become infatuated with. What sort of family does he come from, after all? What prospects does he have? These things are important!"

Kate spoke coldly. "I assure you, you'd have no quibble with Sebastian's family or his prospects. You'll be delighted to know he's eminently respectable. But it's not important, can't you see that? All my life you've been trying to force your standards on me and I'm tired of it. All that's important is that he's a wonderful man and he makes me happier than I've been in my life."

Peter Soames colored hotly. "What about your job? You can't just irresponsibly throw that away!"

"I've arranged to be transferred to London, and they've very kindly given me a leave of absence until September."

"Well then, what about your grandmother?"

"Daddy, you know perfectly well that she doesn't know me when I'm there, so it's not going to make any difference to her one way or the other. You're trying to come up with any excuse to get me home and away from the choice that *I've* made. You might as well save your breath. I'm going to marry Sebastian on Saturday and I'm going to live out the rest of my life with him. You can accept it or not."

"Katie, you're just not being sensible about this! If you think this—this man is so important, then do what you wanted to do with David. Come home where you belong, give it some distance, some time to think it through. Then if in a year you still feel the same way, I'd be willing to give my approval."

"We don't need a year, Mr. Soames, nor do we need your approval, although Kate would be happier for it."

"Sebastian!" Kate smiled and jumped up.

"Hello, sweetheart," he said, advancing into the room and kissing her lightly. "Sorry I'm late—business. Mr. Soames?"

Peter Soames was taken aback. "I—I believe we met earlier?"

"Yes sir, we did. I'm Sebastian Dunn."

"Yes—yes, or course, Mr. Dunn." He rose slowly to his feet.

"I would have explained to you then that I'm the unsuitable man about to marry your daughter, but it didn't seem an appropriate time."

"No, of course not." Kate's father was at a loss. "I don't think I understand . . ."

"No, I don't think you do. If you'll just come outside with me, I believe I can enlighten you. You'll excuse us, Kate?"

Kate examined his face carefully. "No scores please, Sebastian?"

"Only of the sort that are settled between gentlemen," he said with an amused smile. "Mr. Soames?" He indicated the door to the garden.

They didn't return for well over an hour. Kate busied herself in the kitchen to keep her mind off her anxiety. It had come as a shock to learn that her father and Sebastian had already met. That alone was cause for concern. She couldn't imagine what was taking so long, and she'd washed and put down the same potato three times without realizing it, and was washing it for the fourth time when she sensed someone watching her and turned around sharply.

Sebastian was lounging against the kitchen door with a broad smile on his face. "Do you think you can get it any cleaner, my love?"

"What?" She looked down at the potato in her hands. "Oh," she said in confusion.

"Why don't you just peel it and put it out of its misery?"

Kate laughed. "Yes, I think you might be right. But Sebastian . . ."

"Later, Kate. I'd like you to come into the sitting room now. I believe your father has something he wants to say to you." He turned and walked out.

She washed and dried her hands, trying to collect herself, then followed him.

"Katie, dear." Her father looked considerably strained. "I—" He cleared his throat. He looked over at Sebastian who was leaning against the wall with folded arms, watching him intently, and he quickly looked back at Kate. "I believe I have an apology to make to you. Mr. Dunn has explained everything to me, and I realized I have been—I've been wrong."

"Wrong about what?" She shot Sebastian a look of puzzlement and saw the familiar laugh in his eyes.

"Wrong about a lot of things. He explained to me the part you played in all of this business."

"He did?" How much? she wondered. Just how much?

"Yes. I've misjudged you, and I'm . . . I'm very sorry. You did very well."

"Thank you." She waited, watching him carefully.

"Ah, as Mr. Dunn pointed out, I've treated you as a child for far too long, and haven't given you enough credit for the fine woman you've become. I'm sorry about David, my dear."

She looked at Sebastian again with no small surprise, and he nodded.

"I see . . . Then you know? You know the truth about David, about his death?" Her voice had sharpened with anger.

Her father looked away. "Yes."

"You know I was there when he was killed?"

"Yes." He cleared his throat again.

"And you know what he was doing all along?"

"I made an error of judgment."

"I hope you understand now why I couldn't pretend grief. But I also want you to understand that I realized I didn't love David long before any of this, and you were wrong to try to push me into something I didn't want. David was your choice from the beginning and I was foolish enough to go along with it. You do realize that the only reason he wanted to marry me was to get to your contacts in the State Department?"

"Yes, of course—but how was I to know that then? He seemed genuinely fond of you. I never meant for you to be hurt, Katie; you must believe that."

"Of course I do. But while we're on the subject, I think I should point out that the issue really isn't what just happened. That was an extraordinary set of circumstances. The issue is what had been going on since my mother died. You've always assumed that you knew what was better for me than I did, and any decision I've made on my own you've disapproved of. It hasn't been easy to have to fight against you every step of the way and be labeled spoiled and selfish. You may be my father, but you have no right to dictate my life."

Sebastian smiled.

"Yes—I know," said Peter Soames heavily.

"And I also want you to know that I've loved Sebastian since the first day I met him in Jamaica, and I'm going to marry him with or without your blessing."

"I'm sorry about that, too. I have to say that I approve of your young man. I think he'll be a good husband for you."

"Oh, dear," she said with a shaky laugh. "You didn't ask him his prospects, did you?"

"He most certainly did," said Sebastian, moving away from the wall and coming over to her. "And I reassured him that you would be kept in style befitting his daughter. I think we've reached an understanding about things." He slipped an arm around her waist. "Wouldn't you agree, Mr. Soames?"

"Ah yes, indeed. I'll be proud to walk you up the aisle, Kate."

"That makes me very happy." She smiled up at Sebastian.

He laughed and gave her a little squeeze. ''Why don't you be a good little woman and go finish tormenting that poor potato while I finish acquainting your father with the indignities of married life with me?''

''You're going to regret the day you asked me to marry you, Sebastian Dunn.''

''I doubt it,'' he said with a smile.

Much later in the evening after Kate's father had departed, they settled themselves down on the sofa with coffee and cognac.

''Now Sebastian,'' said Kate firmly. ''You're going to explain everything to me. You might have given me some warning, you know.''

''Oh, dear, do I sense a lecture coming? I thought you'd worked that out of your system earlier.'' He laughed. ''I think you took your father somewhat by surprise, darling.''

''Perhaps, but no less than both of you did to me. And you promised me no more alarms! Now tell me, and don't leave anything out.'' She relaxed into his shoulder and looked at him expectantly.

''I didn't want you to know until it was finished, but Colonel Harrington summoned your father in no uncertain terms to make an accounting of himself and his relationship with David.''

''I should have known there was something to all his pointed questions. What happened?''

''Let's just say a satisfactory conclusion was reached and nothing further will come of it.''

''Thank goodness! But you're not off the hook yet.''

''I didn't expect I was.'' His eyes danced with suppressed laughter.

''Well? What did you say to my father outside to make him change his tune?''

''I pointed out to him that he had missed some of your finer qualities, and his loss was my gain.''

''How very gallant of you,'' she said wryly. ''How much

did you actually tell him other than about David? I couldn't quite make that out.''

''With Colonel Harrington's permission I told him everything, including the fact that owing to his bloody-mindedness, you were nearly killed, and I wouldn't have taken it kindly if that had come to pass.''

''Oh . . .'' she said on a long breath. ''How did he react to that?''

''He was rather subdued. I think he realized that he wasn't dealing with someone he could bully.''

''I should think not. But did you really tell him the whole story?''

''Every last nasty shred of it. It was enough, believe me,'' he said grimly.

''Thank you, Sebastian. I'm glad he knows. But it still infuriates me that it took something like this to make a difference in his attitude. I couldn't believe the change in him over dinner. My God, if you only knew the way it used to be—''

''I have a damned good idea, Kate. It took every ounce of control I had not to knock him down when I walked in. He said some fairly choice things about you to Colonel Harrington, and then when I heard what he was laying down on you later . . . Well, never mind. That's something you won't have to worry about again, and more thanks to you than to me. I think you knocked him back quite hard this evening. You certaily proved something to him. It's one thing my telling it, but quite another for him to see it for himself.'' He smiled. ''You're one hell of a woman, Kate Soames, and quite different from the person I met seven months ago. And that reminds me. Colonel Harrington was very taken with you. He said you reminded him of Ernst. That's high praise indeed.''

''It is. I couldn't be more complimented. You know, it's interesting. My grandfather—Guy Jessop, that is—used to talk about how important heredity was. When I first learned that he wasn't really my grandfather, I thought that he was just being kind to me, treating me as a Jessop. But now, of course, I realize that he knew all about Ernst and Giselle and in his own way was encouraging that in me."

"I'm sure he was. He was successful, too. Do you know that Colonel Harrington wanted to recruit you into MI-6?"

"What!" She burst into laughter. "And I can imagine what you had to say to him about that."

"Exactly. I said, 'My dear man, Kate is going to be far too busy cooking and cleaning for me to have any time to gallivant off on missions. And in any case, she'd be extremely unsuitable as an agent. She refuses to follow directions.' And he said, 'You know, Dunn, I sensed a certain—' "

"Sebastian, I don't know why I put up with you."

"Don't you? It's because despite my more appalling faults you love me almost as much as I love you."

"Well, I wouldn't marry just anyone."

"No, you seem to have a penchant for agents, regardless of political persuasion."

"You really *are* appalling! At least I landed on the right side. I must say, it never crossed my mind in my youthful fantasies that I'd end up marrying someone in MI-6."

"In that case, there's something I should show you. I wouldn't want you to marry me under false pretenses." He sat her up and took off his jacket. "Well?"

"Well what?" She looked at him in confusion, and he grinned.

" 'Necessity's sharp pinch.' "

"Sebastian! Your gun—it's gone!"

"Gone for good. I've no more need for it. 'When I said I would die a bachelor, I did not think I should live till I were married.' Do you think you can still love me now that I'm an ordinary mortal?"

"You know I can, you idiot. But tell me something: I've been meaning to ask you this for months. How was it you learned to quote Shakespeare quite so thoroughly?"

"Really, Kate. You don't think you're the only person ever to carry off a First in literature, do you?"

Kate shook her head and laughed. "I might have known. Typical Sebastian."

"But there's a misquote you have yet to explain to me,

and I happen to know this one comes straight from your own complex little mind.'' He drew her to him and lowered his mouth on to hers in a long kiss. ''Now,'' he said when he was finished, ''about Apollo, the lamb . . .''

Epilogue

The afternoon light fell hazily through the ancient chapel windows as Kate walked down the aisle on the arm of her father. Sebastian stood at the altar, Geoffrey next to him, and he smiled broadly at her as she came to his side with a rustle of satin. She turned and gave her bouquet of lilies to Stephanie. They were all there, family and friends, and the entire Jumeau family whom Kate and Sebastian had flown up from St. Mouton and who were in a tremendous state of excitement.

"Dearly beloved, we are gathered here in the sight of God and in the face of this congregation to join together this man and this woman . . ." The Archbishop's voice echoed through the chapel reciting the marriage service.

"Wilt thou, Sebastian Andrew Michael, have this woman to thy wedded wife, to live together after God's ordinance in the holy estate of Matrimony? Wilt thou love her, comfort her, honor and keep her in sickness and in health; and, forsaking all others, keep thee only unto her, so long as ye both shall live?"

"I will . . ." Sebastian and Kate looked at each other with joined hands as the ancient words of commitment fell around them like a binding cloak of love.

". . . I, Katherine Elizabeth, take thee, Sebastian Andrew

Michael, to my wedded Husband, to have and to hold from this day forward, for better for worse, for richer for poorer, in sickness and in health, to love and to cherish—"

"And to obey?" interrupted Sebastian, his eyes dancing. "Will you?" 'Swear to me, Kate, like a lady as thou art.' "

"And to obey," said Kate, choking with laughter.

"Till death do us part, according to God's holy law, and thereto I give thee my troth," finished the startled Archbishop.

"Till death do us part," she said, repeating him dutifully while Sebastian grinned at her.

And then after all vows had been exchanged and the blessing given, the Archbishop declared: "I pronounce that they be man and wife together in the name of the Father, and of the Son, and of the Holy Ghost. Amen."

" 'No worse a husband than the best of men,' " Kate said softly, smiling at Sebastian.

"I love you, Kate," he said simply and kissed her without further ado.